# DEATH FROM THE HEAVENS

Next came the Stuka dive-bombers. These slender, square-tailed demons of the sky spread devastating and demoralizing fear. For one hour, the intense attack continued. It seemed as if it would never end. The cacophony of antiaircraft fire, the roar of airplane motors, the whine of falling bombs, the earsplitting din of explosions, and the shriek of the dive-bombers turned this peaceful countryside into a hell on earth. The siren in the nacelle of each dive-bomber screamed a familiar sound . . . the sound of death descending from the sky.

The battle had begun.

Monks OF MT. TABOR

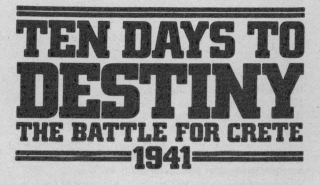

# TEN DAYS TO DESTINY
## THE BATTLE FOR CRETE
### 1941

G.C. KIRIAKOPOULOS

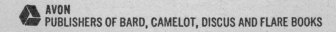
AVON
PUBLISHERS OF BARD, CAMELOT, DISCUS AND FLARE BOOKS

AVON BOOKS
A division of
The Hearst Corporation
1790 Broadway
New York, New York 10019

The Franklin Watts, Inc. edition contains the following Library of Congress
Cataloging in Publication Data:

    Kiriakopoulos, G.C.
    Ten days to destiny.
    Bibliography: p.
    Includes index.
1. World War, 1939–1945—Campaigns—Greece—Crete.
2. Crete—History—20th century.  I. Title.  II. Title: 10 days to destiny.
D766.7.C7K57  1985    940.54′21    85-700

First Avon Printing, June 1986

Printed in the U. S. A.

K-R 10 9 8 7 6 5 4 3 2 1

*O Passer-by, Tell the Lacedaemonians*
*That We Lie Here Obeying Their Orders.*

Simonides' epitaph at
Thermopylae, 480 B.C.

# CONTENTS

# PREFACE

What follows is the documented story of one of the most important yet least acknowledged battles of the Second World War. *Ten Days to Destiny* describes the audacity and horror of Operation Mercury, which involved thousands of soldiers and civilians in the first airborne invasion of an island-fortress in the military history of mankind. It is the tale of a battle that had a decisive effect upon the outcome of World War II.

The germinal idea for the writing of the historic and dramatic events depicted in this narrative began almost a decade ago.

While visiting the land of my ancestors, I decided to include the island of Crete in my itinerary. For many years I had heard of its primitive natural beauty, of the genial hospitality of its proud inhabitants, and of the glorious antiquities of the Minoan civilization that once flourished there.

As I stood in line at Athens' Hellenikon Airport waiting to purchase my ticket for the flight to Crete, I could not help noticing a tall, well-built man several places behind me. He towered over six feet, impressive in appearance, and stood as erect as a granite monument. I eyed his apparel—the costume of his native Crete—a black kerchief with a fringed border adorned his head, and a black vest covered a billowing white long-sleeved shirt. His black pantaloons tapered below his knees and disappeared into his shin-high boots. But it was in his eyes that the pride of the Cretan people could be discerned. I stared at him, trying not to be too obvious. This was my first encounter with a Cretan.

When I arrived in Khaniá, the administrative capital of Crete, I took a taxi to my destination. A few miles westward, on the main northern highway near the village of Galatas, I caught sight of a huge military monument. Later I learned that it was a war memorial built by the German invaders after the battle of Crete to honor their military dead. That this monument of a defeated enemy still stood more than three decades later intrigued me.

By inquiring about the German war memorial at Galatas, I opened the door on a little-known vista in the saga of the Second World War. As my questions prodded their memories, the elders of the many villages I visited began to reminisce about the terrible time in May 1941 when the German parachutists invaded Crete.

In the days that followed, I traveled widely across the length and breadth of the large island, enjoying its natural beauty. I found Crete to be a land steeped in history, and I found its people to be proud yet courteous, cordial, and friendly. I made many friends very quickly, and they were all willing to tell me about their struggle against the German invaders.

Little by little, the more I heard, I began to realize that here was a dramatic tale of heroic human endeavor to resist oppression, and that it was a story well worth telling.

When I returned to Athens, I browsed through the bookstores and bookstalls searching for material related to the battle of Crete. Much had been written by the Germans and the British. It was all objective, informative, yet indifferent. Nowhere, I felt, had the subjectively stark reality of the conflict among the determined German paratroopers, the resolute, gallant British Commonwealth soldiers, or the heroic Cretan civilians been captured. Little had been written and even less was known in the United States of the events that took place in Crete in May 1941; the battle of Crete was a British affair, when Pearl Harbor was still seven months away.

To fill this void, I decided to write *Ten Days to Destiny*.

In the course of the years that it took me to research this book, I traveled an estimated 100,000 miles to England, Germany, Austria, Switzerland, Greece, and, of course, Crete seeking material. I interviewed countless hundreds of people who were directly or indirectly involved. The dialogue is real: it comes from texts, transcripts, stenographic notes, and from the memories of the people I interviewed. (Occasionally, I have taken the liberty of altering the tense to suit the action.) I also read and reviewed hundreds of primary sources, after-action reports, staff journals, published and unpublished monographs, and diaries.

To familiarize myself with the battlefield sites on Crete, I took many trips to the island, trekking over the fields, hills, valleys, and mountains of that beautiful land of Minos.

# PROLOGUE

This is the story of a battle that took place during the early years of the Second World War on an island in the middle of the Mediterranean. For ten dramatic and bitterly fought days, Crete served as a battlefield in the struggle between German paratroopers and free-spirited Cretan civilians fighting side by side with their gallant British Commonwealth allies.

The battle of Crete has been referred to as the Thermopylae of the Second World War. Herodotus tells us in his *History of the Persian Wars* that King Xerxes of Persia invaded Greece in 480 B.C. with a vast army. Most of the Greek city-states put aside their differences and banded together to fight the Persian invader.

The Greek armies attempted to defend Thessaly at the site of Mount Olympus. Defeated, they withdrew southward, leaving only a small army to block the Persian advance. This army decided to fight at a narrow pass between the mountains and the sea, a position that offered some possibility of success. The pass was called Thermopylae.

The whole civilized world has read of the heroic defense that King Leonidas and his 300 Spartans, together with their allies, made at Thermopylae. The defenders fought valiantly until they were betrayed, whereupon they were overcome by the Persian hordes. Leonidas and his Spartans sacrificed themselves in order to delay the Persians.

After Thermopylae the Persians swept onward. They sacked Athens and eventually reached Salamis, where the Athenian fleet was waiting for them. In the sea battle that followed, the Persian fleet was virtually destroyed. Unable to sustain his army, Xerxes was forced to return to Persia. He had won the battle at Thermopylae, but the delay had lost him the war at Salamis.

In World War II, Adolf Hitler did not intend to invade Greece or Crete. Mussolini's failure to conquer Greece, however, caused Hitler to come to his aid, and to put off his plan to invade Russia. Once in Greece, Hitler was persuaded to seize Crete to protect the oil fields in Rumania from Crete-based aerial bombing. This occupied precious weeks of a very tight military timetable, and the delay represented a period of time Hitler would have required to bring Russia to its knees. The campaign in Greece and in Crete forced Hitler to postpone the invasion of Russia until June 1941.

At first the German armies rolled victoriously across the Russian plains, reaching Leningrad and Moscow. However, Hitler never captured Leningrad, and although within sight of the Kremlin towers, he never took Moscow. Then the Russian winter hit with all its ferocity, bringing Hitler's war machine to a standstill.

Stalemated at Leningrad and Moscow, Hitler ordered his southern armies to attack toward Stalingrad. What happened there is history. One million Germans were lost in the military debacle that followed. It was to be the farthest point of the German advance—and the turning point of the war. After Stalingrad the German armies were to travel a downhill road to eventual defeat.

Like Xerxes in 480 B.C., whose delay at the battle of Thermopylae granted the Athenian fleet time to gather and defeat him at Salamis, Adolf Hitler in 1941 was so delayed in Greece and in Crete that he was forced to fight a winter campaign in Russia. Hitler won *his* "battle of Thermopylae" in Crete, but it was a pyrrhic victory. The delay lost him the war in Russia.

If the events that culminated in the battle of Stalingrad marked the beginning of the end for Adolf Hitler, then the events that took place on Crete in May 1941 marked the end of the beginning.

# THE
# ADVENT

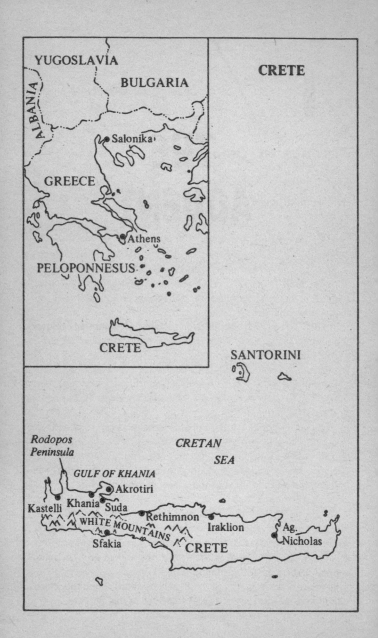

YUGOSLAVIA

BULGARIA

CRETE

ALBANIA

Salonika

GREECE

Athens

PELOPONNESUS

CRETE

SANTORINI

Rodopos
Peninsula

CRETAN

SEA

GULF OF KHANIA

Akrotiri

Kastelli

Khania

Suda

WHITE MOUNTAINS

Rethimnon

Iraklion

Ag.
Nicholas

Sfakia

CRETE

# 1 / "NO, IT IS WAR!"

## OCTOBER 28, 1940

During the early morning hours of October 28, 1940, in the quiet Athens suburb of Kephisia, a huge black limousine drove up to the private residence of Ioannis Metaxas, prime minister of Greece.

The Metaxas household was awakened by the persistent ringing of the front doorbell. It was 2:15 A.M. The maid who answered the door was informed that the predawn visitor was Emmanuele Grazzi, the Italian ambassador, and that it was urgent he see the prime minister. Still half-asleep, the maid misunderstood the announcement. She thought he said he was the French ambassador. She mistook the word *Italia* for *Gallia*.

"The French ambassador is here with an important message from his government," were the first words uttered by the prime minister's personal secretary.

"The French ambassador, at this hour?" grumbled Metaxas. "Haven't the French done enough harm to the world by surrendering to the Germans so easily, without bothering us at such an ungodly hour?"[1]

Metaxas agreed to see the French representative, but he was not going to rush. He took his time washing his face, and sipped a hot cup of coffee to awaken his senses. Throwing a kimono over his pajamas, he decided that enough time had elapsed. He slowly descended the stairs to the drawing room as the clock chimed.

It was 3:00 A.M.

When he entered the room with his secretary-bodyguard, he hesitated momentarily at the entrance. At the sight of the dark, rotund Italian ambassador, he realized the error that had occurred. His heart skipped a beat. A visit from this man at such an undiplomatic hour meant that trouble was afoot.

"Well, what brings you here at this hour, Signore Grazzi? Could you not have waited until the light of day?"[2]

7

"I have an important message from my government which requires an immediate reply,"[3] answered Grazzi, handing the prime minister a large envelope.

Metaxas was now fully awake. He took the document, put on his spectacles, and began to read.

He read through it once in startled disbelief. Removing his glasses, he glared at the Italian ambassador, who looked away. Metaxas replaced his spectacles and read through the document a second time. The silence was so profound one could almost hear the heartbeats of the three men in the room.

The document was an ultimatum. It demanded that Greece open its borders to the passage of Italian troops. Greece was to cede all its major seaports on the mainland and in the Ionian and Aegean islands to the Italian army. All strategic army and air bases were to be turned over to the Italians. In effect, Greece was to be occupied by Italy. All this was to be agreed upon by 6:00 A.M.— in just three hours.

As the Greek prime minister read through the ultimatum once more, he realized he had only two choices: to accede to the demands, or to fight.

Count Galeazzo Ciano, the Italian foreign minister, had forecast the meaning of this ultimatum. "Naturally," he commented in his instructions to Grazzi, "it is a document that allows no way out for Greece. Either she accepts, or she will be attacked."[4]

Grazzi waited for Metaxas to make some response. Finally Metaxas broke the silence. "This note does not give me much time to consider these proposals. I could not set my own house in order—much less surrender my country—in three hours."[5]

Flipping the ultimatum carelessly onto the coffee table in the center of the room, he again removed his spectacles and glared at the Italian ambassador. "The answer is no."

With that curt reply, Metaxas turned and left the room. Grazzi stood alone, mouth agape and speechless. At the door, with tears welling in his eyes, Metaxas repeated his answer to his secretary. "No. It is war!"[6]

The Italian ultimatum to the Greek prime minister was scheduled to expire at 6:00 A.M. on October 28, 1940. However, Mussolini's army did not wait for the set hour to arrive. By 5:30 A.M., 125,000 troops crossed the Greek frontier. Only two Greek divisions stood in defense against the invader, and they were outnumbered six to one. The Greek General Staff had not mobilized its other sixteen divisions earlier, for fear of giving Mussolini some cause for provocation.

The Italian army crept over the rugged mountains of the northern Greek provinces of Epirus and Macedonia in a three-pronged attack. The eastern prong headed from Kónitsa through Florina to Thessaloniki; the central spearhead climbed through the Pindus Mountains toward Metsovon; while the third prong followed the western coast road. The invaders moved southward slowly against light opposition, at a pace of some six miles a day.[7]

It was not a blitzkrieg in the German sense of the word, but it was an advance.

Back in Rome, Mussolini had a huge billboard constructed in the Piazza Venezia. On it was a huge map of Greece, with large red arrows indicating the victorious advance of the Italian army. The public watched and cheered each southerly movement of the arrows.

The newly mobilized Greek army began counterattacking in the Kalamas River area, and the Italians were soon thrown back. By November 2, just six days after the Italian attack began, there was an amazing communiqué that read: "Greek forces had counterattacked in the central region and had captured Mount Pissoderri. . . ."[8] The Greek forces had penetrated three-and-a-half miles inside the Italian border.

This was the beginning of many victories for the small, brave Greek army. Fighting in the rugged, cold, windswept mountains of Epirus amid deep snowdrifts, the Greeks succeeded in decimating the Italian Third Alpine Division—the crack "Julia" division—capturing more than 5,000 prisoners and tons of Italian supplies.

When Greek neutrality was violated by the Italian invasion, Great Britain came to Greece's assistance. On the day following the Italian invasion, British naval forces sailed for Crete from Alexandria with supply ships and auxiliary craft. The Second Battalion of the York and Lancaster Regiment landed on Crete as the first element of a defense garrison.[9]

The Greeks continued to fight the Italian invaders, chasing them over the rugged mountains of northern Greece into Albania. Victory followed victory. Church bells rang continuously and untiringly throughout Greece with the announcement of each Greek victory. The battles for towns such as Kónitsa, Pogradec, St. Ostrovitz, Sarande, Tepelenë, Klissura, and Argyrokastron resulted in smashing victories for the Greeks.

Back in Rome, the billboard with the huge map of Greece was taken down. One official commented that it interfered with the flow of traffic in the plaza.

By November 22, less than one month after Mussolini's troops had invaded Greece, the Italians were in full retreat on the whole front. As 1941 began, not a single Italian soldier was left on Greek soil, unless he was dead or a prisoner of war. The Greeks had chased the Italians eighty miles back into Albania.

Mussolini's attempt to conquer the Greeks left 20,000 Italian soldiers dead on Greek soil, and as many as 40,000 wounded, 26,000 prisoners, and 18,000 men crippled with frostbite from the hard winter of northern Greece.[10] Worst of all, the Greeks had made Mussolini the laughingstock of the entire world. He stood humiliated in the eyes not only of his enemies but also of his Axis ally, Adolf Hitler.

Now it was obvious to Hitler that he would have to invade and occupy Greece, so he could once again push the British off the continent of Europe and bring peace and security to his southern flank.

So it was that on December 13, 1940, Hitler issued War Directive Number 20—Operation Marita—for the invasion of Greece.[11] This meant that Hitler had to postpone the preliminary date set for the German invasion of Russia until the Greek campaign was concluded.

A fateful decision that was destined to alter the course of the Second World War, it spelled doom for the Axis alliance.

On April 6, 1941, Operation Marita went into effect. The German army launched a simultaneous attack against Greece and Yugoslavia.

Through the mountain passes at Monastir and over the mountains into the Vardar Valley came the German legions. Their armored units sped forward over the rough terrain in multiple spearheads across the Greek peninsula.

Outnumbered in masses of troops, outweighed in armor, and continuously harassed by the Luftwaffe's onslaught from the sky, the Greeks gave ground. By April 30 it was all over. What Mussolini could not do in six months, Hitler accomplished in twenty-four days. And now the German soldiers stood on the southern shores of Greece—just 168 air miles from Crete.

* * *

The island of Crete lies like a huge barrier reef in the middle of the Mediterranean.

To the Greeks, the island of Crete is known as Megalonisos, meaning "great island." It is the fifth-largest island in the Mediterranean and lies between three continents: Europe to the north, Asia to the east, and Africa to the south. Because of this geographically strategic position, Crete has played a principal role in the history of the Mediterranean.

It is an island where shadows of artistic giants lurk everywhere. Great artists painted the walls and fashioned the vessels of the Minoan palaces. It is the birthplace of Theophanis, of Georgis, of Michael Damaskinos, and of Doménikos Theotokópoulos, better known as El Greco. It is the Crete of poets and authors—of the idyllic *Erotocritos Erofylli*, *Vascopoula*, and *Abraham's Sacrifice*. It gave us Nikos Kazantzakis, author of *Zorba the Greek* (among hundreds of other works), one of the great literary figures of our century. From Crete, too, came Eleftherios Venizelos, to whom John Gunther referred as the great statesman of modern Europe.

Legends from Crete fill the pages of mythology. It was to the land of the Minotaur—the monster with the body of a man and the head of a bull—that Theseus, prince of Athens, came to slaughter this predator of Athenian youth. Theseus followed the silken thread that led him out of the labyrinth. And it was the builder of the labyrinth, Daedalus, and his son, Icarus, who attached wings to their shoulders and soared skyward.

Beyond the realm of mythology, ancient and modern Crete throughout the centuries has been involved in a continuous struggle among the many peoples that have coursed the surface of this inland body of water. These forces met and clashed on this island, crushing each other through the ages, leaving vivid traces of their existence on the stark face of the land that had been the cradle of the first European civilization.

Crete was first inhabited about 7000 B.C., during the Neolithic period, by tribes from the northern mainland and from the depths of Syria. With the passage of time, Crete developed the illustrious Minoan civilization that became the forerunner of present-day European civilization. The heart of this Minoan culture was Knossos, the strongest and greatest city in Crete. Minoan civilization became preeminent in the Mediterranean, spreading the shadow of its wings across the waters as far west as Gibraltar and as far north as the Black Sea.

According to the natural law of life, every civilization is subject to destruction. To Crete came the natural calamity of earthquakes and the man-made force of war, weakening and dispersing its people and causing the great Minoan civilization to totter and fall.

Then there arrived from the Grecian mainland a new people, ferociously aggressive and better armed, who overwhelmed the weakened and dispersed inhabitants of the Minoan empire. These first invaders of Crete were the Dorians.

They were a crude and rustic horde, ignorant of art or handicraft, and in their ignorance, they destroyed everything that was beautiful or of significance. Their own artifacts were inferior to the wonderful craftsmanship of the classical Minoan civilization. Crete fell into an unexalted existence, a slumbering and neutral state, during the Persian and Peloponnesian wars that racked the ancient city-states on the Greek mainland. In the end Dorian Crete also succumbed to the law of destruction; in 69 B.C. the Romans arrived to add their name to the list of invaders.

The Roman legions, under Consul Quintus Caesilius Metellus, sought to capture the island because of its critical position regarding Roman supremacy in the East. It took three years for Metellus to conquer the island. But with the eventual division of the Roman Empire into Eastern and Western states, Crete became a part of the Byzantine, or Eastern, half of the dual empire.

After the Romans came the Saracen Arabs who built the city of Handox on what is now the site of Iráklion. The Arabs held Crete for more than 130 years until General Nikiforos Fokas, who later became the emperor of Byzantium, liberated the island and made it a province of the Byzantine Empire.

The Crusaders who seized Constantinople in the thirteenth century A.D. divided the conquered provinces of Byzantium among themselves. Crete was taken by Bonifatius, marquis of Monferate, who promptly sold it to the Venetians. The Genoese, not to be left out, overran the Venetians and took possession of the island. After a bitter war, the Venetians succeeded in recapturing Crete in A.D. 1212. Crete was now divided into feudal fiefdoms constantly at war with each other. The Venetians threw out the Greek Orthodox bishops, installed Roman Catholics, and forced the Cretan inhabitants into serfdom. The Cretans, tired of these foreign incursions, finally rose in rebellion. During the 450 years of the Venetian presence, the Cretan population revolted some twenty-five different times to regain their liberty. There was a constant struggle against the great strength of Venetian arms.

In A.D. 1669 Iráklion was captured by the Turks after a bitterly fought war that lasted twenty years. If the Venetians were oppressive, the Turks were cruel beyond all human calculation. For more than two centuries, the Turks treated the people of Crete as subhuman slaves. The decades passed with years of struggle, sacrifice, heroism, and savage torture that embittered the people. It caused the Cretans to revolt against these latest conquerors countless times during the years 1692, 1770, 1821, 1841, 1855, 1866, 1868–69, 1886–87, and 1896–97.

The great Cretan revolt of 1866 was the eruption that shook the very foundation of the might of the sultan ruling the Ottoman Empire. The heroic drama of the rebellious Cretans and the unimaginable torment they suffered at the hands of the Turkish armies of occupation reached such a peak that it stirred the conscience of all free Greeks and of Europeans as well.

The massacre of Christians by the Turks at Khaniá in 1897 forced the Greek government to send an army of 1,500 men under Colonel Timoleon Vassos to Crete. He landed with his troops at Khaniá and took possession of Crete in the name of the king of Greece. Crete then proclaimed itself free of the Ottoman Turks, uniting herself with Greece. Turkey declared war, defeating Greece the same year. However, Crete was able to preserve its autonomy.

In 1898 the Turks again resorted to their inhuman treatment. They massacred both Greek and English subjects at Iráklion. In the furor that followed, the Turkish army was forced to leave Crete, and Prince George of Greece was appointed high commissioner of Crete. With his arrival at Suda Bay on December 9, 1898, the first step in Crete's union with Greece had been achieved.

On October 5, 1912, the prime minister of Greece, Eleftherios Venizelos, a native son of Crete, declared that Crete had been united with Greece. Crete was free at last.[12]

After centuries of foreign invasions and domination, Crete settled into a peaceful existence through the decades that followed, only to be confronted by a new danger—another foreigner was threatening to invade the beautiful island.

The Cretans remembered the Dorians and Romans of ancient times, and the Franks, Venetians, Genoese, Saracens, and Turks of modern times. To this list would now be added the Germans.

# 2 / **WAR COMES TO THE LAND OF MINOS**

## MARCH 26, 1941

The quiet waters slapped the steel sides of the huge warship that was anchored in the middle of Suda Bay in Crete. Not too far away, four freighters were moored closer to the shore. There was not a glimmer of light from the ships, nor from the farmhouses dotting the hills that surrounded the harbor on three sides. Only the blinking stars above marked the sky from the inky blackness of the shore.

The warship was the majestic eight-inch-gun cruiser, HMS *York*. This 10,000-ton ship of the line had escorted a convoy of freighters into Suda Bay the previous day, bringing supplies to the storage depots on shore. The *York* was scheduled to depart the following morning, returning to her home base at Alexandria, where she was to lend the might of her six eight-inch guns to Admiral Andrew Cunningham's ships of the Mediterranean Fleet.[1]

The first alarm came from the lookout astern. He reported a low hum of motors from the direction of the outer harbor. The duty officer checked with the man monitoring the Low Angle Direction Control—or LADCT, as they called it—who confirmed that his detection apparatus had picked up the sound of multiple motors of unknown identity approaching, and gave the bearing. Considering the possibility that the disturbances might be aircraft, the duty officer turned to the ship's newly-installed Air Warning Radio Direction Finder, an early type of radar. If they were aircraft, however, they were too low for radar to pick them up.

A second lookout on the after-superstructure, using infrared glasses, reported the appearance of white disturbances in the water, aft of the port side, which appeared as wakes of small craft. The officer on deck ordered a flare to be fired, then called the captain.

The brilliance of the flare illuminated the whole harbor like daylight, and on the outer fringe of that light there appeared a flotilla

14

of eight motor torpedo boats heading for the freighters near the shore.

The *York*'s captain was still buttoning his jacket when he stepped onto the bridge, to hear a deafening roar accompanied by a fiery red ball. Two fingers of flame reached high into the dark sky from the stricken freighter *Pericles*, sending shadows dancing across the waters and silhouetting the other ships anchored nearby.[2]

The alarm for action stations was sounded aboard the *York*, and the ship's crew of 623 officers and men hurried to their assigned stations and prepared for action. The anchors were raised and the boilers fired to increase power. Slowly the huge turbines began to throb as the ship was prepared for any eventuality. The skipper did not intend to be caught like a sitting duck.

The crew stood ready at their four-inch antiaircraft guns, mounted at the break of the forecastle, abreast of the forward funnel. Other gunners cleared the multiple 20-mm antiaircraft guns and, like the men on the four-inch guns, waited for orders to open fire.

From the bridge the captain and his executive officer followed the course of the speedy little boats with their glasses. Both men, veterans of years of service, were familiar with the German E-type motor torpedo boats, which depended on speed and torpedoes to attack shipping. But these motorboats were smaller, faster, and—more surprising—carried no torpedoes. Yet the flames billowing from the heavily listing freighter gave strong evidence that they were craft to be reckoned with.

"How did they get past the boom of the inner harbor?" asked the *York*'s executive officer.[3]

Both men watched another motorboat veer sharply and head for a second freighter. Racing on a straight course, it plowed into the hapless ship. A few seconds elapsed, and then a huge fiery blast lifted the freighter out of the water, broke her apart, and left her to settle quickly to the bottom of the bay.

"That explains it," said the surprised skipper of the *York*. "The whole bloody boat is a torpedo!"[4]

The explosive motorboats, designated EMBs, were Italy's newest weapon, manned by groups of volunteers who attacked with courage and speed. Each craft had a single crewman, who selected a target and then steered at full speed on an impact course. The forward part of the motorboat contained a warhead of some 6,600 pounds of explosives that would detonate on contact. If the crewman chose, he could alter the explosive setting, allowing the prow with the warhead to separate, sink below the target's waterline, and by hydrostatic detonation, explode with the effect of a depth charge.

The EMBs were difficult to hit because they were so low in the water, and when at full throttle, they sped at thirty knots, driven by powerful Alfa-Romeo outboard motors.[5]

The *York*'s captain ordered all secondary batteries to open fire. The four-inch and 20-mm antiaircraft guns were lowered to zero depression, many of them firing over open sights at the small motorboats dodging and weaving in the waters of the harbor. A curtain of hot metal spouted tall geysers and churned the black waters into foam. One motorboat was hit, exploding in a single brilliant flash.

From the starboard side of the *York*, an EMB spotted the cruiser, now well silhouetted against the flames of the two burning freighters. The EMB zigzagged across the waters as the starboard batteries concentrated their fire on this immediate threat. The motorboat shot forward at thirty knots, knifing through the water and closing fast. It slipped through the ring of shells without being struck.

The single crewman set his controls on a collision course, aiming the prow of his boat to strike the cruiser amidships. With the throttle open to maximum, he locked the rudder controls on target. From his position at the rear of the craft, he pressed a release and was ejected backward into the water, together with his seat. The seat rose to the surface and just as quickly the crewman unfolded it—transforming it into a raft—and climbed aboard. When the warhead exploded against the cruiser's outer plates, the underwater force of the detonation would have little effect on the sailor, now sitting securely on the bobbing raft.

The motorboat churned through the remaining distance to its target while the starboard crew watched helplessly. Orders came from the bridge for a full right rudder, but it was too late. The motorboat with its 6,600-pound warhead struck the cruiser just aft of amidships, with a deafening roar.

A geyser of water shot skyward carrying with it pieces of steel, causing the cruiser to rise slightly out of the water from the force of the explosion. When it settled down again, amid hissing steam and heavy smoke, the *York* had a slight list to starboard.

The men of the *York* picked themselves off the tilting deck. Some had been flung into the water, and lines were thrown to pull them in. Others stood dazed and momentarily frozen by the force of the blast.

Damage control reported that the explosion had pierced the *York*'s four-inch armor below the waterline, opening her to the sea and flooding the forward boilers. The captain ordered ballast to be altered to correct the ship's list and to begin the pumps. However, the pumps could not work fast enough to remove the torrents of water pouring in from the huge hole in the cruiser's side, and she began to settle by the stern. There was no alternative but to beach her.

As the cruiser slowly drifted toward the western end of the bay, the captain remarked that the situation could have been much more tragic. Before her recent refitting, the *York*'s high-angle magazine had been located exactly where she was struck. Since the modification, the magazine had been moved forward of the boilers. This change had saved the *York* from a disastrous explosion that would have torn her apart. Beaching the ship now would keep her from foundering, and repairs could be made.[6]

Less than a quarter mile from the western shore of Suda Bay, the *York* shuddered to a halt. Her bottom had gently come to rest on a sandbar.

Only twenty minutes had elapsed from the moment the first report announced the approach of the EMBs until they disappeared again into the night. They had done their work well, leaving two freighters burning and sinking, and an eight-inch-gun cruiser severely damaged and beached. Of the eight motorboats in the flotilla, three had been destroyed but their crewmen had been picked up.

As the first light of dawn began to streak across the eastern sky, Cretans gathered on the shores surrounding the bay. From their positions on the heights, they could see the awesome results of the previous night. Before them appallingly thick, black smoke rose skyward from the now partially submerged and burning freighters, flames still licking hungrily at their superstructures.

Not too far away lay the sleek cruiser *York,* her afterdeck low and awash in the swirling waters.

The events of the night of March 26, 1941, had rent the tranquility of Suda Bay. Slowly, the conflagration that had already engulfed the millions of people on the European continent would extend itself southward across the Aegean to this peaceful, beautiful island of Crete.

# 3 / MERCURY IS BORN

## APRIL 25, 1941

Within two weeks of the torpedoing of HMS *York* in Suda Bay, the Cretan people heard the news of the German invasion of Greece. No matter how the news reached them, most Cretans stubbornly clung to the belief that war was still far away across the northern waters that separated Crete from the Greek mainland like a great moat.

In the days that followed the German invasion of Greece, plans were formulated that would overcome that watery defensive barrier. Like the Mycenaean invaders of ancient times, who came to destroy the land of Minos, this invader would also come—not by sea this time, but over it.

On April 15, 1941, Colonel General Alexander Löhr, the commanding general of the German Fourth Air Fleet, requested a special conference with his immediate superior—the commander in chief of the Luftwaffe.

It was General Löhr's air fleet, striking from bases in Austria and Bulgaria, that had struck the first blow in the invasion of Greece and Yugoslavia. In the morning hours of Palm Sunday, April 6, 1941, his aircraft pounded into submission the cities and the defenses of those two nations. By punishing and unmerciful bombing, high-level bombers and Stuka dive-bombers from his command completely devastated the city of Belgrade. At the end of that first day's air attack, 17,000 defenseless Yugoslavian civilians lay dead in the rubble of the capital city. By April 15, Yugoslavian resistance had been broken by the air fleet's persistent attacks.

Satisfied that his air command had played a major role in clearing the path for the advance of the German invasion army, General Löhr felt that the time was at hand to discuss further air operations in the Mediterranean.

For several weeks the Luftwaffe General Staff had been considering a tactical plan for the seizure of Crete. The plan could be put into effect immediately after the successful completion of the military operations in Greece, but it first had to gain the approval of the commander in chief of the Luftwaffe.[1]

Hermann Goering first gained fame as a World War I pilot, and after a downhill postwar trek, he rose once again to become the number-two man in the hierarchy of the German Reich.

When the Second World War erupted in 1939, the Luftwaffe soon became its most respected and feared weapon. The Luftwaffe's support of the German armies advancing into Poland, Norway, Denmark, the Low Countries, and France made German victory inevitable. With each Luftwaffe success, Goering's prestige reached greater heights.

Hitler was most grateful. He promoted Goering to the new and special military rank of Reichsmarschall. Greater still was his appointment as deputy Fuehrer of the Third Reich—number-two man and heir to the leadership of Germany. Goering had now fulfilled his dream: both wealthy and famous, his star was at its zenith.

As the commander in chief of the Luftwaffe, he was a law unto himself. Yet, with all his power, Goering feared competition. He was afraid that someone else would displace him in Hitler's favor. Because of this fear, the Reichsmarschall developed a distrustful hatred for the generals of the Oberkommando der Wehrmacht, or OKW (the high command of the armed forces), of the army high command (the Oberkommando des Heeres), and of the Oberkommando der Kriegsmarine (the naval high command). They, in turn, looked upon him as a pompous, arrogant egomaniac interested only in self-aggrandizement. Hitler alone acted as a buffer in the friction between Goering and the commanders of the armed services.

When, in 1940, Goering heard that the retreating British and French armies were fighting with their backs to the sea at Dunkirk, he pompously proclaimed that his Luftwaffe could prevent their successful evacuation. But the Luftwaffe failed. The British survived the evacuation from Dunkirk and came back to fight another day. And the brightness of Goering's star dimmed slightly.

Hitler's next plan was the invasion of England. To succeed in this operation, he first had to gain control of the skies over Britain. Goering's Luftwaffe was given this task.

The Battle of Britain was the first major British victory over Germany. Goering's much-vaunted air force suffered its greatest defeat. The skies over England remained British, and the planned invasion of England—Operation Sea Lion—had to be canceled. It was a crushing blow to Hermann Goering's prestige.

By 1941 Reichsmarschall Goering's credibility and position, relative to his Fuehrer, had waned to their lowest ebb.[2] He would have done anything within his power to be restored to Hitler's favor. It was at this juncture that Colonel General Alexander Löhr arrived with the plan for the seizure of Crete.

Löhr proposed the use of the armed might of the Luftwaffe—and only the Luftwaffe—in an air attack upon Crete. In a sustained program of continuous bombing, aircraft of all types would pound the island into submission. This would be followed by an airborne invasion of the island carried out by glider troops and parachutists. Once the strategic points had been captured, reinforcements would be ferried to the island by air transport. The whole operation was estimated to be completed within a period of three to ten days.

Here was the solution to Goering's dilemma. He realized that this would be the first airborne attack in the history of the world to seize an objective without the assistance of an army moving overland.

The next day, April 16, 1941, Reichsmarschall Goering arrived at Hitler's daily staff conference, a little after 2:00 P.M. The meeting was already in progress, and his tardy entrance disrupted the proceedings. He entered noisily and, with a broad smile, nodded his greetings to Hitler. The other members of the conference received a wave of his baton as their salutation. Hitler responded to his Luftwaffe chief's greeting with a cold, fixed glare. His coolness was obvious to all present.

Resplendent in the full-dress uniform of a Luftwaffe field marshal, Hermann Goering had come to the conference directly from an air force ceremony. His tunic glittering with medals and decorations, around his neck sparkled the Collar of the Annunziata, a gift from the king of Italy.[3]

"Mein Fuehrer!" interrupted Goering. With a quick stride, the Reichsmarschall placed on Hitler's desk a map of Crete. "I have a proposal to make! Now that Greece is finished, I offer you a plan by which my Luftwaffe forces would seize the island of Crete.''[4]

"Goering! Are you not aware of the great plans already in preparation regarding Operation Barbarossa?'' Hitler snapped angrily. "Perhaps you should attend these conferences punctually and more often!''[5]

Goering blushed, then mumbled a few words in his defense: "This plan involves only the airborne units of my Luftwaffe. . . .''

At this point, Field Marshal Keitel saw his opportunity to embarrass Goering further. "Mein Fuehrer,'' he interjected, "the airborne units of the Luftwaffe are inexperienced for such an operation alone. Suppose we put this plan into effect, are we certain that it can succeed? If the airborne units fail to gain their objectives, can we spare the additional men that would be needed to make the attack successful? Time is against us!''[6]

The flush left Goering's cheeks. His eyes flickered in anger. He would take insults from the Fuehrer but not from this lackey, posing as the head of the German High Command.

"My Luftwaffe has proven itself equal to any of the other armed services! My paratroopers are the best trained men in the whole German army. They are second to no one! Look at what they did in Norway and in the Low Countries!''[7]

"Yes,'' retorted Keitel, "we have seen. You promised that your Luftwaffe alone would destroy the enemy ships evacuating the British from Dunkirk. They failed to do so! Did your Luftwaffe fulfill your promise to clear the skies over England?'' Rising to face Goering, Keitel concluded, "And your well-trained paratroopers still are untried for an operation such as as the one you propose for Crete.''

Hitler broke the suspenseful silence. Much to everyone's surprise, he came to Goering's defense: "Goering, you know how I feel about *our* parachute troops. I have always considered them to be men of iron—ruthless men—who would float down from the skies loaded with death.''[8]

Hitler continued, "You know that this operation in the Balkans has delayed our time schedule for Barbarossa, yet, with this knowledge you ask me to delay even more and get further involved with an attack upon Crete?''

Goering finally saw the opportunity to defend his proposal. "That is the reason why this operation becomes necessary. Shall

Crete remain a *Pfahl im Fleisch*—a thorn in our flesh—in our lifeline to the eastern Mediterranean and to the Suez Canal? We had hoped that the Italians would have taken that problem from our shoulders, but they failed. Their failure would be our success."[9]

Goering was himself again. This was the Goering of the early years, displaying an energetic, clear mind, persuasive and refreshing in his argument. All eyes were upon him. "Certainly, you cannot equate the heroic professionalism of the German soldier to that of the Italian. Where the Italian has failed, the German has succeeded." He added, "The seizure and subjugation of Crete would be the crowning glory of our Balkan campaign."[10]

The Reichsmarschall had finished his argument. It was now for Adolf Hitler to accept or reject the proposal. Alfred Jodl, OKW Chief of Operations, spoke up.

"Mein Fuehrer, may I emphasize one point that I had mentioned in my report." Hitler signaled him to continue.

"In that report, I had stressed the fact that the seizure of Crete would keep the enemy from using the island as an air base from which they could bomb the Ploesti oil fields."[11]

The Ploesti oil fields, in Rumania, were just four hours' flying time from Crete. Hitler needed their oil for his tanks and for his airplanes. He could not jeopardize the security of those oil reserves.

Hitler nodded as Jodl's comment struck a warning bell in his brain. His army chief of operations was right. Hitler walked pensively to his desk, head bowed, hands clasped behind him. "Your point is well taken, Jodl," he said. Then, turning inquiringly to Goering, "Who, may I ask, is the creator of this proposal for the airborne operation on Crete?"

Again it was the chief of operations who responded: "Lieutenant General Kurt Student, Mein Fuehrer."[12]

"Ah, yes, of course, Student! I shall give your proposal careful consideration, Goering."

With that, Hitler left the room. The meeting was over.

On April 20, 1941, a well-built, square-faced Luftwaffe officer of average height was ushered into the hallway of Hermann Goering's hunting lodge in Rominten. He was met by Robert Kropp, Goering's personal valet since 1933. Kropp informed the officer that the Reichsmarschall would see him shortly.

This was the first time the visitor had ever seen the interior of this renowned hunting lodge. Seated in a corner in a straight, high-backed chair, he was impressed with the plush, rich decor of the huge room. His eyes feasted themselves upon the paneled ceilings whose crystal chandeliers cast shimmering light upon the huge tapestries that adorned the four walls. Centered before a 400-year-old French tapestry was a long, highly polished table, with one tall bronze lamp at each end. On one side of the table were two large straight-backed armchairs, separated by a coffee table. On the other side, facing the straight-backed chairs, was a huge thronelike armchair. Obviously, this was Hermann Goering's official reception room where he held audience with his visitors.

The visitor had traveled widely in his long military career, but never had he seen such opulence and grandeur. "The Reichsmarschall lives like an emperor," he thought to himself.[13]

Dressed in the uniform of a lieutenant general, the visitor's appearance epitomized the upright, immaculately attired Prussian officer, a member of the Luftwaffe General Staff.

He wore an open-collared tunic with pegged trousers, all in the familiar shade of Luftwaffe blue. The piping cords and insignia of his uniform were in gold, and his breeches bore the white stripes indicating the rank of a general officer. His waist was adorned with a brocade belt of silver interwoven with threads of black and red. It was centered by a gold general officer's buckle with a silver eagle motif.

Over his right breast pocket was a Luftwaffe eagle woven in metallic gold thread. His left breast bore a small silver eagle symbolizing the 1939 bar to the Iron Cross issued to him in the First World War. Below this was pinned a Maltese cross designating the award of the Iron Cross of 1939, First Class. Attached in a circle around this Iron Cross were a silver wound badge and the paratrooper qualification medal. Above his left breast pocket were attached varicolored ribbons representing campaign and service medals of his long career. Perhaps the most impressive medal worn by this much-decorated officer was the black-red-black ribbon that passed under the collar of his white shirt, and from which was suspended the Ritterkreuz—the Knight's Cross[14]

This handsome, well-dressed general was, in fact, the commanding general of the Eleventh Air Corps—the XI Fliegerkorps. Under his command were all the paratroopers and airborne soldiers of the German Army. It was only proper that he should be their commander. This selected, specially trained group of men had been the brainchild of his fertile imagination. Some officers in the higher echelons of command appreciated his genius. But many veteran officers of the German General Staff looked upon his work as too experimental to be successful in actual warfare. In the course of military events, his "too experimental" plans bore fruit.

With the bold use of his paratroop and glider units in the invasions of Belgium and the Netherlands in 1940, and in the rapid capture of the impregnable Belgian fortress of Eban Emael, this ingenious general had proved that his plans could work. The airborne units had become an important component in the German military scheme of surprise and lightning warfare, and their successful operations brought much fame to their commander. There were few officers in the Third Reich who had not heard of the exploits of Lieutenant General Kurt Student.

Kurt Student was not a "Johnny-come-lately" officer who had received his rank because of loyalty to Adolf Hitler or to the Nazi party. All his life, from early youth, he had been devoted to the military in the service of his beloved Germany.

In 1901, at the age of ten, he had entered an army preparatory school as a cadet, beginning his career as an officer candidate. He wore a uniform for the first time and he did not remove it until the end of World War II. In 1911 he received his commission as an officer, making him a member of the German officer corps.

In November 1933 Student had been promoted to lieutenant colonel and appointed director of the technical training schools for the air services. His work dealt with the technical study and construction of airframes, engines, weapons systems, and parachutes. He labored many long hours on the multiple problems posed by this work.

There was a great deal of politics in those early days of Hitler's rise to power. Student knew little of politics and liked them less. He was a member of the German officer corps—an elite group— who wished only to continue serving the fatherland. Because he was not a party member, he was repeatedly passed over for promotion. But he was not discouraged. All he wished was to be instrumental in the development of German air power.

It was not until his forty-eighth birthday, in 1938, that he was promoted to major general. With this rank, he was given command of the Seventh Air Division. Now Student, known in the higher army echelons as the "little adventurer," had been given a command that was an adventure in itself, carte blanche to form an airborne division. It would be his duty to organize, train, and develop an elite group of volunteers to become an exclusive fighting arm of the newly developed Luftwaffe. (In addition, he was appointed an inspector general of the airborne forces.) Student's early experiences with gliders suggested to him the idea of developing glider troops as an adjunct to the paratroopers.

When World War II began in 1939, he sought to put his units into action in support of the Wehrmacht. But the General Staff did not feel that his units had proved themselves. The paratroopers were not used in the blitzkrieg attack upon Poland. But when they were used in the invasion of the Low Countries, they finally had their chance to prove their military value.

On May 14, 1940, during the final hours of the successful campaign in the Netherlands, Kurt Student was struck by a sniper's bullet. Wounded severely in the head, he hung precariously between life and death for many days. In the weeks that followed, he lay in bed half-paralyzed, unable to speak or to recognize anyone. It was a long, arduous path to recovery. His spirit and determination to recover overcame his illness. In September of the same year, he was finally considered fully recovered and returned to duty.[15]

Now a lieutenant general, he was made commanding general of the XI Fliegerkorps and commander of all the German airborne forces. Kurt Student, "the Father of the German Paratrooper," was back.

General Student waited patiently for the conference with his commander in chief. It was known that Goering always kept his visitors waiting; perhaps it added to his image of importance. This did not disturb Student. While he waited he fingered the briefcase resting on his lap. In it were two sets of plans for airborne operations that he wanted to present personally to the Reichsmarschall.

A sound on the step announced the Reichsmarschall's approach. "I am glad you are here, Student," was his opening greeting. "I am leaving for a hunt in an hour. I understand that you wish to discuss the Corinth project."

As Hermann Goering settled his corpulent body into his thronelike armchair, General Student unrolled a huge map upon the table.

"I plan to land the Second Parachute Regiment right at the Corinth Canal. They will secure the bridge and thus sever the Peloponnesus from the rest of Greece. Its success will trap and cut off the British forces." The plan was to go into operation in the morning hours of April 26.[16]

The time was approaching for Goering to leave for his scheduled hunt. He rose to leave.

"Herr Reichsmarschall, has any decision been made regarding our proposed plan for Crete?"

Four days had elapsed since Goering first proposed the plan to Hitler. "I do not think the Fuehrer plans any further campaign in the Mediterranean, once Greece is occupied," he replied.

Student rolled up the maps, seemingly undisturbed by the Luftwaffe chief's remarks. "That is unfortunate. It looks like our Luftwaffe will always play a secondary role in this war!"[17]

Goering's head jerked to attention. He sat down again. Student's remark had a telling effect upon him. Student pressed his point: "This would be strictly a Luftwaffe operation. It need not require assistance from the Wehrmacht nor the Kriegsmarine. We can take Crete with the sole use of our airborne forces. Why should the German Air Force play second fiddle to the army and navy?"

Goering, whose enthusiasm was easy to arouse, fell prey to Student's argument. "Nothing is impossible for the parachutists!"[18]

The Luftwaffe chief was convinced that Student was right. Goering longed to find the opportunity to press his airborne soldiers into action. He believed that Hitler had been misled by the generals of the OKW into relegating the Luftwaffe to a secondary role. "They never would give our Luftwaffe a major vital place in an important battle," Goering muttered dejectedly. "We are always second—but our airmen are worthy of better things!"

"Yes, Herr Reichsmarschall, and this operation for Crete would add great glory for our Luftwaffe and even greater glory for you."

"You are right, Student. I shall go to see the Fuehrer today. He must give his approval!"[19]

The Reichsmarschall was true to his word. He cut short his hunting plans and flew to Hitler's headquarters in time to attend that afternoon's situation conference. He was determined to press for approval of the attack upon Crete.

Much to the Reichsmarschall's surprise, Hitler received the renewed proposal with calm. His only reply to Goering was: "Let me talk with Student tomorrow."

Early the next morning, Kurt Student received a telephone call from the Reichsmarschall.

"The Fuehrer is willing to see you today regarding the plan for Crete." Student's pulse beat faster. He would now have the opportunity to present his plan to Hitler personally. Perhaps he would succeed in getting approval to seize Crete with his paratroopers. It would be a dream fulfilled.

Goering continued, "I will meet you at three this afternoon, immediately following the Fuehrer's daily staff conference. Bring Jeschonnek with you."[20] (General Hans Jeschonnek was the Luftwaffe chief of staff. As an *Oberleutnant*—Lieutenant—he had been Student's assistant in earlier years at the German Air Mission.)

Student and Jeschonnek arrived at Hitler's field headquarters at Münchenkirchen early in the afternoon. They were admitted into the anteroom, an austere, simply furnished chamber. In the adjoining conference room, Adolf Hitler was holding court with the members of the German General Staff. The German leader was elated, for earlier in the day he had received the news that the Greek Army had capitulated to Field Marshal List's Twelfth Army. The operations in Greece were virtually complete. His southern flank was now once more secure.

A military aide appeared at the door of the conference room and beckoned to the two Luftwaffe officers to enter. Goering greeted them at the entrance and escorted them to Adolf Hitler. The Fuehrer stood at his desk acknowledging the Deutsche Gruss—the German salute—tendered by Student and Jeschonnek.

"I have reviewed your plan for Crete, Student," Hitler remarked as the meeting convened. "It seems all right, but I do not think it is practical."[21]

Student was not going to be discouraged by this opening comment. He countered, "Mein Fuehrer, I strongly believe that the conquest of Crete from the air is not only possible, but certain."

Hitler mumbled something to Jodl. Student, undisturbed by the Fuehrer's inattentiveness, continued more firmly, "What I propose is a limited airborne operation of short duration. It would involve only the Luftwaffe forces. The plan is economical in its scope and it will succeed, if given the opportunity! Besides, mein Fuehrer, we have learned from experience that it is harmful for the paratroop units to remain inactive too long."[22]

Hitler faced his airborne commander. With a fleeting glance at Goering, he posed a question tinged with sarcasm: "Are you aware, General Student, that the General Staff has operational plans of greater importance?"

Of course, Hitler was referring again to Operation Barbarossa—the planned attack on Russia. Already the Oberkommando der Wehrmacht was committed to the deployment of one hundred thirty-seven divisions along the eastern front.

"I am aware of those plans, mein Fuehrer. Our proposal for Crete need not disturb the Wehrmacht from their program."[23]

"Why have you not considered the seizure of Malta instead of Crete?" asked Hitler. Field Marshal Wilhelm Keitel, chief of the German General Staff, had repeatedly suggested that Student's paratroopers should be used in the seizure of Malta.[24]

At this point Goering threw in an unexpected question: "Crete or Malta?"

Hitler made a nervous gesture to him to be silent. He knew that Malta had been a hornet's nest. The little island, located sixty miles south of Sicily, stood like a bastion against repeated air attacks. The Aeronautica Regina—the Italian air force—had bombed it day after day. Later reinforced by the German Tenth Air Corps, the bombing continued with even greater vehemence. The island was bombed until clouds of pulverized dust obscured it. Yet, when the dust settled, Malta was still operable. Its aircraft would rise to attack the Axis sea convoys sailing from Italy to North Africa. Not a single convoy carrying supplies to General Rommel and his Afrika Korps escaped damage.

"Mein Fuehrer," answered Student, "I feel that Crete, with its long northern coastline and with those airbases located on the north coast, would be a better objective to seize. An air drop upon Malta might jeopardize our attacking forces, because the island is small and the British could easily transfer their reserve forces from point to point. It would be too risky for our paratroopers."[25]

The Fuehrer nodded his head in agreement. He could not dare risk this elite group of men in an operation that might exhaust their number and destroy their potential.

Student pressed his argument further: "Crete could be the stepping stone to the mastery of the Mediterranean."

Not a single thought or a single plan existed in the German war scheme to extend the battle lines into the eastern Mediterranean. All of Adolf Hitler's thoughts since November 1940 had been centered on the attack upon Russia.

"And the next step?" Hitler asked.

"Cyprus! From there to the Suez, through the back door," replied Student with a self-assurance that startled even Hitler. At that moment new glory for the Luftwaffe, somewhere in the eastern Mediterranean, was conceived.[26]

Hitler now regarded Student closely; a look of interest had crossed the Fuehrer's face. Goering smiled, for he also saw the familiar glitter in Hitler's eyes. Student felt victory within his grasp. It was time to show his trump card.

"The seizure of Crete, mein Fuehrer, would deprive the British of those airfields located on the northern coast of the island. If the British retain those airfields, they could pose a constant threat of bombing, at will, the Ploesti oil fields in Romania. That would be disastrous to our overall war effort."[27]

Hitler rose and walked to the map table. He gazed at Student's campaign map of Crete. He remembered the memoranda about Crete submitted by the chief of staff of the German army, General Franz Halder, and by Grand Admiral Karl Raeder, chief of the Kriegsmarine. Both had mentioned the necessity for the occupation of Crete. Even his chief of operations, Alfred Jodl, had concurred in such an operation. Hitler slowly realized that the seizure of Crete could become a springboard for future operations against North Africa, the Suez Canal, and the whole of the eastern Mediterranean—after Russia had been brought to her knees.

"How much time would you need for this operation?" the Fuehrer inquired.

"The island could be captured within three days!"

"That's impossible!" Hitler countered Student's boast. "I shall give you five days! You would, in any case, have to move with great speed. That is necessary in the interests of the other fronts. Every day lost needlessly is paid for dearly."

Goering and Student exchanged triumphant glances.

"Mein Fuehrer, do your words mean that you approve of the attack upon Crete?" asked Student excitedly.

"I don't know," replied Hitler vaguely, bending once more over the maps on the table before him. "I'll think it over!"[28]

For some reason, Adolf Hitler took four days to "think it over." It was not until April 25 that he finally arrived at the decision to attack Crete.[29]

During those four days, he wrote a letter to his Italian ally, Benito Mussolini. He mentioned to him the proposed plan concerning the seizure of Crete. Since this was in Mussolini's sphere of influence, Hitler felt it was proper to consult him.

General Jodl, however, thought it unusual that the Fuehrer took time now to inform Mussolini of this pending military operation. It was the first time that the younger member of the Axis alliance had ever bothered to take the Italian dictator into his confidence.

It also seemed paradoxical to the generals of the high command that the Fuehrer—who had raged in anger at Mussolini's military failures, and with the date for Operation Barbarossa rapidly approaching—would delay his decision in order to write to this discredited man.

On April 25 the decision was made: Germany would attack Crete. On that date the Fuehrer's headquarters issued a military order bearing Hitler's signature:

DIRECTIVE NO. 28: Order for the seizure of Crete as a base for air warfare against Great Britain in the eastern Mediterranean.[30]

Hitler had imposed two limitations on this operation. The first restriction was that it involve only the units of the Luftwaffe. The second dictated that it should start no later than the middle of May and that it was to be concluded by May 25, just ten days later. The operation was assigned the code name *Merkur.*

Operation Mercury—the plan for the attack upon Crete—was born.

# 4 / "DETERMINE THE NEXT GERMAN OBJECTIVE"

## APRIL 21, 1941

On the same day that Lieutenant General Kurt Student was meeting with the Fuehrer to discuss the proposed plans for an airborne attack on Crete, another meeting was taking place across the English Channel.

The British chiefs of staff, and the service ministers of the coalition government that directed Great Britain's war effort against Nazi Germany, had been summoned to an important conference scheduled for noon, April 21, at the official residence of the prime minister, Ten Downing Street.[1]

As the men who led Britain arrived for the conference, the skies above grew dark with the threat of imminent rain. It was a gloomy Monday; everything seemed bleak and depressing.

The problems that faced these men were harrowing. At sea, the toll of ships sunk by German U-boats was still dangerously high, in spite of efforts to counter the menace. On land, Yugoslavia had capitulated and was almost completely overrun by the German army. British and Greek forces were in full retreat in the face of persistent attacks by overwhelming German armor in Greece. But perhaps the most crucial and startling news came from North Africa.

In February 1941 Hitler had sent General Erwin Rommel to Libya with the first elements of the German troops that were to become the nucleus of the Afrika Korps.[2]

Winston Churchill realized that General Sir Archibald Wavell, Commander in Chief, Mediterranean, had to be reinforced immediately. To accomplish this, Churchill had formulated a daring plan. He had summoned his military leaders to this conference to present it to them.

Churchill proposed that a special convoy be prepared, comprised of fast motor-transport ships. "Let these ships be filled with all available artillery, tanks, and aircraft, and let them be

31

rushed *through the Mediterranean* to Alexandria instead of going around the Cape!"[3]

To remarks concerning the risk involved, he retorted that it *was* risky, "but we must accept the risk." The chiefs of staff still had to be convinced.

"Of course, secrecy is of vital importance, and no one outside the highest circle of command need know of our intention to turn off, eastward, at Gibraltar. Even those aboard the convoy must think they are going around the Cape of Good Hope!"[4]

The conference members stirred, yet not one offered any encouraging word of acceptance. Undismayed, Churchill pressed forward. "The fate of the war in the Middle East is at hand. Let us not forget," he reminded them, "that the loss of the Suez Canal would have a calamitous result for our interests in that area. The loss of this vital waterway would end all prospects of future American cooperation through the Red Sea. Yet, gentlemen, all this may hinge upon a few hundred armored vehicles reaching Wavell on time."[5]

"It is obvious that our operations in Greece will end shortly. We are rapidly approaching the need for the withdrawal of our troops from the Greek mainland." Churchill went on to say that it would again be up to the Royal Navy to help evacuate the troops. The majority of these men were to be taken to the island of Crete. There, they would be rearmed and amply supplied for the defense of that Mediterranean island. "I have made repeated injunctions these past six months," Churchill emphasized, "that Suda Bay be fortified. We must have a strong, well-armed garrison there, with a strong air force as a protective cover. The island must be stubbornly defended! *I strongly feel that the Germans will strike next at Crete!*"[6]

"We do not agree, Prime Minister!" the chief of the Imperial General Staff demurred. Churchill raised his head, and with his eyeglasses resting halfway down his short nose, he frowned at General Sir John Dill.

In the light of the events then taking place in Iraq and in the western sands of North Africa, General Dill continued, "We feel that the next German objective would *not be Crete, but Iraq!*"[7]

Pointing to the map with a long unlit cigar, Churchill queried, "If the German plans to occupy Iraq, why is he even now concentrating his bombing efforts upon our defence positions in Crete?"

"It is possible that the German wants us to *think* that he is planning to attack and occupy Crete," was Dill's unhesitating reply.

"His air attacks upon Crete would be a feint to divert our attention, while his real plan would be directed at Iraq. I might say that General Wavell concurs with me that Crete might be a coverup!''[8]

Churchill's frown had been replaced by a pensive expression. "If Hitler follows the strategy that Dill set forth," he thought to himself, "then we might well be in dire straits." What gave Churchill consolation, however, was that Dill's strategy was too logical; Hitler did not always follow sound military logic.

Admiral Dudley Pound, the First Sea Lord, raised his hand to speak. "[British] air attacks have been staged from our air bases on *Malta*. The German knows this, and he also realizes that he must have a supply line free from attack if he is to succeed in North Africa. The German must get rid of Malta!'' Now everyone in the room stirred. Admiral Pound continued, "This is the reason we feel that Hitler's next objective in the Mediterranean is neither Crete nor Iraq, but rather the island of Malta!''[9]

"I know only too well of Malta's strategic value to our Mediterranean war effort," Churchill replied, "but what makes you think that the German would attempt to seize Malta *now* that she stands like a bastion of defence when he did not do so last year when she lay as naked of defence as a newborn babe?''[10]

Winston Churchill remained unconvinced. He admitted to himself that each argument was strategically sound. However, there were also plausible arguments against each theory. The innate ingenuity that made him a great leader still argued that the next German goal was Crete.

Though undaunted in his conviction, Churchill did not wish to counter the professional expertise of his military leaders. He would still press for Crete's defensive buildup.

"Gentlemen," concluded the prime minister before adjourning the meeting, "we have a distinct difference of opinion which must be resolved immediately. I shall recommend that our intelligence people find out for us in what direction Hitler will march next!''[11]

That same afternoon orders were dispatched to all British intelligence sections, to the effect that every effort should be made to determine the next German objective in the Mediterranean.

Thus, on the afternoon of April 21, following the meeting at Ten Downing Street, W. Cavendish-Bentick, director of the Joint Intelligence Board, received a memorandum from Winston Churchill, asking him " . . . *to determine the next German objective in the Mediterranean.*'' [author's italics][12] Would it be Malta, Iraq, or Crete?

# 5 / "ANY DAY AFTER THE SEVENTEENTH"

**MAY 14, 1941**

On the morning of April 7, a man in his early thirties arrived at the Athens railroad station. The dirty, wrinkled appearance of his clothes and the streaks of dust on his round face told of the ordeal that he and his fellow passengers had undergone during this particular trip.

The train, one of the last to leave Saloniki, had departed just ahead of the advancing German columns. Twice it had been bombed and strafed by German Messerschmitts, the second attack causing several casualties among the passengers. Only the darkness of night protected the train and its passengers from total disaster.

The young man did not resemble the average Greek, for he was taller and lighter complexioned than most, blue-eyed, and had a tousle of light brown, almost blondish hair.

As he passed through the exit gate, his height and Nordic appearance raised the suspicion of two officers of the National Security Police. An alert had been issued for them to be wary. It was not unlike the Germans to sneak an espionage agent into a swarm of arriving refugees. The two officers following the tall young man felt that he was suspect; they decided to detain him.

Searching him from head to toe, rummaging through his valise, and carefully scrutinizing his identity papers, they found nothing extraordinary. The papers identified him as one John Drakopoulos, a teacher from Thessaloniki. Inasmuch as his name did not appear on the secret police wanted list, and finding nothing else to substantiate their suspicions, they reluctantly released him.

John Drakopoulos walked along Delighianni Street, past Platia Kariskaki, and down St. Constantine Avenue to Omonia Square. He took a room in a second-rate hotel and rested from the ordeal of his trip.

For the next few days, he did not leave his room except to eat or to buy the latest editions of the Athens newspapers. Back in his room, he ignored the headlines that reported defeat in Thrace, Thessaly, and Attica. Instead, he thumbed through the pages of each newspaper searching for one particular item. This became a daily practice, and when he did not find it, he threw down the papers in dismay. It was only a matter of days before Athens would fall to the invader. The Greek government already advised evacuation. King George II had left for the safety of Crete, while Athens had been declared an open city.

On April 25, eighteen days after his arrival in Athens, John Drakopoulos finally found the item he had been anxiously looking for. It was a five-line insert in the classified section of the Acropolis newspaper:

WANTED

CIVILIAN MAINTENANCE ENGINEER
GRANDE BRETAGNE HOTEL
MUST HAVE APPROPRIATE CREDENTIALS
APPLY IN PERSON

The time had arrived for Drakopoulos to go into action. Leaving his hotel, he stopped momentarily on the corner of Athena Street and looked up its length to the distant Acropolis, glowing majestically in the morning sunshine. He walked quickly past the milling throngs of Athenians, who had gathered on each corner reading the latest headlines, and turned up Panepistimiou, or University, Street, toward Constitution, or Syntagma, Square. As he hastened past the National Library and the neoclassical buildings of Athens University, the crowds thickened noticeably. He finally reached the corner of Kriezotou Street, where the density of the crowds made his passage almost impossible and the echoes of their voices had risen to a steep crescendo. Pushing to the corner of Queen Sofia Avenue, Drakopoulos saw the cause of the uproar.

There in the middle of Syntagma Square, in front of the Parliament building, was a long armored column of Royal Artillery. The battered, exhausted men clearly demonstrated the pitiful signs of soldiers who had fought hard in continuous, futile battle. The Athenians were swarming all about them, cheering, clapping, and shouting words of encouragement.

This unit belonged to Major General Harold Eric Barrowclough's brigade—possibly the last defending unit between Athens and the advancing Germans. The column could not proceed in its southward retreat to the ports of evacuation because of the crowds that had gathered around them. The Athenian men and women jumped onto the running boards of the vehicles. The girls kissed and hugged the startled, smiling soldiers, while the men shook their hands with a heartfelt gratitude. They did not know how to thank these gallant soldiers who had traveled halfway around the world to fight on Hellenic soil in order to save the Greeks from German conquest.

One woman ran up to the staff car, which led the convoy, and gave a bouquet of flowers to an officer. Lieutenant Colonel R. Waller smiled in embarrassment as another woman kissed him on both cheeks. Other women threw bouquets at the vehicles, shouting in Greek: *"Ef haristo"*—"Thank you."[1]

The column finally resumed its movement through the streets of Athens. These soldiers would never forget the kindness, affection, and expressions of goodwill that the Athenians bestowed upon them. Some of these soldiers were to gain even greater glory and everlasting affection in Greek hearts by their heroic deeds in the battle that would soon follow on the island of Crete.

Just opposite from where John Drakopoulos stood was his destination. The Grande Bretagne had long been, and even at that time remained, the most luxurious and renowned hotel in Athens. It was also British headquarters. When the British forces arrived in October 1940 to aid the Greeks in their war against the Italian invaders, they converted this hotel into the General Headquarters of the British Expeditionary Forces in Greece under the command of General Henry Maitland Wilson.

Darting between the vehicles of a British armored column, and struggling through the crowds, Drakopoulos reached the entrance of the hotel.

The main lobby was bustling with activity; soldiers of all ranks were racing to their assigned duties. Drakopoulos stopped a sergeant and in precise English asked for the civilian personnel officer. The young captain who was the personnel officer listened patiently and glanced briefly at the classified advertisement that Drakopoulos showed him. "We really have nothing to do with this anymore, old chap," he replied, handing him back the folded newspaper. "As you can see," he continued, "we are in the midst of departing. This is no longer our concern." Then he suggested that Drakopoulos apply to the civilian directors of the hotel for employment.

In 1941 there were two associate directors of the Grande Bretagne Hotel: One was a Swiss named Walter Schmidt; the other was a Greek, George Canellos. It was Canellos who interviewed Drakopoulos for the vacancy, and since no one else had applied, Drakopoulos was given the position of maintenance engineer for the hotel.[2]

By the evening of April 26, all British troops had left Athens. In their wake there remained a suspenseful vacuum—a void of silent anxiety. In the early morning hours of April 27, the first elements of Field Marshal Wilhelm List's Twelfth Army entered Athens. The Athenians glared at them from street corners and from behind shuttered windows. A silence of imminent doom prevailed. All that was audible was the grinding squeal of tanks and the tramp of hobnailed boots beating a harsh tempo on the city pavements. Athens, the birthplace of democracy, had lost its freedom as the Greek flag on the Acropolis was replaced by the Nazi swastika.

Shortly after the Germans entered the capital, a Volkswagen jeep followed by four armored personnel carriers drove up to the entrance of the Grande Bretagne. This advance headquarters billeting party lost no time in taking over the hotel. All vestigial reminders of the British presence were quickly removed. In their place appeared German eagles and a host of swastika banners. On the pavement outside, two tanks took up positions as guardians of the entrance. In no time at all, the beautiful, plush, Victorian-style hotel had assumed a Germanic flavor. What had been the headquarters of the British Expeditionary Army the previous day now became German headquarters in Greece.

A few hours after the Germans commandeered the Grande Bretagne, a sleek, black Mercedes limousine drew up before the hotel, followed closely by another vehicle filled with black-uniformed soldiers. These troops belonged to the Schutzstaffel—the dreaded SS.

The tall, lean officer who got out of the limousine was dressed in the black duty uniform of an SS colonel. He was the commanding officer of this headquarters security unit, Standartenfuehrer Heinz Gellermann. Under his command, the SS set up its own headquarters within that of the Wehrmacht.

The German military organization was unique in that it held within its fold two distinct armies. One was the regular army—the Wehrmacht—under the Oberkommando des Heeres, as the army high command was called. The other army was composed of selected units collectively called the Schutzstaffel, or the SS.

Perhaps the most important subgroup of the Schutzstaffel was the National Central Security Office—the Reichssicherheitshaup-tamt, or RSHA for short. In 1941, Reinhard Heydrich, whose assassination in Czechoslovakia led to the terror of the town of Lidice, was the director of the RSHA.

This National Central Security group had within its body several departments: Bureau III with the SD (Sicher Dienst) was a security service inside Germany; Bureau IV, the Gestapo, was the State Security Police; Bureau V, the criminal police; and Bureau VI dealt with foreign intelligence.[3]

Standartenfuehrer Heinz Gellermann was a member of the Gestapo, or Bureau IV.

It was the duty of the SS unit to enforce security in the Greek capital and to establish even tighter security at German headquarters. To begin with, SS Colonel Gellermann ordered the immediate investigation of all civilian personnel employed at the Grande Bretagne.

John Drakopoulos was in the first group of hotel personnel to be interviewed by Colonel Gellermann's Gestapo staff. Afterward, Gellermann read the dossiers very carefully and found Drakopoulos' background to be the most interesting of all. What he read about Drakopoulos pleased him.

It appeared that John Drakopoulos had spent the last ten years of his life in Germany. He had received his engineering degree at Kiel University. His student days had been spent amidst the political turmoil preceding Adolf Hitler's rise to power.

When Germany went to war, the young student from Greece returned to his home city of Saloniki. In this second-largest city in Greece, he obtained employment as a high school German teacher. When Germany invaded Greece, Drakopoulos fled before the tide of battle with countless thousands of other refugees— arriving in Athens in the morning hours of April 7.

It was obvious to the SS colonel and his Gestapo staff that this young Greek engineer was a Germanophile. There was something Germanic about his appearance. It would be advantageous to have Drakopoulos working for the German occupation forces. But Standartenfuehrer Gellermann was an officer in the hated Gestapo. A member of an organization that from its inception was nurtured on suspicion and raised on deceit, the SS colonel was not going to accept the young engineer's statements at face value. The validity of Drakopoulos' dossier would have to be confirmed. Gellermann wired Gestapo headquarters on Prinz Albrechtstrasse in Berlin requesting all available information on John Drakopoulos, the former student at Kiel University.

Within thirty-six hours the colonel had his reply. It confirmed everything in the Drakopoulos dossier. The Gestapo report added that on several occasions Drakopoulos had participated in pro-Hitler student rallies. The information was enough to satisfy Colonel Gellermann.

The next day John Drakopoulos was summoned to Gellermann's office. It was a nerve-racking moment when the two burly SS guards pushed him gruffly through the door. Standing before the colonel, watching his pen scratch across a page, Drakopoulos did not know what to expect. The silence became ominous. Finally Gellermann closed the file before him, looked up, and smiled.

"I congratulate you, Herr Drakopoulos," Gellermann remarked, rising from his chair. "It is obvious from your record that you are one of us! We shall be pleased to have you work with us."

Drakopoulos released an inaudible sigh of relief.

Without further word, Colonel Gellermann handed Drakopoulos his pass. This passport-size document carried more authority than any other similar permit issued by the German occupation forces. It gave Drakopoulos permission to go anywhere in Athens and its environs. It also indicated that he was in the good graces of the Gestapo.

The tall Greek glanced quickly at this vital permit. There was his picture with his vital statistics on the right side, while the left bore the imprint of the German eagle with Reichsfuehrer Heinrich Himmler's signature. Below the eagle there appeared the Gestapo seal, signed by the SS commandant in Athens.

When Drakopoulos left Gellermann's office, a broad smile slowly crossed his face as a feeling of elation welled up within him. He had fooled the Germans. Not only had he fooled them, he had also fooled the *Gestapo*—and seldom did anyone succeed at that.

In reality, John Drakopoulos was a Greek working for the British, with the rank of major in British military intelligence. He had been planted in the Grande Bretagne as an employee and his orders were specific: Find out if the Germans planned to invade Iraq, Malta, or Crete?

During the first week in May, John Drakopoulos noticed an increase in Luftwaffe personnel at the Grande Bretagne. The Luftwaffe command had taken over the entire second floor of the hotel. The largest room on the floor had been converted into a carefully guarded war room, with access granted only to members of the Luftwaffe General Staff and their aides. From photographs, Drakopoulos easily recognized Colonel General Alexander Löhr, who commanded the Fourth Air Fleet in the Balkans; and General Wolfram von Richthofen, cousin of the famous "Red Baron" of World War I fame, who was the commander of the Eighth Air Force in Greece. What impressed Drakopoulos most of all was the continuous presence of Lieutenant General Wilhelm Suessmann, a parachute commander; and that of the commanding general of all German parachute units, Lieutenant General Kurt Student, who had set up residence in the hotel. Their constant presence in the war room gave clear evidence that the pending operation would involve the entire parachute corps.

Drakopoulos knew the answers he sought were in the war room. However, with tight Luftwaffe security, and the ubiquitous Gestapo always present to scrutinize the identity of each person entering the inner sanctum, gaining access would be the most difficult part of his assignment. Drakopoulos asked the cleaning women to bring him all war-room refuse. Perhaps, he thought, he could piece together some clues of what went on there daily. This plan, however, failed, for all refuse was personally dealt with by the SS. Attempts at planting listening devices also proved futile. Drakopoulos was stymied. Then he got lucky.

On a clear, hot, humid morning in the second week of May, the Grande Bretagne was inundated with Luftwaffe officers of all ranks arriving en masse. John Drakopoulos observed the ranks—generals, colonels, majors, captains, even a few Oberleutnants—as they were quickly ushered into a huge salon at the rear of the hotel's first floor. As each officer entered the heavily draped, hermetically sealed meeting room, he was handed a writing pad. It was evident to Drakopoulos—who made mental notes of the proceedings—that the simultaneous arrival of predominantly general and field-grade officers, with only a smattering of company-graders, meant that the major briefing of the planned operation was about to take place.

Throughout the meeting John Drakopoulos positioned himself behind the main reception desk, helping a young communications corporal wire a switchboard. He worked slowly, hoping that the meeting would adjourn before he completed the wiring. For three long hours he labored, doing and undoing the wires, until the huge double doors opened and the swarm of officers emerged.

Drakopoulos watched with chagrin as Gestapo personnel collected the writing pads from each officer. Whatever had happened in that room was meant to remain a secret.

The hotel lobby rapidly emptied as each officer returned to his unit. Two officers—one a major, the other an Oberleutnant—remained in the outer foyer chatting amiably. It was obvious to Drakopoulos that they were renewing an acquaintance. But what caught his quick eye was that the young Oberleutnant had neglected to surrender his writing pad. The major also noted this omission and cautioned the young officer as the two finally took leave. Before exiting, the Oberleutnant turned, walked over to the main desk, and placed the writing pad on the counter—right in front of John Drakopoulos.

Drakopoulos' heart skipped a beat. He eyed the writing pad momentarily, then—pretending that the midday heat had become unbearable—he removed his jacket and threw it on the counter, directly over the pad. A little later, his work finally completed, Drakopoulos nonchalantly picked up his jacket, being careful to hide the writing pad within its folds, and casually left for his room.

Once in his room with the door locked, Drakopoulos examined the writing pad carefully. It was devoid of any writing, but he could make out an imprint on the top sheet. He took a piece of charcoal from a censer that stood on a corner shelf together with some icons, and crumbled it over the top sheet. He smeared it smoothly over the whole page, then blew off the excess. Removing the shade from his bedside lamp, he tore off the page and placed it against the naked light bulb. The imprint, which was previously barely discernible, now appeared clearly in white against the black background.

What appeared to Drakopoulos as a jagged, broken line, similar to a thunderbolt, streaked halfway down the page. It was obvious that the Oberleutnant had been doodling. At the end of the jagged streak appeared the letters $K,R,E,T,A$. The $K,R,E$ were quite clear; the $T$ was faint; and the $A$ was barely distinguishable. But it was enough for Drakopoulos, for in German the word *Kreta* meant Crete!

Farther down the page there appeared another scribbled symbol. It was in the form of a huge $V$ followed by the Arabic numeral 17.

Drakopoulos knew that the Fifth German Mountain Division was stationed outside Athens. The Germans designated their divisions with Roman numerals. Could this young lieutenant, who had so carelessly disposed of his writing pad, have been the commanding officer of the seventeenth company in the Fifth German Division? It was not a plausible inference, for there had not been many Oberleutnants at the briefing. It appeared that $V$ 17 had a different connotation. He then gave credible weight to the thought that the letter $V$ designated the Roman numeral for the fifth month of the year, while the Arabic numeral 17 denoted the day of the month. He felt that this was a more logical conclusion.

Drakopoulos left the Grande Bretagne for his prearranged "drop-off" point. At the corner he was stopped by two Gestapo troopers. When he showed them his Gestapo pass, they gave him the Nazi salute and let him proceed with a nod and a smile. The tall young engineer strode quickly down University Street until he reached a basement bookstore located directly opposite the University of Athens. He walked to the rear of the shop where the shelves were filled with out-of-print books in Greek, English, German, and French. From the top shelf, he removed a moldy, weatherbeaten volume entitled *A Popular History of Greece.* Opening the book to Chapter 7, ''Characteristics of the Minoan Empire,'' he placed in it a piece of paper containing three digits: 17—5. He returned the book to the shelf and left.[4]

Two blocks away and parallel with University Street is an equally lengthy thoroughfare called Akademias, or Academy, Street. At a point left of where Academy curves to join Queen Sofia Avenue and Constitution Square, there is a narrow street named Canaris Street. In those dark days of the German occupation, a person walking up Canaris Street immediately encountered a barbed-wire barricade at the first street on the right. This barricade marked the beginning of Merlin Street, a two-block connection of Canaris Street with Queen Sofia Avenue. Merlin Street became a place of foreboding and nightmare for the victimized citizens of Athens—for it was the center of Gestapo terror activity. The cellars of the buildings on both sides of the street testified in blood to the tales of broken bodies, of torture, terror, and death.

At 5 Canaris Street, there was a four-story town house. On the top floor, in an apartment whose windows overlooked the Gestapo buildings on Merlin Street, the British had a wire transmitting station. It was typical of the phlegmatic British to place such an apparatus directly under the nose of the dreaded Gestapo.

An hour after Drakopoulos left his message in the book, a fourteen-year-old boy arrived at the same bookstore. Like Drakopoulos, Athanasios Tziotis was employed at the Grande Bretagne.

Each day at the same hour, he would come to the bookstore and pick up several newspapers for his employer, George Canellos, the associate director of the hotel.

On certain occasions the bookstore proprietor would ask young Athanasios if he would deliver a book or a newspaper to a special customer. The thought of earning a few extra drachmas appealed to him. The person to whom he made these deliveries lived on the top floor of a town house at 5 Canaris Street. It was many months before Athanasios Tziotis became even remotely aware that he was a runner for the Greek underground in the British intelligence service.[5]

Drakopoulos' message, hidden within the pages of the newspaper *Estia,* was delivered to 5 Canaris Street the same afternoon. That night the message was transmitted across the waters to a British submarine stationed on special picket duty off the western tip of Crete. The submarine relayed the message to Gibraltar, and from there it was transmitted to Admiralty House in London.

As Winston Churchill's personal bodyguard, it was Inspector Walter Henry Thompson's official duty each morning to awaken the prime minister and to deliver a large yellow sealed box that contained all communications received during the night.

This morning Thompson left the box as usual on the little table at Churchill's bedside. As Thompson turned to leave the room, he was startled by Churchill's jubilant exclamation. In an exhilarated, almost boyish voice, Winston Churchill cried out, "I knew it, Thompson, I knew it would be Crete! Send in my secretary! I must send a message!"[6]

Within the hour the message was transmitted to the commanding general of all the British forces in the Mediterranean:

PRIME MINISTER TO GENERAL WAVELL     14 MAY 1941
ALL MY INFORMATION POINTS TO [the invasion of Crete] ANY DAY
AFTER THE SEVENTEENTH.[7]

# 6 / SCORCHER ON COLORADO

## MAY 16, 1941

The hour of reckoning was rapidly approaching. From the day in October 1940 when Greece found itself at war with Italy, Churchill had insisted that military aid be rushed to his Balkan ally, even though this meant stripping the defenses from General Wavell's army in Egypt. Not only did Churchill insist that troops be dispatched to the Greek mainland, but he repeatedly exhorted Wavell to convert the huge natural harbor at Suda Bay in Crete into another Scapa Flow. It was difficult for Wavell to comprehend how Suda Bay could be fortified into a Scapa Flow. That famous naval base north of Scotland was well out of German bomber range, while Suda Bay lay exposed and defenseless to the might of the Luftwaffe. However, Churchill's enthusiasm for Crete's defense would not be dampened by such a reality; long before the Germans came to the aid of the Italians, Churchill had recognized Crete's strategic importance in the Mediterranean.

The responsibility of providing men for the defense of Crete fell upon the broad shoulders of the British commander in the Mediterranean, but Wavell did not have the soldiers to spare. His defenses covered a vast perimeter: In the Western Desert, his troops were defending themselves against Rommel's threatening incursions; to the south, they were fighting the Italians in Ethiopia; and now it appeared that more troops would be required to put down a rebellion in Iraq. In the face of these problems confronting his beleaguered command, Wavell gave the defense of Crete a lower priority.[1] In spite of this, Churchill insisted that steps be taken to convert Crete into an island bastion.

British Intelligence had become aware that the Germans were planning an airborne operation against Crete. As early as April 18, Churchill had informed Wavell in Cairo that an airborne invasion of Crete was to be anticipated. The British had been suc-

44

cessful in intercepting and decoding German messages originating in the highest command echelon via an apparatus known as *Ultra*.[2] As more and more information was intercepted, the magnitude of the attack became alarmingly impressive. It was enough for Churchill to telegraph Wavell:

> PRIME MINISTER TO GENERAL WAVELL 28 APRIL 1941
> IT SEEMS CLEAR FROM OUR INFORMATION THAT A HEAVY AIR-BORNE ATTACK BY GERMAN TROOPS AND BOMBERS WILL SOON BE MADE ON CRETE.
> LET ME KNOW WHAT FORCES YOU HAVE ON THE ISLAND AND WHAT YOUR PLANS ARE. . . .
> . . . IT OUGHT TO BE A FINE OPPORTUNITY FOR KILLING THE PARACHUTE TROOPS.
> . . . THE ISLAND MUST BE STUBBORNLY DEFENDED.[3]

The next day, Churchill received a reply:

> GENERAL WAVELL TO PRIME MINISTER 29 APRIL 1941
> CRETE WAS WARNED OF POSSIBILITY OF AIRBORNE ATTACK ON APRIL 18.

He went on to describe the disposition of the troops arriving daily from the Greek mainland:

> BESIDES ORIGINAL PERMANENT GARRISON . . . CRETE NOW CONTAINS AT LEAST 30,000 PERSONNEL EVACUATED FROM GREECE. THESE ARE BEING ORGANIZED FOR THE DEFENSE OF THE VITAL PLACES ON THE ISLAND: SUDA BAY, CANIA, RETIMO, AND HERAKLION.

Wavell proposed to visit the island on the next day for a personal inspection. However, the final paragraph of his reply disturbed Churchill:

> IT IS JUST POSSIBLE THAT PLAN FOR ATTACK ON CRETE MAY BE A COVER FOR ATTACK ON SYRIA OR CYPRUS, AND THAT REAL PLAN WILL ONLY BE DISCLOSED EVEN TO [their] OWN TROOPS AT THE LAST MOMENT. THIS WOULD BE CONSISTENT WITH GERMAN PRACTICE.[4]

When John Drakopoulos' message was received on May 14, confirming the date of the German airborne assault, Churchill wondered if Wavell had done everything possible to fortify the island.

In a seven-month period, the command of Crete had changed hands seven times. How was it possible to build up a strong defense structure under such conditions?

Back on December 1, Churchill had forwarded a memo to General Hastings Lionel "Pug" Ismay, his liaison with the Imperial General Staff, with a specific inquiry:

EXACTLY WHAT HAVE WE GOT DONE AT SUDA BAY . . . ? I HOPE TO BE ASSURED THAT MANY HUNDREDS OF CRETANS ARE WORKING AT STRENGTHENING THE DEFENSES AND LENGHTENING AND IMPROVING THE AERODROMES.[5]

The response was long in coming, but when it finally arrived, Churchill discovered that in spite of all his exhortations and suggestions, *nothing* had been done. The inhabitants of Crete, though eager to defend their native soil, had not been mobilized to strengthen defense positions or to improve the airfields. Nor had a reserve division been organized into a well-trained fighting force. All those months had gone to waste. Churchill knew the reason: The command structure on Crete was at fault. It was time he personally intervened again as he had had to do in the past. He would have to designate his own choice for the next commanding officer of the Cretan garrison.

The man he was going to appoint would bear the whole responsibility for the defense of Crete. For that position he chose a personal friend held in high esteem, who was also a hero of the British Empire.

Respectful of protocol and not wishing to override the echelons of military command, Churchill submitted the name of his choice to the chief of the Imperial General Staff. General Sir John Dill concurred with Churchill's recommendation and forwarded the name to General Wavell in Cairo.

The man who was appointed commanding officer of all forces on Crete was a fifty-two-year-old New Zealander, Major General Bernard Freyberg.

Although born in England, Bernard Freyberg had spent most of his early youth in New Zealand. Churchill first met him in September 1914, when Freyberg arrived as a young volunteer seeking a commission. Great Britain was at war, and Churchill, as First Lord of the Admiralty, was instrumental in organizing the Royal Navy Division. Bearing the First Lord's recommendation, Freyberg was assigned as a junior officer to a battalion in that naval division.

In the four years of trench warfare that followed, Freyberg proved himself a man of extraordinary courage. His days in the trenches were filled with legendary feats of gallantry and valor. He became a national hero and was awarded the Victoria Cross and the Distinguished Service Order with two bars in recognition of his unsurpassed service. By the end of the war, Freyberg had risen in rank from a sublieutenant to commander of a brigade.

After the war Freyberg remained in the British army but—more suited to the daring deeds of battle than the pomposity of garrison life—he was unhappy. To overcome the dull existence of a peace-time officer, he sought diversions such as attempting to swim the English Channel, a feat in which he failed by only a few hundred yards.

During that period, Freyberg also often met with his old friend and patron Winston Churchill. At one such meeting, Churchill inquired about Freyberg's war wounds. When Freyberg obligingly stripped to the waist, Churchill was able to count twenty-seven scars on his body.

As the years passed into the thirties, men of Freyberg's caliber were becoming a liability to the penny-pinching bureaucrats of the War Office. Thought was given to retiring and pensioning off the old war-horses—when war erupted again in Europe.

As early as September 1940, Winston Churchill had great plans for his old friend. The prime minister looked upon Freyberg as a man who would "fight for King and Country with an unconquerable heart anywhere he is ordered, and with whatever forces he is given by superior authorities, and he [thus] imparts his own invincible firmness of mind to all around him."[6]

These were the qualities that Churchill sought in the man who should command in Crete. They were qualities that would drive a commander to a resolute defense of the island and, in so doing, deny it to the enemy.

True to the promise given in his April 29 message, General Wavell left the next day for a visit to Crete. He arrived early on the morning of April 30, fatigued by the uncomfortable flight and weary from the many problems that burdened him. Upon his arrival, he immediately summoned a conference of all the senior officers on the island.

About the time that Wavell arrived in Crete by air, Bernard Freyberg sailed into Suda Bay aboard a warship, with troops that had been evacuated from the Greek mainland.

New Zealand had shipped its only division of three brigades to fight in the Mediterranean. With defeat in Greece and in the ensuing evacuation, the Fourth and Fifth Brigades were deposited on Crete, while the Sixth Brigade was transported directly to Egypt. As division commander, it was Freyberg's hope to reunite the three brigades in Egypt and reconstitute the whole New Zealand Division. For that reason, he left the warship in Suda Bay just before it sailed with the rest of the convoy for Egypt. He planned to visit the two brigades of his division and make plans for their transfer to Egypt. No sooner had Freyberg stepped ashore, however, than he was handed a message summoning him to the conference with Wavell.

The meeting took place on the rooftop terrace of a villa in the village of Platanias, halfway between the airfield at Maleme and the capital at Khaniá. Under the shade of a huge awning, the people who would resolve the defense situation in Crete gathered.

Wavell immediately realized that he faced a protocol problem, for he had too many senior commanders on hand. General Henry Maitland Wilson was senior to the island's garrison commander, General Edward Weston. Any message from Wavell to Weston required, out of courtesy, that a copy be sent to Wilson. Wavell would not "order" Wilson, but would only "suggest" that he act in conjunction with Weston. To add to the problems, Freyberg was expected momentarily, and he was junior to Wilson and senior to Weston. Someone would have to be sent away.

"Henry, what is your appreciation of the problem we face in defending Crete?" Wavell asked of Wilson when they were finally alone.

Wilson thought for a moment before answering. "I consider that unless all three services are prepared to face the *strain of maintaining adequate forces up to strength,* the holding of this island is a dangerous commitment, and a decision on the matter must be taken at once."[7]

"That is what you stated in your report. Then you haven't altered your opinion," replied Wavell, referring to the report Wilson had submitted to him on April 28. To the commanding general of the Mediterranean forces, Wilson's remarks represented an abdication of responsibility.

"You realize, of course, that it would be beyond our ability of 'maintaining adequate forces,' " commented Wavell, simultaneously remembering Churchill's exhortations "that Crete be held." Obviously, Wilson's thinking—although logistically sound—was at cross-purposes with that of the prime minister. Clearly, it was Wilson who had to go. Wilson was not too displeased when Wavell said: "I want you to go to Jerusalem and relieve Baghdad. . . ."[8]

Bernard Freyberg appeared on the terrace just as Wavell and Wilson were concluding their conversation. When Wilson departed, Wavell greeted Freyberg warmly.

"I want to tell you how well I think the New Zealand division has done in Greece. I do not believe any other division would have carried out those withdrawals as well."[9]

Freyberg, though never unduly impressed by compliments, accepted these warm words. He agreed that his New Zealanders had performed well.

Wavell took Freyberg by the arm and led him to a chair in the center of the terrace.

"I want you to take command of the forces in Crete!" Wavell stated without preamble, and then he added, "We expect Crete to be attacked in a few days. . . ."[10]

Taken by surprise, Freyberg still had other thoughts on the subject: "General, I would much rather get back to Egypt and concentrate the division and train and re-equip it. Besides," he added as an afterthought, "my government would never agree to the division being split permanently."

Wavell studied the tall, husky New Zealander for a few moments. "You realize, of course, that these orders come from the highest echelon in London."[11]

Freyberg took a deep breath. Then it must have been Churchill who had proposed his name for this assignment, he thought to himself. As if reading his mind, Wavell leaned forward and touched him lightly on the knee with his riding crop.

"It is your duty to take on the job."[12]

Freyberg shrugged his shoulders, replying, "I could do nothing but accept, under the circumstances."

"Good. Now let us take a close look at the problem," Wavell said as he opened a map of Crete.

When General Wavell stretched out the map before him on the table, it was Freyberg's first opportunity to make a critical observation of the island he had been asked to defend.

A cursory glance told him that Crete lay like a huge barrier reef in the middle of the Mediterranean, controlling the sea-lanes that connected the three continents of Europe, Africa, and Asia through Asia Minor. Whoever held possession of this island *could* maintain strategic control over the fortunes of enemy armies in southern Europe, North Africa, and the Near East. Now he appreciated Churchill's demands that Crete be defended and held.

After a light lunch, Freyberg was met by Colonel Keith Stewart, his chief of staff when he had commanded the New Zealand Division in Greece. Together they drove to the capital of Crete, Khaniá, to visit Crete Force Headquarters. What they found there was complete disorganization; there *was* no headquarters. No one seemed to know anything about the new command setup. Freyberg was horrified to learn that he had no staff officers and not even a single clerk to write out a general order.

Later, when he met his predecessor, General Weston, he asked if any defense plan had ever been drawn for Crete. Weston, who had held the command of Crete for only four days, smiled and shook his head. Much to Freyberg's chagrin, it was obvious that he would have to start from the beginning.

Freyberg appointed Colonel Keith Stewart as his chief of staff on Crete and ordered him to select a complete headquarters staff. He also requested an estimation of the strength of the forces available to defend the island. In the meantime, Freyberg would make a personal study of the lay of the land.

From the beginning, he was aware of Crete's primitive existence. The first point that impressed him was that not a single railroad existed. Only a narrow, paved road ran approximately 160 miles of the island's 186-mile length. It started at the western end of the island at Kisamos Kastelli and, running parallel to the north coast, went through the capital of Khaniá to the city of Rethimnon, and beyond to Iráklion. From Iráklion it proceeded inland past the village of Neapolis to Ayios Nikolaos, and then it deteriorated into a dirt road. This was the only paved road in Crete. One narrow, rocky, dirt road was the only passable connection to the southern coast, reaching the village of Timbakion. The other secondary roads leading inland began as dirt paths but soon narrowed into trails as they ascended into the foothills of the mountains that ran along the southern face of the island like a huge monolithic barrier. The mountains rose from 6,000 to 10,000 feet and were almost always snow-covered. The trails along the foothills disappeared amid the rugged crags, only to reappear on the southern coast, where the mountains ended in cliffs that fell in a sheer drop to meet the waters of the Libyan Sea.

To a military man like Freyberg, it was obvious that only the paved main northern road could be used for vehicular transportation by an army that had to maintain communications from one end of the island to the other.

Most of Crete's inhabitants lived on the northern coast of the island. Some of those near the main road had electricity in their homes; the rest still used kerosene lamps and candles. The few telephones that were available were used only by the rich or by businessmen in the cities.

Freyberg would have to create his own telephone communications system.

He observed that the northern coast was fertile and verdant— the reason why most of the Cretans lived in that area—covered with vineyards, olive groves, and fields of grain. But the fields were intersected by deep ravines, gullies, dry riverbeds, stone walls, dense bamboo glades, and tall grass sprinkled with angry cactus. To the military eye, such terrain posed a problem for a body of men that might have to move crosscountry rapidly for a counterattack. Such broken ground would make a mobile attack force almost useless.

On the western extension of the northern road lay the sleepy town of Kastelli, little bigger than a village, nestled around a deep harbor between the Gramvousa and Rodopos peninsulas. Traveling eastward, Freyberg passed through the town of Tavronites, crossed over a dry river on a three-span steel-girder bridge, and just beyond the bridge, he came to a small, singlestrip airfield named after the adjacent village of Maleme.

Across the road from the airstrip, there rose a height the Cretans called Kavzakia Hill. Freyberg noted that the hill and the airfield would have to be well defended.

From Maleme, Freyberg traveled along the road passing through the village of Platanias and the other villages that lay further inland, returning to Khaniá early in the evening.

On the map the barren hills of the Akrotiri Peninsula, where

Freyberg now had his headquarters, appeared as the left profile of a human skull. The capital of Khaniá was at the Adam's apple, while the huge natural harbor of Suda Bay lay at the nape of the neck. The harbor was littered with sunken hulls of freighters that had suffered at the hands of the Luftwaffe.

Farther east, the village of Georgeopolis stood near the sandy shore. The village had no significance except that its beach could be a possible landing site for a seaborne invasion.

The north coast road continued eastward beyond Rethimnon for another forty-eight miles until it entered the walled city of Iráklion, the largest city in Crete. The harbor was the best of the three cities, second only to Suda Bay. Its airfield was the largest and most modern on the island, with a double landing strip.

When Freyberg finished with the study of his map, he counted the circles he had drawn around Maleme, Khaniá, Suda Bay, Georgeopolis, Rethimnon, and Iráklion. Slowly a defense plan was forming in his mind.

In the corner of his makeshift desk several sheets of paper caught Freyberg's eye. Neatly handwritten—there were no head-quarters clerk-typists—was a report on the total manpower situation on the island. Freyberg's chief of staff had done his homework.

Except for the men of the original island garrison, the majority of troops arriving in Crete were evacuees from the Greek mainland. Countless thousands poured onto the island, with few weapons and fewer supplies. Dirty and disorganized, they had just the clothing on their backs; all their personal equipment had been left behind in Greece in their haste to leave. Most of the men were unassigned, and lacking the supervision of junior officers—of which there were too few—they wandered aimlessly through the fields and villages at will, hungry and thirsty. Some resorted to stealing; some fought among themselves; there was even a report of a civilian murder. Many of them had become ill-disciplined and disrespectful of authority. It was time to bring order out of this turmoil and restore the discipline that marks a military fighting unit. Court-martials were put into effect for the malefactors, and there were field punishment centers for the incorrigibles. To a punctilious person like Bernard Freyberg, this was a bad sign of the breakdown in morale.

As far as equipment and supplies were concerned, the report continued, matters were equally bad. Many of the men who arrived unassigned had no rifles or any other infantry weapons, much less ammunition. The units that landed intact were devoid of artillery or antiaircraft weapons. There was no transport or any adequate reserves of equipment or supplies with which to arm the arrivals.

Of the meager rations and arms supplies sent from Egypt, only one-third arrived safely in Crete. Nothing entered Suda Bay during daylight, when the Luftwaffe was always present to attack the defenseless supply ships.

Attached to Colonel Stewart's summary, which painted such a grim picture of the situation in Crete, was a military appreciation dated April 29 from the War Office, which reported the extent of the expected German attack in numbers of aircraft and shipping. Freyberg thought for a moment, shocked by what he had read. Then he picked up a pencil and scribbled a message to be telegraphed to Cairo.

GENERAL FREYBERG TO GENERAL WAVELL  1 MAY 1941
FORCES AT MY DISPOSAL ARE TOTALLY INADEQUATE TO MEET ATTACK ENVISIONED. . . .
URGE THAT QUESTION OF HOLDING CRETE SHOULD BE RECONSIDERED. . . .
IT IS MY DUTY TO INFORM NEW ZEALAND GOVERNMENT OF SITUATION IN WHICH GREATER PART OF MY DIVISION IS NOW PLACED.[13]

True to his threat, a few moments later Freyberg scribbled a second message, addressed to the prime minister of New Zealand, Mr. Peter Fraser:

P.M.–N.Z.  1 MAY 1941
FEEL IT IS MY DUTY TO REPORT MILITARY SITUATION IN CRETE . . . WOULD STRONGLY REPRESENT TO YOUR GOVERNMENT GRAVE SITUATION IN WHICH BULK OF NEW ZEALAND DIVISION IS PLACED, AND RECOMMEND YOU BRING PRESSURE TO BEAR ON HIGHEST PLANE IN LONDON EITHER TO SUPPLY US WITH SUFFICIENT MEANS TO DEFEND ISLAND OR TO REVIEW DECISION [that] CRETE MUST BE HELD.[14]

Freyberg's worry about the Royal Navy was needless.

The evacuation of the British troops from the Greek mainland was a monumental task that was borne successfully by the Royal Navy—despite the Luftwaffe—after many trying days of great effort and greater courage. Churchill forwarded a message to Admiral Andrew Cunningham, commanding the Mediterranean Fleet:

> I . . . CONGRATULATE YOU UPON THE BRILLIANT AND HIGHLY SUCCESSFUL MANNER IN WHICH THE NAVY HAS ONCE AGAIN SUCCOURED THE ARMY AND BROUGHT OFF FOUR-FIFTHS OF THE ENTIRE FORCE. . . .[15]

Perhaps the prime minister, with the foresight of his genius, was priming the commanding officer of the Mediterranean fleet for the tremendous task he would face in the days ahead.

In the year that Admiral Cunningham held the command of the Mediterranean fleet, he was determined to transform the vast Mediterranean into a British lake. With Admiral James S. Somerville's fleet guarding the strait at Gibraltar, Cunningham planned to protect the sea-lanes from Malta in the west to the Suez in the east. It would be a formidable task, with the most immediate dangers being the presence of the Italian Supermarina and the German Luftwaffe.

To keep the Italian fleet in check, Cunningham ordered an all-air attack on their naval base at Taranto in November 1940. It was a successful raid, which surprised them by its audacity and shattered the aspirations of the Italian navy.

With the threat from the Italians diminished, there remained the foreboding shadow of the ever-present Luftwaffe. The only counter to that threat would be the intervention of the Royal Air Force. Unfortunately, the RAF could not spare the aircraft required to defend Crete and the waters around the island. There were not enough fighters or bombers available to protect the Western Desert, Malta, Suez, and the Near East all at the same time, particularly after the losses suffered in the Battle of Britain.

Although Freyberg raised the question of the logistics of holding Crete with the prime minister of New Zealand, Peter Fraser's silence indicated that there was no alternative but to stay and defend. Wavell's response was the proposed delivery of equipment, supplies, and men. Freyberg replied that he had ample numbers of men, but was in dire need of equipment and supplies. However, getting the supplies past the Luftwaffe to Crete still remained the major obstacle. On this problem, Freyberg was to comment humorously that the fault lay with the topography of Crete; the mountains should have been on the northern coast, with the harbors on the south, facing Egypt.

By the end of the first week in May, Freyberg's force on Crete had reached a total of 32,000 British and Commonwealth troops, to which could be added 14,000 partially armed Greeks.

Once again Freyberg referred to his map with its red circles. It was time to put his defense plan into effect.

He decided to divide the island's defense system into three major sectors, with the greatest consideration given to areas that appeared most vulnerable to air and sea invasion. The criteria used to designate a sector were the presence of an airfield and a harbor. The sector divisions were Iráklion, Rethimnon, and Maleme (the latter extended to include Suda Bay). Looking at his roster, Freyberg saw that he had ample general officers to command these sectors.

For the Iráklion sector, he appointed Brigadier General B. H. Chappel, who had been the commanding officer in Crete two months earlier, before the arrival of Weston and Freyberg. The Rethimnon sector was placed under the command of Brigadier General G. Vasey, an Australian who had fought brilliantly in Greece and now was to command the Australians again in Crete. The third sector, Maleme, was given to Brigadier General Edward Puttick to command the Fourth and Fifth New Zealand Brigades.

Because of the extensive ground covered by this third sector, Freyberg subdivided it to include Khaniá, Akrotiri, and Suda Bay. General Weston, who had been Freyberg's predecessor in Crete, was appointed to command this subdivided area, which included the commanding general's headquarters.

Freyberg left the disposition of troops to each sector commander, but he did emphasize one specific condition: He wanted the airfields to be defended during an attack by at least one-third of the troops allocated to each sector, while the rest would be available as a mobile force to counterattack and overcome any threat to the landing strip. "You must deny the airfields to the enemy at all costs!" he warned the sector commanders at a briefing.[16]

The airfield at Maleme, with its adjacent high ground, soon to become known as Hill 107 on the war map, was given to the Fifth New Zealand Brigade to defend. Its commander, Brigadier Janies Hargest, was a short, plump New Zealander who assigned the defense of the airfield and its Hill 107 to the Twenty-second Battalion, while two other New Zealand battalions, the Twenty-third and Twenty-first, were echeloned further east of the airfield. The Twenty-eighth Battalion, composed of Maori New Zealanders, was kept in reserve at Platanias village, where Hargest established his brigade headquarters.

Antiaircraft guns protecting the airfield at Maleme were controlled by the gun operations room at Khaniá under General Weston, the Royal Marine general.

Thus the disposition of the troops was completed. The whole system formed a straight line of defense in which each sector was linked to the others by the frail means of radio, telephone, cable, or runner—all of them vulnerable to disruption during the course of battle.

Four days after General Freyberg sent his telegrams to Wavell and the New Zealand prime minister protesting the decision to defend Crete, he regretted his impetuous action, wondering if his remarks had created an unfortunate stir in London. After all, his appointment as the commanding general in Crete had come upon the recommendation of his old friend Winston Churchill. It would be improper to cause Churchill undue embarrassment by his negative attitude toward this new command. It was time to make amends.

GENERAL FREYBERG TO PRIME MINISTER          5 MAY 1941
CANNOT UNDERSTAND NERVOUSNESS: AM NOT IN THE LEAST
ANXIOUS ABOUT AIRBORNE ATTACK; HAVE MADE MY DISPOSI-
TIONS AND FEEL CAN COPE ADEQUATELY WITH THE TROOPS AT
MY DISPOSAL. . . .[17]

But on May 5, the date of this message, Freyberg had *not* completed his dispositions. The Second Battalion of Leicesters, assigned to Brigadier Chappel at Iráklion, did not arrive in Crete until May 16.

By that date, too, Bernard Freyberg had completed his final tour of the Cretan defense system, and he was elated. His earlier doubts seemed to have been alleviated. He thought it best to inform his superior in Cairo.

FREYBERG TO GENERAL WAVELL                16 MAY 1941
HAVE COMPLETED PLAN FOR THE DEFENSE OF CRETE AND HAVE
JUST RETURNED FROM FINAL TOUR OF DEFENSES. I FEEL

GREATLY ENCOURAGED BY MY VISIT. EVERYWHERE ALL RANKS ARE FIT AND MORALE IS HIGH. . . .[18]

The tired, heavily burdened Wavell breathed a sigh of relief. He was so pleased with the message that he forwarded a copy to Winston Churchill.

Wavell's staff in Cairo had adopted the code name Colorado for Crete, and Scorcher for the pending German attack.[19] Freyberg's headquarters on Crete was designated Creforce.[20]

Thus, while the Germans made their plans for Operation Mercury, the defenders of Crete completed their defenses and waited for Scorcher to come to Colorado.

# 7 / "JUST A CIRCLE ON THE MAP"

## APRIL 21, 1941

One evening, the quietude that usually prevailed after sunset along the main road in the village of Pelikapina was disturbed by the approach of vehicles on the darkened highway. The sound intensified as a motorcade, traveling with dimmed lights, came down the highway from Khaniá. The vehicles turned left and proceeded up the tree-lined road, halting before the main entrance to a villa.

The neighbors in the surrounding homes peered through their shuttered windows and, in the dim shadows of early evening, saw many people enter the house. They concluded that their respected neighbor, Constantine Manos, had late visitors.

By the next morning, the grounds of the villa had undergone a great change. The beautiful grass of the front lawn had been furrowed by the tires of the many military vehicles parked in the courtyard before the main entrance. Men in uniform stood everywhere. There were guards at each entrance; at each pathway around the house; at the juncture of the main road with the path to the house; even at the shore north of the Manos home. Overnight, the once-quiet residence had become a military compound.

The fact that the military guards would not reveal the identity of the new resident, obviously for the sake of security, only whetted the neighbors' curiosity. And then, one day, they all knew.

A single villager, Peter Lazerakis, got a brief glimpse of the guest in the villa. The newcomer was standing on the front terrace in clear view. He appeared tall and regal and wore the uniform of a Greek army field marshal. Lazerakis had seen that face before. The old villager's jaw dropped as he recognized the royal profile.[1]

The presence of the king of Greece in Crete gave Freyberg added concern. The king's safety and that of his government was also considered to be the general's responsibility.

Freyberg had considered the possibility that the king might be captured by a German raiding force and held as a war prize. From London came the order that the Greek king should be exposed to no undue risk. That order made the situation quite impossible. Even with additional guards stationed at the king's residence, a clear danger existed. To this order from London, Freyberg replied tactlessly that he "would prefer to see his Royal Highness killed or wounded in battle, rather than be taken a prisoner of the Germans!"[2] The Creforce commander decided that King George must leave Crete for the safety of Egypt.

Freyberg dispatched Colonel J. S. Blount, who was liaison officer between Creforce headquarters and the British minister in Greece, to see King George, with orders to tell him that he must leave Crete for his own safety. Provisions would be made to take him to Alexandria and then to Cairo. The Greek king would not see Colonel Blount but, through his aide-de-camp, refused curtly and emphatically.

Now it fell upon Freyberg's shoulders to see the king personally in order to persuade him to leave the island. Sir Michael Palairet, the British minister in Greece, made the appointment for the interview. The commander of Creforce arrived at the Manos villa in Pelikapina promptly at the appointed hour. He was ushered into the living room, which doubled as the royal audience chamber.

King George met Freyberg at the entrance to the room. The king's lean, taut, smooth-shaved face was slightly pale with fatigue, but his keen blue eyes twinkled cordially, and the deep lines around his mouth broadened in the warmth of his greeting. Regal in appearance, he lacked the stiffness of his office.

The New Zealander quickly came to the purpose of his visit. In clipped phrases, he reviewed the dangers to the king's safety— the possibility of assassination by any pro-German agent, or kidnapping by German parachutists. The situation pointed to one solution: It was imperative that King George leave the island.

In his zeal, Freyberg had forgotten royal tact. He had not suggested that the king depart; he had ordered him to leave. The general had spoken as if he were addressing a junior officer.

King George disregarded this lack of courtesy and graciously attributed it to Freyberg's concern for the royal safety. "My dear General," interrupted the king, "we appreciate your concern for our safety, but what you ask is quite impossible."

The king stood up and walked to the large French doors that

opened onto the terrace. At last Freyberg remembered royal etiquette: he also stood up. The king resumed, "As long as a single Greek soldier fights on Greek soil, my place would be at his side. Remember, General, that I am the King of the Hellenes!"[3]

The interview was over. The decision was final—King George did not intend to leave Crete. At least, not yet.

Soon Freyberg received a cable from General Wavell in Cairo, confirming "that the king and his government should remain on Crete even if the island were attacked." This was the decision formulated by Churchill, the war cabinet, and the Foreign Office in London.[4] But the responsibility of King George's safety still remained like a lead weight upon Freyberg's shoulders. It was one more problem in addition to the many already confronting the commanding general of the Cretan defenders.

A few days later, King George requested that General Freyberg attend a meeting to be held in Khaniá, the capital of Crete. The king ordered that the commanding officers of all Greek regiments serving in Crete also attend. Freyberg arrived with his chief of staff, Colonel Keith Stewart.

The Greek king and the New Zealand general mounted the stage of the large auditorium. Standing at attention before them were the commanding generals of the four Greek army commands in Crete, with their regimental, battalion, and attached unit commanders. It was a collection of brass that filled the meeting hall to capacity.

The king greeted the commanders courteously, but did not put them at ease. Then he introduced General Freyberg.

"Gentlemen," announced King George, "from this moment forward, I commit all Greek units on Crete to the command of General Freyberg."[5]

With a formal hand salute, the laconic monarch left the stage, got into his waiting automobile, and returned to his residence. Thus the commanders of all Greek units were placed under the direct command of Freyberg's Creforce headquarters. The next day a royal proclamation made this commitment official.[6]

General Freyberg was surprised but not pleased by this additional burden of command. He requested and received from the Greek General Staff the order of battle of all Greek units in Crete. Reviewing the listing, he had 350 officers, 300 officer cadets, 11,000 infantrymen, 200 airforce personnel, and 3,000 gendarmes—a total of 14,850 men.

On paper this total looked impressive. However, the figures

belied the facts. Of the armed infantrymen, most had old weapons with only ten to thirty rounds per rifle. Many had no weapons at all. Of all these men, approximately 2,000 officers and other ranks were veterans of the fighting on the Greek mainland. The only other Greek units with any semblance of military training were the Cretan gendarme units—just 3,000 of the total. The rest were raw, untrained recruits.

Freyberg referred to the Greek troops as "ill-equipped, ill-trained polyglot units."[7] He strongly felt that if they were to be directly involved in the anticipated fighting, they would be a hindrance rather than an asset. He issued instructions to his sector commanders that the Greek units be assigned to areas that would not be factors in the defense of the island. In a sense, his order implied that these units be placed out of harm's way.

The First Greek Regiment was assigned to the command of Brigadier James Hargest of the Fifth New Zealand Brigade. Hargest's Fifth Brigade had the task of protecting the airfield at Maleme, the prominent height below the airfield—designated as Hill 107—the surrounding villages, and the highway bridge over the Tavronites River.

The ground west of the river was unfortified because Hargest had no men to place in those defense positions. The small port town of Kisamo Kastelli, just twenty-six miles west of Khaniá, was located on the western edge of this undefended area. With its dozen or more limestone buildings, it stood at the southern end of Kisamos Bay, formed by the fingerlike projections of the Gramvousa and Rodopos peninsulas. The town's only claim to importance lay in its unfinished airfield and its brokendown wooden wharf. Brigadier Hargest decided to place the First Greek Regiment in that undefended area west of the Tavronites River. Such an assignment would serve a twofold purpose: First, it would cover a weak spot in his defense perimeter; second, it would keep this "ill-trained, ill-equipped" Greek unit from interfering with the defense plans of his Twenty-first, Twenty-second, and Twenty-third battalions, which together with the Twenty-eighth comprised his Fifth Brigade.

The Greek regiment had a complement of approximately 900 men—a little larger than battalion strength. More than half of them were new recruits from the surrounding Cretan hills, with only a few weeks of fundamental basic training.

Approximately 300 of the new recruits had no rifles or any other weapons. Those who did have rifles had such a vast variety that bullets from one type did not fit the others. The men who possessed no firearms armed themselves with axes, curved Syrian swords, ancient shotguns, and flintlocks that had been used against the Turks early in the century. The regiment had two machine guns of World War I vintage, both of which had a sad history of multiple breakdowns.

When Hargest inspected these men, he protested to his superior, General Puttick, that they were unfit for any battle assignment. As a compromise, Puttick dispatched several New Zealand officers from his staff and a few NCOs for the purpose of training this Greek "rabble," as Hargest had referred to them. The New Zealanders brought with them the welcome additions of two Bren guns with ammunition.

This New Zealand cadre came under the command of Major Thomas Bedding. His orders were explicit: Put up a token defense if attacked, then retreat to the hills in the south and link up with any other unit. In the meantime, he was to train the men of the First Greek Regiment in the art of military defense.[8]

Bedding immediately took over advisory command of the Greek regiment, dividing it into two battalions. One battalion was deployed west of Kastelli and the other was positioned east of the town. The best-trained men of the regiment were the members of the Cretan gendarmerie. They all had the same rifles and at least thirty rounds per man. Kept as a mobile reserve between the two deployed battalions, they were situated in the center of the town where Bedding had established his headquarters.

The Greek regimental commander, Colonel Socrates Papademetrakopoulos, had an amiable smile as long as his name. He greeted Major Bedding with courtesy and warmth and ordered his two battalion commanders, Lieutenant Colonels Skordilis and Kourkoutis, to accept the military orders of the New Zealand junior officer.

"Listen to him and learn," were his instructions. "Forget your seniority in rank and your pride. When the time comes, we will show these gentlemen that it takes more than weapons and training to fight a battle."[9]

His words were to prove prophetic. In due time this "ill-trained, ill-equipped rabble," whose existence had taught them fieldcraft and mountain marksmanship—and whose past was characterized by a long history of valorous opposition to servitude—would astound their British allies with their heroism in battle.

* * *

The other Greek regiments were distributed among the other brigades of the New Zealand division. General Puttick, the division's commanding general, had assigned the Sixth and Eighth Greek Infantry Regiments to Colonel Howard Kippenberger, the commander of the Tenth New Zealand Brigade.

Kippenberger was just getting the feel of command. Although his brigade was newly formed—composed mostly of gunners and truck drivers without infantry training—he felt that he had a good core of men. He would mold them into a fine military unit, ready to meet any offense the enemy had to offer. All he needed was time to train them.

When the 900-man Eighth Greek Regiment was assigned to his brigade, Kippenberger regarded them skeptically. He felt at home with his own men, but these Greeks were a different lot. He protested their assignment to his brigade. Puttick listened patiently to Kippenberger, just as he had listened to Hargest earlier.

"Why, these men are nothing more than malaria-ridden little chaps from Macedonia, with only four weeks service," objected Kippenberger.

"I know," replied Puttick somewhat condescendingly. Then he suggested, "Put them someplace where they would not interfere with your basic defense. Put them down at the village of Alikianou." He placed his finger on the map at a village in the Prison Valley area south of the town of Galatas.

"But, General, in this position, they would only be just a circle on the map!" the brigade commander continued. "It would be murder to leave such troops in *any* position!"

General Puttick rose to leave, giving Kippenberger a parting comment, "Remember, Colonel, that in war, murder sometimes has to be done."[10]

The other Greek unit that Kippenberger reluctantly had to accept and situate within the defense perimeter of his brigade was the undermanned Sixth Greek Regiment, under the command of Lieutenant Colonel Gregoriou. Its two battalions were commanded by Major Moraites and Major Papadakis.

This was a newly formed regiment, and the men that filled its ranks were for the most part green recruits with little or no training. Their arms varied in caliber and vintage. Kippenberger was at wit's end where to position them so that they would do the least harm to his defense perimeter. He decided to assign the Greeks to the high ground—called Cemetery Hill—south of the village of Galatas. The position would not be too far forward of his own brigade headquarters, and it would conveniently sandwich the Sixth Greek Regiment between two of his own New Zealand battalions. Kippenberger felt that his dependable New Zealanders, on both flanks, would be able to offer the inexperienced Greeks some support to offset their weakness. As for Lieutenant Colonel Gregoriou, the CO of the Sixth Greek Regiment, Kippenberger had little respect for him as a regimental commander.

First Lieutenant Aristides Kritakis had been a reserve officer in the Greek army before the war. In civilian life he had been a newspaper correspondent and a free-lance writer. When war came to Greece, he returned to active duty and was assigned to Greek Army Headquarters in Athens. With Greece's capitulation, Kritakis became one of the countless thousands who were evacuated by the Royal Navy and ferried to Crete. There he reported to the headquarters of the First Greek Army Command in Khaniá, and was assigned to the newly formed Sixth Greek Regiment stationed at Galatas.

A motorcycle carried Kritakis westward out of Khaniá on the main highway and, after a few miles, took the left turn that led south to Galatas. It was a dusty, bumpy ride over a deeply rutted dirt road, the vehicle finally stopping in front of a coffeehouse in the Galatas village square. The coffeehouse was the headquarters of the Sixth Greek Regiment.

Kritakis dusted himself off, happy to get out of that uncomfortable sidecar. The whole square bustled with Greeks, New Zealanders, trucks, jeeps, and motorcycles. The lieutenant cast a quick eye over the scene, noted the double-belfried church that dominated the square and the New Zealand Service Club in the building adjacent to the church, and then he turned and entered the regiment's headquarters.

The regimental adjutant, a young first lieutenant, greeted Kritakis and asked him to remain until the return of the regimental commander, who wished to meet him. Kritakis took a seat in the corner and waited. He watched with amusement at first, and later with impatience, as the bureaucratic complexities of a headquarters office unfurled before him. From the experience of his previous assignment in Athens, he realized that all headquarters offices were the same, except that this one was primitive compared to its plush Athens counterpart.

A tall, slender infantry captain entered and headed for the adjutant's desk. His height, ramrod bearing, and military demeanor caught Kritakis' eye immediately.

"I have come for the ammo and rations I was promised two days ago!" he rapped sharply at the young lieutenant. The adjutant rose from his seat, somewhat surprised by the captain's brusqueness, mumbling a few words of greeting.

"Look here, Lieutenant," the captain continued, ignoring the greeting, "my men are hungry and so are their rifles." Leaning over the desk, he added, "I want those supplies and I want them now!" There was anger flashing from his blue eyes.

The lieutenant stammered, "Yes, sir, they are ready for you."

"Good," smiled the captain, his anger suddenly softening. "I have a detail of men waiting outside."

Kritakis witnessed the whole episode and admired the captain's concern for his men. That is a good officer, he remarked to himself.

Colonel Gregoriou arrived a few minutes later and greeted Kritakis cordially. "I am glad to have an experienced man like yourself in my regiment, Kritakis. Most of my young officers are just out of school, with only six weeks training. I am going to send you to a good company—let's see, ah yes, here we are." He leaned over his desk and picked up a manila envelope. "The CO is tough, but he is one of my best company commanders." Lieutenant Kritakis was assigned to the Sixth Company, encamped in a valley before the village's Cemetery Hill.

Lieutenant Kritakis refused the offer of a motorcycle ride to his company. One such motorcycle trip a day was enough for him, he thought; besides, he preferred to walk the distance. Before taking the road to his new assignment, he strode across the village square and entered the Church of St. Nicholas, lit a candle and said a few prayers, ending with the sign of the cross. Though not a deeply religious man, Kritakis felt that he was now prepared for whatever was to come.

Following the posted signs, he took the left road exiting from the village square. It was a dirt road that wound past the stone houses of the village and ascended gradually to the cemetery. At the entrance to the cemetery, Kritakis passed a small chapel and followed a path among the rows of tombstones.

At the far end of the cemetery, there was a tall stone wall like a parapet, the hilly terrain beyond dropping gradually into a deep valley. Kritakis stood on the wall and scanned the breathtaking view.

To his right he could see a series of flat oblong buildings, marking the location of the prison compound that gave the area its name of Filakes, or Prison Valley. Beyond lay the village of Aghia, with its glistening water reservoir. To Kritakis' extreme right were the multihued, undulating hills that bounded Galatas on the west. To his left he could discern the varicolored rooftops that marked the city of Khaniá, near the horizon, with the deep azure of the sea beyond.

In the valley below him was a tented encampment. A road, forking at the entrance to the cemetery, descended into the valley toward the encampment. That must be the company area, Kritakis thought.

The headquarters tent for the Sixth Company was a huge square tent pitched under a group of trees. Aristides Kritakis introduced himself to two officers he found in the tent. They were Second Lieutenants Koulakis and Piperis, platoon leaders, waiting for the company commander.

"What's the CO like?" Kritakis inquired, hoping to get an opinion of his new commanding officer.

"He is a good officer, is Captain Emorfopoulos. We call him Captain 'E' for short—but with respect," replied Piperis.

"He does everything for the soldier in the field. He wouldn't ask a single man to do what he himself wouldn't do first. The men love him," continued Koulakis, adding, "I served as a sergeant under him in Albania. He is a good man!"

"His only drawback," interjected Lieutenant Piperis, lowering his voice as if to lessen the critical aspect of his remark, "is that he is often moody and too philosophical."

Both Koulakis and Piperis snapped to attention as a tall shadow fell across the entrance to the tent. Kritakis turned, and there standing before him was his new company commander. Kritakis had not forgotten the captain's bearing, his blue eyes, his smile. It was the same man he had seen in the regimental headquarters a few hours earlier. He had already drawn his own conclusions about this officer.

Captain Athanasios Emorfopoulos introduced himself to Kritakis and, ignoring military protocol, warmly shook the lieutenant's hand. A close attachment was born between the two men. It was obvious that Captain E knew how to gain the immediate respect of the men under his command.

Because of Kritakis' seniority, Captain E appointed him company executive officer.

"I need you here looking after the company's paper work while

I train the men in the field. You know, my dear Kritakis," he added prophetically, standing in front of the tent looking out at his men just back from a field exercise, "we don't have too much time."

In the days that followed, Lieutenant Kritakis observed his company commander carefully. Captain E was in the field continuously from sunup to sunset, working tirelessly to train his company in the rudimentary aspects of infantry life. In the mornings he had his men undergoing manual-of-arms and short-order drill and weapons familiarization. In the afternoons he led them in target and bayonet practice and basic field defense. Hour after hour he was out there, sweating with his platoons under the hot sun. After dusk he roamed through the encampment listening to the men and their gripes, giving them inspiring pep talks. They loved him for it.

Whenever he learned, through the grapevine, that a supply of rifles or ammunition was available, he would take a few of his sergeants and sweep in like a vulture to snatch them for his ill-equipped men.

One evening, after a long day of training, Captain E sat quietly in the headquarters tent, alone with his executive officer. The captain was in one of the philosophical moods Lieutenant Piperis had mentioned. Kritakis broke the long silence.

"It looks as if the company is shaping up," he remarked, hoping that Captain E would snap out of his mood. There was no response, and he tried again: "How does it look to you?"

Suddenly Captain E realized that Kritakis was speaking to him, and his eyes cast off that distant look.

"The men will do well," he replied, "in spite of the fact that they have not completed their basic training. They will do all that is asked of them, even if they don't have enough rifles, bayonets, or ammunition. I am satisfied with them; they are not the weak link. The weakness lies in those pompous asses on the staff in regimental headquarters."

Kritakis was shocked that his company commander would criticize the regiment's leadership.

"Take our jolly good Colonel Gregoriou," Emorfopoulos continued. "He has let himself get too fat in mind and in body. Did you notice the New Zealand officers? They are lean and hardy. Don't misunderstand, our regimental commander is an excellent soldier. Why, I've seen him throw a can five feet into the air and hit it three times with his pistol before the can fell to the ground. He is a good soldier, considerate of the officers in his command—

but that is not enough in war today! His worst fault is that he lacks *initiative*. His thoughts deal with a war of a bygone era, not what we expect to hit us tomorrow or the next day.''

The captain left his chair, lit a cigarette, and resumed. "Did you know that in Khaniá there is a whole warehouse filled with rifles and ammunition, just waiting to be distributed? Yet the Colonel makes no effort to requisition the rifles, even though he knows that many of our men have *no* weapons. He claims that the English will distribute them when the proper time arrives—can you imagine that? Someday the Luftwaffe will discover the warehouse's location and blow it to hell!

"He leaves everything to our allies, the British and New Zealanders. He has made no effort to set up a secondary regimental defense or make provisions for an open supply line to the frontline companies. He doesn't even allow us to distribute ammunition to our men, just in case we are attacked suddenly.

"As a matter of fact, from what I can see of the overall picture, our whole regiment presents a stagnant, walled-in defense. There are no provisions for a mobile attack force to hit the enemy at his weakest point. When he comes, we will sit here waiting for the enemy to land and to come to us—instead of us going after him and killing him before he is massed and reinforced.

"I have made my suggestions to Regimental in writing, but they have been ignored. There is an air of defeatism up at Regimental, but not here in the ranks. *My men will fight!*

"Mark my words, if they don't change their attitude at Staff, we can lose this battle even before it begins, and it will begin sooner than they think.''[11]

Angered at his own words, the captain picked up his helmet and walked out of the tent, leaving his executive officer with a stark picture of the regiment's situation.

The island of Crete was now rapidly becoming a bastion of armed men. More than 46,000 troops filled the island-fortress from Kisamo Kastelli in the west to Sitia in the east.

The civilian inhabitants of Crete were aware of the existing danger. Even before the final occupation of the Greek mainland, light German air attacks had been made upon Crete. By the first week of May, the attacks had become increasingly heavy. In time, they began at sunrise and did not cease until sunset. Their fury pinpointed the defensive positions located in the hills about the airfields at Maleme, at Rethimnon, and at Iráklion. More concentrated bombing focused on the Suda Bay defenses. The waters of Suda Bay were choked with debris and submerged hulls of sunken ships. A heavy layer of black smoke rose skyward for thousands of feet from the burning ships in the bay. Even the superstructure of the beached HMS *York* had been shattered by the persistent attacks of the Stuka dive-bombers in their all-out effort to silence the antiaircraft batteries on the eight-inch-gun cruiser.

All ships arriving by daylight were trailed by a string of dive-bombers or were constantly strafed by ME-109 fighter aircraft. These persistent bombings aggravated the island's critical supply problem. Of a total of 27,000 tons of munitions sent to Crete in the first weeks of May, only 3,000 tons were landed safely.

After May 15 the scope of these air attacks was expanded to include the cities of Khaniá, Rethimnon, and Iráklion. With an earsplitting, earthshaking roar, the bombs fell upon the defenseless cities. They whistled as they plummeted to earth, erupting into flames and spewing pieces of concrete, steel, lumber, and human bodies into the air.

The first bombing raid caught most city inhabitants by surprise. They had not sought shelter—nor were there any adequate shelters available. People died like flies in the rain of explosives, as tons of steel slammed into their dwellings and into the streets. The concussion was so stupefying that those who survived that early attack would never forget it. In a matter of a few days, the cities were a mass of ruins. Skeletal, fire-blackened remnants of walls, shattered streets, and corpses became a common sight.

Below this debris and destruction lay the bodies of more dead and of the dying, pinned under timbers, fallen walls, and roofs. In the heat of day, the dead began to decompose, and the stink of death permeated the dust-filled air, making rescue work even more difficult.

Yet the German air attacks continued relentlessly on a daily schedule from sunrise until dusk.

The Cretan inhabitants took even this hardship in their stride. Most city dwellers left for the fields, the hills, and the caves of the southern mountains. Others sought refuge with relatives in distant villages. They had to alter their routines, but life went on.

While the city dwellers left their destroyed homes for the safety of villages in the hills, many other Cretans left their homes in the safe villages in order to serve in the island's defense.

Manoli Paterakis was one of these. Leaving his family and his home in the village of Koustogeriko, located high in the White Mountains of southern Crete, he descended to the northern coast. A gendarme by profession, he had come to serve in the defense of Crete. Indeed, Manoli Paterakis would fight well. In the months ahead, his heroic deeds were destined to thrill many adventurous hearts.

There were others. George Psychoundakis was twenty-one and, dressed in a typical black Cretan shirt, black trousers, and patched black boots, he was an example of the simple poverty that prevailed among the mountain people. But heroism gave no ground to poverty. He left his home in Asi Gonia, in western Crete, for the same purpose as Paterakis. A man of small stature, lithe, agile, with soft dark eyes, his timid personality belied his tremendous nervous energy. Psychoundakis, too, was destined to leave his name in the historic pages soon to be written.

Kostas Manousos, a six-foot six-inch giant, made plans to leave his home in Sfakia, a fishing village on the southern coast of Crete. His trip would take him across the White Mountains to the northern shore for the same purpose that drew Paterakis and Psychoundakis.

Manousos was typical of the Cretan warrior: tall, wiry, and virile. (The Cretan is the second-tallest Caucasian in the West—second only to the Montenegrin.) His father, Kapetan Manousos, had fought the Turks for Cretan independence in the late 1800s and early 1900s. He wanted to accompany his son to the north so that he too might join in the fight to protect the island from enemy invasion. Kostas tried to dissuade him, but to no avail. It was destined to be their last trip together.

As had been his habit for many years, Kapetan Vasili Kazantsakis began his daily task of fishing in the earliest hours of daybreak, with the rising sun still low in the eastern sky. His father and his grandfather had been fishermen before him.

Before the war, Kapetan Vasili would sail out in the company of the other fishing boats belonging to his brother Dimitri and to his two cousins Pavlos and Stelios. This small fishing fleet sailed at daybreak and returned in the early hours of the evening. Their produce—the fish caught during their daily excursions—would be brought to the agora, the central marketplace in the city of Khaniá.

The first to fall victim to the war were the fishing vessels belonging to Kapetan's cousins Pavlos and Stelios. It occurred after

the Greek mainland had been occupied by the Germans. Having
made a wide fishing sweep, the little fleet stopped at the island
of Milos to refuel. Kapetan Vasili and his brother, Dimitri, had
an extra supply of fuel aboard; thus they did not have to enter
the harbor. Pavlos and Stelios went into the harbor. Before the
two cousins had a chance to sail, their caïques were seized by the
German port command. Although they protested the confiscation,
their remonstrances proved fruitless. So intense were their objections that the German commander ordered their detention.

With the increase in the air attacks upon Crete, the Germans
flew sortie after sortie of Stukas and ME-109s on their bombing
and strafing attacks. This heightened enemy air activity had no
effect upon Kapetan Vasili or Dimitri. They took their vessels out
early each morning and returned late each evening. At those hours,
the sky was empty of enemy aircraft.

One day Vasili and his brother Dimitri decided to return to
their home port of Khaniá earlier than usual. Dimitri's caïque had
developed engine trouble, and they hoped that by returning earlier
they might make repairs before the next morning's sailing tide.
A few miles outside Khaniá harbor, Dimitri's boat failed. Kapetan Vasili brought his caïque alongside to offer aid. The two fishing vessels wallowed in the trough of a rough sea. It was at this
moment that a passing flight of ME-109s sighted them.

The German aircraft made four passes, as Vasili and Dimitri
cowered behind the bulkheads of their boats for protection.

Finally, luck ran out. A solitary rocket struck Dimitri's fuel
tank. The ensuing blast tore the craft apart. When the smoke
cleared, all that remained on the frothing waters was a piece of
wood—a remnant of Dimitri's boat. Dimitri had disappeared.

Kapetan Vasili recovered slowly from his shock. Then, unable
to find any trace of his brother, he hastened to depart in order to
salvage the sole surviving vessel of a once-proud fishing fleet.
Luckily the aircraft broke off their attack and disappeared into the
gathering dusk of the northern horizon.

In the days that preceded the German invasion, Kapetan Vasili
continued his daily fishing trips. He would not be deterred by the
ubiquitous enemy aircraft. He simply altered his routine: He left
port long before sunrise and returned long after sunset.[12]

Life had to go on.

# 8 / THE HUNTERS FROM THE SKY

Lieutenant General Kurt Student, Commanding General of Fliegerkorps XI—the Eleventh Air Corps—had spent days refining his
plan for the seizure of Crete.

He studied the island's lengthy expanse carefully and observed
that it possessed seven critical objectives that had to be seized for
the success of the operation. His plan was designed to include the
simultaneous capture of these seven points, all to be taken on the
first day of the assault.

Student proposed that his parachutists attack from west to east,
beginning in the western part of the island with the seizure of the
strategic village of Kisamo Kastelli; eastward to Maleme airfield
with its dominantly strategic Kavsakia hill, Hill 107; then the
Cretan capital of Khaniá, with its adjacent natural harbor of Suda
Bay; then on to the village of Georgeopolis; and the cities of
Rethimnon and Iráklion with their respective airfields and harbors. The seventh objective would be the Askifou plateau, which
was really a valley, in the central part of Crete.

Student's immediate superior, General Alexander Löhr, the
commanding general of Luftflotte IV—the Fourth Air Fleet—objected to this aspect of the plan. Löhr proposed instead that the
spearhead of the attack—what he called the *Schwerpunkt*—should
concentrate upon one objective only—Maleme airfield and its adjacent Hill 107.[1]

Student turned a deaf ear to Löhr's modified proposal. He was
adamant that all seven objectives be attacked simultaneously. Even
General Hans Jeschonnek, Luftwaffe chief of the general staff,
concurred with Löhr. A stalemate had been reached, and Operation Mercury was in jeopardy. Jeschonnek suggested that the con-
flicting proposals be placed before the Luftwaffe commander in
chief for resolution.

Hermann Goering was not going to permit this plan to fall apart under any circumstances. He appreciated Löhr's conservative approach and realized that logistically the air fleet commander was correct. However, Goering did not wish to contravene Student's well-conceived plan.

Goering weighed the problem carefully, then arrived at a decision. He announced a compromise. Student's proposal that all seven objectives be attacked on the first day would stand.

Student smiled; Löhr shook his head dejectedly.

"However," Goering continued, "the attack will be undertaken in two stages."[2]

Now both generals frowned.

Goering ignored the frowns as he clarified his decision. He explained that the objectives in the western part of Crete would be attacked during the first stage of the invasion, which would take place in the early morning hours. The second stage would concentrate on the objectives in the eastern part of Crete, and would take place in the afternoon of the same day. In this way the air transports used in the morning attack could return to their respective bases in Greece to refuel. In the afternoon the same transports would ferry the rest of the troopers to the remaining objectives.

"I think that is a fair compromise," Goering commented with a satisfied sigh, knowing he had resolved the difficulty. "Now, go ahead and work out the details."[3]

For reasons of their own, neither Student nor Löhr cared much for the decision. But Goering would brook no further discussion.

Reichsmarschall Hermann Goering was proud of his paratroopers. He was almost as proud of them as was General Kurt Student—the man who had trained and developed them.

It was a paradoxical situation in the hierarchy of the Third Reich that each major personality had created autonomous formations of troops, as a means of personal insurance, personal aggrandizement, and for expansion of his personal sphere of influence in governmental circles. They all had one goal: to insure a position of strength within Adolf Hitler's inner circle. Hermann Goering had called his own police force the Landespolizeigruppe "General Goering."

When the German Fuehrer announced the official creation of the German air force in October 1935, Goering—as commander in chief of the Luftwaffe—incorporated his special police units into the air force and entitled them the "Regiment General Goering.'' One month later, 600 members from this regiment volunteered to serve as Germany's first airborne unit. It was designated as the IV Falschitzer Battaillon, detached from the parent unit, and placed under the command of Major Bruno Brauer. Thus the nucleus of the future German paratroopers had been created. Three years later, in 1938, this unit became the I Battaillon/Fallschirmjäger Regiment I, or the First Battalion of the First Paratroop Regiment.[4] The German high command appreciated the potential value of such troops—who could drop directly onto a target from the air—and ordered the creation of a Fallschirm Infanterie Kompanie, a company of airborne infantry under the command of Major Richard Heidrich. This unit was later augmented to battalion size and given wide recognition in public military displays. They were placed under the command of the Luftwaffe in 1939, becoming II Bataillon/Fallschirmjäger Regiment I—the Second Battalion of the First Paratroop Regiment.

These two battalions were eventually raised to regimental strength and were incorporated within the newly formed Flieger Division 7, the Seventh Airborne Division. The divisional commander was Kurt Student, at the time only a major general.

So great became its renown and so restricted was the selection of recruits that it rapidly developed into the most elite unit in the German armed forces. German civilians looked in admiration at the Fallschirmjäger, girls even swooning at sight of the badge with the golden plunging eagle—the symbol of the paratrooper. The word *Fallschirmjäger* soon became an electrifying one in the German military lexicon. It means ''hunter from the sky.''[5] The flower of German youth sought to join their ranks.

They were all highly trained and molded into a finely disciplined, organized unit. They were ruthless and fearless. Their skull-shaped helmets and their strange uniforms, reminiscent of something out of a Jules Verne novel, were meant to be forbidding.

German youth were not the only group to volunteer. Professional soldiers, officers of all ranks, and personnel from other branches of military service sought admission as well.

Old professional soldiers like Major General Eugen Meindl, who was admitted to the paratroopers at the age of 48 after having served many years in the Wehrmacht; or Colonel Hermann Bernhard Ramcke, a veteran of the First World War, who joined the paratroopers at the age of 51, admittedly because it offered him an opportunity for promotion to higher rank; Major Richard Heidrich, who had transferred from an instructorship at the Potsdam War College to the command of the Third Parachute Regiment of the Seventh Airborne Division.

The paratroopers also attracted men from Germany's aristocratic families. These families, with such famous names as Von Braun, Von Plessen, and Von Blücher, had always distinguished themselves in military service.

A Von Plessen had been military aide to Kaiser Wilhelm II in the First World War. The Von Blüchers' ancestor had assisted the Duke of Wellington in defeating Napoleon in the Battle of Waterloo. In the Battle of Crete, the Von Blücher family was destined to lose the last three heirs of that famous name.

Baron Friedrich August Freiherr von der Heydte was another member of Germany's aristocracy who entered the newly formed paratroop units.

Captain Friedrich von der Heydte was thought to be too scholarly to be a battalion commander. In fact this slender officer seemed out of place in a military setting. His quiet, intellectual bent added to the incongruity. At first glance, his fellow officers felt that he belonged in a university classroom rather than in command of an elite body of paratroopers. Yet not one person doubted his courage or his ability as a leader of men.

He excelled in the problems undertaken during training periods, and he went through each phase of training with his men. Nothing was asked of them that he himself would not do. The officers and enlisted men in his command realized this, and their respect for him increased.

In the Battle of Crete he was to command the First Battalion of the Third Parachute Regiment. Thus, on the eve of battle, this student of international law was to put aside his scholarly robes and textbooks and exchange them for a uniform, a pistol, and a canopy of silk. He was to lead a group of men into a battle destined to enter the pages of history.[6]

Karl Schoerner was born and raised in Linz, Austria, Hitler's favorite city. When Schoerner reached military age, he rushed to enlist in the glorified Fallschirmjäger Korps. He was sent for his basic paratrooper training to a camp at Stendal, about 100 miles from Berlin. He would be carefully tested for stability and intelligence—prime requisites for the rigorous training of a paratrooper. Those who failed this part of their indoctrination were transferred back to their original units. Schoerner successfully completed this period and entered the first phase of his "ground" Fallschirmjäger training.

In the initial weeks of this period, paratroopers were taught basic skills. From a dummy aircraft fuselage, they learned how to position themselves for jumps and how to roll on impact with the ground. Proper handling of the parachute harness and the correct methods of packing parachutes were additional skills instilled in the trainees. It was felt that no man would be careless with his parachute packing if his life depended on his work. It was good psychology.

The air phase of training involved six successful jumps. During this period, Schoerner and his classmates learned the science of falling bodies. They learned how it felt to jump into space from a moving airplane and float gently to earth.

Aside from being sick with nervousness, the paratrooper's first descent was exhilarating. He had been taught how to station himself in the open doorway of the transport plane and, with the rushing wind slapping him in the face, to assume a squatting position with his feet far apart. From this pose, he would launch himself out into space—almost like diving from the edge of a swimming pool. Jumping from a JU-52 transport, his first drop was a solo, from a height of 600 feet. During his descent, he had to master the technique of landing accurately on a given target. As he approached earth, he would twist his body and face downwind, so that he would be thrown forward onto his hands and knees to break his momentum. Many suffered wrist and knee injuries during touchdown. Schoerner was luckier than most.

The parachute descent had an initial arc of about 85 feet, in which time the chute would be fully opened. After a few seconds of oscillation, the paratrooper would float steadily downward, reaching earth in about fifteen seconds. His rate of fall would be anywhere from twelve to nineteen feet per second.

The RZ-16 parachute was made of silk, with all the shroud lines culminating in two straps attached to the *back* of the harness. There was a distinct disadvantage to this type of attachment because it limited the paratrooper's control of the drift of his descent. Ironically, the shroud lines of parachutes issued to Luftwaffe air crews terminated in two straps, one on each shoulder. This more conventional system gave the air crewmen better control of drift during descent. It was odd that the paratroopers, who required the greatest drift control, were given the RZ-16s.[7]

The next four jumps were also made from 600 feet, but they were made in groups. The sixth and final jump was made from an altitude of 400 feet, in battle groups landing under simulated combat conditions. Once the paratroop trainee had successfully completed six jumps, he became a full-fledged Fallschirmjäger.

After twelve months of hard, grueling training, Karl Schoerner received his parachutist's qualification badge. To retain it, he would have to make six jumps a year.

The third phase of training now began. The paratrooper arrived in battle with the dual advantages of surprise and mobility. However, once the objective on the ground had been reached, his success depended upon his effectiveness as a member of a combat team. So the next period of training focused on light infantry combat tactics. The paratrooper was taught how to function in a team to disrupt enemy lines of communication, to move quickly against an enemy, to attack enemy positions, and to hold those positions once captured.

By necessity, the paratrooper was very lightly armed. When he jumped, he carried only a 9-mm Parabellum Luger automatic pistol, a few grenades, and a large, flat, gravity knife whose blade would be activated by gravity once the spring in the handle was released. One man in four carried a folding-stock MP.40 Schmeisser 9-mm submachine gun. The rest of the weapons were dropped in special supply canisters. These had to be located and opened on the battlefield and the weapons had to be distributed before the parachutists could become combat-effective. This was a disadvantage, as the paratroopers were to learn in Crete.

The cylindrical canisters carried the standard German rifle, the Mauser K.98; the rest of the MP.40 submachine guns; and the MG.34 light machine guns. Per squad the rifles outnumbered the submachine guns two to one.

To give the attacking paratroopers additional firepower, an effective airborne artillery piece was developed as early as 1940. It was a 75-mm recoilless gun resembling a bazooka, mounted on a wheeled carriage. Readily dismantled, it could be dropped in two supply canisters and easily reassembled in the field. In addition, each battalion was also issued thirteen .81-mm mortars as mobile fire support.[8]

The parachutes used during these drops were of different colors:

Officers' parachutes were pink, while other ranks' were black. Arms and ammunition canisters had white canopies, and medical supply canisters floated to earth under yellow parachutes.

With the final phase of his training completed, Karl Schoerner graduated and awaited assignment to a Fallschirmjäger unit.

By 1941, like Schoerner, enough trainees had qualified for a third regiment to be formed and added to the Seventh Airborne Division. With this division fully manned and combat ready, General Student now relinquished his command in order to concentrate on his duties as commanding general of the Eleventh Air Corps. In his place, he put Lieutenant General Walter Suessmann. He also decided to organize an additional unit.

This new unit would be a specialized assault force comprised of parachutists and glider-borne stormtroopers. It was to be called the Luftlande-Sturm-Regiment, or the Air Assault Regiment. If the paratroopers were the elite of the German army, the men of the Air Assault Regiment would be the elite of the elite.

The regular parachute division was now composed of three regiments; each regiment had three battalions; and each battalion had three companies. With attached antitank, engineer, medical, and heavy machine-gun units, this represented a force of about 12,000 men.

The assault regiment differed from the others of the Seventh Airborne Division in that it was composed of four battalions. Each battalion, in turn, had four companies. This regiment represented a total force of approximately 2,000 men.[9]

It had another special feature, too: Its First Battalion was composed of glider-borne troops—600 men to be transported into battle by seventy gliders. The gliders would prove to be unique newcomers to mobile air warfare. (After World War I, there developed among the Germans a great craze for gliders. The demand was such that gliders were being constructed privately and commercially.)

The glider was a direct outgrowth of the restrictions imposed upon Germany by the Versailles treaty. Prohibited from construction of any motorized aircraft, the Germans were later allowed to develop a transport plane for commercial use. The JU-52 air transport thus became the workhorse of the German Luftwaffe, as a troop carrier, supplier, and glider-tow.

As far back as 1932, the Rhön-Rossitten-Gesellschaft had built a newly designed widespan glider that was to be used for mete-

orological measurements from high altitudes. In 1933 the design
of this glider was taken over by the German Institute for Glider
Research, known more succinctly as the DFS, located in Darm-
stadt.

Ernst Udet, a veteran pilot in the German air force during the
First World War, had been appointed by the Luftwaffe commander in chief as Generalluftflugmeister. This position made
him the director of the Luftwaffe Experimental Unit. He was the
overseer of all experimental air models that might be developed
for military use.

When Udet had been advised of this glider model's existence,
he requested a demonstration. He immediately realized its military potential. He likened it to "a modern-day Trojan Horse—a
wooden horse which would land amidst the enemy and discharge
its secreted soldiers . . . to the enemy's surprise. . . ." Udet ordered that various refinements of the original prototype model be
developed in order to conform to its ultimate use as a troop carrier.[10]

This militarized glider was the size of a fighter plane of World
War I vintage, weighing about 1,600 pounds. Its long, tapered
wingspan was set high, well braced to the fuselage. The body
was a box-shaped fuselage with a framework of steel tubes covered by a tightly drawn canvas, which had thick, translucent
portals for windows. These steel tubes were built with *Soll-
bruchstellen,* or breaking points, which were joints of purposely
weakened construction in order to allow a certain flexibility to the
body of the glider once it came into contact with a hard surface.

It had a wooden floor with a central beam that ran the full
length of its body. On this beam, ten armed men would sit, one
behind the other, while in flight.

The undercarriage of this propellerless craft possessed a set of
wheels that were released and discarded when the glider was airborne. When it returned to earth, it landed on a central skid. This
central skid was often wrapped in coils of barbed wire for break-
age. Some of the gliders had a barbed hook that could stop the
craft within thirty-five yards of contact with the level surface.

Tests proved that this glider model was easily adaptable for
towing behind a JU-52 transport or a HE-111 bomber, and that
it could undergo speeds of up to 100 miles an hour. Once released,
it had a descent rate of 240 feet per minute.

This militarized model performed so successfully during tests that Udet ordered its immediate production. It was designated as the DFS 230 glider.[11]

When, in 1932, General Student was apprised of these successful tests, he decided to introduce it into his scope of airborne operations. He recognized the glider's distinct advantage over parachutists. Whereas the parachutists would be betrayed by the noise of the transports as they approached the target, the gliders would slip silently upon their target, having been released at some distance from their towing aircraft. Whereas the parachutists would swing helplessly for fifteen seconds before touchdown, and whereas they would have to regroup on the ground and obtain their weapons before being ready to fight, the gliders brought the attackers within twenty yards of point zero, already armed and grouped to enter battle. The glider definitely had multiple advantages in this new form of air warfare.

The DFS-230 glider was introduced to the surprised world during the German invasion of the Low Countries in 1940. General Student had dispatched fifty-one gliders, under the command of Captain Walter Koch, with orders to seize various bridges, forts, and crossroads in Holland and Belgium, in support of the invading German army. Eleven of these gliders attacked and seized the fortress of Eben Emael on the Albert Canal in Belgium.[12] So well-constructed and so heavily fortified that it was thought to be impossible to capture either by land or by sea, it was almost impregnable—"almost" in the sense that the Belgians discounted the possibility of a landing from the sky. But that is exactly what happened.

From April 25, when Adolf Hitler gave his approval for the promulgation of Operation Mercury, General Student had less than one month to put the gears of the operation into full motion. In that short time, he had to overcome all the difficult problems of logistics and supply.

The air staff was ordered to collect all available gliders and ship them to Greece; most of them had to be dismantled and shipped by truck. The gliders could have been flown to Greece in JU-52 transports, but those planes were needed for Operation Mercury. These slow, lumbering workhorses would be needed to tow the gliders and ferry the parachutists in the attack on Crete, and they were being overhauled for that purpose. From airfields scattered all over Europe, the JU-52s were collected into one massive fleet and flown to maintenance centers at Brunswick and Cottbus in Germany, Prague and Brno in Czechoslovakia, and Aspern in Austria. By May 15, 493 transports had been overhauled and were ready for their new assignment. They were immediately flown to the Athens area.

The Athenians observed the daily arrival of these huge, trimotored square-boxed aircraft. Soon the airfields around Athens were filled with JU-52 transports. And there was another type of aircraft that confounded the curiosity of the Athenians—the propellerless planes that were lined up wing tip to wing tip at the outer perimeter of Eleusis Airfield.

To General Student's satisfaction, this phase of the logistical problem was slowly but successfully being resolved. There now arose a new difficulty.

As the days passed rapidly toward May 17, hundreds of bombers and fighters, together with the JU-52 transports, were arriving daily at the many airfields in Greece. They had to be refueled and made ready for the day of attack. However, an incident that had occurred on April 26 during the Allied defense against the German invasion now presented a critical supply problem, and it would also cause the delay of the scheduled attack on Crete.

Two brave British engineers who were trying to reach their evacuation point on mainland Greece stole a munitions truck and were inadvertently instrumental in destroying the bridge over the Corinth Canal, keeping the German tanks from rushing into the Peloponnesus in pursuit of the retreating British army. This allowed most of the British troopers to be evacuated so they could fight another day at another place. Some British troops were transported to Crete, where a month later they would fight the Germans.

However, the debris of the fallen bridge blocked the Corinth Canal so effectively that no German tankers could pass through; not a single barrel of fuel could reach Piraeus to supply the German aircraft. With plans for the attack on Crete in full force and the deadline drawing near, some 650,000 gallons of fuel were needed to supply the huge air armada scheduled to participate in the first-day assault.

The bridge had been destroyed in the morning hours of April 26, yet by May 17 not a single drop of gasoline had reached the empty tanks of the German aircraft waiting on the airfields around Athens.

The canal was not cleared of debris until the quartermaster of the Eleventh Air Corps, Lieutenant Colonel Seibt, requested that divers be sent to Corinth from the submarine base at Kiel, Germany. And not until May 17 was the first tanker able to pass through the connecting waterway.[13]

The attack on Crete, which had been scheduled to begin on May 17, had to be postponed. It was rescheduled for the morning hours of May 20.[14]

There was another meeting of the German air command at the Grande Bretagne. Staff cars and jeeps arrived all morning at the hotel entrance, discharging officers of various ranks. They were ushered into a huge salon that had been converted into a conference room. At the double-door entrance, a Gestapo officer with a squad of armed men checked credentials.

John Drakopoulos observed the entire proceedings.

No sooner were the officers assembled than General Kurt Student strode in with his staff, and the meeting began. An aide walked over to the map board and removed a sheet, revealing the huge battle plan for the island of Crete. The map was filled with arrows and punctuated by tiny colored flags representing the position of each attacking unit.

Student began to describe how the invasion would be preceded by a one-hour bombing of the objectives by Von Richthofen's Eighth Air Corps. Following this heavy bombing, the Eleventh Air Corps would send its troops into action.

Student explained that the operation would be divided into two phases. The first phase would be the assault on the western part of the island, which would take place in the morning. The attack on the eastern sector of Crete, the second phase, would follow that same afternoon.

The morning attack would consist of a center and a western Kampfgruppe, or battle group. The western group, Task Force Komet, would have three parachute battalions and one glider battalion of the assault regiment and it would attack and seize Maleme airfield and the heights around it. The center group would have two companies of gliders, and it would attack the capital of Khaniá. The Third Regiment of the Airborne Division would be landed around Galatas and Alikianou village and sweep northward to capture the capital of Khaniá from the south.

In the afternoon the second phase of the assault would attack and seize the cities of Iráklion and Rethimnon and their respective airfields.

All of these objectives were to be achieved, and the cities to be in German hands, by nightfall. A convoy of steamers carrying elements of the Fifth Mountain Division as reinforcements would land the first night of the invasion at Maleme and at Iráklion.[15]

Student was followed by the Eleventh Air Corps' intelligence officer. Briefly, he sketched a summary of the defense situation on the island of Crete. Then he gave two pieces of intelligence that sounded reasonable enough yet were grossly erroneous. First he stated that there were only 10,000 Empire troops on the island, with remnants of two Greek divisions. Second, he said that most Cretans were sympathetic to the Germans and would welcome them as allies. This group would identify itself by the code name "Major Bock."[16]

No one at the staff meeting thought to challenge these assertions, so the German commanders left the meeting with the opinion that Crete would be underdefended, and that the civilian population would be hospitable to the Germans.

# 9 / *IT IS ONLY A RUMOR*

**MAY 19, 1941**

King George of Greece carefully followed the defense plans for Crete. Although he had placed the Greek regiments under overall command of the British, he studied their disposition with exceptional interest. His questions and suggestions did not endear him to Freyberg or his staff.

Besides the defense of Crete, the king was concerned with another matter. He felt that it was up to him, as the leader of the Hellenes, to fan the flame of national fervor. It was important that he give courage and succor not only to the Greeks on Crete but to the Greeks on the mainland.

On May 18 King George paid a visit to the residence of his prime minister, Emmanuel Tsouderos. He proposed a royal proclamation to be circulated among the Greeks in Crete and in occupied Greece, reminding them of their ancestral heritage of freedom:

> Nations that uphold their national honor and respect their commitments to their allies are placed upon a holy pinnacle of esteem. Our honor has been written in blood and circumscribed by sacrifice and heroism.
>
> Be certain, people of Greece, that a bright new day shall soon dawn for the greater glory of Greece![1]

Tsouderos, who had become prime minister after the suicide of his predecessor, Alexander Korysis, was staying in the home of George Volanis in Malaxa, a small hamlet located high in the foothills of the White Mountains. The house was located some six miles south of the royal residence at the village of Pelikapina.

The Greek king arrived on Sunday afternoon, May 18. He worked with the prime minister throughout the next day, and the proclamation was drawn up the night of the nineteenth.

With this task completed, the king wished to return to his own residence near the north shore. Tsouderos dissuaded him from leaving at such a late hour. He stressed the danger of traveling in total darkness. The king reluctantly agreed to remain another night and to depart early the next morning. He did not know it at the time, but his decision was to save him from certain capture or even death.

General Weston, the Royal Marine general commanding the defenses around Suda Bay, had given specific orders that all antiaircraft guns remain silent during the continuous German air attacks. They were under *no* circumstances to fire at the enemy aircraft. "Let them think that they have silenced our air defenses!" was his retort to objections raised by the antiaircraft gun commanders. The general did not wish to reveal the well-camouflaged defense positions to the Germans. It would be better to surprise them when the actual day of attack arrived.

Weston's orders affected the Germans exactly as he had planned. The Luftwaffe commanders were surprised by the silence of the defense batteries; their aircraft flew over the hills of Suda Bay without a single shell being fired at them. They reached the conclusion that the weight of their massive and continuous attacks had actually destroyed the defense positions. They reported these conclusions to the intelligence section of Fliegerkorps VIII.

General von Richthofen, the commanding general of Fliegerkorps VIII, was not so easily deceived. He ordered that reconnaissance and photographic sorties be flown over the Suda Bay area.

Private Dimmy Rose of the Royal Marines was positioned behind a mounted Lewis machine gun in the hills west of Suda Bay. For days his gun had remained silent, obedient to orders, while German aircraft crossed the sky above him.

On this day, May 19, an ME-110 reconnaissance aircraft slowly and repeatedly circled the harbor in a wide sweep. It was obvious to ground observers that it was on a photographic mission.

Gunner Rose followed the low-flying aircraft in the sights of his Lewis gun, swinging it in a wide arc on its tripod. The German plane was a very tempting target. Taking courage from the lack of defensive fire, it swooped in even lower on its photographic mission. Once again it flew past Rose's gun position, and once again he followed it in his sights. When the ME-110 flew past him a third time, almost at eye level to his hill position, Rose could no longer resist the temptation. He opened fire.[2]

A string of tracer bullets arched toward the German aircraft, seeming to disappear into its fuselage. The men in the other gun positions stood aghast as the low rattling sound of the machine gun echoed through the valley.

No sooner had the echoes subsided than a wisp of smoke trailed from the aircraft's port engine. The ME-110 dropped into the choppy waters of the bay.

A motor launch manned by Royal Marines of the MNBDO (Mobile Naval Base Defense Organization) raced out to the downed plane. As they cleared the island of Suda in the outer bay, they could see that a fisherman's caïque had already reached the Germans. One of the pilots was being lifted out of the water, while the second stood on the wing, clutching a map case in his arms. The fisherman pulled him off the submerged wing just as the aircraft disappeared below the waves.

As the airmen were being transferred from the fishing skiff to the marine launch, the fisherman shouted in comprehensible English, "This fellow says that the invasion will come tomorrow."[3]

When the marines landed, they took their two German prisoners to Freyberg's Creforce headquarters for interrogation. They repeated the fisherman's warning remarks to the interrogating officer, who just shrugged his shoulders. He did not know that a valuable source of information was missing from the interrogation—the map case with its contents. Earlier the German crew had boasted to the Greek fisherman that they would invade the next day, but now they both kept their silence. The fisherman had withheld the pilot's map case out of curiosity. He wanted to see if it contained anything of value for himself. All he found were a map and some typewritten papers.

When the fisherman docked his caïque in Khaniá harbor, he took the map case with its contents to Greek Army Headquarters Command. After explaining how he happened to be in possession of the German documents, the crafty fisherman waited for a reward. All he received was a curt smile of appreciation for "doing the right thing."

The map case eventually passed into the hands of Major Hector Pavlides, an officer on the staff of the Greek army commander in Crete, General Achilles Skoulas. Pavlides was curious about the contents of the map case and decided to study them. One typewritten sheet in particular caught his attention. The word *secret* was stamped across the top, with the additional precautionary admonition that it be burned and not carried into battle. His eye ran quickly down the page, and his eyebrows arched in surprise. As the meaning of the translation slowly penetrated, his excitement grew and his heart beat faster. Carefully he translated the remaining sentences, often cursing the Germans for always putting the verb at the end. When he completed the translation, he realized the enormous value of the document before him. It was a copy of a German operational order for the pending attack upon Crete!

Specifically, the operational order was for the Third Parachute Regiment of the Seventh Airborne Division. It was dated May 18, and briefly summarized the initial objectives of the attack:

> Group Central was to capture Khaniá and Suda Bay in the initial wave of attack. . . . Rethimnon was to be attacked in the second wave, eight hours later, capture its airfield, then turn west toward Suda. . . . a Western Group was to attack Maleme, capture its airfield for subsequent reinforcements by air . . . then turn eastward join Group Central, and help capture Khaniá and Suda Bay. . . .

The document then referred to the specific objects of the Third Parachute Regiment:

> It was to seize Prison Valley, storm Galatas . . . then turn northward to join the Western and Central Group in their sweep to capture Khaniá and Suda Bay.

All this was to be accomplished by sundown of the first day of attack.[4]

Pavlides rushed to the office of the chief of staff of the Greek Cretan command, Colonel I. Vachlas. The chief of staff lost no time in taking the document to General Achilles Skoulas.

"Freyberg should know about this," said Skoulas, after he had digested the contents of the document. Then he picked up the phone to personally contact the Creforce commander.[5]

Pavlides was ordered to transcribe into English his Greek translation of the German document, and was then sent immediately to Freyberg's headquarters on Akrotiri Peninsula.

Freyberg's chief of staff, Colonel Keith Stewart, did not share stupid

Pavlides' excitement over the importance of the captured operational order, but he agreed to inform the commanding general.

"I think you should see this, sir," Colonel Stewart remarked as he handed the English copy of the translation to General Freyberg. Pavlides stood at rigid attention near the entrance of the dugout that served as the general's office.

Freyberg read the translation slowly, without the slightest change of expression on his face. "Interesting, indeed. Thank you, Major Pavlides." Pavlides did not budge. He expected the general to exhibit some degree of excitement and to issue a bevy of orders alerting the whole garrison. None were forthcoming.

Colonel Stewart glared at Pavlides, who finally took the hint. Still disappointed by the lack of reaction, Pavlides snapped to attention and, with a smart salute, wheeled and left Freyberg's headquarters.[6]

Freyberg turned to his chief of staff, "What do you think, Jock?"

"General, I believe that this is a ploy to deceive us. Why would the Germans allow such a classified document to be carried in the pilot's map case, in a reconnaissance aircraft—particularly when the danger of being shot down is so great?"

Freyberg listened attentively, then handed Stewart a single sheet of paper from the pile on his desk. It was a carbon of a letter from General Wavell that had been forwarded on April 29 to Prime Minister Churchill and to the chiefs of staff in London. The letter reported on Wavell's plans for the defense of Crete. Paragraph four of the letter had been circled in red:

[It] is just possible that the plan for attack on Crete may be cover for attack on Syria or Cyprus, and that the real plan will only be disclosed even to [their] own troops at the last moment. This would be consistent with German practice.[7]

The information given by the two captured German pilots flowed like electricity from mouth to mouth. In a matter of hours, Cretan civilians and Greek soldiers of all ranks had heard of the attack due the next day, May 20.

The news did not escape the ears of the New Zealand troops in the western zone of the Cretan defense. However, no orders of any kind were forthcoming from Freyberg's Creforce headquarters. In the absence of official confirmation, the warnings had to be taken as rumors by all officers in authority.

First Lieutenant Kritakis heard about the rumor from his company commander, Captain E. The captain stormed into his headquarters tent in Galatas as Lieutenant Kritakis was completing the company orders for the next day.

"Can you imagine," growled the captain, as he flung his helmet onto the cot, "can you imagine the idiocy of it all? It is sheer stupidity!"

The lieutenant looked up in surprise. He had never seen his CO so angry. He opened his mouth to speak, but the captain cut him off.

"That's what I meant when I said 'no initiative'—by our own general staff officers. Here we are on the eve of being attacked, and the regimental C.O. orders a *dress parade* rehearsal by the whole regiment for tomorrow. Incredible, isn't it?"

Again, the lieutenant opened his mouth to speak and again the captain cut him off.

"Look at these orders—a dress parade rehearsal in order to look well for an inspection by General Freyberg at 10:00 hours on May 23. Can you imagine that?" repeated the seething company commander. The captain stalked back and forth in the close confines of the tent, removing his field tunic and pistol belt as he did so.

"You have heard the rumors about the Germans attacking tomorrow—I believe them! And what do we do about it?" queried the captain sarcastically, "we get orders to prepare for a dress parade!"

With one final grunt of disgust, he threw himself, half-dressed, upon his cot and pulled a sheet over himself.

Lieutenant Kritakis read the written order that the angry captain had flung on the desk. He shook his head, realizing that the captain was right. The order was illogical—but, after all, since when did any army reason logically? In the course of history, battles had been won by that army whose reasoning was less illogical than that of the army opposing it.[8]

Across the blue waters separating Crete from the Greek mainland, the Germans were completing their preparations for the attack. On the afternoon of May 19, the various detachment and battalion commanders held a final critique. It was at this conference that the last assignments were issued to the various companies and platoons.

As afternoon passed into evening, the paratroopers received special rations of beer and brandy.

Karl Schoerner from Linz, Austria, the newly trained paratrooper, had been assigned to the First Company of the First Paratroop Battalion of the Third Fallschirmjäger Regiment. Being a new face in the company, he was befriended by Gefreiter Hans Kreindler. Private First Class Kreindler was a veteran. He had already undergone the baptism of fire, making his first parachute jump in combat during the invasion of the Netherlands.[9] Schoerner looked up to Kreindler as a boy looks up to his older brother. It was a pleasant relationship.

Both of them had just spent the last few hours on special detail, assisting the ground crews fueling the transports and bombers that were to be used in the next day's attack. The blockage of the Corinth Canal had so delayed the passage of gasoline barges that, in the few remaining hours before takeoff, many aircraft had still not been fueled. Fueling was being done by hand pump, a slow and grimy task. So the call had gone out to the paratroopers for volunteers. The sergeants selected the "volunteers" for this special detail, Schoerner and Kreindler among them.

When the two returned to their encampment, they were exhausted. Karl Schoerner was too tired and nervous about tomorrow to enjoy the special rations. He slumped to the ground in the shade of a lemon tree and sniffed its fragrant scent. He decided to write to his mother:

May in Greece is hot, but its fruit trees do give off such a cooling fragrant breeze. . . . Tonight I shall sleep under the stars. . . . When the war is over, I shall return to live here.[10]

Unlike Schoerner, the veteran Kreindler was not going to let his fatigue prevent him from enjoying his ration of beer and brandy. He remembered an old soldier's slogan: "Eat today and be merry for there may be no tomorrow."

While Schoerner wrote to his mother and Kreindler enjoyed his drinks, their battalion commander, Captain von der Heydte, was too concerned with responsibility to be as carefree as his enlisted men. After his final staff conference, the commanding officer of the First Paratroop Battalion returned to his headquarters tent, where he busied himself with the last minutiae of the pending attack.

On this same day, the British air officer commanding in Crete, Group Captain G. Beamish, requested that the remainder of his aircraft be excused from further service in Crete. The request was granted.[11]

It was a difficult decision but the problems that had confronted the RAF in Crete were insurmountable. The air battle over Britain was now in its waning stages, but there were few surplus aircraft available for transfer to the Mediterranean theater of operations. Air Marshal A. Longmore, the air commander in Cairo, had only ninety bombers and forty-three fighter aircraft to cover all of North Africa, Syria, Iraq, Cyprus, and Crete.

The remnants of four squadrons, which had been evacuated from Greece, were now based on Crete.

Aircraftman Ryder was stationed at Maleme airfield in Crete. On the morning of May 13, thirty ME-109s struck the field in an unannounced surprise attack. The air was suddenly filled with the exploding crash of their cannon shells and the rattle of their machine guns, as wave after wave attacked the field from all directions.

Unlike the Battle of Britain, the RAF in Crete had no radar stations to help them locate the enemy or to advise them of their approach. No sooner were the Germans sighted than they dove into the attack.[12]

In this morning's attack, Ryder sat behind his Lewis machine gun, firing as each airplane sped past. The sky was filled with ME-109s. There were so many of them they were difficult to count. Wherever Ryder turned his gun, a German aircraft loomed into his sights.

Momentarily, something else caught his attention. He watched anxiously, with growing apprehension, as two Hurricane fighters taxied down the runway in an attempt to take off while under attack.

Flight Sergeant Reynish raced his aircraft down the strip at full throttle, while enemy planes came at him from all directions. Miraculously, he rose into the air, banking his Hurricane sharply with three ME-109s on his tail. He skillfully looped onto the tail of a German, gave him a short burst from his machine guns, and watched as the Messerschmitt rolled over out of control. Reynish's victory was shortlived. Twelve ME-109s now raced after him as he fled for the protection of the hills.[13]

Reynish's CO, Squadron Leader Edward Howell, raced the second Hurricane with open throttle down the same runway as six Germans sped after him in pursuit. Howell was flying a Hurricane fighter plane for the first time that day, handling it superbly against great odds. That day, alone, he shot down three German planes, landing safely when the raid had ended.[14]

Again, unlike the Battle of Britain, the defenders of Crete did not possess the appropriate equipment with which to communicate to the pilots when the raid was over, or, more important, when it was safe to land and refuel.

A Hurricane fighter came in to land during an air raid. It was obvious to the pilot that the airfield was under attack, but he was out of fuel and had to land. He was followed down by a swarm of ME-109s.

He lowered his landing gear, and as he made his final approach with full flaps down, all eyes of the airfield's defenders and ground crew watched him, rooting for him to land safely. Then the Germans hit him—it was like shooting at a sitting duck. He flamed, arched upward, turned over and fell into the sea with a splash, disappearing below the waves.[15]

Flight Lieutenant Woodward had made two attempts to take off while the airfield was under attack. Each time, his aircraft was riddled by bullets from the attacking fighters, never getting off the ground. On his third attempt, with a new Hurricane, he succeeded.[16]

With the coming of dusk, the sky cleared of all German aircraft. An eerie quiet settled over the island. Soldiers and civilians alike could move about without fear of strafing bullets or falling bombs. It was hard to imagine the sense of relief that prevailed when another day of bombing had passed. In those hours of dusk, before the darkness of night cast its cover, the island came to life. Motor vehicles carried supplies to their designated units; entrenchments were repaired or modified; messengers sped on their motorcycles with the orders for the next day.

Australians and New Zealanders left their foxholes, their entrenchments, and their encampments, removed their clothes and plunged into the cool waters that lapped the shores of Crete. They swam and frolicked, forgetting the dangers of the day and those that would come tomorrow. Passing Cretans gazed at them, wondering with amazement at the love these foreigners had for the ocean.

While these men cooled themselves, others ventured to the surrounding villages to visit the homes of civilian friends or to enjoy a drink of ouzo or retsina at a village tavern.

With the sun slowly descending behind the western horizon, the crimson colors of sunset deepened as night settled over the island. Suddenly it grew dark, as if a shade had been drawn. Not a light was to be seen; not a sound was to be heard; only the fragrant scent of the island's subtropical flora floated gently on the cool evening breeze.

Around 2:00 A.M., May 20, General Kurt Student's telephone rang with a loud urgent sound and an aide answered it. Colonel Heinz Trettner, Student's personal staff officer, was calling. It was imperative that he speak to the general immediately.

Student was awakened, and he listened to Trettner's apprehensive voice. In excited tones Trettner referred to an air reconnaissance report that had sighted British warships in Khaniá Gulf.

"Could it be possible that the British Fleet knows of our scheduled attack tomorrow, Herr General? Shall we postpone the hour of the attack?"

Student considered the question. Both Goering and General Löhr had repeatedly stressed the importance of time; Student had promised Hitler that he would take Crete in three days, with May 17 as the initial target day. Already the date of attack had been postponed once; besides, all units were prepared, eager, and ready to go.

"We have to risk that danger," he replied after a long moment's silence. "I appreciate your anxiety, Trettner, but it was really unnecessary to awaken me. Let the attack go on as scheduled."[17]

The decision was final. The attack upon Crete would begin in four hours, at 6:00 A.M. Operation Mercury was ready to be launched.

In the early predawn hours of Tuesday, May 20, Kapetan Vasili Kazantsakis untied his fishing boat from its mooring post in the small harbor of Khaniá. As he left the harbor behind him, the first brilliant rays of the ascending sun scattered the shadows of night. It looked as if it would be another bright and cloudless day. A stillness prevailed over the whole expanse of the island. To the Kapetan, it was a foreboding silence—the calm that proclaimed the approach of a storm.

At 6:00 A.M. that bright, sunny morning of May 20, the storm broke over Crete.

# THE
# ATTACK

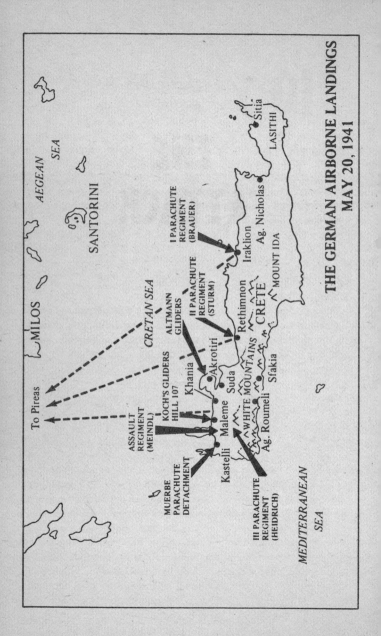

THE GERMAN AIRBORNE LANDINGS
MAY 20, 1941

# 10 / MERCURY IS AIRBORNE

## MAY 20, 1941

In the darkness of the predawn hours, the many Germans who were to participate in the first phase of the attack upon Crete were awakened. Some of them had slept soundly after an extensive beer party. Others had been too excited even to close their eyes, much less sleep. Their moment of truth would soon arrive.

Some of the assault companies were bivouacked adjacent to the airfields. All they had to do was march to their assigned transports. Others had to be trucked across bumpy, dusty roads to their respective fields.

Captain von der Heydte, the CO of the First Battalion, Third Regiment, sat in the passenger seat of the jeep leading the convoy of trucks carrying his battalion to their assigned section of the airfield. As they approached the field, he turned to speak to his adjutant. His voice was lost in the roar that broke the silence of the night.

At that moment, 120 JU-52 trimotor transports started their engines. The sound of 360 whirring propellers was deafening. Von der Heydte could not even hear his own words in the rush of noise.[1]

His convoy left the roadway and was guided by traffic control officers to its assigned aircraft. It was very difficult for the drivers to see the traffic directors because of the darkness and the heavy dust that seemed to fill the air. Silhouettes of the nearby troop carriers would periodically emerge from the dust cloud. This fine, powdery dust, coming from the parched soil that covered the airfield, was stirred into cyclonic swirls by the spinning propellers. It rose like a red pillar almost a thousand feet into the sky, covering men and machines alike. It crept into the cylinders of the motors and into the nostrils of the men. In the dim light, the moving formations of men appeared as grotesque shadows.

Group after group, in multiples of thirteen to fifteen men per group—called a "stick" in paratrooper language—followed a beckoning pale beam from the boarding officer's flashlight. The only signal that would guide the men to their assigned aircraft, it brought order out of possible chaos.

Gefreiter Hans Kreindler walked closely behind his guide. He was followed by his squad, each man dressed in the bulky equipment of the paratrooper, from the dome-shaped steel helmet on his head to the rubberized pads on his knees to the parachute on his back. Karl Schoerner was second in the file of fifteen men, keeping in step behind Kreindler.

Slowly and patiently the men waited to enter the transport, each one holding his parachute static line in his gloved hand. As they entered the plane, they would take the white cords between their teeth, leaving both arms free to grasp the grabirons on either side of the door.

It was a slow, time-consuming process, as the men of the Third Parachute Regiment and the assault regiment boarded the troop carriers, but it was completed even against the difficulties of darkness and dust. By 4:00 A.M. the paratroopers were settled in their transports. All was in readiness, waiting for the signal to depart.

At 4:30 A.M., the first heavily laden bomber trundled down the runway and lifted itself into the sky. Other bombers taxied from their stations, taking their place in line, waiting for the signal to take off. At thirty-second intervals, each aircraft followed the one before it down the strip, slowly rising and disappearing into the deep blue sky of approaching dawn.

These bombers were the first group of aircraft scheduled to leave. They were to provide the final pulverizing destruction of the defenses on Crete—the "softening-up" phase before the actual invasion.

The Dornier, Heinkel, and Junker bomber groups were to strike their objectives from an altitude of 6,000 to 10,000 feet. They were to discharge their bombs and return to their respective airfields to refuel and rearm for the afternoon phase of the attack on the eastern half of Crete.

From airfields in the Peloponnesus and from the island of Karpathos (known during World War II as Scarpanto), located midway between Crete and Rhodes, came the "glamour boys" of the Luftwaffe. These were the pilots of the Stuka dive-bombers, who had been assigned to this mission from Dive-Bomber Group 2.

Two groups of these JU-87 dive-bombers came from airfields at Mycenae and Molaoi in the Peloponnesus, under the command of Lieutenant Colonel Oskar Dinort. A third group of Stukas, led by Captain Brücker, came from Karpathos.[2]

The JU-87 Stuka dive-bomber had established a dreaded reputation in the early part of the war. Its narrow silhouette, its large square-tailed rudder, its fixed undercarriage, and its reverse gull wings were the outstanding characteristics of this aircraft. Its shrill shriek, during its dive, struck terror into the hearts of retreating troops and fleeing refugees during the German conquests of Poland, the Low Countries, France, Yugoslavia, and Greece. It was already familiar to the defenders of Crete.

While the medium bombers performed from high altitude on a given target, the Stukas were used tactically, attacking any feasible target at random, in support of ground forces.

Finally came the aircraft of Fighter Group 77. This unit consisted of three groups of fighter planes, two of them under Major Woldenga and the other under Captain Ihlefeld, all based on Molaoi.[3]

These groups were comprised of the famous Messerschmitt 109, the best single-seat fighter of the Luftwaffe—if not in the world—in that period of the war. A beautifully designed aircraft, its slim, sleek contours, light weight, and excellent maneuverability made it a fighter pilot's dream.

The ME-109 was used as a protective escort for bombers on short-range targets, as an attack fighter to engage in air duels, and as a tactical fighter to harass and destroy ground troops. It was perhaps the most versatile airplane in the air in 1941. In the days that preceded the battle, the defenders of Crete had come to fear this fighter more than the Stuka or any other aircraft.

In his headquarters, the commanding general of this vast air armada, Major General Wolfram Freiherr von Richthofen, was pleased with himself. He had successfully mustered 650 aircraft of all types from his Eighth Air Force for this operation. When the report arrived that his last available groups were airborne, he settled back to await the results of the attack.

Slowly the many aircraft from all the airfields in Greece rose to a point of rendezvous over the Greek mainland. It had taken them almost an hour to overcome the visibility problems caused by the huge clouds of dust blanketing the airfields. Now they were above the clouds.

In the east, the huge red ball of the sun rose slowly over the Aegean Sea. It would be another beautiful, sun-filled day with a cloudless blue sky—a perfect day for the task ahead.

At last the mighty armada was airborne and turning southward, in the direction of Crete.

At Topolia air base, Colonel Rüdiger von Heyking, the commanding officer of three bomber groups for special assignment, was studying the landing gears of the trimotor transports in his command.

"How can these machines be expected to take off with their landing gears buried in sand almost to their axles?" he protested. He shook his head pessimistically. "It would take a miracle if some of these aircraft don't bog down or crack up on take-off!"

He scooped up some soil with his gloved hand and remarked disgustedly, "These airfields are a sea of sand—they are nothing but deserts!"⁴

Von Heyking was standing outside the operations van and, half-choking in the dust, tried to determine if the transports of his group were ready to take off. He had before him 150 Junker-52 transports of Air Groups 60, 101, and 102—all half-hidden in a cloud of dust.

His remarks had been addressed to his superior officer, General Gerhard, standing beside him. Major General Gerhard was the air service commander for Operation Mercury. He was the officer responsible for the availability and serviceability of the transports and gliders to be used in this operation. He had ten groups in his command, consisting of 500 JU-52 transports and about 70 DFS-230 gliders.

"I agree, Colonel, but there was little time to lay down metal runways. I ordered that the fields be sprayed by water wagons, but it has not helped. We must do the best we can," said General Gerhard. "Conditions are no better at Tanagra, Dadion, Megara, or at Corinth!"⁵

It was a fact that the other transport groups located at these airfields were also confronted with the same problems of poor visibility caused by the swirling dust. It was a situation that was to affect the whole operation.

* * *

Near the runway at Eleusis airfield rested the many gliders that were to take part in the opening phase of the assault upon Crete. This group of gliders represented the task force assigned to the capture of Khaniá. In one of these gliders, the commanding general of the Seventh Airborne Division and his whole divisional staff had taken their places.

Lieutenant General Wilhelm Suessmann, who sat in the lead glider, was not only in command of the paratroop division but also commanding officer of the central attack force, designated as Task Force Mars.

A veteran of the First World War, he had only recently joined the airborne forces. Prior to his transfer, he commanded an infantry division in the Polish campaign, and later served in the attack on Norway. Since Suessman had worked with General Student on the details of Operation Mercury, the commanding general of the Eleventh Air Corps decided to place him in charge of this elite paratroop division.

In the dim light of the canvas-bodied glider, General Suessmann glanced at his watch. It was 5:25 A.M.

Suessmann knew that the bombers of the Eighth Air Corps were already flying toward Crete. Shortly the signal would be given for the gliders to become airborne and follow the bombers to the same destination.

There was silence in the gliders and the transports as the minutes ticked by. Few noticed that the air was becoming stifling.

An Obergefreiter, acting as a starter, stood outside the operations shack, a red flag in his left hand—the signal to hold—and a white flag with a green cross in his right, indicating "all clear for takeoff." He waved the white flag. Nothing happened. The pilot of the lead transport could not see the signal for the heavy cloud of dust. The Obergefreiter dashed into the shack and returned with a flare gun.

At 5:30 A.M. a huge green flare arched into the sky. It was the signal. General Suessmann leaned forward in his seat, satisfied that they would finally depart. He had no way of knowing that fate had willed he would never reach Crete.

The pilots of the transports throttled their motors to an ear-shattering roar. The lead transport began to move slowly across the field, followed by another and then another. Behind each transport trailed a glider of the First Assault Regiment. With the added burden of a fully loaded glider in tow, the transports taxied sluggishly down the runway.

As each transport rolled forward, the tow line extending from its tail grew taut with the attachment in the nose of each glider. The gliders jerked forward slowly, bounced unevenly, then picked up speed as they rolled down the strip in the wake of the towing transports. At the end of the runway, the first transport left the ground. The glider pilot slowly pulled back the control stick. The rumbling sound of the fuselage ceased. He was airborne. In a matter of seconds, his glider lifted noiselessly and majestically over the fields and rooftops of the surrounding countryside, gaining altitude behind its towing mother transport.

In half-minute intervals, transport after transport soared into the sky. It was daylight as the many Junkers rendezvoused over the blue waters of the Saronic Gulf. All in all, 500 JU-52 transports comprised this second great armada that filled the skies in the early hours of May 20. Behind them were seventy assault gliders in tow.

Operation Mercury was airborne.

The Junker transports, carrying the paratroopers and towing the gliders, reached their proper altitudes and settled into formation for the flight to Crete. They trembled and vibrated as they struggled through periodic air turbulence over the Mediterranean. The machines carried approximately 6,000 men in the first airborne invasion ever attempted in modern history.

The elation and exuberance that each paratrooper had felt at takeoff was diminishing. Slowly they fell into a solemn silence. Each man contemplated the approaching moment when he would jump into space and descend into battle. They were all anxious for that moment to arrive, to get it over with. The new recruits had not been in combat before and were visibly apprehensive. Some tried to smile nonchalantly at their comrades sitting opposite. Others removed their skull-shaped helmets and unfastened their harness straps for comfort.

Gefreiter Hans Kreindler, the veteran of the Netherlands campaign, was the ranking noncom in his aircraft. By virtue of his rank, as prescribed in the paratroop training manual, he occupied the first seat and would be the first to leave the transport. From his position, he glanced to his right at both ranks of men sitting quietly. Although experienced in battle, he was nervous; his throat was dry to the point of choking, and his stomach was queasy. He turned his head in order to hide any expression that might betray his feelings.

If he was nervous, he wondered what his buddy Karl Schoerner was feeling. Whereas Kreindler had undergone one airdrop into combat, Schoerner had not as yet tasted battle. Schoerner kept his head bowed and his eyes closed. Kreindler hoped that his friend would remember his advice to stick close once they touched ground.[6]

As silence pervaded the aircraft, Kreindler's eyes scanned the printed cloth attached to the inner lining of his jacket. Each paratrooper had the same message sewn to the identical spot. It was the code of the German paratrooper. Kreindler's eye ran down the list of ten "commandments," remembering his training days when he had to commit them to memory.

1. You are the chosen ones of the German army. You will seek combat and train yourself to endure any manner of test.

2. Cultivate true comradeship.

3. Beware of talking.

4. Be calm and prudent, strong and resolute.

5. The most precious thing in the presence of the foe is ammunition.

6. Never surrender.

7. You can triumph only if your weapons are good.

8. Grasp the full purpose of every enterprise, so if your leader is killed you can help yourself fulfill it.

9. Against an open foe fight with chivalry, but to a guerrilla extend no quarter.

10. Keep your eyes open.[7]

In another transport, carrying the paratroopers of the Third Parachute Regiment, the commanding officer of the First Paratroop Battalion, Captain von der Heydte, removed his helmet and carefully studied his map. He was cool and collected. He closed his eyes, hoping for a few moments of relaxing sleep. Shortly, he became aware of someone standing before him.

"Herr Hauptmann, may I speak with you?"

Von der Heydte looked up at a tall, bushy-browed paratrooper. "What is the matter, soldier?"

"I feel ill to my stomach, Herr Hauptmann."

Von der Heydte recognized him. This paratrooper had achieved international fame as a boxing champion before the war. Now he was going into combat and he was pleading illness. Was he really ill or was he feigning illness because of fear?

The battalion commander gazed out through the porthole and thought, A man who was a national hero in the boxing ring certainly could not be a coward in battle. Yet fighting in the boxing ring is not quite the same as a soldier jumping into battle. A soldier who has tasted the life-or-death baptism of combat is a hero of a different stature.

Captain von der Heydte said, "My dear fellow, there is nothing I can do for you now. You may report sick when we arrive in Crete. You know that our medical staff is flying with us."[8]

The remark was not very comforting to the anguished paratrooper, but it was practical. The former heavyweight boxing champion of the world, Max Schmeling, nodded and returned to his seat.

The airborne glider troops also sat in anticipatory silence, strapped into position, astride the central beams of their aircraft. Little light penetrated into the interior of each glider, except through the thick celluloid windows on either side of the canvas-covered fuselage.

At first, the interiors of the gliders were stiflingly hot. The heavy combat uniforms they wore added to the paratroopers' discomfort, and some of them became airsick.

As the towing transports rose to higher altitudes, the air in each glider became cooler and more comfortable. A few holes in the canvas body allowed little airstreams to filter in and circulate. It was an invigorating stimulus to the men, a fair compensation for the sickly feeling of flight, as the gliders responded to the varying air currents.

Each glider carried a team of specially trained paratroopers. According to their assigned tasks, the number in each glider varied from eight to twelve men, equipped with weapons and explosives. Each paratrooper had been trained to do a specific task, and they were considered to be masters at them. These men represented the "point of the lance" in the attack.

The huge armada of gliders and transports moved slowly through the radiantly blue sky of early morning. Here were the gliders of Major Walter Koch, the hero of Eben Emael, assigned to capture the strategic Hill 107, which overlooked Maleme airfield. To his right were the nine gliders of Lieutenant Wulff von Plessen, whose task would be to seize the antiaircraft batteries at the edge of the airfield and then seize the airstrip itself. Behind him followed the gliders of Major Walter von Braun, ordered to seize the main bridge over the Tavronites River, thus sealing the western approach to the airfield. To the left of the huge column flew the gliders of Captain Gustav Altmann and Lieutenant Alfred Genz, whose assignment would be the capture of General Freyberg and the seizure of Creforce Headquarters.

From the lead glider General Suessmann could see a sky filled with trimotor transports and gliders. It was a stirring sight, and he was proud to be in command.

The sun had fully risen above the horizon. Below, the beautiful Mediterranean appeared a brilliant blue, glistening in the angled rays of the early morning sun. High above, Suessmann could pick out silvery specks traveling north. These were the first flights of high-level bombers returning to the mainland. They had already discharged their bombs over Crete and were returning home to refuel and reload.

The pilot of Suessmann's transport, Sergeant Franz Hausser, marveled at the vast panorama of aircraft that filled the sky around him. He was still gazing leisurely about when his eye caught a metallic speck flickering in the rays of the morning sun. In a matter of minutes, this speck loomed larger. It was another aircraft flying a course perpendicular to his transport, and it was traveling at a greater speed. He became alarmed—if the pilot of the approaching plane did not veer from his course, they would collide in midair in a matter of minutes.

The aircraft in question was a bomber. It was, in fact, an HE-111 that had been delayed in its departure from Eleusis airfield by engine trouble. Now it was racing at top speed in order to catch up. In his anxiety to reach his squadron, the pilot, Lieutenant Paul Gerfehr, did not realize that his aircraft had intersected the flight pattern of the transport-glider group.

Sergeant Hausser had only minutes to decide what to do: Should he alter his course to avoid a possible collision with the rapidly approaching bomber or should he remain on his present heading and hope that the bomber pilot would spot him in time? It was obvious that the bomber pilot was not aware of the danger—the sun's glare must have blinded him.

Others in the huge formation had also spotted the intruder. Now all eyes in the lead flight of transports were riveted to the danger ahead.

With seconds to spare, the pilot of the endangered transport took the only possible action. Sergeant Hausser pushed his controls forward, and the huge plane's nose dropped. The JU-52 went into a steep dive, giving its attached tow-rope a sudden, sharp, and vibrating yank, as it pulled its glider in its wake. Everyone held on breathlessly.[9]

In the bomber, Lieutenant Gerfehr, seeing the Junker suddenly drop into a steep dive, followed by its glider, finally realized that he had entered the flight path of another formation. Abruptly he throttled his engine, pulled back on the control stick and rose upward, above the diving transport. A midair collision had been avoided by just a few yards.

General Suessmann and the other occupants of his glider braced themselves as the glider followed the diving transport. Slowly the transport returned to level flight. The Heinkel 111 had passed over them and was already out of sight. However, the air turbulence created by the slipstream of the passing bomber now placed a great strain on the heavy hawser that linked the glider to its mother transport. The glider vibrated uncomfortably while its pilot struggled to cope with the changes in air pressure.

The glider pilot was alarmed at the new danger now presenting itself. The towline had been stretched dangerously taut. Even before he could express his concern, a dull twang was heard, not unlike the snap of a thick elastic band. The towline had parted.

Released from its mother ship, the glider now floated free. "How, in God's name, do we reach our objective with one hundred and fifty miles remaining to Crete?" General Suessmann knew that from a height of 4,000 feet, it would be impossible for the glider to reach the distant objective. The only possibility would be to land safely on some island or glide back to the mainland. Then, perhaps, another JU-52 would fly them directly to Crete.

Suessmann's glider soared upward, aided by the rising warm air. Soon it had risen hundreds of feet above the flight of gliders, continuing on their course. Suessmann's pilot made every effort to control his machine. He decided to attempt a landing on the island of Aegina.

As the pilot banked the glider into a wide turn, he heard a dull thud to his left. He could not at first pinpoint the source of the noise.

Even before the pilot could identify the cause of the dull sound and thus appreciate the new danger, the sharp, rasping crack of tearing metal echoed like a pistol shot through the glider's fuselage. The left wing had fallen off!

The pilot of the JU-52 transport that had towed this ill-fated glider was still following the glider's upward trajectory. So were the pilots of the other transports that passed below them. To their horror, the stricken glider now began to fall, cartwheeling downward. Then the other wing separated from the glider. Now completely wingless, the hapless craft fell earthward, toppling end over end.[10]

From the courtyard of the Convent of the Holy Trinity, the abbot and the church acolytes followed the fall of the glider as it hurtled toward earth like a stone falling from a high precipice. Only a huge puff of dust rising upward indicated that the glider had returned to earth.

There on the mountainous terrain of the beautiful island of Aegina in the Saronic Gulf, near the ancient Temple of Aphoea, General Wilhelm Suessmann and his staff were killed. The first casualties of the German assault upon Crete, they were destined to be joined by thousands more before the day ended.

# II / "THEY ARE COMING!"

## MAY 20, 1941

The hour was approaching 6:00 A.M. In the deep blue of the northern sky, a vast dark shadow appeared just above the horizon. The stillness of the early morning was disturbed by a continuous low hum. As the shadow loomed larger, the low hum increased in pitch to that of a drone. It was a sound that reminded the Australians and the New Zealanders who had worked in the fields back home as farmers, of approaching locusts. The Cretans likened it to a swarm of bees.

A lookout posted on a hill some 500 yards north of Creforce Headquarters also heard the distant drone. He lifted binoculars to his eyes, focused quickly, and carefully studied the evergrowing shadow on the horizon.

Captain Theodore Stephanides was a doctor attached to the British forces at Creforce Headquarters. More recently, he had been assigned as medical officer to the dock-operating companies at Suda Bay.[1]

On this brilliant morning of May 20, he stepped out of his tent and took a deep breath of the fresh early morning air. He felt that it was too beautiful a day to fight a war. He greeted a fellow officer, Captain Fenn, and together they walked toward the tent that served as the headquarters mess. While waiting for breakfast to be served, Stephanides chatted with several headquarters staff officers. They all heard the drone from the sky. It did not interrupt their breakfast, but they knew that they were in for another day of bombing.

Lieutenant Kritakis, the executive officer of the Sixth Company of the Sixth Greek Regiment, encamped in the valley before the village of Galatas, had also stepped out of the headquarters tent to bask in the sunshine of this beautiful day. He observed his commanding officer, Captain E, out in the field, instructing the platoon leaders on the procedures for the dress parade rehearsal scheduled later that day. It was obvious that he also heard the sound of the approaching bombers. The company commander decided to dismiss the formation, ordering his men to take shelter from the forthcoming attack.[2]

Just outside the cave in the quarry that served as his headquarters, the commanding general of the allied forces in Crete, Major General Bernard Freyberg, had just been handed a message from the lookout post on the Akrotiri heights. The huge dark mass on the horizon had been identified as approaching German bombers, numbering in excess of 400. Air alarms were sounded and church bells rang from east to west. It was the warning that an enemy air attack was imminent.[3]

Trucks left the road; men sought shelter in slit trenches or in the protective shadows of grape arbors and olive trees.

Flying high above Crete, the Dornier 17s, the Heinkel 111s, and the Junker 88s began their bombing runs.

All hell broke loose. The air was torn by the sounds of Bofors guns firing at the enemy aircraft. Simultaneous with the sound of the air alarms, a battery of 3.5-inch antiaircraft guns, located at the neck of Akrotiri Peninsula, opened fire on the approaching enemy. Everyone scattered except the men firing the guns. The crewmen stood bravely by their weapons, completely exposed to the aerial attack.

Captain Stephanides dashed for the foxhole that served as his air-raid shelter. He jumped in just as the first bombs whistled down on their targets.[4]

The high-level bombers released their destructive missiles in strings of twelve. In a crisscross bombing pattern, from north to south and from east to west, the Heinkels and Dorniers, under Colonel Reickhoff, and the Junker 88s under Captains Hoffman and Kollewe, left no sector of Cretan soil unscathed. Squadron after squadron of bombers passed overhead. The roar increased to an ear-shattering din. The whine of bombs filled the air as their deadly detonations blasted everything in sight.

Soon the blue sky over Crete was obscured by a thick mantle of dust—a cloud that rose from the dry ground ripped by the hailstorm of aerial bombs. A black smoky shroud hovered like a widow's veil over the transport ships burning in Suda Bay. It was the heaviest concentration of aerial bombing since that of the English cities during the Battle of Britain.

Men of the Twenty-second New Zealand Battalion, protecting Maleme airfield from their positions on the heights of Hill 107, were entirely helpless and at the mercy of these bombers. All that stood between them and the slicing shards of exploding bombs was the dry Cretan soil. The men lay in their foxholes, and as the bombs fell, each man prayed that the pattern would miss his

hole. Most of the bombs did miss the earthen shelters of the New
Zealand defenders, but many were covered with dirt and debris
from the earthshaking concussions. They shook dirt from their
ears and spat grit from their mouths. The brain-rattling detonations left many of these men temporarily deaf. Occasionally, a
bomb fell into a trench, its explosive force leaving a scar in the
earth where once soldiers had sought shelter.

The intensity of the attack was such that even the disdainful
Cretans thought it best to seek shelter from this madness. Ala-
baster dust rose hundreds of feet into the air over the city of
Khaniá, as the bombs tore apart buildings and their occupants.

Stephanides and the other personnel of Creforce Headquarters,
who sought safety from the aerial assault in slit trenches, could
hear the persistent and continuous roar of the antiaircraft guns.

Next came the Stuka dive-bombers. These slender, square-
tailed demons of the sky spread devastating and demoralizing
fear. They flew at 4,000 feet, stacked in grids, one above the
other. At a signal from their group leader, Lieutenant Colonel
Dinort, the planes moved into line astern. Each pilot switched on
his bombsight, let out his dive brakes, and closed his radiator
flaps. Then they nosed over into the attack.

The Stukas plunged into their seventy-degree dives, each plane
following the other down to the target. The siren in the nacelle of
each dive bomber screamed a familiar sound that foretold that death
was coming. Plane after plane, squadron after squadron, dove down
at a speed of 275 mph, peeling off at 300 feet. Their bombs, released
at 1,500 feet, plummeted toward their targets. One of the first was
the battery of antiaircraft guns located on Akrotiri Peninsula.

Stephanides watched the air strike in morbid fascination. When
the dirt from the exploding bombs fell back to earth and the dust
cloud lifted, he saw that of the four antiaircraft guns in the battery,
only one remained intact and firing. The other three guns had been
destroyed by the attacking Stukas. Bodies and parts of guns lay scattered in all directions on the churned-up, bomb-cratered ground.

While the dive-bombers gathered in the sky for further attacks
on other targets, the air was ripped by the roar of strafing fighters.
Messerschmitt 109s took up the fight. In groups of three, they
flew low across the terrain, machine-gunning anything that moved.

For one hour, the intense attack continued. It seemed as if it
would never end. The cacophony of antiaircraft fire, the roar of
airplane motors, the whine of falling bombs, the earsplitting din

of explosions, and the shriek of the dive bombers turned this peaceful countryside into a hell on earth.

Cretans knelt before their icons and prayed for safety. Soldiers, some of whom had never believed in an Almighty Being, now prayed to God for salvation.

At 7:00 A.M. the attack suddenly came to an end.

An eerie silence followed. Heads appeared above the tops of trenches. Civilians emerged from the bombed remnants of their homes.

Just then Captain Stephanides heard a low, prolonged sibilant sound. It reminded him of wind passing through telegraph wires. A huge object blocked the sun momentarily and fleetingly cast an eaglelike shadow across the ground. The men once again dove for the security of their trenches. Over them passed a square-bodied fuselage with long tapering wings, sweeping toward the heights of Akrotiri Peninsula.

Stephanides was puzzled by the aircraft's appearance, for it had no propeller. He had never seen such an aircraft before. It was the first glider of the assault regiment descending earthward toward its objective.[5]

At Creforce Headquarters, General Freyberg's aide pointed to the appearance of aircraft in the west. With his field glasses, Freyberg saw transport planes flying over the Maleme area. From these aircraft, multicolored plumes appeared, slowly drifting to earth like flower petals.[6]

All over the western part of the island, gliders and paratroopers began to drop on Crete. From the ground, soldiers and civilians alike watched the sky above Crete fill with colorful, blossoming umbrellas floating toward earth. There were thousands of them, from Maleme to Khaniá and from Suda Bay to the foothills of the White Mountains. It was a spellbinding sight.

A Cretan farmer yelled, "They are coming . . . they are coming!" gesticulating wildly at the sky. In seconds the warning was repeated, "They are coming!"

Somewhere in the distance, a single rifle shot broke the prolonged silence. The sound echoed over the western hills and valleys of the island. It was followed almost immediately by the multiple bark of rifles and the low, repetitious rattle of machine guns.

The battle had begun.

# 12 / "IT WAS LIKE A TERRIBLE DREAM"

## MAY 20, 1941

Having flown in close formation throughout their southward flight, the paratroop-glider armada began to separate into various approach patterns. The huge yellow-nosed, black-bodied, trimotor transports headed toward their assigned drop zones. As they approached the island, the pilots could see in the distance the last of the bombers returning from their missions. There, ahead of and below the lead transport, was the major objective—the airfield at Maleme.

Events occurred in rapid succession. As the transports containing the paratroopers headed for their drop zones, the transports towing the gliders released their charges.

The three-pronged attack on the Maleme area was to be carried out by the special assault regiment of the western battle group, known as Task Force Komet. While parachutists were to seize and secure the western and eastern approaches to the airfield, the glider troops would capture the airfield itself and its commanding height, Hill 107. The Schwerpunkt—the main punch—of the attack thus fell to the men being carried to the objective in fifty-three gliders.

These glider troops represented the middle prong of the attack. Their specific objective was the seizure of the bridge over the Tavronites River, with the neutralization of the Bofors antiaircraft battery located at its mouth, and the capture of Hill 107. Capturing the hill, which rose approximately 350 feet above ground level, was particularly essential, for whoever controlled it also controlled the airstrip.

As Major Koch's detachment of thirty gliders emerged from the low-lying dust cloud lingering from the bombardment, their objective came into view. Kavsakia Hill—Hill 107—stood like a towering sentinel over the small airfield on its northern flank.

These great gliders dropped like soaring eagles from the sky. The silence that prevailed in the few moments following the termination of the aerial bombing was broken by the sibilant sound of air being cut by the enormous wingspan of each glider as it descended toward earth.

Koch had planned to attack the hill from two directions. He divided his force into two groups of fifteen gliders each. The first group would land on the northeast side of the hill, and Koch and his group would touch down on the southwestern slope. Once the 150 men of each group had landed, the two groups would advance toward the crest of the hill.

Major Koch sat behind the pilot in the lead glider of the second group. Behind him, strapped into their seats on the glider's center sill, were ten troopers of the battalion staff. They were ready to pounce upon the enemy as soon as they touched ground. The towing JU-52 transport had released them when the target hovered into view.

Koch's glider was on course, coming in from the southwest, heading for a small clearing on the slope below. Slowly the pilot pushed the controls forward, and the huge machine dipped into a gentle glide. All was still; nothing could be heard but the hissing of air streaming past the wings.

"Hold tight!" ordered Koch in a loud voice as the glider touched down. The glider careened off a stone wall, spun clockwise, and broke in two, coming to a full stop in a cloud of dust.[1]

There was a moment of stunned silence. Then the occupants emerged through the broken fuselage, their weapons at the ready. With Koch landed the headquarters staff of the First Battalion of the assault regiment. It was 7:15 A.M., fifteen minutes before zero hour.

No sooner had Walter Koch stepped out of the smashed craft than he realized that his glider had come to rest in a huge hollow. He saw the trajectory of tracer bullets from the New Zealand positions pass harmlessly overhead. The troopers from his glider immediately took defensive positions at the rim of the hollow.

Koch looked about him and was surprised at the hilly terrain surrounding the landing site. Air reconnaissance had not disclosed the existence of so many hills. This created an immediate problem. It had been planned that the glider troops land as complete fighting units ready to be led into battle. Now Koch saw the gliders of his group disappear over the summits of many hillocks, landing in other hollows. The troopers of each glider lost visual contact with each other. Koch ordered runners to be dispatched to contact the troopers of the other gliders in his group. They were to assemble at his glider, which would serve as a temporary command post. While he waited for the troopers to arrive, he followed the flight of the other gliders coming in for landings.

He winced as he saw one glider plummet to earth minus its tail section, which had been severed by a direct hit from a Bofors gun. It dropped like a rock, and not a single trooper emerged from the wreckage after it hit the crest of a nearby hill.

Some gliders came in too high. One of these banked very sharply in its descent; its wing dipped low and struck the rocky prominence of a hill. It cartwheeled several times, until the wing crumbled and the fuselage smashed itself against a grove of olive trees. The glider's occupants were strewn along the trail of its fatal path; some lay dazed, but most were killed on impact.

Another glider floated down with its nose up and tail down. It hit the rocky ground, and the fuselage split into two parts, spilling its live cargo. Despite the shock of impact, the surviving troopers quickly emerged with their weapons, ready to enter combat.

Still another glider dropped down into a clearing of the valley. Striking the ground with force, it shot forward between two olive trees, shearing off its wings. The fuselage bolted onward until it smashed into a stone wall. A few survivors emerged dazed from the broken remnants of the glider.

However, most gliders did succeed in landing intact on the rocky terrain of the lower slopes, but they were too dispersed to form a cohesive fighting unit. Koch waited impatiently while his runners sped off to guide these men to his command post.[2]

Nine gliders of eighty men together with the skeleton staff of the assault regiment dropped exactly on target into the dry riverbed of the Tavronites. This assault detachment was under the command of Major Walter von Braun. He landed at the exact moment that Koch touched down on Hill 107. While Koch waited for his men to assemble, Von Braun turned to seize his objective—the Tavronites bridge.

The paratroopers of the Von Braun group came under the immediate fire of D Company of the Twenty-second New Zealand Battalion, entrenched on the eastern bank of the river, south of the bridge. Captain T. C. Campbell, the company commander, ordered his men to concentrate a withering fire on the glider troops. The deadly stream of bullets from the defenders tore into the canvas-covered fuselages of the gliders as they attempted to land, taking a fearful toll of the attackers. Major von Braun was one of the first to be killed while still seated in his glider.[3]

The members of the assault regiment's headquarters staff withdrew under heavy fire to the western bank of the Tavronites, and sought shelter in the nearby village of Roponiana to await the outcome of the battle.

The Germans pressed their attack. Using the steep riverbank for shelter, they fought stubbornly until they reached their objective. Once the bridge was within their grasp, they attacked the few New Zealanders who held the western end. The stout resistance put up by the isolated defenders was quickly overcome. With a rush, the attackers raced across the double span, removing any demolition charges.

Lieutenant Wulff von Plessen's gliders came over the northern coast of Crete, swung in a wide semicircle, and approached the landing site from the south. That brought them in behind the New Zealand antiaircraft positions. Nevertheless, the gliders of this attack force did not escape the New Zealander's defensive fire unscathed.

One glider was hit by tracer bullets while still in flight, setting it on fire. The stricken craft fell to the ground, enveloped in flames and black smoke, roasting the troopers still inside. Some fell or jumped out, their uniforms in flames as they plummeted to their death.

As another glider came to a stop it was hit point-blank by a British Bofors gun firing at zero elevation. The glider disintegrated, flinging bodies and parts of bodies in all directions.

The rest of the gliders landed successfully, and immediately the glider troops focused their automatic fire on the crews of the antiaircraft guns. Most of the men manning these Bofors guns had only pistols with which to defend themselves, and even these weapons were short on ammunition. Their defensive fire was no match for the well-armed glider troops of Von Plessen's detachment. Those gunners who were not killed outright had no alternative but to surrender to the Germans.

Having achieved his initial objective, Von Plessen ordered his men to advance against the western perimeter of the airfield. The

Bofors crews may have been ill-armed, but it was a different story with the New Zealanders defending the airfield.

Leaving the protection of the undulating sand dunes, Von Plessen's men now entered an exposed position. They immediately ran into the blistering fire of C Company of the Twenty-second New Zealand Battalion, which was covering the northwest perimeter of the airstrip. The Germans were caught in the open, in a crossfire between C Company's 15th and 13th platoons. Von Plessen's men took to ground with heavy casualties. Even the arching fire from the crest of Hill 107 found targets in Von Plessen's troops. There was no choice; he ordered a withdrawal.

He decided to follow the Tavronites riverbed upstream and make contact with Von Braun's men. As he rose to signal his men, a burst of fire tore him in two. Von Plessen fell dead. The young medical officer attached to this assault group, Oberarzt Doktor Weizel, assumed command of the detachment. He was the only surviving officer.[4]

Once again the objective had been gained, but the heavy casualties in officers and men turned it into a costly achievement.

While the Von Braun and the Von Plessen detachments were meeting their fate, on Hill 107 Major Walter Koch was still waiting for the men of his detachment to gather at his command post.

Koch looked impatiently at his watch. At 0730 hours, the Third Assault Battalion of the assault regiment was scheduled to drop in the Pirgos-Platanias area, east of the airfield and Hill 107. It was to cut off a major segment of the important northern road, thus securing the eastern approach to the airfield. According to the timetable, Koch and his detachment of glider assault troops were to have captured and secured Hill 107 by the time the Third Assault Battalion of paratroopers had gained its objective.

The minutes were passing quickly. Only twenty-five troopers had assembled at Koch's command post. Of the 150 men of his detachment, only a handful had been able to gather. The rest had been killed during the landings or had landed too far away from the target site.

At the base of the northeastern slope of Hill 107 and running south on the eastern flank of the hill, there was a dirt road called the Xamoudokori. This road ran parallel to the dried-up Sfakoriako River, which was no wider than a stream. Across the Xamoudokori road, on its eastern side, were the gently ascending slopes of many vineyards. Called Vineyard Ridge, this was the defense position of the Twenty-first New Zealand Battalion.

The battalion's observers easily spotted the men of Koch's second group of glider troops clustered on the northeastern slope of Hill 107. They immediately concentrated a heavy barrage of mortar and machine-gun fire on that slope.

The Germans were now enfiladed, receiving fire from their front and from their flank. Within the first hour of battle, this group ceased to exist as a cohesive fighting unit: they were decimated; it was each man for himself.

On the southwestern side of the same hill, Major Koch heard the din of battle and assumed that the second group from his detachment was attacking up the northeastern slope. He could not wait any longer for the stragglers of his own group; he decided to attack with the handful of men available.

With the twenty-five men and officers of his battalion staff, he pushed off toward the summit of Hill 107. The first objective they encountered was the RAF tented encampment on their side of the slope. The attack was originally planned to be a surprise, hoping to capture the occupants in their cots. But there was no surprise—the camp was empty.

"One less problem," remarked Koch. "On toward the summit!" he ordered, enthusiastically waving his men forward. Forward and up they charged—only to be met by another wall of blistering small-arms fire from the entrenchments of the New Zealanders defending the hill.

These New Zealanders of the Twenty-second Battalion were satisfied that they had contained the German assault from the northeastern slope, and now they turned their fire on the enemy approaching from the southwest. It was a cruel concentration of machine-gun and rifle fire. Again the Germans were caught in the open; officers and men dropped along the whole slope. Some were killed; others fell badly wounded. The survivors sought to find the slightest depression in the ground for shelter. They could not move forward nor could they retreat. They were pinned down.

In a hollow behind a bush lay Major Walter Koch. Three bullets had pierced his body, severely wounding him. The hero of Eben Emael had come to Crete to receive almost mortal wounds on the rock-strewn terrain of Hill 107.[5]

The central prong of the attack had been dented. The airfield, with its commanding high ground of Hill 107, remained in the hands of the New Zealand defenders. In the first hour of battle the Germans had been dealt a serious setback.

The eastern jaw of the huge nutcracker that was to crush the defenders of Maleme airfield was represented by the Third Assault Battalion of the assault regiment under the command of Major Otto Scherber.

The six hundred paratroopers of this battalion were being flown to their target by fifty-eight transports. Their assigned objective was the capture of the area between the village of Pirgos, located east of Maleme, and the village of Platanias, a few miles farther east along the northern coast road. Once landed, the paratroopers were to consolidate, secure their objectives, and then advance against the airstrip, attacking from the east.

The enormous black transports flew over the Gulf of Kisamos, the hills of the Rodopos Peninsula, and the blue waters of the Gulf of Khaniá. They flew a west-to-east course parallel to the north coast of Crete. As they came abreast of the village of Maleme, they made a ninety-degree starboard turn and headed inland.

The transports crossed the coastline in elements of three to five aircraft per group, flying in tight formation at the low altitude of 500 feet. The air groups extended from Maleme in the west to the island of St. Theodore off Platanias village in the east. The pilots of this flight had been instructed at their briefing to release the paratroopers before crossing the coastline in order to concentrate the assault on the beaches north of the coast road. But the pilots of the lead transports feared that premature release of the paratroopers might accidentally drop them into the sea. They decided to delay the drop until the sandy beaches of the northern coast had been crossed.

As soon as the great black iron birds crossed the shoreline, all the antiaircraft guns from Pirgos to Platanias opened up. One transport blossomed into a huge orange fireball, both plane and paratroopers disappearing in the smoke and debris. Another transport swayed side to side, out of control, with only two paratroopers jumping from the plane before it tipped over into a perpendicular dive, ending in a loud explosive roar as it struck a terraced hillside.

Yet the transports continued on their flights as if nothing had happened. The fire from the defense positions increased in intensity as 20-mm and 40-mm Bofors guns barked, releasing a furious hail of incendiary and tracer bullets on the huge targets flying over them. The tight formation of transports was now scattering and rapidly losing its cohesion as a strike force.

Another transport, black smoke gushing from its port engine, tried to no avail to steady itself until the paratroopers were released. Rapidly engulfed in flames, it fell into the sea with most of its paratroopers still aboard.

The remaining transports continued onward, descending to a height of 400 feet, with all engines throttled back to reduce speed. Slowing the aircraft would allow the paratroopers to land closer together. However, this reduction in airspeed delighted the crews of the Bofors guns. The transports were like sitting ducks; and now the roar of heavy antiaircraft fire was augmented by the lighter, more rapid staccato sound of machine guns. Dropping to an altitude of 400 feet protected the transports from the devastatingly accurate fire of the three-inch antiaircraft guns, which could not be depressed to fire below 500 feet, but the Bofors guns poured a continuous stream of lead at the targets, until their barrels glowed red from overheating.

Four hundred feet was also the predetermined altitude for the paratroopers to jump. From this height, it would take a paratrooper only fifteen seconds to reach the ground.

It was obvious to the officers and NCOs that the assault battalion had passed its assigned drop zone. Major Otto Scherber, the commanding officer of the battalion, flying in the lead plane of the second group of five transports, left his seat and approached the cockpit.

"When the hell are you going to drop us?" he yelled impatiently at the pilot over the roar of the motors.

He did not know that some of his company commanders had instructed their pilots to fly farther inland in order to avoid the dense antiaircraft fire. He knew only that the paratroopers were getting uneasy with each passing moment, and that this delay in minutes seemed like hours. They were eager to jump and meet the foe face-to-face.

Finally the signal to jump was given. It was now 7:35 A.M. The battalion was five minutes behind in its time schedule.

First Lieutenant Werner Schiller made an uneventful descent from his aircraft. His transport had discharged him and his "stick" of men over a quiet sector. As he floated to earth, he studied the terrain below him. It was unfamiliar; not a single landmark resembled the objectives discussed during their briefing. He came to the realization that they had been dropped too far off course. In the distance, about four miles to the west, he noticed the smoke that hung like a low dark pall over the airfield at Maleme.

He cursed the transport pilots for deviating from the set course. They had tried to skirt the heavy antiaircraft fire that struck them as they crossed the north coast of Crete. As a result, Lieutenant Schiller and his parachutists were dropped too far to the east. In fact, his whole company had been too widely dispersed and it would be a problem to assemble them. He resigned himself to this stroke of bad luck, as his chute floated into the village of Platanias. Platanias was the headquarters of the Fifth New Zealand Brigade.[6]

Modhion, a village about one mile south of the north coast road and lying midway between Maleme and Platanias, had become the landing ground for scores of parachutists of the 10th Company of Scherber's Third Assault Battalion.

It was at this village that the New Zealanders had established a divisional Field Punishment Center for errant Creforce troopers. Apprehensively watching the approach of the German bombers earlier that morning, Lieutenant W. J. T. Roach, the CO, had ordered his sergeant to have the prisoners taken under guard to the dugouts provided for protection from air attacks.

Few bombs fell in the area of the detention camp, but tactical dive-bombers did concentrate on the bridge just outside the town on the south road. On the heights around the bridge and overlooking the flat-roofed houses of Modhion, the New Zealand engineers had established their defense positions. Into the center of this small village floated the parachutists of the 10th Company.

Almost from the first appearance of these ill-fated parachutists, a heavy concentration of small-arms fire echoed over the rooftops and into the hills and orchards of the surrounding countryside. The machine guns, dug into ground emplacements, picked off the paratroopers as they landed. Riflemen, too, took careful aim before firing. There were dead Germans wherever the eye could see.

One German fell into a grape arbor. While still struggling to get out of his parachute harness, a few rifle rounds were fired at him. He hung limply from his harness. Gunner McDonald, from the artillery battery protecting the Modhion bridge, walked up to the German. He felt that the parachutist was faking death.

"You'd look at me like that, you bastard, would you?" And he emptied his weapon into the German.[7]

Lieutenant Roach watched the paratroopers as they descended in the area south of his camp. He ordered his prisoners released and issued them all his available weapons. Then, taking his place at the head of the column of prisoners to lead them into battle, he gleefully remarked, "Let's go headhunting for bloody Huns."[8] Replenishing their arms and ammunition from the enemy dead, the men from the New Zealand prison camp celebrated their newly won freedom with a "turkey shoot." These sixty prisoners succeeded in killing over 110 Germans during the next few hours.

Many German paratroopers landed in the town square of Modhion. Before they had a chance to reach the canisters containing their weapons, they were set upon by the townspeople.

Disregarding the danger from bullets fired by the New Zealanders, Cretan civilians, both men and women, charged out of their homes and fell upon the paratroopers. Fighting furiously in defense of their homes, they struck the enemy with scythes, axes, hoes, and spades—anything they could use as a weapon.

It was an unbelievable sight to behold. One New Zealand machine-gun squad stopped firing at the Germans in order to watch a group of civilians pursuing six Germans in the town square. Only when another parachutist fell within a few feet of their machine gun did the New Zealand gunners return to the business at hand.

Four Germans racing toward a white-parachuted canister were met by a volley of fire from two old men. The four paratroopers fell victim to bullets fired by two ancient flintlocks captured from the Turks a half-century earlier.

When the two old men disappeared to reload, three other parachutists made their way to the same weapons canister. Instantly five adults and a child charged them with hoes and axes. Two women of this group fought one paratrooper; the three men quickly dispatched the other two troopers and turned to assist the women. No assistance was required, for the luckless victim lay motionless at their feet.

The Germans paid a heavy toll at Modhion. Of the total complement of the 10th Company, more than 60 percent were killed or wounded. This high casualty rate was partly due to the furious fight put up by the villagers. But these heroic people were to pay a heavy price in retribution in the days ahead.[9]

Major Otto Scherber, the commanding officer of the Third Assault Battalion, was the first man to jump from his aircraft. No sooner had his pink parachute opened and its oscillation stopped than he surveyed the many other chutes that filled the sky. In one quick dissatisfying glance, he realized that his battalion was in trouble. Scattered over a total of four miles, they would be too far apart to support each other as a concentrated attack force.

Halfway down, Scherber became aware of a greater danger. The heavy concentration of antiaircraft fire from the Bofors guns had shifted from the departing transports to the descending para-troopers. To the syncopated boom of the Bofors was now added the staccato bark of machine guns and the hollow crack of rifle fire. The sky was filled with the crisscross trajectories of tracer bullets. The German paratroopers had become the targets of an-other turkey shoot.

The delay in releasing the paratroopers over their original drop zones had brought them further inland—right over the defense positions of the Twenty-third New Zealand Battalion.

As the parachutists floated toward earth, they came within easy range of rifle and pistol fire. Major Scherber had only one object in mind: to land quickly and rally the men who had survived the descent.

From a height of fifty feet, he realized that he was dropping near a command post. Under some trees below him, he noticed a huge open-sided tent, men around it firing upward in all direc-tions. Scherber removed his pistol from its holster. In the direct path of his descent, he saw a New Zealander crouching behind a half-fallen rock wall. As he dropped closer, observing the enemy to be a sergeant, Scherber raised his pistol to fire at him, but the New Zealander turned and fired in Scherber's direction. His bul-lets struck the German in the body and his pistol fell from his hand. Scherber struggled in the throes of death and then went limp as his body finally touched earth. He lay still where he had fallen, his parachute enveloping him like a death shroud. The commander of the Third Assault Battalion was dead.

The New Zealander, Sergeant Ray Striker, realized that he had killed a German officer.[10] He ran to Scherber's side and detached a map case from the German's belt. It might contain information of some importance. With the case neatly tucked against his chest, he turned and headed for the buff-colored, open-sided tent located in an adjacent field, headquarters of the Twenty-third New Zealand Battalion.

When Sergeant Striker reached the tent, he found the staff officers busily shooting at the paratroopers dropping all around them. At the front of the tent, the sergeant recognized the commanding officer of the Twenty-third Battalion, Lieutenant Colonel D. F. Leckie, who was firing his pistol at a group of paratroopers. The CO stood right in the open, issuing orders and firing simultaneously. In just a few minutes, he had fired his pistol five times—killing five paratroopers.[11]

It was obvious that the colonel was too busy to be bothered.

The Cretan and New Zealand defenders were exacting a heavy price from the Germans. In less than two hours after the first paratrooper of the Third Assault Battalion had touched Cretan soil, these elite German soldiers had ceased to exist as a fighting unit. Of the 600 men who comprised Major Scherber's battalion, more than 400 were killed or wounded in the first hour of battle. The remainder survived as scattered, isolated units seeking relief from the debacle. Of 126 paratroopers from one company of this battalion—which had landed between Cretan defenders on one hill and New Zealanders on the other, in the village of Gerani just north of Modhion—only fourteen survived.

When nightfall came, the remnants of the 9th Company of the Assault Battalion fought their way westward in order to reach their own lines somewhere behind the Tavronites River. They were the sole survivors of Otto Scherber's assault battalion. To the survivors of this day's battle, "it was like a terrible dream!"[12]

# 13 / "IT WAS MAGNIFICENT, BUT IT IS NOT WAR"

## MAY 20, 1941

The first group of nine gliders commanded by Captain Gustav Altmann, swept silently toward the Akrotiri Peninsula. As they descended toward this rugged, rock-strewn terrain that resembled the profile of a human skull, they were exposed to intense anti-aircraft fire. Three gliders were totally wrecked when they smashed against the rocky hills and stone walls that ran the length and breadth of the peninsula.

Captain Altmann gathered the survivors of his scattered force, and they advanced on their first objective—the nearby antiaircraft batteries.[1]

When Altmann and his men arrived, they were surprised to find the gun emplacements empty. There were no guns and no gun crews. In place of guns, there were wooden logs. The batteries were dummies—the Germans had been fooled.

General Freyberg watched these gliders during their descent. They were not too far from his headquarters. He turned to his chief of staff and issued a terse order to attack them.

The Northumberland Hussars were sent out on this search-and-destroy mission. Moving rapidly on foot and with tracked Bren-gun carriers, which resembled miniature tanks, the British rushed to meet the invader.[2]

Altmann's force was too dispersed to offer a concerted resistance in the face of the Hussars' determined counterthrust. In a matter of a few hours, half of Altmann's men were killed or wounded. The remainder were captured or had to surrender when their ammunition was spent. They never had the opportunity to undertake the second phase of their mission—the seizure of Freyberg's headquarters.[3]

South of the city of Khaniá, the second group of assault gliders landed safely and precisely on target—the gun emplacements of the 234th Heavy Antiaircraft Battery at the crossroads of the Mournies-Khaniá road. This group of five gliders was commanded by a scholarly, English-speaking officer, First Lieutenant Alfred Genz. His group originally had six gliders, but one had been lost at sea during the flight.

Once his group landed, Oberleutnant Genz led his fifty men in an attack on the crews of the antiaircraft battery. The gun crews had no weapons whatsoever with which to defend themselves; they were no match against the well-armed Germans.

Some of the gun crews were still hiding in the slit trenches that had protected them from the earlier aerial bombing. The Germans found them there and machine-gunned them where they lay. Of the 180 men comprising the battery's gun crew, 173 were killed and the surviving 7 fled to the hills.[4]

Genz and his men now turned their attention to their second objective, the powerful wireless station located to the south. At the turn of the Mournies road, they ran into stiff rifle fire from the vineyards on their left. The firing increased in strength, pinning the Germans down; their advance had come to a halt.

A small force of Royal Marines from the nearby Suda garrison was putting up a strong defense against Genz's men. In a sharp counterthrust of shouting men wielding their bayonets freely, the Royal Marines pushed Genz and his men back to their starting point—the antiaircraft battery. There the Germans remained pinned down for the rest of the day, with increasing casualties, as steady fire picked them off one by one.

It was to remain that way until nightfall, when Genz and his survivors would make an effort to escape through the encircling British lines. Lieutenant Genz's major objective—the powerful radio station—remained untouched and still in British hands.[5]

The transports carrying the First Battalion of paratroopers from the Third Regiment of the Airborne Division approached the area called Prison Valley intact.

The island's prison colony lay one mile south of the village of Galatas and three miles west of Khaniá. It was composed of several oblong one-story buildings in a huge clearing.

From the rolling hills around Galatas a broad, undulating plain swept southward five miles toward the foothills of the White Mountains, its cultivated fields intermittently broken by the darker hues of vineyards, olive groves, and orchards. The huge expanse of land was bounded on its eastern side by a dirt road that descended southward from the heights of Galatas and ended in the village of Alikianou. From Alikianou another dirt road stretched to the western side of the plain to Aghia, a village nestled on the shores of a small lake that served as the reservoir for the entire area. This whole plain was called Prison Valley.

The First Battalion of paratroopers had flown southward across the northern coast of Crete; then they circled counterclockwise, approaching their objective from the south. In this way, once the men had been dropped, the troop carriers could continue on their northern course, returning to their respective airfields on the Greek mainland to prepare for their subsequent assignments.

As the JU-52s carrying the First Battalion approached the objective, the hooters in each plane sounded the "get ready" signal. Captain Friedrich von der Heydte, the commanding officer, had awakened moments before. Now he prepared himself for his parachute jump into combat.

He placed his steel helmet on his head and gave a final check to his harness straps, casting a quick glance at the faces of the men in his transport. Only his batman and sergeant were familiar to him; the rest were all new. By their smiles, he was satisfied that they would do what was expected of them. Even Max Schmeling was smiling now.

At a given signal, the fifteen men in the transport stood up in single file facing forward and hooked their static lines to a wire that ran the length of the aircraft. The transport's low hatch was now opened, and Captain von der Heydte stood poised at the door. True to the dictates of the paratroop manual, as battalion commander he would be the first to jump. Von der Heydte felt the rush of air strike him full in the face, taking his breath away momentarily. He looked up at the blue sky above and at the green fields rushing rapidly past below. The great black shadows of the transports, fleeting across the landscape, reminded him of ominous birds of prey ready to swoop down on a victim. His thoughts were interrupted as a dispatcher shouted over the roar of the engines, "Get ready!"[6]

Von der Heydte's knuckles blanched as his hands tightened on the grabirons at each side of the open hatch. The rest of the men stood anxiously behind him. There was no talking now—just the silence of nervous tension, broken only by the roar of the engines and the whistle of the wind as it swept past the open hatch.

The dispatcher dropped his arm—the signal to jump.

The battalion commander dived into empty space. It was like diving into a swimming pool, except that instead of water, hard earth rushed up menacingly to meet him. The force of the wind tore at his face, distorting his cheeks and roaring in his ears.

Suddenly he felt a tremendous snap that pulled his harness straps backward and up. It was as if some huge hand had grabbed him by the shoulders, stopping his free fall instantaneously with a force strong enough to knock the breath out of his lungs.

Now his rapid fall was quickly replaced by a smooth, slow descent. Breathing normally again, he looked up to see a great pink silk canopy billowing above him like a protective angel.

It took Von der Heydte fifteen seconds to reach earth. He unhooked his parachute and quickly gazed into the sky, now filled with hundreds of parachutes, the pink parachutes of the officers and the black chutes of the lower ranks. Here and there he spotted the yellow parachutes bearing canisters of medical supplies. Typical of his concern for his men, Von der Heydte had the fleeting thought that now Schmeling could report to the medical officer, if he still felt ill.[7]

His battalion sergeant-major had landed nearby and immediately dispatched a group of paratroopers to a canister floating to earth below a white parachute. It contained rifles, machine guns, and ammunition.

Throughout the whole valley south of the prison complex, the men of the First Battalion landed unscathed, meeting little or no resistance.

Also in the First Battalion, Private First Class Kreindler, as the ranking noncom in his aircraft, was the first to jump. He half-squatted by the open hatch and waited for the signal. The delay in jumping added to his tension. He watched the rush of landscape below him; he saw the mirrorlike reflection of Lake Aghia on the left, and the white buildings of the prison complex below him.

"Why the delay in jumping?" he thought.

His anxiety increased when white puffs appeared in the sky before him. He could not hear the sound of the detonations over the roar of the motors, but he knew it was enemy antiaircraft fire. The transport slowed and descended to a height of 400 feet. Nearby flak bursts caused the aircraft to lurch just as the dispatcher gave the signal to jump.

Kreindler dived out into space, followed by his buddy Karl Schoerner. The thirteen other men of this "stick" followed in sequence.

When his black chute opened above him, Kreindler was jolted upright and he swayed rhythmically side to side as he descended toward earth. He looked about him and spotted his friend Schoerner floating to his left. Schoerner waved to him.

In the fifteen seconds it took Kreindler to float to earth, he became aware of yellow and orange streaks of light arching up toward him. He recognized the danger and his heart skipped with alarm. Those streaks were tracer bullets. The enemy on the ground was shooting up at him and his men. Bullets streaked past Kreindler with a snapping sound; some made a solid thump as they buried themselves in the bodies of parachutists. One or two already had been killed and hung limply in their harnesses. Kreindler was horrified at the thought that he made such a perfectly defenseless target in his slow descent. Fifteen seconds seemed like fifteen minutes. He had only 200 feet to go!

Incendiary bullets hit Schoerner's parachute, igniting it. The parachute began to smolder. If only he could reach ground before it was too late, thought Kreindler.

Schoerner began to descend at a faster rate. The rush of air fanned the smoldering silk into a flame. One by one the parachute risers began to snap. Schoerner's face was frantic; he looked to Kreindler for help. Kreindler pulled on his own risers in an effort to alter his direction. If he could swing to his left, he might put himself into position to grab Schoerner as he dropped past him.

Kreindler was still tugging at his risers, completely oblivious to the increased whip of bullets flying past him, when he glanced up to give Schoerner a hopeful sign. All he saw was the burning remnants of a chute, floating off into space; a figure dropped past him, just beyond his reach. It was Schoerner, with that look of frantic terror still in his eyes, falling 150 feet to his death.[8]

The staccato beat of gunfire echoed over the hills from the Galatas area. Von der Heydte's executive officer looked at him apprehensively, but the battalion commander smiled.

"It is a relief to hear the sound of fighting," he said. "It is at least a token that we are not alone in this hostile land."[9]

It was now 7:40 A.M.

While the battalions of Colonel Richard Heidrich's Third Parachute Regiment were still descending into Prison Valley, the remaining two units of the First Assault Regiment were being discharged in the Maleme area. Eighty-seven JU-52s had ferried 1,300 paratroopers of the Second and Fourth Assault Battalions to their objective.

In perfect formation, without a single threatening burst of antiaircraft fire, the troop carriers released the parachutists. The sky filled with the multicolored blossoms of billowing umbrellas. It was a riveting sight for the villagers from Spilia, from Voukoulies, and from Kolimvari, on the northeastern corner of the drop zone. An awesome spectacle, it was frightening, yet beautiful.[10]

Major General Eugen Meindl jumped into the Battle of Crete with the paratroopers of the Second Assault Battalion.

Once he had landed, he issued orders that contact be made with all the units of his assault regiment. It was at this time that several bedraggled officers from the regimental staff that had been ferried to Crete in Von Braun's gliders arrived at Meindl's headquarters to report the death of Major von Braun and Lieutenant von Plessen.

Meindl had further disquieting news when he was informed that not a single wireless set had survived the descent. The major radio units, 200- and 80-watt transmitters, had been shattered on impact.

"Can you repair them?" Meindl asked his communications officer.

"Yes, Herr General," Oberleutnant Göttsche replied, "I will try to reconstruct one operable wireless from an assortment of parts available from the broken sets."

"Do your best—we must have communication with the other units!"[11]

A detachment of seventy-two German paratroopers fell in two groups at the eastern end of Kastelli, into the defense positions of the First Greek Regiment's A Battalion. Right from the start, the paratroopers were in trouble in their attempt to seize the village of Kastelli.

Many paratroopers succeeded in shedding their harnesses and raced for the canisters containing their weapons. The Greeks chased after them into the high grass. Hiding in irrigation canals and behind bushes, trees, and stone walls, the men of A Battalion followed the trail of each German like hunters stalking their prey.

Each time a German was found, the Greeks fell on him with any weapon at hand. Bayonets, axes, curved Syrian knives, sticks, stones, and even bare hands became weapons to kill the enemy. In those eventful moments of conflict, the only sounds audible from the battlefield were the oaths of fighting men and the screams of the dying.

As the men of A Battalion killed paratroopers, they took their weapons. In no time at all, the poorly equipped Greeks had armed themselves with German pistols and machine guns and turned to fight the rest of the parachutists with their own weapons. The combatants were now more evenly matched.[12]

Certainly untrained and ill-equipped for combat against a foe disciplined in the regimen of modern warfare, these Cretans possessed certain innate traits the paratroopers lacked. They were a hardy lot who lived a primitive day-to-day life. Toiling the fields from sunrise to sunset beneath the searing-hot Cretan sun had steeled them to the hardships of life. To these men, fieldcraft and marksmanship were as natural as the breath of life.

Above all, the Cretans held one principle more sacred than life itself—their freedom. So it was of little surprise that these civilian soldiers of the First Greek Regiment should fight so fiercely against the elite of the German army.

In a matter of an hour, most of the paratroopers had been killed or wounded. Their CO, Oberleutnant Peter Muerbe, was among the slain. The survivors gathered in confused groups as the Greeks fired on them with their own weapons. The toll was heavy. Their only chance for survival was to fortify themselves within some nearby buildings and hold out until relief arrived.[13]

Led by a noncom, the survivors raced for a cluster of four stone houses that formed a rectangle surrounded by a stone wall. At a given signal, in twos and threes they retreated to these shelters. Bullets from Major Bedding's machine guns bit the dirt at their feet, but once inside, they bolted the doors and closed the shutters of each window. From cracks in the shutters and holes in the walls, the deadly muzzles of their own weapons emerged. In every direction, MG-34 machine guns, pistols, rifles, and tommy guns spit out flames at the Greeks.

The few Greeks who chased them were now caught in the open and cut down by a few bursts of fire. The surviving pursuers sought refuge behind a stone wall 100 feet away.

In a room in one of the stone houses, the paratroopers found four frightened civilians. It was the family of Spiro Vlahakis, which included the old man, his elderly wife, and their two grand-children. His son was somewhere out front with the men of A Battalion.[14] In a murderous disregard for human life, one of the paratroopers fired a burst at them, killing them as they huddled fearfully in a corner of the dark room. Gefreiter Walter Schuster, who led this group, scolded the paratrooper for the needless slaughter. The paratrooper only shrugged his shoulders, replying nonchalantly, "Anyway, they would have been killed in the crossfire."

It became obvious that the Germans were well positioned behind the thick walls of these farmhouses. Their field of fire made an open approach impossible. The houses had been converted into a miniature fortress.

Major Bedding was satisfied to keep it that way. He was willing to keep them surrounded until they ran out of ammunition, food, and water.

"Let us wait them out," he advised the Greek regimental commander.[15]

But the Greek colonel was not pleased with this advice. Colonel Papademetrakopoulos spoke rapidly in Greek to his battalion commander: "Remember what I had said to you in the past? Now is the time to show these gentlemen that battles are won by men with brave hearts. Give the order!"

At a signal the Greeks rose up from behind the stone wall—on all four sides. Major Bedding was shocked to see the Greeks race across the open field toward the farmhouses. It was an old-fashioned do-or-die bayonet charge.

The Germans fired at them, but the Greeks swept forward yelling at the top of their lungs.

"What is that they are yelling?" Bedding asked.

"It sounds like—'Aeria,' " replied a New Zealand sergeant.

"Aera!" corrected the Greek colonel. "It is the battle cry of the Evzones!"

"These men are not Evzones, Colonel!" Bedding said sarcastically, remembering their lack of training. Evzones were special regiments in the Greek battle for independence, known for their valor and heroism.

"No, but they are Cretans—and this is their soil," the Greek commander answered angrily.[16]

Even intense German machine-gun fire could not stem the fury of the charge, and the Cretans reached the main buildings.

It was a heroic, almost miraculous feat. The Greeks seemed to defy the wall of lead that met them as the German bullets ate at their vitals. Some of them continued their forward momentum even after bullets struck their bodies—so great was their determination—until they fell dead. The field was soon covered with dead and wounded Greeks, but still the rest came rushing.

When they reached the houses, they smashed in the bolted doors and the shuttered windows and leaped into the muzzles of the German guns. Once inside, the frenzied Greeks fell on the Germans. The air was rent with groans, screams, and shrieks as men fought hand to hand.

It was a slaughter.

One by one the German guns were silenced. Slowly the Cretans emerged from the houses into the open air—smiling.

Eighteen German survivors walked out with their hands over their heads in surrender. As they emerged, a wounded Greek, one arm hanging at his side in shreds, lunged with his bayonet at a paratrooper—killing him. Now there were only seventeen.

Another Greek picked up a German tommy gun and pulled back the bolt. Everyone knew what he was going to do, and the Greeks stood aside.

Just then Bedding stepped forward.

"Remember, Colonel, the rules of the Geneva Convention—these men are now officially prisoners of war."

The Greek colonel nodded his head, and the prisoners were reprieved. But Bedding did not trust the Greeks. Their blood was boiling, and their thirst for revenge had not yet been slaked.

Bedding ordered the seventeen German survivors to be placed in the Kastelli town jail for their own safety. To make certain, he ordered the men of his own advisory staff to stand guard over them.

When the survivors of A Battalion stood for roll call, Major Bedding looked upon them with admiration.

"It was magnificent," he commented to the Greek regimental commander, "but it is not war!"[17]

# 14 / "THAT THE GERMAN SHALL NOT PASS!"

## MAY 20, 1941

Colonel Howard Kippenberger, the commanding officer of the Tenth New Zealand Brigade, had begun his day as usual with the first light of sunrise. He completed the morning entry in his personal diary and went downstairs to the officer's mess for breakfast.

Kippenberger wondered if the meal served the lower ranks was as bad as his, when his attention turned to the roar of two ME-109 fighters, which raced back and forth machine-gunning everything that moved along the Khaniá-Alikianou road.[1] It was strange, he thought, that these two fighters should concentrate on such close ground strafing unless it was in support of . . . He never finished the thought, for no sooner had it crossed his mind than a shout went up. There above them swished four longspanned gliders, heading northward, casting ominous shadows over the ground. Immediately thereafter, the sky filled with scores of trimotor transports. Amidst the roar of motors came the frightened screams of civilians and the alarmed shouts of soldiers. Men jumped from these low-flying transports, and soon the sky was filled with billowing parachutes strung out in all directions.

Kippenberger jumped to his feet, shouting, "Stand to arms!" and ran into his quarters. In his room he grabbed his Lee-Enfield rifle and his binoculars.[2] As a battle-wise veteran of the Greek campaign, he knew that an officer had a better chance of survival carrying a rifle rather than the official pistol. In his haste, he neglected his diary, which lay open on his desk. He was not to see it again for four years; it was returned to him by a Cretan girl after the war.

Rifle in hand, Kippenberger raced down the main road toward his battle headquarters. To the din of roaring aircraft was added another sound—the rising crescendo of rifle and machine-gun fire. He knew that the battle had begun.

Although short in stature, he quickly outraced the two communications men who had accompanied him. When he reached the pink stone house that served as his battle headquarters, he dashed up the path toward the entrance. A burst of machine-gun fire shook him as it cut the huge bush at his side, missing him by inches. Veteran infantryman that he was, Kippenberger quickly rolled into a hollow. Slowly and carefully, foot by foot, he crawled up the path to the house. Once within the safety of his command post, he found that his staff members were out shooting Germans. He was all alone.

From the side window, he spied the German who had shot at him hiding in the protective shadow of a huge cactus bush. Kippenberger could not get a clear shot at him from this position; he had to get closer. His ankle now began to hurt, and he realized that he must have injured it when he rolled down the embankment. Pain or no pain, he was determined to kill that German. He exited from a window on the opposite side of the house and stealthily worked himself to the rear of the building. This maneuver brought him behind the German. Taking careful aim, Kippenberger fired one shot, and the German fell dead with a bullet in his head.[3]

Colonel J. R. Gray, commanding the Eighteenth New Zealand Battalion, lost no time rounding up his men and hastening off in pursuit of the invaders. The order went out to men of all ranks in all capacities—including cooks and clerks—to pick up their weapons and go after the Germans. Colonel Gray led the pursuit through olive groves, over hills, and into valleys. Accompanying the battalion commander were his batman, his sergeant-major, and one of the clerks from the orderly room, Corporal Dick Phillips. As soon as Colonel Gray and his men reached the drop zone, they went to work in the deadly game of hide-and-seek.

Gray noticed a parachute hanging from a branch and shrewdly surmised that its former wearer must be close by. He saw a movement behind a cactus and fired at it with his rifle. (Like Kippenberger, Gray also felt safer behind a rifle than an officer's pistol.) When Gray approached the spot, his prey made a dash toward a weapon-filled canister. The colonel fired again, hitting the paratrooper in midair.

From behind an olive tree, a young paratrooper aimed and fired at him. The bullet passed unnoticed through Gray's sleeve while he spun and returned the fire, wounding the German. As the bat-

talion commander was relieving the wounded youth of his pistol,
Corporal Phillips, who was standing next to him, uttered a sharp
cry of pain and fell to the ground with a bullet in his knee. Off
to the left, behind some bushes, two paratroopers shot at them.
Colonel Gray, the sergeant-major, and Private Andrews—the
colonel's batman—all fired at once in that direction. Two Germans leaped up as the avalanche of lead hit them; they fell back
dead.

Andrews took aim at another cactus bush.

"Steady," cautioned the colonel. "You might be shooting at
one of our chaps!"

"No bloody fear," Andrews replied. He fired once and another German fell dead.[4]

Oberleutnant Werner Schiller was one of the many paratroopers
who came down far from his designated drop zone. Being one of
the first to be released from his transport, he landed farthest from
the target, in the western outskirts of the village of Platanias,
which was the headquarters of the New Zealand Fifth Brigade.

Once he had touched ground and discarded his parachute, he
raced for the protection of some tall cactus bushes. He appeared
to be alone, for not a single man from his "stick" of fifteen
paratroopers was anywhere in sight.

He lay there motionless, cursing the transport pilots once again
for scattering the unit over such a wide area. From the sound of
rifle fire in the distance, he realized that his comrades were in a
firefight. Carefully and methodically, he evaluated the situation;
his only choice was to follow the sound of battle and join his
men.

As he rose to leave, he heard a rustle in the branches of a tree
to his rear. He turned sharply, pistol at the ready, only to come
face to face with a paratrooper dangling from his parachute, his
feet just inches off the ground. Schiller stood momentarily in horrified shock, staring into the glassy eyes of the dead trooper,
whose chute was caught in the tree's upper branches. One neat
bullet hole over the heart had brought a huge red smudge seeping
through the dead man's jacket.

Werner Schiller turned away from his dead comrade, more
determined than ever to make contact with the other members of
his unit. Crouching in the shelter of an olive tree, he had the
weirdest sensation that someone was watching him. He thought

he saw movement, but before he could fire his pistol, he felt a sharp pain in his arm. Simultaneously, the force of the bullet spun him around, knocking him to the ground. Holding the wound tightly, he gasped with pain as blood plowed through his fingers and down his sleeve. He almost blacked out.

When he opened his eyes, he found himself staring into the muzzle of a rifle aimed by a huge man with wild, piercing eyes. He was not dressed as a soldier, but wore instead a black jacket, black trousers, and black boots; and his weathered face sported a thick moustache. Schiller did not realize that he was confronted by the pride of Cretan manhood—the heroic Kapetan.

The Cretan leaned over, picking up Schiller's pistol and bandolier. His keen eyes never leaving the wounded man, he stuck the weapon into his trouser belt and threw the bandolier over his shoulder. He gave a fast glance at the dangling paratrooper and a longer stare at Schiller. The Cretan then counted the bullets in his belt and shook his head, as if to say that it was not worth wasting another bullet to kill this German.

With a quick step, the tall Cretan disappeared behind some bushes just as quickly as he had appeared.[5]

In a matter of a few hours, singly or in small groups, the scattered paratroopers of the 11th and 12th Companies of Major Ludwig Heilmann's Third Parachute Battalion of the Third Regiment were hunted, found, and killed or taken prisoner.

The third company of this battalion—the 10th Company—was destined to meet a similar fate.

They had been dropped on a promontory north of the main east-west road at a point east of where it is intersected from the south by the Alikianou-Khaniá road. This high ground had been selected by General Freyberg as the site for a major hospital station for all Commonwealth forces west of Khaniá. To this area the Creforce commander assigned the Seventh General Hospital with the Sixth Field Ambulance Unit attached.[6]

The Germans felt that this installation was tactically important and should be seized in the initial attack. The 10th Company of Heilmann's battalion was assigned to its capture. Strangely, this company was the only one in the battalion to be dropped on target.

Private George Denker had been painfully wounded in the right shoulder and, as a result, had been sent to the Seventh General

Hospital for treatment. Throughout the remainder of the morning's bombing, he and the thirty other men assigned to this large rectangular tent lay on their cots. Denker was hoping that "they would all go away."

From his position in the shadows of the far corner, right against a canvas wall, Denker thought he heard guttural voices speaking German. Suddenly the flap flew open and a paratrooper carrying a tommy gun stuck his head in. He entered, followed by two other Germans.

Private Denker spied the Germans moments before the paratroopers' eyes could get accustomed to the darkness inside the tent. Rolling himself carefully off his cot, he eased himself beneath it and lay there motionless, hoping to escape detection.

The Unteroffizier (sergeant) ordered the men in the tent to be marched outside. Denker remained unobserved in the shadow of his hiding place. He lay there breathless, watching through a slit in the lower part of the canvas, as the Germans rounded up a large group of wounded. All in all, about two hundred patients were gathered in a field in front of the main hospital tent.

Lieutenant Colonel Plimmer, the medical commander of the hospital installation, surrendered to the Germans in the hope of protecting his patients. It was a fruitless gesture.

From a nearby tent, a smaller group of twenty wounded prisoners had been gathered. Watching closely, George Denker paled, and his heart skipped a beat when he saw a paratrooper open fire on the hapless group, killing them in one long burst. It looked as if the Germans did not intend to take any prisoners.

Colonel Plimmer ran up to a Feldwebel (class 2 warrant officer) and protested heatedly, shouting and flailing his arms. The German NCO looked at him disdainfully, raised his pistol and shot the colonel several times. The dead doctor fell back into a slit trench.[7]

The Germans of the 10th Company collected a total of 300 walking wounded. As the paratroopers stood with their tommy guns poised to fire, it became evident that they planned to execute them. An Oberleutnant approached the Feldwebel and, after a brief discussion, the prisoners were reprieved. They were marched down the slope of the hospital promontory, across the main northern road, and up the Galatas heights toward Galatas village, where the Germans hoped to make contact with the other units of their battalion.

The hospital prisoners were used as a protective screen by the advancing paratroopers of the 10th Company. But when the Germans reached the outskirts of the village of Efthymi, the New Zealanders of Colonel Gray's Eighteenth Battalion were waiting for them. Gray was determined to do to them what he had done to the same battalion's 11th and 12th Companies. He was outraged when he discovered that the paratroopers were holding hospital wounded as hostages. His orders were brief and to the point: "Get them!"

In the firefight that followed, the Germans were picked off one by one or in small groups. Many hospital patients were also killed, but most of them made a break for freedom, while others helped the New Zealanders seek out the hunted paratroopers. Many of the Germans surrendered; those who fought were wounded or killed.[8]

The Second Battalion of Colonel Heidrich's Parachute Regiment had been assigned to capture the hilltop village of Galatas and the surrounding area. It was strategically obvious that once Prison Valley was occupied and Galatas and its heights were taken, the gateway to the capital of Crete would be open.

Major Wulf Derpa, commanding officer of the Second Paratroop Battalion, was one of the first of his unit to land. From the start, it was obvious to him that all was not well. The battalion had been scattered in the many hills that encircled the village like a ring. Two companies had fallen south of Galatas, while the third descended into the center of town.

Stabsfeldwebel Karl Neuhoff was the first sergeant of the company that came down in Galatas. When Neuhoff and his "stick" of fifteen men received the signal to jump from the transport, they dropped into a cauldron of pistol and rifle fire.

New Zealanders and Greeks stood in the village square shooting up at the descending paratroopers. Germans fell everywhere; some were dead before they touched the ground, and others were set upon the moment they landed.[9]

Private First Class Hans Kreindler landed with a heavy thud amid cacti and lay momentarily stunned. Although Kreindler was in the First Battalion, the delay in releasing his "stick" from the transport had brought him into the zone of the Second Battalion. The noise of pistol, rifle, and machine-gun fire filled his ears, and bullets snapped through the air. Once out of his harness, Kreindler glanced about for the men of his group and for the location of the nearest weapons canister. At that moment he felt a sharp sting on the back of his left hand, followed by another. His first thought was that he had been hit. Instead of blood on his hand, there were two huge welts. A big Cretan wasp was crawling up his sleeve. In its brush with a tree, his parachute had disturbed a hive, and the wasp stings were the first shots from their patrol! In minutes he was beset by other wasps. He rose and raced across the field, while bullets chewed the earth at his heels. He finally reached shelter behind some rocks near a farmhouse, where he was immediately pinned down by sniper fire.

Kreindler grumbled to himself. His first thought on landing had been to search for Schoerner's body, but enemy fire was now too heavy. From his position, he was able to observe soldiers running about, shooting and shouting. They did not sound English, and he wondered if they were Greek. Suddenly, from behind the farmhouse, he heard a yell: "Natos o diavolos!" Still shouting "Here is the devil!" a tall soldier charged with his bayonet. Kreindler was momentarily startled, but he quickly fired his Luger from the hip.

Kreindler had scored his first kill in battle, and the very thought of it, as he pushed the corpse away with his feet, chilled him. His position now exposed, he raced for a nearby stone wall, behind which two other paratroopers had set up a machine gun.[10]

Captain Emorfopoulos—or Captain E, as he was known to his men of the 6th Company of the Sixth Greek Regiment—was stationed in the Galatas area.

The Greek regiment was composed of green troops under the command of a veteran of the Balkan Wars, Lieutenant Colonel Gregoriou. Heavily shackled by the outmoded training of bygone campaigns, Gregoriou was totally inept in the practice of modern warfare. He had given his two battalion commanders, Major K. Moraites of the First Battalion and Major P. Papadakis of the Second, a free hand in deploying the men of the regiment. They had deployed their units in the hills to the south of Galatas, while a small reserve was kept in the village near the regimental headquarters.

The men of this regiment were numerically at battalion strength; however, these newly conscripted recruits were poorly trained and equipped, with little knowledge of the fundamentals of defense, and less of attack. Colonel Gregoriou placed the whole respon-

sibility of his regiment's defense on the battleworthiness of his
flanking allies—the Tenth New Zealand Brigade. Colonel Kippenberger, the brigade commander, thought little of the battle
qualities of the Sixth Regiment and even less of Gregoriou. He
was soon to be pleasantly surprised.

The commanding officer of the 6th Greek Company watched
as the paratroopers descended into the rolling valley below his
company's positions. Although alarmed, he appeared calm as he
gave rapid and precise instructions to his platoon commanders.
He ordered them to deploy their men amid the olive trees and
high grass on either side of the field below Cemetery Ridge.

Captain E and his first sergeant were the only combat veterans
in the whole company; both had fought in Albania during the
early months of the Greco-Italian war. Emorfopoulos was worried
about his newly conscripted men. (Although each had a rifle,
ammuniton was in short supply.) He had no fears about their spirit
or their will to fight, but he was very concerned by their lack of
the most basic infantry tactics.

The Greeks could not help but admire the coolness with which
the German paratroopers went about their business under fire.
Once they reached the ground and removed their harnesses, they
helped the other men of their groups and then ran for the weapons
canisters. Armed with tommy guns and rifles, they joined the
battle. While their comrades fell dead all about them, they carried
on their routine almost with drillfield precision. It was unnerving
and heroic. "If only my men were as well trained," thought the
Greek captain.

That German training eventually made a significant difference.
In time, the paratroopers' concentrated fire began to tell on the
Greek soldiers. Slowly but surely, Captain E's men fell victim to
German pressure, and they had to retreat to the wall that formed
the southern boundary of the Galatas village cemetery. The untried Greek troops suffered many casualties in this firefight, but
German losses were heavier. What concerned Captain E most of
all, as his men entrenched themselves on Cemetery Ridge, was
that they were short of ammunition.

The other two companies of the Second Parachute Battalion,
which had fallen south of Galatas, were immediately ordered to
attack the village. Major Derpa, the battalion commander, was

short one paratroop company; it had been retained in Greece but was to follow later by sea. In its place, Derpa had been given two attached paratrooper companies with antitank guns. He ordered one company to advance toward Galatas from the east by way of Cemetery Ridge. The other would seize the high ground named Pink Hill and attack the village from the west.

Thus, one company of paratroopers was preparing to attack Galatas from the east, and Major Derpa was leading the other— the 7th Company—to a point west of the village. This attenuated column extended in double ranks on either side of the road that bisected the rising ground above Prison Valley, and worked its way westward. It was a forced march, and the going was foul. Once the road was left behind, the men had to hike through a maze of deep gullies, rocky ridges, and boulder-strewn, dried-up watercourses. With time of great essence, there was no resting. This company had to reach its point of attack quickly in order to coordinate its advance on Galatas with the other company's from the east.

Most of the men walked as if in a trance. With each step, their boots raised dust clouds in the wavy currents of the sunbaked air. The immediate enemy confronting the paratroopers of this company was neither the Greek soldier, the New Zealander, nor the Cretan civilian, but the scorching Cretan sun. The tropical heat was an enemy to be reckoned with; it was brutal.[11]

Rising thickly, the dust compounded their misery. It became an almost palpable barrier through which they had to thrust their sweating bodies. It settled quickly on their faces and hardened into a heavy crust that even made breathing difficult.

The standard paratroop uniform added to their problems. Designed for the cold air of northern continental Europe, it proved far too heavy for the Cretan heat. Uniforms clinging to their bodies like wet tissue paper, steel helmets like hot ovens baking their brains, the well-trained, well-disciplined Fallschirmjägers took these hardships in stride as they hiked to their destination.

When the men finally reached the hill west of Galatas, they were given a few minutes' respite. Some staggered off the trail and sought the shady shelter of the olive trees; others sat in their tracks, too exhausted by the heat even to drink the warm water from their canteens or to nibble on their rations. Still others found their compact food rations impossible to eat. The hard chocolate had become a brown mushy mix; just to lick it would add to the insatiable thirst that not even the warm canteen water could quench.

Finally Major Derpa ordered his company commander to begin the advance and occupy positions atop the vital hill. As the paratroopers formed a skirmish line, waiting for the signal to attack, they momentarily forgot the natural enemies of sun, heat, and dust and concentrated instead on the human enemy entrenched on the crest of the hill before them.

Stabsfeldwebel Karl Neuhoff, the company first sergeant who had earlier witnessed the destruction of his company as it dropped into the center of Galatas village, had succeeded, with some of the survivors, in reaching this company of paratroopers. He fell into rank and prepared to take part in the forthcoming attack.

Like the attackers of Pink Hill in the west, the paratroopers of the company attacking from the east marched off in an extended skirmish line. Slowly but deliberately they advanced up the ridge. There was no enemy fire, only a silence intermittently broken by the sharp commands of German officers and noncoms.

As the Germans passed the midway point of the hill without a shot being fired in opposition, they felt increasing tension. Now they took heart and, with an exultant yell of pending victory, raced for the cemetery wall. Then it happened.

From behind the wall, the men of the Sixth Greek Regiment popped up and opened fire. The whole German company was caught in the open, and the first blasts of rifle and machine-gun fire had a devastating effect. Men fell in all positions of instant death, the hail of lead cutting through their ranks as a scythe cuts through wheat. They sought shelter behind every available rock, bush, or hollow. Attempts to rise were limited by the crossfire from the ranks of the Nineteenth New Zealand Battalion on the right. The attack had been stopped in its tracks.

Unable to advance in the face of such withering fire and unable to remain in such an exposed position, the German company was ordered to withdraw. In groups of twos and threes, the stricken paratroopers retreated slowly down the ridge. They left half their company as casualties on the slope of the ridge.[12]

While Derpa's Second Battalion was fighting for its life in the hills around Galatas, southwest of Colonel Heidrich's command post, the Fallschirmpionier Bataillon—the attached engineer battalion under Major Liebach—was meeting heavy resistance in the attempt to capture its objective.

Where the southbound Alikianou-Khaniá road junctions with the road going west to the village of Aghia and its reservoir, lies the village of Alikianou. A small, nondescript collection of ten to twelve scattered white stone farmhouses settled amid the olive groves and citrus trees covering the foothills of the White Mountains, the village never had any claim to fame. In the ensuing days, however, it would take its place next to Galatas as the most important piece of real estate in Crete. Its seizure would secure the southern boundary of Prison Valley and simultaneously cut off any escape routes into the White Mountains. Alikianou was the objective of the German engineer battalion.

Defending the village and its surrounding hills were the raw recruits of the Eighth Greek Regiment, under the command of Lieutenant Colonel Peter Karkoulas. Colonel Karkoulas had deployed his first battalion, commanded by Major John Valegrakis, in the hills to the left of the village, while his second battalion, under Major George Vamvakis, protected the right flank. The regimental command kept a reserve force in the village itself to throw in if any breach occurred in the defense line.[13] Like the Sixth Regiment at Galatas, the Eighth had a complement of 800 men—approximately the strength of a battalion. It had only a small supply of ammunition and fewer rifles than men. This was the regiment to which Colonel Kippenberger had referred as "those malaria-ridden chaps," and whose defense positions he had dismissed as "just a circle on the map." The events that followed in the next few days changed his mind.

As soon as the engineer battalion concentrated its forces after the parachute drop, it set out to capture Alikianou. When the Germans reached the foothills leading to the village, they confronted withering fire from the men of the Eighth Regiment. The paratroopers scattered at first, but soon pressed on toward their objective. The Greeks continued to shower them with bullets, causing heavy casualties. Once the Greeks had used up their ammunition, they charged with bayonets. Charge followed countercharge, the Greeks even using rifles as clubs in hand-to-hand combat in their attempts to break the German attack.

Slowly but surely the Germans were pushed back to their original assembly line. One Greek bayonet charge advanced into the

German command post before it was finally stopped. The ferocity of the Greek attack was unbelievable.

As the battle swayed back and forth across the hills of Alikianou, the Greeks were solving the problem of their weapons shortage. Each time a Greek killed a paratrooper, he took his dead foe's weapon and ammunition. After a few hours of battle, the Germans were startled to hear the familiar burp of their own P-40 tommy guns and the fast rattle of their own MG-34 machine guns firing into their own ranks.

Besides the fury of the Greek counterattacks, the Germans had to contend with the wrath of the Cretan civilians. Like the civilian population at Modhion, which had rushed out to attack the paratroopers in the town square, the residents of Alikianou raced from their houses and fell upon the Germans in a blind fury. Attacking the Germans singly or in groups and using anything at hand for weapons, they left scores of dead Germans in the fields around their village.[14]

The Greek regiment suffered severe casualties during the day's battle, casualties that included the regimental commander and most of his staff. But the spirit of their determination was such that from their hearts they shouted the battle cry: "That the German shall not pass!"[15]

The German engineer battalion finally withdrew from the attack, having suffered such heavy losses that Major Liebach decided to regroup and wait for reinforcements. He informed Colonel Heidrich of his plans to stand fast, stating that Alikianou "was strongly held by at least 4,000 Greeks, partisans, and British."[16]

His pride would certainly have been broken had he known that his attack had been repulsed by only a small group of ill-trained, ill-equipped but resolutely determined men of the Eighth Greek Regiment.

# 15 / "WITH AXES, WITH SHOVELS, AND WITH THEIR BARE HANDS"

## MAY 20, 1941

Crete represented several firsts in the early history of World War II. The airborne invasion marked the first time that any such military venture was launched without the supporting assistance of ground troops. It was also the first battle in which the civilian population stood shoulder to shoulder with Greek and British Commonwealth soldiers in the defense of the island-fortress. This brave resistance set the example for the guerrilla warfare that followed in later years in all the German-occupied nations.

Nicholas Manolakakis lived on his family farm in the hills between the villages of Spilia and Voukoulies. Like his father before him, Nicholas had been born and raised on this farm, had married a woman from a nearby village, and had three sons.

With the war on the mainland over and German troops occupying Greece, he didn't know whether his sons were alive or prisoners of war. He hid his pained concern and turned his attention to his youngest son, thankful that at least he was safe at home.

Nicholas Manolakakis was a man of habit. Each morning at sunrise, he would go out to his properties and there like all farmers in his time—and his father's time before him—he pruned the fruit trees, tilled the soil, repaired the fences, and collected the fruit. By 8:00 A.M. he returned to his home, hung his pruning sickle on the kitchen door, and sat with his wife for a brief morning repast of fresh bread, white goat cheese, and homemade wine.

From 9:00 A.M. until 1:00 P.M., he was back in the fields. When the sun reached its zenith, he returned home for lunch, followed by an afternoon siesta until 4:00. The late afternoon and early evening hours found him doing chores about the house. This was his life, day in and day out. But on May 20 the man of habit became a man of action.

On this fateful morning, Manolakakis returned from the fields earlier than usual. The thunderous sound of the heavy bombing to the northeast and the constant presence of German airplanes in the sky worried him.

As he ate his breakfast, he watched his son working in the field in front of the house, bundling the long thin branches that would serve as fuel for the oven fire. He smiled to himself proudly, wrinkling his sun-hardened face. His wife was doing her morning wash in an old wooden tub just outside the kitchen door.

The shadow of a low-flying aircraft momentarily darkened a path across the fields below. Young Manolakakis looked up and stood mesmerized, his mouth agape. Then, suddenly alert, he raced across the field toward the house, pointing upward and shouting in the high-pitched voice of a thirteen-year-old, "They're here, they're here!"

His father had heard the din of the transport, but it did not disturb him, for such aircraft had passed over him in the fields from early morning. The roar of its motor drowned out his son's shouts and muffled the report of a pistol shot.

Manolakakis watched as his son stumbled and fell forward on his face. Slowly he tried to rise, only to stagger a few feet and fall forward once again. This time he lay very still.

His mother uttered a cry and rushed to the boy's side. A muffled sob escaped from her lips.

The sharp report of a pistol again echoed through the morning air—more audible this time, since the passing aircraft's roar had diminished. The mother staggered, then fell near her son. Slowly and painfully, she crawled toward him and cradled his head in her lap. Then, gently slipping to her side, she, too, lay still.

Manolakakis watched with disbelieving eyes. "It isn't true," he thought to himself. "It is a bad dream." But there, descending before his very eyes, was the killer of his wife and son. In a rustling rush of wind, a German paratrooper, a pistol still in his hand, landed not more than ten feet from the front entrance to the house, the black canopy of his parachute following behind him.

Now Manolakakis was alert to the realization that this was no dream but a cruel reality. With the wide-legged stride of his huge frame, he charged out the front door, clutching in his right hand the only weapon within reach—his sickle.

The paratrooper had no chance to turn toward the sound of footsteps behind him. The sickle buried itself deeply in his back, at the base of the neck. He stood momentarily transfixed as if hung from a nail on the wall. When the blade was withdrawn, blood gushed from the triangular wound and the soldier crumpled soundlessly to the ground.

Manolakakis stared down at the dead German. Then, with tears welling in his eyes, he started toward his stricken wife and son. Hearing the same rush and rustle of wind, he turned and saw a portion of a parachute catch on the chimney at the back of the house, its wearer struggling to disengage himself from his harness. Thirsty for revenge, his blood racing with hate, Manolakakis ran to intercept him.

At the rear corner of the house, he came face to face with the second paratrooper. The German looked up at this towering specter of a wild man with hate-filled eyes and bristling black mustache. The sight was enough to startle any man. As the trooper pulled his pistol from its holster, Manolakakis swung his sickle in an upward stroke. Still coated with the blood of its first victim, the blade streaked upward with a hiss and it caught the paratrooper in the throat. Manolakakis' wrath was still not spent. He was poised to strike again when he heard that familiar hissing sound. There was another paratrooper, this one armed with a tommy gun, just fifty feet away. Having witnessed what the maddened Cretan had done to his two comrades, the German raised his automatic weapon to fire. In his haste to shoot Manolakakis, he neglected to unhook his parachute harness. It was a fatal mistake. As the paratrooper raised his weapon to fire, a brisk breeze filled the canopy of his parachute, pulling him off his feet. His shot missed. With catlike agility, the alert Manolakakis fell upon the German, his sickle striking repeatedly.

Now the field about him was filling with other paratroopers. Manolakakis took the dead man's machine gun and continued his one-man rampage. He fired short bursts at three paratroopers, killing them instantly. With a yell of hate, he charged like a crazed bull into the south field of his farm, where five other paratroopers had just reached the ground. He fired wildly, but the spray of bullets found their targets, and the men fell dead where they landed.

Two more paratroopers were dropping to earth. Manolakakis fired at them in single-shot bursts. The Germans kicked their feet wildly in their anxiety to reach ground quickly and escape the deadly bullets. But one by one the bullets struck home, and each man, in turn, hung limply in his harness. When these last paratroopers finally reached the ground, they were dead. Their parachutes, still filled with air, dragged them across the field. Manolakakis raced after them, emptying his last bullets into their bodies. He fired again and again until the weapon fired no more. Then all was still except for the slap of a parachute here and there, fluttering in the breeze.

Nicholas Manolakakis stood there for a long time, staring at the still forms lying in the fields in the various positions in which death had come to them. Finally, he returned to the bodies of his slain wife and son. Gently, with tender care, he picked them up and carried them into the house. He laid them on the master bed, folding their arms across their chests. He placed an icon between them, and at their heads he lit a holy light.[1]

On the morning of May 20, Manoli Paterakis found himself on the lower slopes of the White Mountains, south of the village of Gerani.

When the morning bombing had begun, he had reached the outskirts of Gerani, not far past Modhion. For an hour, he hid behind the twisted trees of an olive orchard as the whole area was subjected to the opening attack of the invasion. When the bombers left, the paratroopers arrived.

From where he stood, he could observe thousands of parachutes blossoming in the sky as far as he could see. He was fascinated by the panorama that passed before his eyes. So this is modern warfare? he thought to himself.

Suddenly, Paterakis awakened to the immediate danger. Raising his rifle, he fired quickly at a paratrooper. It was a young face that kept staring at Paterakis as it came closer. When his feet finally reached the ground, he crumpled in a heap, his dark parachute falling over him. The German was dead—his first one!

Some fifty feet away, another parachutist had just touched earth. Paterakis noticed an elderly couple approaching the German from the rear. They crept forward slowly, barefooted, each carrying a huge rock. Paterakis watched, wondering what the old man and his wife were up to.

The German turned suddenly and saw them. Just as he reached for his pistol, Paterakis fired a shot and the paratrooper fell.

"Be careful, old man," Paterakis cautioned, "he may be feigning death!"

To make sure, Paterakis fired two more times at the still body of the German. Now he was certain the man was dead.

"Can I take them?" asked the old farmer.

"Take what?"

"His boots—I need his boots," responded the old man, pointing to his own bare feet as his wife started unlacing the dead man's boots.

Paterakis nodded. What do these well-fed, well-clothed soldiers from a rich land want with poverty-stricken farmers like us? he thought. He started down the trail after the rest of the paratroopers.[2]

King George II had awakened early, as was his custom, on the morning of May 20. He dressed himself casually and stepped through the French doors separating his bedroom from the vine-covered terrace of the Volanis house. Leaning over the balustrade, he surveyed the countryside.

The view was the familiar scene of orchards filled with fruit trees, of olive groves, and of green-carpeted land rising to hilltops and dropping into the valleys beyond. It was a panorama of green offset by the deep blue sky of early morning. A cool, refreshing breeze drifted in from the north. The king took a deep, invigorating breath and thought to himself, Why must the ravages of war destroy this natural beauty?

The sky to the north over Khaniá was filled by a great dust cloud. To the east of Khaniá, the town of Suda, with its huge harbor of Suda Bay, was receiving its share of Luftwaffe attention this morning.

Thick black clouds rose hundreds of feet into the sky. The vessels in the bay still smoldered from earlier attacks, but the appearance of additional black clouds indicated that a new ship had been caught in the harbor and was burning. To the west, the dust and din over Maleme showed that the airstrip was also under attack.

Captain Basil Kiriakakis, the commanding officer of the forty gendarmes who served as the bodyguard to Prime Minister Tsouderos, stood on the terrace of the Volanis house and, through his binoculars, watched the fury of the aerial attack. Few planes passed over the villages of Perivolia and Malaxa; most of them were concentrating their attack on the region to the north from Maleme to Suda Bay.

The king and his prime minister were in conference over breakfast in the main room of the Volanis home. The massive stone structure of the house plus its location, cradled as it was in the foothills of the White Mountains offered some safety for the royal entourage. Yet Captain Kiriakakis still felt a danger existed; he wanted the king to go below into the wine cellar. One errant bomb from a passing plane could deprive the Greek people of their king and of their prime minister. But King George shunned the danger as too remote a possibility, preferring to continue his conference in the main room of the Volanis residence.

Colonel Blount, British liaison officer from Creforce Headquarters to King George, was now the senior officer in charge of the detachment of Royal Marines assigned to protect the royal party.

Blount watched in particular one black trimotor aircraft as it flew low over Perivolia, to the north.

From this transport, an object seemed to fall out and trail backward. Another followed. In seconds a whole string of them trailed each other obliquely, floating gently to earth. Shifting his binoculars to the other transports, he saw that they, too, were releasing paratroopers. He lowered his binoculars momentarily, blinked his eyes, and looked back into the sky—this time without the aid of the glasses. The sky was filled with multicolored parachutes descending from all directions. Blount quickly recovered from his surprise: "Paratroopers! By God, we're under paratroop attack! The invasion is on!" In rapid-fire order, he issued instructions to his executive officer: "Make plans to leave immediately!"

Colonel Blount returned to the terrace for a last glance. With his binoculars he followed the movements of the paratroopers in the countryside around Perivolia. From his position, he could see that the village of Pelikapina was swarming with Germans. Fate had been kind to the Greek king. Had the king returned to his home in Pelikapina the previous night as he wished, he would already have been a prisoner of war.

With that chilling thought in mind, he hastened to present himself to King George.

"Your Majesty, we must depart immediately! German parachutists have landed in the valley below us. They are only a mile or so away."

Prime Minister Tsouderos was not worried. He placed his official papers in a briefcase, put on his jacket, made certain that a few personal belongings had been packed in keeping with instructions to his personal valet, and then descended to the main room. Seating himself in a comfortable armchair, he waited quietly for the moment of departure.

The Greek king seemed even less concerned. Much to Colonel Blount's anxiety, the king hurried out the front door of the Volanis house with his uncle, Prince Peter, accompanying him through the front garden. At the garden wall, they stared in disbelief at the surrounding countryside. Wherever they looked there were paratroopers.

Prince Peter, pistol in hand, stood beside the king, shaking his head. King George realized the imminent danger: "Blount was right, we must leave."[3]

King George reappeared soon after, dressed in the full regalia of a field marshal of the Greek army. On his head he wore the officer's cap with its royal crest, while his left breast was emblazoned with multiple lines of colorful decorations. Pistol at his side and baton in his hand, the king signaled that he was ready to depart.

Finally the king, his prime minister, and the whole entourage—which also included the British ambassador, Sir Michael Palairet, and his wife—began a harsh trek, amid the din of aircraft above and battle in the valley below. It was a long and arduous climb, leading them over the rough-hewn, slate-gray crags of the White Mountain range. There were no paved highways or dirt-covered secondary roads, only goat trails leading ever upward to end abruptly at a cliff's edge above a deep ravine. Continuing under a hot, blistering sun, this was the meandering, tortuous trail that would eventually lead the royal party to safety.[4]

Oberleutnant Rudolf Toschka and the survivors of his thirty-man detachment struggled to keep alive throughout the afternoon of May 20. From the moment their gliders swooped into Venizelos Plaza in the heart of Khaniá, they were in trouble.

Toschka's survivors had left their first position behind a garden wall and were now holed up in a courtyard whose high wall offered them protection from three sides. Rations were gone and their ammunition was running low. It was almost impossible for Toschka's medics to care for the wounded. Their only chance for survival was to slip through the lines under cover of darkness—if they could hold out that long.

Their most imperative need was water.[5]

A young Gefreiter volunteered to carry a few water canteens to a well in the yard of a nearby house. He had to cross an open area of the plaza and enter the house to reach the yard; Toschka ordered his men to cover him with a volley. The young corporal ran across the plaza but never got to the well. No sooner had he reached the open ground than he fell victim to a sniper's bullet.

Another soldier, desperate for water, volunteered to attempt the same run. He raced across the open ground, past the corporal's body, to the door of the house. A bullet struck the soldier as he reached the threshold.

Toschka spotted the sniper but could not believe his eyes. It was a woman!

In one final attempt, a sergeant picked up the rest of the canteens and zigzagged across the plaza to the house. Bullets picked at his heels, spurring him to run faster. In a desperate dash, he leaped through the door, but no sooner had he entered the house than he was captured and quickly disarmed. His captors were women!

"Hello, Teufel!" The greeting came from a woman who spit the word *devil* at him in heavily accented German.

The sergeant stared at her in disbelief. She was dressed in male clothing, as were the other six women in the room. All carried rifles or German tommy guns—obviously captured from paratroopers, and all wore bandoliers across their chests.

"How do you like fighting Cretan women, Devil?"

"Why do you oppose us?" he asked hoarsely through parched, thirsty lips.

She laughed at him. "You want us to be hospitable to you—when you come to destroy us?"

"Come, Georgalakis, let's kill him and hang his body out the window for the other devils to see," interrupted one of the taller women.

"Let *me* kill him," added a huge, heavyset woman, brandishing a curved Syrian knife in her huge hand. "Why waste a bullet?"

Mrs. Georgalakis, whose husband was a member of the Greek Parliament and was at this time a prisoner somewhere in Athens, put an end to the debate. "No, we're going to send him back, without his rifle or his pistol—and *no water!* Let him tell his leader that unless they surrender to us—the women of Khaniá— we are going to kill all of them!"[6]

* * *

Corporal Hans Kreindler joined the two paratroopers who had set up a machine gun behind the protection of a garden wall. When he reached them, he flung himself down to catch his breath. The mad dash over open ground with the enemy shooting at him had been exhausting. The heat had become unbearable, sapping the very core of his strength. He drew his sleeve across his forehead, wiping the perspiration before it dropped into his eyes, and sat still for a few minutes, taking deep breaths.

Suddenly there was a red flash followed instantly by a thunderous, earsplitting explosion. Kreindler felt himself lifted off the ground and slammed down again. He lay there half-dazed, the wind knocked out of him, his ears ringing.

Gradually he raised his head and looked about him. The two machine gunners lay sprawled over their guns—dead. There was a big hole where the wall had been. Carefully Kreindler ran his good hand over his body; he seemed to be unhurt except for the shock. It must have been a shell burst or a hand grenade, he thought. The fact that he was at the other end of the wall had saved his life. He noted that the force of the blast even had twisted the barrel of his tommy gun.

With a painful effort, he raised himself and took his bearings. Some 100 feet to his left was a narrow trail that ran through some trees and seemed to dip toward the valley. In that valley he would find Von der Heydte's paratroopers and the rest of the men from his unit.

Slowly he rose to his feet, only to hear a voice behind him shout, "There's another blighter—still alive!" It was followed by a scattered burst of rifle fire. Kreindler dashed down the trail hoping to lose himself among the trees. At a clearing he ran into three New Zealanders sitting around a fire brewing tea. Before they had a chance to recover from their surprise, Kreindler retraced his steps back up the trail. When he reached the crest of the hill, he followed the trail to the left, past a small chapel and into what appeared to be the village cemetery. He stopped momentarily behind a tombstone to catch his breath. His weary body ached, his heavy paratrooper's combat uniform weighing heavily on him.

From his position Kreindler spotted soldiers at the far wall of the cemetery, firing down the hill, from which came a noisy clamor of rifle and machine-gun fire. It did not take Kreindler long to realize that he was trapped between the Greeks at the cemetery wall and the New Zealanders coming up the trail. Quickly he glanced about him and decided to seek refuge in the small chapel he had just passed at the cemetery entrance.

The iron door opened with a grating squeal, admitting Kreindler into a small, dark chamber, in which he could barely discern a small altar with a cross on it. It was quiet, and the sudden coolness was a relief from the outside heat. He closed the door, shutting out the sounds of battle, and curled up in a corner to rest. He would wait until darkness to make his escape to his own lines. It was a comforting thought, and in a few minutes he was sound asleep.

A sharp pain in the ribs awakened him abruptly. Kreindler rubbed his side and through half-closed eyes distinguished two figures standing before him in the dark. He reached for his pistol, but it was gone.

The two men before him spoke a strange language. It was not English—which he would have recognized—so he assumed them to be Greek. One of them pushed the muzzle of a rifle against Kreindler's chest and motioned him to rise. The second grabbed Kreindler by the collar and pulled him to his feet, half dragging him out the door. It was still bright daylight outside, and the sudden light hurt Kreindler's eyes. The taller of the two men pushed the German against the chapel wall, and the other closed the bolt and raised his rifle. Kreindler realized that he was going to be executed. He scowled at them, fearful, weary, yet defiant.

As the Greek soldier took aim, a deep, commanding voice stopped him. Both men snapped to respectful attention as a third appeared out of nowhere, tall, pistol in hand, and with the bearing and authority of an officer. Kreindler could not understand what was said, but it was obvious that the officer was reprimanding the two soldiers. Then he turned to Kreindler and said in fair English: "You are a prisoner of war and shall be treated as such."[7]

Manoli Paterakis succeeded in shooting five paratroopers from the "stick" that fell in front of him after the episode with the elderly couple. The rest he lost in the heavy underbrush.

Later that morning he met a group of ten Cretans who had obviously been busy all morning fighting the invader, for they all carried German weapons.

Word reached the Cretans that a column of paratroopers was

advancing up the road. After a brief discussion, Paterakis and the rest of the men scattered amidst the high ground that paralleled the road. When the Germans came into view, the Cretans opened fire. It was this sound of battle that attracted Oberleutnant Werner Schiller.[8]

Painfully pushing himself through a thick glade of bamboo, Schiller came to a little rise, beyond which he heard the loud sound of rifle and machine-gun fire. Carefully he crawled to the crest of the knoll and looked down the other side. What he saw frustrated him. There in a shallow hollow was a squad of paratroopers completely surrounded by a group of men without uniforms, looking much like the Cretan he had encountered earlier that morning.

He lay there helpless for about an hour. Gradually the firing from the hollow ceased. When he looked again, Cretans were swarming all over the dead Germans. His comrades had been beaten by civilians. In the brief moment that he was exposed, one of the Cretans spotted him. Schiller rolled down the hill and raced for cover with the Cretans following close behind.

Exhausted, thirsty, out of breath, and weakened by his wound, he pushed himself through the thick underbrush. In a little clearing, he came across a dry irrigation ditch. He crawled in and, with his good arm, dragged some dried bamboo stalks over himself for cover. He lay there for what seemed an eternity, hiding from the approaching Cretan guerrillas.

The Cretans passed without noticing Schiller, the sound of their footsteps diminishing gradually over the uneven, rocky trail. Schiller stayed there, hardly breathing and too weak to stir. Eventually he felt that someone was staring at him. Slowly he opened his eyes, only to peer into the tough, weatherbeaten face of a Cretan standing beside the ditch with a rifle in the crook of his arm. Schiller would never forget that face or the fear that coursed through his body. He closed his eyes again and held his breath, waiting for the bullet that would end his life. It never came, for the Cretan turned and walked away.

The events of the morning were too much for the weakened Schiller, and he lapsed into unconsciousness. When he awakened hours later, he found himself in a German first-aid station.[9]

# 16

## "HENCE, THEY HAVE TO PRESERVE MY HEAD"

### MAY 20, 1941

Throughout western Crete on the morning of May 20, the Germans were running into trouble in their struggle with the New Zealand and Greek defenders.

General Eugen Meindl, the commanding officer of the assault regiment fighting in the Maleme area, waited anxiously at his command post for word from his various units. The initial news was not good—in fact, it was demoralizing, even to an officer of his experience. Meindl realized that the situation was going against him. Almost in a daze, he followed the battle developments from scattered reports, watching helplessly as his units were systematically decimated. To this veteran officer it seemed the beginning of a nightmare. He had never conceived the possibility of German troops being so quickly destroyed in the face of enemy resistance. It had never happened before on the continent, and they had not expected it to happen here in Crete.

One of the major problems facing Meindl was the lack of communication with his unit commanders. The wireless sets, shattered during the landings, had not yet been repaired by the communications officer, Oberleutnant Gottsche, leaving Meindl temporarily incapacitated. However, he was not deaf to the sound of battle resonating from the perimeter of the airfield and from Hill 107.

He heard nothing from Major Scherber's ill-fated Third Assault Battalion on the eastern perimeter of the airfield. After the initial storm of battle, the firing from that direction had slackened, yet not a single German paratrooper appeared on the airfield from the east. Meindl had to assume that Scherber was in trouble. He had no way of knowing that Major Scherber had been killed and his whole battalion wiped out.

Of course, the CO of the assault regiment had no inkling that the commanding general of the Seventh Airborne Division, Gen-

eral Suessmann, had also been killed during the flight to Crete.
Nor was Meindl able to discern whether Colonel Heidrich's Third
Parachute Regiment had been successful in its drop into Prison
Valley. Worse yet, he could not communicate with General Stu-
dent at Luftwaffe headquarters in Athens. It was indeed a hardship
to fight a battle without any modern means of communication.
Meindl's meager information was derived only from slow, vul-
nerable runners and from stragglers.

A small reconnaissance patrol sent westward toward Kastelli returned with the news that they had run into stiff opposition from
Greek troops outside the town. They added that the fields and valleys east of Kastelli were dotted with empty parachutes and dead
bodies. From this fragmentary report, General Meindl assumed that
Muerbe and his detachment had failed in their purpose at Kastelli.[1]

Meinld searched frantically for a way to stop what looked like
the beginning of a military disaster. In a little less than three
hours, he had lost more than half his regiment. It was obvious
that the solution lay in the capture of Maleme airfield and its
crowning height, Hill 107. Only if the airfield were taken could
reinforcements be ferried to Crete. The forces that might be able
to turn this pending disaster into victory were the paratroopers of
his Second and Fourth Assault Battalions, which had landed successfully west of the Tavronites River.

After a cursory meeting with his two remaining battalion commanders, Meindl ordered them to attack the airfield and Hill 107.
He planned to send the Fourth Battalion, under the command of
Hauptmann Walter Gericke—the energetic, intelligent officer who
had assumed command after Major von Braun was killed—across
the captured Tavronites bridge and attack Hill 107 from the north.
Captain Gericke's battalion was composed mostly of heavy machine guns and mortar squads, with few infantrymen. To fill that
gap, Meindl assigned one company of paratroopers from the Second Battalion and the survivors of the glider force to join the other
three companies of the Fourth Battalion.

The two remaining companies—the Fifth and Sixth Companies
of the Second Battalion, led by Major Stentzler—were to cross
the Tavronites, circle counterclockwise in an enveloping maneuver, and attack Hill 107 from the south. Meindl's strategy would
bring this vital ground under fire from two directions.

As the battalion commanders assembled their troops in their
respective staging areas, General Meindl arrived at the line of

departure from which his men would begin the attack. Earlier that same morning, he had left for Crete with approximately 2,500 men in his assault regiment. Now he had fewer than 900 troopers.

Lieutenant Colonel L. W. Andrew, commanding officer of the Twenty-second New Zealand Battalion defending Hill 107, had witnessed the parachute and glider landings. At 7:30 A.M. he dispatched a message to brigade headquarters informing General Hargest of the attack. Then, from the command post dug into the side of Hill 107, he tried to maintain contact with his five companies spread out on the crest of the hill and around the slopes leading up to the airfield.

Within the opening minutes of the bombing, the telephone lines to two of the New Zealand companies and to Andrew's Headquarters Company were ruptured. The battalion telephone connection to brigade headquarters in Platanias was next to go. The wireless was Andrew's only communication with Hargest, and from 9:30 A.M. until 10:00 A.M., even that failed.[2]

Meanwhile, the men of Andrew's battalion became engaged in fierce combat. Paratroopers of the Von Plessen detachment were attacking one of the slopes of Hill 107 and, led by Oberarzt Dr. Weizel, these young soldiers fought with such ferocity that they quickly overran the New Zealanders' platoon positions, killing many and taking few prisoners. Although Von Plessen had been killed earlier, his men pressed their attack from the north and south, exposing the New Zealand troops of the perimeter companies to heavy crossfire.

The major problem now facing the New Zealanders was their dwindling ammunition. When they ran low in hand grenades, they manufactured their own by filling ration cans with concrete and nails and exploding them with gelignite.

Headquarters Company, protecting the area between the villages of Maleme and Pirgos northeast of Hill 107, had a field day shooting Germans. Not a single paratrooper landing in Maleme and Pirgos survived once his feet touched the ground. But many of them did land safely in the fields, and once they concentrated themselves into a striking force, they attacked the clerks and supply men of Headquarters Company. The German assault overran the defenses of one of the company's isolated platoons, but the rest of the New Zealanders rallied behind Lieutenant G. Beaven and held their ground. The hard-pressed Beaven dispatched a runner to battalion headquarters with a note he had received from one of his section leaders, citing his dilemma:

NO MACHINE GUNS, NO HAND GRENADES, EIGHT RIFLES, AND TWO BAYONETS . . . [3]

But the runner never got through.

On Hill 107 itself, the men of A and B Companies were faced by the attack from the scattered troops of Major Koch's glider force. The withering fire set up by the New Zealand defenders extinguished that major threat to their position.

But the Luftwaffe was still present overhead, and periodic attacks by Stuka dive-bombers and strafing ME-109s kept the men of Colonel Andrew's battalion on their toes. As the dust cloud cleared slowly and the increasing heat of day burned off the morning mist, through his field glasses Andrew could see troop movements across the west bank of the Tavronites River. He knew the danger this posed to his own defense position, yet he had no way of knowing how many men had landed in that area.

Before the attack began, Andrew had dispatched several men with a wireless set down to the village of Roponiana across the Tavronites, to act as an outpost. They were based exactly where the Second and Fourth Battalions of the assault regiment had landed. Without a word forthcoming throughout the morning hours, Andrew assumed their outpost had been wiped out, as indeed it had.

Even as he watched the paratroopers moving into position across the Tavronites, sporadic mortar bursts and a few shells from light mountain cannon were hitting the slopes of Hill 107.

At 10:00 A.M. communications with brigade headquarters were restored. Andrew immediately summarized a report of the enemy landings. At 10:55 A.M. he reported to Hargest, without the slightest hint of alarm, that:

400 PARATROOPERS . . . LANDED IN THE AREA, 100 NEAR THE AIRFIELD. 150 TO THE EAST OF THE AIRFIELD BETWEEN MALEME AND PIRGOS AND 150 WEST OF THE RIVER. [4]

General Meindl signaled his battalion commanders to begin the first major coordinated attack of the day against a specific defense position in the Maleme area.

At first there was the usual snap of sporadically fired bullets from scattered points on the hill and airfield perimeter. When the platoons were completely exposed, the firing increased to a roar of thunder, with bursts of rifle and machine-gun fire arching down on the paratroopers. Caught in the open, the front ranks were shot dead. Others fell wounded and, lying where they had fallen, they were hit again and again by the spray of bullets. The rest could not proceed; some paratroopers attempting to dash back to the safety of the olive trees were quickly cut down.

Ignoring the initial plight of the attacking platoons, Meindl ordered the assault to continue. But then something caught his eye halfway up Hill 107.

It was a flag signal, and it was German. A group of twenty-four surviving paratroopers from Koch's glider force were holed up in a New Zealand trench they had captured after a brief hand-to-hand skirmish. Once these glider troops had taken the position, they were unable to advance any further; sniper and machine-gun fire cut down anyone who ventured to raise his head above the parapet of the trench. New Zealand fire from farther up the hill was accurate and treacherous.

Looking down toward the airfield, these surrounded paratroopers decided to announce their presence at all costs, hoping that their attacking comrades would relieve them of their plight. When he saw their flag, General Meindl pointed to the spot and enthusiastically shouted over the din: "It must be Koch's men signaling to us!"

Grabbing a green signal flag lying on the ground and starting to wave a reply, he took his staff by surprise. This was the duty of the communications officer, not of the commanding general.

In his enthusiasm to signal Koch, Meindl partly raised himself above the edge of the stone wall behind which he had sought shelter. His aide turned to warn him of the danger, but it was too late. A sharp crack sounded, followed by the singing whistle of a bullet cutting through the air. With hardly a sound the bullet struck the general's hand; the signal flag fell to the ground, covered with blood.

It took a few seconds for the general to realize he had been hit, after which he grabbed his wrist to quell the first stab of pain. In doing so, he rose up again, completely exposing himself a second time. There was a renewed burst of rifle fire with bullets ricocheting off rocks and trees. A few of them ripped into Meindl's body. He slumped forward to the ground, severely wounded in the chest.

His alarmed staff hurriedly gathered around their fallen leader. Now there was a continuous concentration of fire raking the entire area, making any movement difficult. They dragged his body behind a half-fallen stone wall, where the doctor and his medical assistant began to attend the wounded general.

The staff officers frowned with apprehension as they looked down at the pale face of their commander. They were relieved to hear that the wounds, although severe, would not be fatal.

After his wounds were dressed, Meindl was moved to a nearby farmhouse. He grimaced from the sharp pain that racked his body each time he breathed. It was more painful when he spoke, but he made it clear to his staff that he was still in command and that he intended to remain in command until properly relieved.

"Order the men to attack that damn hill—take it at all costs!" he gasped. "Don't come back until it is in your hands!"

He paused to catch a painful breath, and then with perspiration rolling down his face, he added: "Schnell!"[5]

Meindl's men now struck in full force against the positions on Hill 107. Amid the despoiled foliage and bomb-cratered earth, the paratroopers of the Fourth Battalion raced forward in the face of a rising storm of fire.

Their first ranks were shot down, as were the second and third that followed. But the rest leaped over the bodies of their fallen comrades and raced up the western defense perimeter, gaining a foothold at the base of Hill 107. The whole northern slope of the hill was ablaze with the fire of battle.

The hard-pressed men of the Twenty-second Battalion were taking heavy casualties, but their fire continued unabated. These brave soldiers fought magnificently in the face of the German attack. When their rifles were empty, they resorted to the bayonet, as the first line of trenches became the scene of hand-to-hand encounters.

The Germans could not dislodge the New Zealanders, who clung to their positions as shipwrecked sailors cling to their rafts. Beneath that blazing hot Cretan sun, the struggle for this valuable hill was to continue throughout the day.

When General Meindl was informed that the Fifth and Sixth Companies of Stentzler's Second Assault Battalion had paused in their attack for a brief respite while search parties went out hunting for wells to get water for the thirsty troopers, he was furious. Although blood was seeping into his lungs from his wounds, and although speech was becoming increasingly difficult for him, he nevertheless gasped out orders that the Second Battalion must continue in the attack without delay.

By 11:00 A.M. shelling from light mountain artillery and heavy mortars, firing from beyond the Tavronites, was accelerated, taking an increasing toll of the men on Hill 107. A wounded straggler from D Company arrived at Andrew's headquarters with the disheartening news—completely incorrect—that D Company had been overrun and destroyed. The inroads that the paratroopers of the Fourth Assault Battalion had made in the defense perimeter at the base of Hill 107 might have indicated to Andrew that even C Company had been wiped out. There still was no word from Beaven and his Headquarters Company at Pirgos. Lacking direct communication with his companies at the defense perimeter of the airfield, Colonel Andrew had no way of knowing that Companies C and D were still holding out despite heavy casualties.

He informed his brigade commander that he had lost communication with his forward companies and could not report on their situation. The report should have alarmed the brigade commander, considering the value of Hill 107.

Colonel John Allen, commanding the Twenty-first Battalion, was also having communication problems. His wireless was inoperable and all his messages had to be dispatched by runner to the Twenty-third Battalion; from there all messages were transmitted to brigade headquarters using the Twenty-third Battalion's wireless. Having destroyed the paratroopers of Major Scherber's ill-fated Third Assault Battalion earlier in the day, the men of the Twenty-third Battalion were now involved in mopping up the surviving stragglers.

In a message forwarded by the Twenty-third Battalion to brigade headquarters, Colonel Leckie informed Brigadier Hargest that the situation in the area was well under control.[6]

Colonel Allen of the Twenty-first Battalion sent a similar message a short while later.

At brigade headquarters, Brigadier Hargest, the politician-turned-soldier, was pleased with this news. He dictated the following message to the commanders of his Twenty-first and Twenty-third Battalions:

> GLAD OF YOUR MESSAGE . . . WILL NOT CALL ON YOU FOR COUNTERATTACK UNLESS POSITION VERY SERIOUS. SO FAR EVERYTHING IS IN HAND AND REPORTS FROM OTHER UNITS SATISFACTORY.[7]

Thus while Colonel Andrew was hard-pressed in his defense of Hill 107 and hoped for some response to his message, Brigadier Hargest sat down to his noon meal, ignorant and unmindful of the danger that prevailed at Maleme. *Typical British*

King George of the Hellenes and his entourage continued, against great hardships, the climb up the rugged crags of the White Mountains to elude the invading Germans.

Their effort was becoming more difficult with each passing hour. Many times when the group had to pause for rest, they looked down on the panoramic landscape of the northern valleys and fields. It was an appalling sight.

In the northeast, toward Khaniá and Suda Bay, the now familiar black smoke from burning ships hung like a dark smudge against the blue sky. A light-gray cloud was suspended like a canopy over the airfield to the northwest. The green acres below them were strewn with parachutes that looked like miniature flower petals—red, white, yellow, pink, and black wherever the eye could see. Many were on the ground, and others hung from the trees. There were so many of them that it shocked human imagination for any one nation to have put into effect such a feat of arms as this tremendous air invasion.

When they resumed their climb, the king discarded his tunic and cap. His blouse was drenched with perspiration but it retained the semblance of neatness which was so characteristic of him.

By noon the royal party reached a village cradled in a valley between two huge mountains. This was the village of the Virgin Mary of Keramia.

The men of the village appeared with hoes, axes, and ancient rifles to meet the trespassers. They were prepared to defend their homes. But when the men of the advance guard revealed their identities and those they were escorting, the villagers put down their weapons. Their eyes lit up. "The king is coming here?"

"The king *is* here!"

Immediately the mayor of the village, together with the town elders, rushed forward humbly to greet the royal guest and his party. In no time at all the aroma of barbecued lamb filled the mountain air, fresh warm bread was placed on the tables, and cool red wine filled the glasses.[8]

The German timetable dictated that all the major objectives in the Maleme and Prison Valley areas were to be secured by noon on the day of the attack.

In keeping with this timetable, a Junker-52 transport revved up on Elevsis airfield in Greece. This transport was the first of several that were to fly to Crete carrying the Eleventh Air Corps Airfield Service Company. It was the specific duty of this servicing unit to prepare the airfield for the transports that would carry the first elements of the Fifth Mountain Division as reinforcements that afternoon. It was projected that by nightfall, the troop carriers were to have ferried close to 9,000 men to Maleme. The rest of the Mountain Division was to arrive by sea—the follow-through of the invasion, taking over the fighting from the paratroopers. If the paratroopers represented the spearhead, these mountain troops would be its head and shaft.

Once over Maleme, Lieutenant Colonel Snowadzki, the commanding officer of the unit, sitting in the copilot's seat, scanned the airfield with his field glasses. It was difficult to see clearly through the mistlike layer of dust that hung over the landing strip. He spotted the many downed gliders, lying at grotesque angles in the hills and fields around the airstrip.

As the transport circled the field a second time in a wider sweep, Snowadzki was able to distinguish a huge red banner with its centered white circle upon which was emblazoned a black swastika. It had been placed at the base of the northern slope of Hill 107 by the men of Walter Gericke's Fourth Assault Battalion in order not to be bombed or strafed by their own aircraft. The flag represented the farthest advance by the paratroopers in their penetration of the New Zealand defense perimeter. Snowadzki assumed incorrectly that the flag meant that the airfield had also been captured.

He ordered his pilot to land.

The aircraft slowly lumbered over the field, lining up with the landing strip. It dropped lower and lower, its wheels almost touching the ground. Suddenly the sides of the transport were ventilated by countless holes as bullets bit into the fuselage. A spray of bullets shattered the observation glass behind the pilot's seat. The men in the body of the aircraft were showered with slivers of glass as bullet after bullet smashed through the portholes on both sides. In seconds the transport had become the target of every rifle and machine gun in the area. Streams of tracers arched from all directions at the Junker rolling across the runway.

Startled, Colonel Snowadzki shouted: "Take off!"

The pilot gave the transport full throttle and lifted the plane back into the sky with string after string of tracer bullets following in its wake. He veered and banked his aircraft to avoid enemy fire. In a matter of minutes, he was flying again over the green-blue waters of the Gulf of Khaniá, safely out of reach of enemy fire.

Much to Snowadzki's surprise, Maleme airfield was still in the hands of the New Zealanders. For the first time, the Germans realized that their timetable was inaccurate.[9]

In his headquarters office on the second floor of the Grande Bretagne Hotel in Athens, Kurt Student was anxiously waiting for the first reports of the invasion.

It was difficult to sit blindly 168 air miles from the battle zone, waiting for the first information as to how his paratroopers were faring. The only news he had received was the debriefing reports the transport pilots had given upon their return, after releasing the paratroopers over Crete—and that information was not totally accurate.[10]

Many pilots were not truthful. They did not report that heavy enemy antiaircraft fire caused many transports to veer from the drop zone, resulting in a wide dispersion of the parachute units, possibly decreasing their effectiveness. No pilot wished to indict himself for failing to drop his "stick" exactly on target. So for the first hours of the invasion, General Student had nothing more to go on than glowing, albeit inaccurate, information.

Student sat at his desk, checking through his papers. One of them was a transcript from General Gerhard, the Air Service Commander, reporting that the returning transports were having difficulty landing at their home bases because of the heavy dust clouds that reduced visibility to zero in broad daylight. The dried, parched soil, agitated by propeller turbulence, suspended its sandy particles in a dust-filled fog over the airports, making landings hazardous. Several transports had crashed on landing because of this lack of visibility. Other Junker-52s had to fly in circles over their respective airfields as long as two hours waiting for the dust to settle. When they finally did come in for a landing, many of them ran off the runway, damaging their landing gear.[11]

Of the 493 Junker-52 transports that had taken part in the first-wave assault, two had been lost over Crete, while five had crashed on their return to their home field. Countless others had sustained lesser damage from the difficulties created by the dust clouds. It was a problem that further threatened the German timetable. The question that lodged in Student's mind was whether these troop carriers could be refueled in time for the second phase of the attack on the eastern part of Crete, scheduled for that afternoon.

His thoughts were interrupted by the arrival of his communications officer. The time was a little past noon.

The staff officers who watched Student saw his face begin to pale, a frown furrowing his brow. The message was from Admiral Karageorg Shuster, the commander in charge of southeast naval operations. It forwarded a report from a German E-boat (motor-torpedo boat) patrolling off Aegina in the Saronic Gulf that a glider had crashed on the island. Confirmation of the original report added that the ill-fated glider had been carrying the commanding general of the Seventh Airborne Division and his immediate staff.

Student took the news in stride and immediately issued orders that Colonel Richard Heidrich, commanding officer of the Third Parachute Regiment of the Seventh Airborne Division, then landing in Prison Valley, was to assume command of the airborne division. Heidrich was to be informed as soon as contact had been established with him.[12]

More alarming news followed.

At 1:15 P.M., Student's private telephone rang. He immediately recognized the distinctive voice of Lieutenant Colonel Snowadzki on the other end. Student listened, thanked him quietly, and without the slightest show of emotion, put down the receiver. He sat there for a long time, disregarding the anxious stares from his subordinates and deaf to the constant ringing of the field phones.

Then came the third piece of bad news. Hauptmann Mors of the intelligence section reported a signal from the Maleme area. Meindl's communications officer, Oberleutnant Gortsche, had finally succeeded in repairing a wireless set. He had spent all morning cannibalizing parts from all the broken sets to produce one that would function. At approximately 4:15 in the afternoon, a weak message began to filter into Athens. It told of an impending military disaster:

> ALL MAJOR OBJECTIVES, INCLUDING MALEME AIRFIELD AND HILL 107, STILL IN ENEMY HANDS . . . VON BRAUN, KOCH, SCHERBER, VON PLESSEN, MUERBE . . . KILLED IN ACTION . . . MEINDL WOUNDED SEVERELY[13]

Student sat stunned for many minutes as his staff evaluated the import of this alarming message. Finally he came to a decision, and with a rap of his fist on the arm of the chair, he muttered aloud—more to himself than to anyone else—"I must go there!"

In a burst of energy, he walked hurriedly down the corridor to General Löhr's office. Without waiting for a response to his knock, he entered and briefed his commanding officer. Löhr received the news calmly.

"I must leave for Crete immediately," Student added forcefully, declaring his intent rather than asking permission.

"That is out of the question," snapped Löhr, annoyed at the proposal. "If you go to Maleme, you would be out of touch for the second phase of the attack against Rethimnon and Iráklion. No, your place is here, in case the pattern of fighting should suddenly change."

Crestfallen, Student returned to the map room, informing his chief of staff, General Schlemm, that his request had been denied.

Then, turning toward the tall French windows, Student added, "You see, Schlemm, if this attack fails, they want to be sure I will be around for they will need a scapegoat. If we fail to take Crete, someone has to be held accountable. That is my responsibility. Hence, they have to preserve my head in case it should be wanted at an inquiry."[14]

# 17 / "BE BACK BY 4:30 P.M."

**MAY 20, 1941**

The German timetable for the invasion had indeed gone awry. The 1:00 P.M. deadline for the second part of the assault against the eastern portion of the island was rapidly approaching. In light of the paratroopers' apparent difficulties in the Maleme area, the question of postponing the afternoon attack was raised, along with that of withholding the other two regiments or sending them instead to aid the forces at Maleme.

Student needed time to think this out. Further reports from the Maleme area were scarce, and those from Prison Valley were insufficient for him to order such a dramatic alteration in the detailed plans of the overall assault. He had to wait until his information was more conclusive. One item of bad news followed another: first the item of Suessmann's death on Aegina, followed by Snowadzki's report of the situation at Maleme. At 4:15 that afternoon, Meindl's weak radio transmission put the question to him again.

Now Student recalled the Air Service commander's earlier report about the difficulties the returning transports were experiencing in landing on their home airfields amid the confusion created by the tremendous dust clouds. General Gerhard had expressed concern that this difficulty might delay the refueling of the transports in time to begin the second phase, scheduled for 1:00 P.M. Student hoped that this delay might be a blessing in disguise.[1]

He picked up the phone to call Gerhard's command post, but the line had been cut by the Greek underground. Like Snowadzki, Student had to resort to the use of the civilian exchange, with all its inept difficulties. When he finally got through to the airfield, it was too late. Some transports had already left, while others were on the departure line. Student shrugged his shoulders, somewhat pleased by the news, for now he would not have to change his original plan. Perhaps, he thought, the second phase of the invasion would achieve the immediate success he expected, thus tipping the scales in his favor.[2]

The objectives of the second part of the day's airborne assault were the cities of Rethimnon and Iráklion together with their respective airfields. The seizure of Rethimnon had been assigned to the Second Parachute Regiment under the command of Colonel Sturm. The First Regiment, commanded by Colonel Bruno Brauer, was to capture Iráklion. Their sister regiment of the Seventh Airborne Division had been fighting for its very existence since early morning in Prison Valley.

Colonel Sturm had chosen to divide the attack force of his regiment into three groups. It was an attack pattern similar to the one taken by the assault regiment at Maleme. The western, or right, prong of the attack was assigned to Captain Wiedemann with a force of some 800 men comprised of the Third Battalion of Sturm's regiment, two sections of airborne artillery, and a company of heavy machine guns. His objective was twofold: the seizure of the village of Perivolia and the city of Rethimnon. The capture of Perivolia, some three miles west of the airfield, would cut the northern road and secure the western approach to the field, after which Wiedemann was to wheel westward and take Rethimnon.

The left flank, or eastern prong, of the assault was to be led by Major Hans Kroh, whose force of 550 men consisted of two companies of the regiment's First Battalion, the regiment's heavy weapon detachment of mortars and mountain artillery, in addition to a heavy machine-gun company.

Sturm assumed personal command of the central prong of the attack. He planned to land on the airfield with his headquarters staff and one-and-a-half companies of some 200 paratroopers. From this central command position he planned to coordinate the attack. All three groups were to seize their objectives, and while Wiedemann held Rethimnon, Kroh was to head toward the center and help secure the airfield. With the airfield in their hands, the whole force would then swing to the west and approach Suda Bay from the east.[3]

The whole operation appeared logistically sound, for Sturm's attack group represented a powerful and well-balanced force of some 1,550 men. Flushed with European victories the Germans still considered themselves invincible. What happened in the Maleme sector was still unknown to them, and so Sturm's plan gave little consideration to the possibility that a resolute and determined defense might make the difference between success and failure.

The defending force of Australians and Greeks that was to oppose the landing was outnumbered in men and equipment. But to a scrappy Australian like Lieutenant Colonel Ian Campbell, such a weakness was meaningless. Campbell realized that the most strategic objective in his sector was the airfield located five miles east of the city of Rethimnon. He was determined to deny the Germans that goal.

All Campbell had with which to stop the German attack were two understrength Australian battalions of 600 men each and two poorly trained and equipped Greek regiments of some 2,000 men. He had no antiaircraft guns, only four captured Italian 100-mm cannon and four 75-mm French fieldpieces. The artillery pieces had no sights, in addition to which he possessed only 80 shells for his four three-inch mortars. His men lacked a sufficient amount of grenades and they were even short of rifle ammunition. Of the men in the Greek regiments, many had no rifles and those who did had only ten bullets per weapon. Yet despite all these short-comings, Campbell was determined to repel the invader.

Campbell surveyed the lay of the land personally during the days before the attack and disposed his units in well-camouflaged positions. So well were they hidden that German photographic reconnaissance aircraft failed to uncover them. In his determination to deny the Germans the airfield, Campbell strung out his units over the uneven terrain surrounding the airstrip. To the east of the landing field there was a steep plateau of broken rock formations that Campbell had penciled on his map as Hill A. A narrow ridge running perpendicular to Hill A and extending approximately three miles westward as far as the village of Platanes was divided by two dried riverbeds; the easternmost, just west of Hill A, the Australians had happily named Wadi Bardia to honor their victory in North Africa. The second riverbed, Wadi Pigi, lay one mile farther west. Between the two riverbeds there rose a small rocky prominence designated as Hill D. The ridge from Hill A continued for two miles in its westerly direction until it terminated in another hilly prominence just south of Platanes. Campbell called this high ground Hill B. Farther west, a mile south of the village of Perivolia, there was yet another rise of ground, standing alone between the village and the city of Rethimnon. This was Hill C.

Along this terrain, well suited for defense, Campbell strung out the companies of his battalions. On Hill A he positioned a company from the First Australian Battalion, which was under his direct command. The rest of the companies were dug in on the ground between Hill A and Hill D. To support the companies of his First Battalion, he had emplaced six of his fieldpieces together with a machine-gun platoon. Dug in on the forward slopes of both hills, they had an excellent range of fire over the airfield.

Campbell's Second Battalion, the Eleventh Australian under Major R. L. Sandover, was positioned two miles farther west on Hill B, with the remaining two artillery pieces and a machine-gun platoon in support.

Between the two Australian battalions, Campbell put the Fourth and Fifth Greek Regiments. Like the Greek regiments at Kastelli, Alikianou, and Galatas, they were only in battalion strength. The Fourth Greek Regiment, under the command of Lieutenant Colonel John Tryfon, was in the area between Hills A and B, near the coast road just west of Wadi Pigi. The other Greek unit, the Fifth Regiment, commanded by Lieutenant Colonel Serbos, was positioned in the foothills beyond the ridge near the village of Adhele. Campbell hid his two infantry tanks near them on the southern slope of the ridge.

Inasmuch as Campbell had concentrated his men to protect the airfield, he allocated the defense of the city of Rethimnon and its surrounding area to a well-armed, aggressive force of Greek gendarmerie under the command of Major Jacob Chaniotis. These men were to give a good account of themselves in the days ahead.[4]

The communications setup between all these units was intolerably inadequate and incomplete. Campbell established his command post on Hill D in the center of the defense line, from which he had telephone communication with his companies on both Hills A and B. All other areas in the defense perimeter had to depend on runners, who could always fall prey to marauding Messerschmitts overhead. Campbell's single cable line to Creforce Headquarters must have been cut much earlier in the day, for—strange as it may seem—as of four o'clock in the afternoon of May 20, he had not received a single word of the intensive battle in progress in the western part of Crete, a battle then in its tenth hour!

With his battalions well entrenched in their defensive positions, Campbell sat back and waited for the German onslaught.

\* \* \*

Zero hour for the attack on Rethimnon and its airfield had come and gone. Unlike the punctuality that marked the morning bombings in the Maleme and Khaniá areas, the afternoon attack rapidly deteriorated into a haphazard affair.

At 4:00 P.M. the fighters and bombers finally made their appearance over the Rethimnon area. The bombing had been assigned, of necessity, to Messerschmitt 109s and the ME-110 light fighter-bombers.

The strafing and light bombing continued for only a fifteen-minute period, after which the aircraft departed. The fuel wasted waiting for the delayed and scattered squadrons to rendezvous over their respective airfields had abbreviated the time allowed over the target. Their departure was followed by an extended lull, the first indication to the defenders that the attack lacked synchronization.

Then a dull drone was heard from the east. At that point, the first of twenty-four JU-52 transports crossed the coastline and turned westward. No sooner had they made their appearance than the Greeks and Australians opened fire. Tracers reached out at the slow, low-flying Junkers like little red fingers, searching for them and digging into their midst. Bren and Lewis guns, firing from high angle tripods, released a hot lead screen that began to take its toll.

One transport, still carrying its human cargo, suddenly banked sharply to avoid ground fire and sliced into another that was just releasing its "stick" of paratroopers. Amidst screams of horror, both men and pieces of aircraft plummeted into the waters beyond the shore. Other transports caught fire and turned back out to sea, trailing smoke. Some had already released their paratroopers, while others continued to release them over the water.[5]

In the center of the attack, Colonel Sturm and the men of his headquarters staff descended with the attached paratroopers in support. They immediately came under fire from Campbell's Australians positioned between Hills A and D on the right and the men of the Fourth Greek Regiment on the left. Lieutenant Colonel Tryfon's Greeks had only ten rounds for each rifle, which they soon used up; thereafter, they did not hesitate in attacking the descending Germans with their bayonets.

Most of the paratroopers who fell in this sector were picked off in that fifteen-second descent that left them so vulnerable. Those who survived the drop were quickly chased off the airstrip, across the road that bounded it on the north, and into the dunes of the sandy beach beyond.

Here Sturm was pinned down and cut off with the other survivors of his force. No man was able to raise his head without being picked off. No runner dared rise to carry out his errand to the scattered men of Sturm's central force. The middle prong of the attack had failed.

For the rest of the day and well into the night, the beleaguered Sturm was to remain with the rest of his survivors, hiding behind dunes and tufts of tall grass in complete isolation from the other two prongs of the attacking force.

On the left, Captain Wiedemann's group did not fare any better. The transport pilots' prolonged delay in dropping Wiedemann's men had strung them out, scattering the paratroopers over a wide area and wiping out their attack-effectiveness. They became easy targets for the intensive fire from the rifles and machine guns of Major Sandover's eager Australians of the Eleventh Battalion, positioned in this area. One "stick" of fifteen men fell in a perfect line, each paratrooper dead before he touched the ground, his body riddled with bullets.

Even the Greeks took part against Wiedemann's men. The company on the left flank of the Fourth Greek Regiment charged the paratroopers as they landed. They captured twenty Germans while they were still shedding their harnesses.

The paratroopers who did succeed in landing safely quickly gathered for protection among the trees and tall grass. Many of the canisters carrying their weapons were too scattered to be reached. Nevertheless, Wiedemann collected his men amidst the protective foliage and returned the fire with what little he had on hand.

As evening approached, Major Sandover decided to end this threat in front of his defenses and ordered an attack. With an excited determination, the Australians left their protected positions and charged the Germans, pushing them back toward the village of Perivolia and beyond, taking some eighty-four prisoners in the rush of the attack.

During the advance, Sandover came across the body of a German officer. A search revealed a list of signal codes. The battalion commander translated the list himself and decided to make use of it. Such resourcefulness was to help Sandover replenish his dwindling ammunition. The next day, German supply aircraft replied well to his coded signal requests for hand grenades, mortar and rifle ammunition—invaluable supplies to be used against Wiedemann's men.[6]

Sandover's knowledge of German was put to good use a second time. From a captured German officer he learned there would be no enemy reinforcements that day. Relieved, he pressed his attack against the paratroopers at Perivolia village.[7]

The second flight of transports released their "sticks" of paratroopers over the same positions. In that fifteen-second interval, it was terrifying for these men to look down at the fields below littered with the dead bodies of their comrades. As they descended, they could see the flaming trajectories of bullets arching up to follow them down.

Major Kroh, however, landed safely with a good portion of his men, despite the heavy concentration of fire from the defense positions of the First Australian Battalion around the slopes of Hill A. Four Australian machine guns, entrenched on the forward slopes of the hill, laid down a devastating fire that pinned the Germans down. For two hours they kept it up, taking a severe toll of the enemy. But then, one by one, the machine guns either ran out of ammunition or jammed from overheating.

Slowly Kroh mustered his men, and as each gun fell silent, the paratroopers advanced toward Hill A. The two companies from Wiedemann's force that had been wrongly dropped in these positions now served to assist Kroh in attacking Hill A. Using the mortars from his heavy weapons detachment, Kroh unleashed a withering barrage against the Australian company that held the hill. In addition to mortar fire, the Germans brought an antitank gun and a howitzer to bear on the Australians. In the face of such heavy fire, the surviving defenders of the hill position had to withdraw from the crest to the reverse lower slope.

At 5:15 Campbell decided to strengthen the counterattack by releasing his only two infantry tanks in support. He ordered them to clear the airfield and strike the Germans on the forward slopes of Hill A from the north. Both failed in their mission: The first crossed the perimeter of the airfield, where its treads got stuck in a gully—without firing a shot; the second succeeded in reaching the eastern slope of Hill A and fired a few rounds at the Germans. Kroh's men were not in the least frightened by the tank's appearance, for they had an antitank gun to counter it. As they wheeled the gun into position, however, the tank backed off and slipped into a deep ravine where it lay useless.[8]

With that threat overcome, the Germans strengthened their hold on Hill A. It was to prove their only success that day in the Rethimnon sector.

* * *

By early evening Campbell realized that his position on the hill was in jeopardy; the outnumbered men of his First Battalion were being hard pressed by the better-equipped Germans. If the Germans continued to hold this strategic piece of terrain, they would, in effect, control the airfield. He was determined to dislodge them before any German reinforcements arrived to make the task impossible. Campbell did not know what Sandover had already learned from his prisoners—that there would be no reinforcements.

As it had been since early morning, communication with Creforce Headquarters was still out. At 6:00 P.M., Campbell got his radio working and was able to send a message to Freyberg for help:

I AM HEAVILY ENGAGED ON BOTH FLANKS AND WOULD APPRECIATE HELP.[9]

In Athens, Kurt Student faced a dilemma. All day the news from Maleme had been bad, and by 7:00 P.M., he had not had a single report from Sturm at Rethimnon. There was not a single response to the regimental call letters sent out repeatedly over the wireless. In final desperation, Student decided to send a reconnaissance plane to contact Sturm.

Within the hour, a Feiseler Storch monoplane took off from Athens for Rethimnon. The pilot's orders were simple and direct: Find out what you can and report back to Student in person. The plane never returned.

At midnight Ian Campbell finally received Freyberg's reply to his earlier request for help. It was terse:

REGRET UNABLE TO SEND HELP. GOOD LUCK![12]

Undaunted, Campbell set out to push the Germans off Hill A. He planned to collect all his men and attack the Germans by dawn.

Colonel Bruno Brauer decided to land with the men of the First Battalion three miles east of the Iráklion airfield, where his men would secure the approaches from the east and from where he could maintain overall command of the regiment.

A little after 1:00 P.M., Brauer ordered the men of the First

Battalion to board their assigned transports, joining his headquarters staff in the lead plane. He sat down near the open hatch and waited for the signal to depart.

Brauer seemed calm and undisturbed, yet he wondered what had caused the delay in the departure for Iráklion. The old warhorse wanted to get under way. As yet he had no inkling that the morning attack at Maleme still hung in the balance, dangling between success or failure. Nor did he know that at this very moment Kurt Student was desperately trying to contact Elevsis airfield in an attempt to alter the plan of the operation. Unaware of all these problems, Brauer sat quietly in his seat, perspiring profusely in the stuffy confines of the Junker transport, smoking and waiting.

The signal finally came at 3:00 P.M.

One by one, the huge black trimotor JU-52s lumbered slowly down to the end of the runway, where they rose unmajestically into the air. Once assembled, they pointed their noses to the southeast and headed for Iráklion.

In the early afternoon of May 20, Major A. W. Nicholls, a company commander in the Leicester Battalion, requested permission from his commanding officer to take three of his platoon lieutenants on a reconnaissance of the defense perimeter.

"Get off by two o'clock," the colonel suggested, "but be back by 4:30 P.M.—no later!" It was odd, Nicholls thought, that the colonel should specify a time limit."

Nicholls planned to visit the Greek defense positions in the city, check the Royal Marine gunners at the Bofors batteries, then drive east to the airfield and visit a friend in the Black Watch. It would be a casual trip. No one had mentioned to him—*since no one knew*—that the Germans were landing in force in the western part of Crete. When the colonel set a time limit for Nicholls's reconnaissance, he did not know how prophetic his stipulation would be.

Major Nicholls spent the greater portion of the afternoon completing his rounds. A little after 3:30 P.M., he and his three platoon leaders left their vehicle for the short stroll back to their company positions. A familiar roar was soon audible from the north; within minutes, fighters and bombers crossed the coast signaling the approach of an air attack.

Nicholls's lieutenants raced across Buttercup Field—as the Iráklion airstrip was called—to seek shelter among the rocks and crevices of one of the two heights known as Charlie. Winded, they hid and watched as the bombers began their devastating work.

For less than an hour, ME-109s, ME-110s, JU-87s, and a few JU-88s circled, bombed, and strafed the Iráklion defense positions. Bombs fell on the airfield, the antiaircraft emplacements, and the city with unerring accuracy. When the bombers finished their work, the fighters came down to strafe anything that moved.

From his perch among the rocks, Nicholls watched the bombing spectacle in fascination. The bombers and fighters had a free run, for—following strict orders—not a single shot was fired in opposition. The young pilots smiled with satisfaction, assuming that their bombing runs had silenced the defenders' batteries.

As soon as the bombers turned north over the water, Major Nicholls and his three junior officers made a dash for their company's position within the Leicester Battalion perimeter. At 4:30 P.M. JU-52 transports were sighted flying low over the water. The general alarm was sounded in the Black Watch positions; elsewhere, in the distance, church bells echoed the warning of the enemy's approach.

Slowly the Junkers came in over the coastline and headed for their respective drop zones. The whole sky filled with the slow-moving transports, now settling to their familiar 400-foot height before releasing the paratroopers.

The defenders remained in their entrenchments, watching the tableau before them. It was the first time in their lives that they had witnessed such a colorful aerial spectacle. The air vibrated with the roar of triple-motored aircraft, while the sky filled with thousands of colorful parachutes slowly descending to earth.[12]

It did not take long for the British, Australians, and Greeks to awaken from this spell.

The silent antiaircraft batteries were the first to fire; their gunners at last had the gleeful satisfaction of telling the Germans that they were alive and well. Their announcements had a telling effect on the low-flying transports.

One aircraft took a direct hit, bursting into flames and leaving a black, smoky wake as it plummeted to earth with all its human cargo. Another Junker was hit as it released its paratroopers. The flames scorched some of them before they jumped, while those who were able to get out found their parachutes aflame.

The sky soon filled with the black puffs of shell bursts and the red glows of burning transports. Many Junkers crashed, and others headed out to sea followed by a long smoke trail. From one such blazing aircraft dangled a single paratrooper, his parachute caught in the tail.

Many parachutists, jumping from stricken transports, dropped to earth like rocks, their chutes unopened. Others left their planes, slowly descending to earth below billowing, swaying parachutes, only to meet the ire of the Australian, British, and Greek soldiers.

The defenders now emerged from their hiding places, the crack of their rifles echoing over the fields. Their rattling machine guns struck down the descending paratroopers, rapidly carpeting the fields with German dead and wounded. Most of the paratroopers died before they completed their descent; others hung limply from trees and telegraph wires. Those who were not shot in the air were soon killed on the ground, as the defending patrols sought them out in the fields.

One group of paratroopers hid in a barley field.

"Let's set the bloody barley on fire," yelled one of the Australians.[13]

Several matches were thrown into the dry barley, turning it into a blazing inferno. Hiding among the tall barley stalks, the paratroopers were now caught between two enemies—the Australians at their rear and the raging fire before them. The flames raced through the field, forcing the Germans to flee. One by one or in groups they rose from their positions, only to be picked off by Australian riflemen or to be cut down by machine-gun fire. Not a single German survived.

For three hours the parachute drop continued. As at Rethimnon, where the attack was already in progress, the JU-52 transports arrived over the drop zone in scattered instead of concentrated formations. This staggered drop gave the defenders ample time to seek out and destroy the enemy.

The delays caused by the dust clouds at the airfields on the mainland now took a heavy toll of the battalions of paratroopers at Iráklion, as it had further west at Rethimnon. It proved to be a slaughter.

At 6:15 P.M. General B. H. Chappel ordered his reserve battalion—the Leicesters—to flush out any stragglers hiding in Buttercup Field. The Leicesters pushed the surviving Germans back toward the beaches, where, their backs to the water, they were forced to surrender.

However, five men were determined not to give up. Three survivors from the Sixth Company and two from an attached machine-gun platoon discarded their heavy uniforms and waded out into the surf. They struggled for several hours in deep water, swimming along the perimeter of the airfield until they reached safety well east of the drop zone.[14]

By 8:00 P.M. the Second Battalion was no more. It had lost twelve officers and three hundred men killed, while eight officers and one hundred men lay wounded as prisoners of war.

The Third Parachute Battalion, commanded by Major Karl Lothar Schulz, landed scattered and piecemeal in the hills beyond Iráklion. They were immediately engaged on the outskirts of the city by the Greek battalions. The paratroopers suffered heavily in that first hour, as the Greeks chased them through the fields and orchards with their bayonets.

Major Schulz, a tall paratrooper, quickly collected the survivors and led them in a concentrated attack toward the city gates, against strong Greek resistance. By dusk he had driven his men along Martyron Road toward the northwestern gate, and along Kondilaky toward the western entrance to the city. Once through the gate, several groups of paratroopers succeeded in reaching the harbor docks. With nightfall, however, resistance stiffened as the civilian population picked up arms in a determined effort to throw the Germans out of the city. It quickly became a cat-and-mouse affair as Cretans stalked Germans through the dark city streets. Every flash from a rifle meant that another sniper had added a victim to the toll. Major Schulz found himself trying to hold his meager gains for the night. He hoped that daylight would turn the battle to his advantage.

Colonel Bruno Brauer landed in Crete with his regiment's First Parachute Battalion, three miles east of the airfield near the village of Gurnes. The battalion's scattered and delayed descent was only lightly opposed, for it had dropped well beyond the eastern extent of Chappel's defense perimeter.

Once on Crete, Brauer was determined to fight in proper dress uniform. From a separate satchel he removed a blue Luftwaffe service tunic, which he immediately put on, making certain that his Ritterkreuz was properly displayed around his neck. In place

of the steel helmet he wore the Luftwaffe officer's service cap—
the Schirmmütze—and around his waist he strapped his pistol belt,
from which hung a holstered Luger. His appearance now assumed
that of a field-grade officer on review rather than one who had
just landed in a combat zone. With a lit cigarette held smugly in
a holder, the dapper, if not eccentric, commander was finally
ready to direct the battle fortunes of his regiment.[15]

Turning his attention to the other battalions, Brauer contacted
Major Schulz by wireless, only to learn through a feeble signal that
the Third Battalion had encountered very stiff resistance in its landing zone. Schulz's casualties were heavy and his progress was slow.
The battalion's objective was still in enemy hands.

From the Second Battalion on the airfield, there was no response to Brauer's signals.

Cretan irregulars had arrived on Brauer's eastern and southern
flanks. These mountaineers, well accustomed to the field tactics
that characterized the basic elements of guerrilla warfare, positioned themselves among the rocks and picked off any paratrooper
who showed himself. The accuracy of their fire took a heavy toll
of the men in the First Battalion. It was to last into the night and
for the many days that were to follow.

By nightfall Schulz signaled that his men had entered Iráklion at
two points, but the outcome was still in question. He hoped that his
advance unit could hold its position in the city until daylight.

As of nightfall on May 20, at least 1,000 of the 2,000 men of
the First Parachute Regiment that had been dropped over the Iráklion sector lay dead.[16]

# 18 / "IF YOU MUST, THEN YOU MUST"

## MAY 20, 1941

At 1700 hours—five o'clock in the afternoon—Colonel Andrew lost his patience waiting for Brigadier Hargest's reply to his request for reinforcements. He turned to his executive officer and, in a voice tinged with anger, ordered that another message be forwarded to brigade headquarters.

"Ask Brigade if I can expect reinforcements for a counterattack—correct that! *Tell* Brigade that I need—repeat, *I need*—reinforcements for a counterattack!"

The executive officer jotted the message on his pad, stopped, and stared at the colonel in mid-sentence. The vehemence of the note was not characteristic of the otherwise subdued battalion commander.

"Dress it up and send it!" was Andrew's only response to his executive officer.[1]

While the battalion commander waited, he evaluated his headquarters staff. The first signs of weariness from the long day's events were beginning to show on their faces. Andrew thought to himself that if his headquarters personnel were tired, what about the lads out there in the trenches under constant fire? At that moment, Colonel Andrew made up his mind: He would counterattack to take the strain off those men, whether he got reinforcements or not.

At 5:20 P.M., twenty minutes later, he received his reply from Hargest:

THE 23RD BATTALION CANNOT ASSIST YOU BECAUSE IT IS ITSELF ENGAGED AGAINST PARATROOPERS IN ITS OWN AREA.[2]

Turning to his second in command, Major John Leggatt, Andrew ordered, "See what men are available as infantry support for a counterattack. And send a runner to the two 'I' tanks in the field. Tell them that their time has come. I need them!"[3]

* * *

In the Prison Valley area, Colonel Kippenberger, the commanding officer of the Tenth Brigade, had taken a brief respite to evaluate the situation.

It was clearly apparent to him that the objective of the German paratroop regiment was the village of Galatas, nestled atop the high ground behind its protective walls. Kippenberger's undermanned brigade had taken a severe lashing during the morning phase of the attack. Yet, despite this, the Germans had been prevented from capturing their objective. As long as Galatas and the surrounding hills were in New Zealand hands, the rear door to Khaniá remained closed.

The Petrol Company of the brigade's Composite Battalion withstood several sharp attacks by the Germans, and their defense of Pink Hill took a heavy toll of the attacking parachute company. But the Germans rallied, and although they lost their company commander, they resumed their attack against the Pink Hill defenders. The Petrol Company commander, Captain McDonagh, kept his men under control until he himself fell dead from a sniper's bullet. Lacking his leadership, the men of Petrol Company withdrew, giving the Germans of Major Derpa's parachute battalion a foothold on Pink Hill.

Kippenberger had not received any word from the Eighth Greek Regiment fighting at Alikianou. From the heavy firing in that direction, he realized they were under attack. A false rumor, carried by a New Zealand runner, informed him that the Eighth Greek Regiment had broken before the German attack and fled from the battlefield. The brigade commander was not to learn until much later of the stout defense mounted by Lieutenant Colonel Peter Karkoulas' men against Major Liebach's Paratroop Engineer Battalion—a defense that caused Liebach to withdraw his force in order to regroup and lick his wounds.

Closer at hand, Kippenberger did not need a runner to tell him that the other Greek regiment attached to his brigade—the Sixth Regiment—was in trouble. In fact, the Sixth faced near annihilation. From the first moment of the paratroop attack in the Galatas area, these green, ill-equipped men had borne the full fury of the assault. They were no match for the disciplined, well-armed Fallschirmjägers.

The regiment's First Company, commanded by First Lieutenant Stavroulakis, had been deployed in a gully west of Cemetery Hill—

due south of Galatas village. Within the first hour of battle, this company was surrounded by paratroopers, and when a German flanking thrust captured their commander, the company surrendered.

The same fate befell the Fifth Company, led by First Lieutenant Constantinidis. The men of this unit were surrounded without firing a shot because ammunition had not been distributed to them in time. The prisoners were quickly rounded up and marched off toward Prison Valley.

The regiment's Machine Gun Company, under First Lieutenant Ksirgianakis, put up a stiff wall of fire until their ammunition ran out. When their company commander was killed, the survivors fled toward Galatas village. The Second Company fought stubbornly among the graves and tombstones of Cemetery Hill, but when their company commander, Lieutenant Gianoulakis, fell wounded, the rest of the raw recruits also broke and fled toward Galatas.

Captain Silamianakis' Third Company held its ground east of Cemetery Hill against repeated German attacks. The Third Company's men met each German thrust with a fierce counterthrust. It was the only company of the regiment to hold its ground all day.[4]

When the Fifth Company surrendered, it exposed the Sixth Company's right flank. Captain Emorfopoulos—Captain E—and his executive officer, Lieutenant Kritakis, became aware of this new danger from the right. Having taken severe casualties and running low on ammunition, Captain E ordered his men to fall back behind the cemetery wall. Gathering the survivors of the Second Company who fought in the cemetery, he linked up with a third company and set up a stable defense line. On his right he had contact with the Petrol Company, which had withdrawn from Pink Hill, and on the left he had the New Zealand Nineteenth Battalion. In the hours ahead, Captain E and the survivors of his company were to give a good account of themselves in the face of repeated German attacks up Cemetery Hill.[5]

In order to bolster this defense line, Colonel Kippenberger ordered that the 190 men of the New Zealand Divisional Cavalry Detachment take their place in line along Cemetery Ridge.

Typical of the aloofness exhibited by the British Commonwealth commanders regarding their Greek allies, Kippenberger seemed nonchalant when advised of the troubles faced by the Sixth and Eighth Greek Regiments. Yet he had said nothing when the Petrol Company withdrew from Pink Hill, nor did he admonish the Divisional Cavalry Detachment for having retreated from the foothills above Alikianou village.

As early as 10:40 A.M., he realized that the German attacks toward Galatas were fragmented and that the attackers were off balance. Kippenberger's aggressiveness spurred him to conclude that a sharp counterattack in force against the whole Prison Valley area would throw the Germans back.

Not too far away from Kippenberger's brigade was the Fourth New Zealand Brigade commanded by Brigadier L. M. Inglis.

Inglis was of the same opinion as Kippenberger—an immediate counterattack in force would succeed in clearing Prison Valley of Germans.

Inglis proposed that the Eighteenth and Twentieth Battalions of his brigade mount an attack against the Germans in Prison Valley. The force of the attack should push the enemy out of the valley in confusion and help relieve the beleaguered force at Alikianou village. Once Prison Valley had been cleared, his brigade would wheel northward in a clockwise sweep and attack the Germans at Maleme from the south. The whole advance would follow a course that had been reconnoitered before the battle. Inglis's proposal was a clever, aggressive plan of attack, typical of his nature. It bore that distinct flavor of success, and Colonel Stewart at Freyberg's headquarters liked it. "The plan seems sound, old chap," commented Feyberg's chief of staff, "but you have to put the proposal up to Puttick—after all, you are now under his direct commmand."[6]

General Edward Puttick, the New Zealand divisional commander, who believed that World War I tactics were equally sound in World War II, did not like Inglis's proposal when he heard it. He considered it too bold a plan, for it depended on many contingencies— such as proper coordination in the face of communications difficulties, movement across open fields while in danger of Luftwaffe attack and, last but not least, the problem of supply. In any case, Puttick took the responsibility off his own shoulders when he remarked to Inglis that he would put the plan before Freyberg.

No sooner had Brigadier Inglis returned to his own headquarters than he received the answer to his proposal:

*I Blunder*

GENERAL FREYBERG DOES NOT APPROVE THE COUNTERATTACK.[7]

Thus passed General Puttick's first and only opportunity to salvage the day's battle. General Freyberg's failure to approve the proposal and order the counterattack—he did not wish to countermand Puttick's wishes since Puttick was senior in rank—proved to be a costly lost opportunity for early victory.

After repeated messages by Kippenberger requesting a counterattack, Puttick was finally moved to action only when he was erroneously told that the Germans might clear Galatas valley for a landing field. At 8:00 P.M. Puttick ordered Inglis to attack, yet he failed to tell Kippenberger—the man who would lead the attack!

Kippenberger first learned of the counterattack when he heard the roar of motors as three Vickers light tanks entered Galatas village from the north. In command of these tanks was Lieutenant Roy Farran of the Third Hussars, who brought them hastily over the twisting dirt road into Galatas. He reported to Kippenberger that he was ordered to attack by 8:30 P.M. "but it was not clear what their objective was!"[8]

When the attack finally began, it was almost dark. The three tanks immediately ran into a roadblock just beyond Cemetery Hill. Farran's machines were vulnerable to mortar and machine-gun fire, and he had to exercise great care. By the time the infantry of the Nineteenth Battalion cleared the roadblock, darkness had blanketed the battlefield. Farran pushed his tanks forward hoping to reach Prison Valley and cover the potential landing field with fire, even in darkness. They succeeded in doing so, until a mortar shell blew a track off his tank. Unscathed, Farran left his demolished machine, just missing capture.

Now, in the night hours of pitch blackness, Kippenberger and C. A. Blackburn, the CO of the Nineteenth Battalion, concurred that the attack had begun too late, and was too weak to achieve success. The two remaining tanks and supporting infantry were recalled and the attack cancelled.

Sergeant Dick Fahey was in his foxhole when the runner from Colonel Andrew arrived with the order to move the tanks out.

The crews of the two infantry tanks had dug a series of entrenchments in front of their hidden vehicles. All about these entrenchments lay the lifeless bodies of German paratroopers. Although the tank squad had taken a few casualties, they were still operational, and when Fahey got the message, he and his tankers sprang into action. At last he and his men would see the kind of action for which they had trained, instead of sitting in their fox-holes fighting as infantrymen.

Off came the broken olive branches, uprooted cacti, and hunks of sod covering a huge camouflage net. The forward end of the tank pit had been graded like a ramp to facilitate exit. Fahey revved up the motors of the first tank and slowly crawled up the incline into the open, the second tank following right behind. Like two huge metallic turtles, they trundled over the rocky terrain of the eastern slope of Hill 107, heading for the main northern highway. The first element of the counterattack had moved into position.

The second element would be the infantry support. Colonel Andrew's battalion had taken a severe pounding all day, not only from the German ground attacks but also from the ubiquitous Luftwaffe. Although the air attacks had tapered off during the afternoon, pressure on the ground increased. As each paratroop assault was repulsed, the casualties among the defenders increased. By late afternoon, things had reached a point where no men were available to fill the gaps opened in the battalion defense line. And now, amid the fury of battle, these fatigued men would be asked to leave the somewhat supportive shelter of their entrenchments and expose themselves in a counterattack.

It is militarily axiomatic that such a maneuver is most likely to succeed when it is launched with fresh troops. Colonel Andrew had no such reserves available. In view of the increasing pressure exerted from two directions by the Germans, Companies A and B could not be spared from their positions on Hill 107. Company D and Headquarters Company were considered lost by Andrew. Only Company C presented a possible solution to the problem.

Captain S. H. Johnson of Company C had kept two sections of his unit in a secondary defense line along the coast road. These two sections were still intact, and their proximity to the road made them an obvious choice as the source of the men required for the counterattack. Thus, the nineteen battle-weary men of these two sections of C Company were ordered to do the work originally assigned to a whole battalion of 600 men. They were ordered to attack the Germans, rout them, and recapture the bridge over the Tavronites River.

Seeking some possible sign that would confirm the stupidity of the order, the sergeant in command of these seemingly expendable men stared at Captain Johnson while the company commander slowly repeated the orders given to him by the battalion commander. Captain Johnson completed his instructions and looked away; he could not endure the sergeant's penetrating stare, for he acknowledged to himself that it was a suicide mission.

Just then a young officer entered Andrew's headquarters. With a sharp, snappy salute, punctuated by a click of his heels, he presented himself to Major J. Leggatt, the second in command. The enlisted men, noncoms, and officers in the headquarters looked up in surprise at the sound of clicking heels. The sound also drew Colonel Andrew's attention.

"This lieutenant has a detachment of six men who were formerly the crew of a Bofors gun," remarked Major Leggatt, introducing the young officer. "The Bofors is out of action, sir, and he volunteers himself and his six men for the counterattack."[9]

Colonel Andrew nodded assent. "Have him and his men bring up the rear of Johnson's two sections. So now we have twenty-six men for our great attack. Things are looking up, Leggatt!"[10]

South of the main highway just east of the Tavronites River was Captain Campbell's D Company, which Colonel Andrew thought was wiped out. Only forty-seven men remained of this gallant New Zealand company. They were well situated in their defense positions, but their other problems were becoming vastly acute.

At about 5:30 P.M., the roar of motors from the direction of the coast road lightened the spirits of each of the forty-seven men. The sound was the familiar one of tanks; the long-awaited counterattack was finally coming.

The New Zealanders stirred in their trenches, and they noted that German harassing fire was no longer directed at them but toward the coast road. There was much movement and shouting by the Germans as they left their positions in order to repel the approaching counterattack, and the pent-up New Zealanders let loose a deadly fire on them.

One group of paratroopers was pulling a 20-mm mountain gun over the rocky terrain in order to site it on the coast road. A concentration of rifle fire from the flank of the D Company positions dropped each of the Germans around the cannon. Now it was the New Zealanders' turn to pick them off.

The first infantry tank moved slowly along the highway. Rifle fire coming from all directions struck its sides with little or no effect. The sound of ricocheting bullets bouncing off the superstructure made Sergeant Fahey's ears ring.

Through the narrow aperture, he spotted a group of Germans

in an irrigation ditch to his right. He ordered that one round be fired at them and rotated the turret in order to sight his gun on the target.

There was no response.

"What the hell you waiting for? Load it!" yelled Fahey over the roar of the tank's motor.

"The shell won't fit—it's too big!" came the reply from the gunner. Hardly believing what he heard, Fahey stepped down from the observer's position, grabbed another shell from the rack, and placed it into the gun's breech. It would not go in. He tried another, with the same result, then another. They had been supplied with ammunition suited for a larger-caliber cannon! Fahey was livid.

"What the bloody hell! Here we are leading an attack and we can't even spit at them!"[11]

The second tank followed the first by an interval of thirty yards. Strung out between them were the twenty-six men serving as infantry support. They were using the tanks for protective cover.

The commander of the second tank had also spotted a good target and ordered his gunner to load the two-pounder cannon. But when he tried to rotate the turret in the direction of the target, he found that it was jammed. Unable to fire his cannon at will, the leader of the second tank ordered it to withdraw from the attack.

Without wireless equipment, when the second tank in the column decided to withdraw, it could not inform the advance tank. Thus Fahey assumed that the rest of the column was following him, and continued onward.

Fahey's Matilda (the affectionate name the Australians called their tanks) churned up the road until it approached the Tavronites River bridge. The Germans felt helpless before the advance of this interloping monster, for their light-caliber weapons could not penetrate its steel skin. One hundred yards from the bridge, Fahey left the road and headed for the river's edge, hoping to strike the Germans from the rear. The tank skidded down the steep embankment and passed under the concrete pylons of the bridge, Germans everywhere running from its path. Although its cannon was mysteriously silent, its machine gun cut a swathe in the fleeing ranks of the enemy.

Fahey continued along the dried-up river bed at the base of the embankment. Directly in his path were three members of a mortar section. Before they could climb out of their shallow entrenchment and run for safety, the tank ran over their position, crushing the men beneath its treads.

Advancing toward the far side of the river, Fahey found the going more difficult when his vehicle entered a muddy patch. The tank struggled forward and then slid into a shallow gully, its spinning treads chewing deeper and deeper into the mud. After exhausting attempts to disengage the tank, Fahey finally realized that it had become hopelessly mired in the muddy soil of the river bottom.

"Bail out!" he yelled, and through the turret and lower escape hatch, the crew wriggled out and raced for the protective cover of the embankment. The Matilda tank was left an abandoned derelict, as it had been once before in the sand dunes of North Africa.

The column of supporting infantry could not keep up with the lead tank, and when the follow-up tank withdrew, they were left in the open, unprotected.

Now a concentration of rifle and machine-gun fire fell upon these hapless men. Those caught in the middle of the road had no chance for survival, and dropped in all the grotesque positions of instantaneous death. Some of the others who were advancing along the side of the road hit the ground at the first volley of enemy fire, rolling into the protective hollow of an irrigation ditch that paralleled the road.

Gone was the lead section from C Company, with its gallant sergeant. Dead were the six volunteers from the Bofors gun crew. Their officer, that young, earnest lieutenant, screamed and shook his fist at the retreating tank, until bullets ripped into his body and he too fell dead.

Of the twenty-six men who constituted the infantry support of the counterattack, only eight demoralized survivors returned from this fruitless and tragic sortie.[12]

Colonel Andrew watched dispiritedly the eight men file past his command post. Suddenly he lost faith in his ability to hold Hill 107.

At 6:00 P.M., he signaled brigade headquarters that his counterattack had failed. Over a wireless set whose weakened batteries were transmitting a fading signal, he repeated his appeal for reinforcements. He added emphatically that in view of the counterattack's failure, if he did not receive reinforcements soon, he would have to withdraw from Hill 107.

To Andrew's surprise, Brigadier Hargest replied, "If you must, then you must."[13]

A curtain of darkness heralded the approach of night. The German commander who opposed Kippenberger also took time to consider his situation. Colonel Richard Heidrich, the newly appointed commander of the Seventh Airborne Division, still commanded the paratroopers of the Third Parachute Regiment in the Prison Valley area.

When Heidrich finished reviewing his position, it left him in a state of "extreme nervous tension."

He issued orders to his Engineer Battalion, recalling them from Alikianou in order to protect his rear in Prison Valley. Derpa's Second Battalion was to remain in place and regroup its men into a cohesive force after the day's bitter losses. To Captain von der Heydte, he issued orders to collect any stragglers from Heilmann's destroyed Third Battalion and together with his own men return and guard Prison Valley on the east, holding the Alikianou-Khaniá road.

Captain von der Heydte was with the battalion field hospital when he received the message to withdraw to Prison Valley. The aristocratic battalion commander, who bore a slight resemblance to the actor Leslie Howard, had spent some time in the hospital assuring himself that his wounded were being as well treated as circumstances allowed. He walked past the litter cases lying in the open under the cooling shade of olive trees and paused before a youthful, badly wounded paratrooper who lay unconscious. Von der Heydte lightly stroked the hair from the young man's eyes and remained kneeling beside him, gazing absentmindedly at his face. The dying soldier reminded the battalion commander of a familiar face from the past. Then he remembered. The youth had once been his aide.

In a hollow, the surgical team had rigged up a canvas top suspended from tree branches, below which stood an old kitchen table stained crimson with blood. This was their operating room.[14]

All night the messages received from Puttick's headquarters overflowed with confidence. Not a single reference had been made to Colonel Andrew's almost monotonously repetitious appeals for assistance. On the basis of the messages, Freyberg assumed that the airfield at Maleme was in no immediate danger.

At 2200 hours—10:00 P.M. that night—Freyberg decided to inform General Wavell in Cairo of the prevailing situation in Crete at that hour. It was a message tinged with an undercurrent of anxiety:

TODAY HAS BEEN A HARD ONE. WE HAVE BEEN HARD PRESSED.
SO FAR I BELIEVE WE HOLD THE AERODROMES AT MALEME, HER-
AKLION, RETIMO, [RETHIMNON] AND THE HARBORS. MARGIN BY
WHICH WE HOLD THEM IS BARE ONE AND IT WOULD BE WRONG
OF ME TO PAINT OPTIMISTIC PICTURES.[15]

Shortly after Freyberg dispatched his message to Wavell, a young
man appeared at his headquarters. He was Geoffrey Cox, a junior
officer attached to Freyberg's improvised intelligence section.

In the first hours of the German assault, Lieutenant Cox had
joined a platoon of the Twentieth New Zealand Battalion, which,
together with the men of the First Welsh Battalion, were out
rounding up the paratroopers of Captain Gustav Altmann's glider
force. Later that afternoon, Cox returned to Creforce Headquarters. He sat at the makeshift packing case that served as Colonel
Blount's desk. On the desk was a pile of reports scheduled for
shipment to Cairo by the first available means. Next to this pile
was a captured German officer's briefcase; it did not appear to
have been opened. Attached to its handle was a brief notation
reporting how the item had come into British possession.

Cox was a journalist by profession, and in the days before the
German invasion of Crete, he had edited two issues of a garrison
newspaper, the *Cretan News*. Now, as he sat quietly at the desk,
his reporter's curiosity got the better of him. He wondered about
the contents of the briefcase and decided to glance through it.

It contained maps and an assortment of papers. One document in
particular caught his attention. The words TOP SECRET were stamped
across the top—with the additional precautionary admonition that it
be burned and not carried into battle. Using a pocket-size English-
German dictionary, which he had carried since his prewar days as
a reporter in Vienna, Cox began to translate the document. It was
a tediously slow task that took many hours. As the meaning of each
translated word fell into place, he realized the significance of this
piece of paper. What he had before him was a carbon copy of a
German operational order for the invasion of Crete!

Cox scribbled the last words of his translation hastily, then
rushed to Freyberg.

General Freyberg listened attentively to the translation. The
words—the phraseology—stirred his memory: A western group
would attack Maleme. . . . Group Central was to capture Khaniá.

. . . Third Parachute Regiment . . . to seize Prison Valley. . . .
Rethimnon and Iráklion to be attacked in the second wave.

The words were all too familiar. Freyberg had heard them before—no, he had read them! But where?

"What is the date of the order?" queried the Creforce commander.
"The eighteenth, sir," answered Cox.[16]

Freyberg remembered. It seemed so long ago, but just yester-
day a Greek liaison officer—Major Hector Pavlides—had appeared at Creforce Headquarters, sent from the Greek Army
Command in Khaniá, with a captured copy of an order describing
the plan for the German attack on Crete.

That was the document taken by a fisherman from two downed
German pilots outside Suda Bay. After the Greek commanding general read the captured document, he sent it to Freyberg's headquarters. But Freyberg did not believe that a classified document of such
importance would have been carried in a pilot's map case on a flight
that ran the risk of being shot down, as indeed had happened. Although the Greek command believed in the authenticity of the captured document, Freyberg had regarded it as a German ploy.

Cox's translation proved that the original document had been
authentic. From this translation, Freyberg perceived that the Germans had failed to achieve their major objectives and that they
were just holding on. Now was the appropriate time for action—
to strike them while they were still weak and off-balance. Yet he
issued not a single order to prepare for attack.

*For the second and final time in a twenty-four hour period, Cre-
force Headquarters was informed of the German plans for their
military operations in Crete, and for the second time, this valuable
information was ignored.* It would prove to be a fatal error.

General Student was seated at the broad table that stood in the
center of the war room in the Grande Bretagne Hotel. Under a
brilliant light, the table's surface was covered with maps, reconnaissance photographs, and official reports. A wisp of smoke rose
from an ashtray filled to overflowing with butts and half-smoked
cigarettes. Major Reinhardt, Student's staff intelligence officer,
stood next to him going over the latest reports. Nearby stood
Student's immediate superior, the Fourth Air Fleet commander,
General Löhr, together with General Julius Ringel, the commanding general of the Fifth Mountain Division.

The news from Crete continued its disturbing trend; no one felt

this tension more than General Student. The success or failure of
this operation rested entirely upon his shoulders.

Certainly Adolf Hitler, who regarded the Fallschirmjägers as
the ultrasecret weapon of his arsenal, would not look kindly upon
the casualty lists incurred in Crete. Hitler must have had little
confidence in the success of this operation, even though he approved it, for he had instructed his propaganda minister, Joseph
Goebbels, to withhold all press releases of the invasion. Not a
word of it had been printed in the German newspapers or reported
over the German radio. Had Student realized this on the night of
May 20, he would have been frantic. A telephone call from Berlin
warned him that detractors in Hitler's capital were even now turning wheels to persuade the OKW to suspend operations in Crete.
A brief message mentioned that if an airfield had *not* been secured
by the next day:

WE MAY CONSIDER SUSPENDING THE OPERATION . . . AND
WITHDRAW ALL AVAILABLE UNITS.[17]

This struck Student hard. Were he to accede to this "suggestion"
his career would be ruined and with it all the work that had gone
into developing the theory that an airborne division could be effective in an independent military operation. Still, the news from
Crete was not good.

There were no reports from Colonel Sturm and the Second
Parachute Regiment at Rethimnon. This worried Student even
more. Reevaluation of the earlier reports, which described the
problems encountered by the assault regiment at Maleme and by
the Third Parachute Regiment in Prison Valley, revealed that a
great number of senior officers had been killed or wounded. Student concluded from this that losses in the lower ranks must have
been equally heavy. His depression might have reached its nadir
had he known that in Crete he was destined to lose more men
than had been lost by the whole Wehrmacht since the beginning
of the war.

At 2345 hours—fifteen minutes before midnight—Student received the latest casualty totals for Maleme and Prison Valley.
Major Reinhardt turned to him and softly inquired, "Should I
make any preliminary plan for the possibility of breaking off the
engagement . . . if it seems advisable?"[18]

There it was! His own staff was now asking the same question:

Should the attack be suspended? Upon Student's answer rested the success or failure of Operation Mercury—and of his career. But Student was an able, conscientious officer who would not—could not—give up so readily.

He responded with a firm no. The attack would continue; he would concentrate all his remaining forces upon the Maleme area.

"Maleme will become the [focus] of the follow-up attack!" he asserted. [19]

A question still rankled in his mind: Could transports be landed at Maleme? Colonel Snowadzki's earlier attempt had shown it was impossible; but he had to try again—to be certain. He sent for Hauptmann Kleye, a staff officer with a reputation for dash and cool nerves.

"Fly to Maleme tonight," he ordered Kleye, "and see if you could land on the airfield!" [20]

Within the hour Captain Kleye was in a JU-52 racing for Crete. He reached Maleme and, in complete darkness, put his aircraft down successfully on the western edge of the airfield. Kleye did not encounter the fiery reception that the defenders had given Colonel Snowadzki earlier. He taxied his transport and, with throttles revving the three BMW motors to their full thrust of 830 horsepower, he took off for the return trip to Athens. An hour later he reported to Student that the airfield was usable. That was all Student needed to know. Rapidly he issued a series of orders— the forceful tactician at his best.

He ordered that six JU-52 transports prepare to fly to Maleme immediately carrying medical supplies and ammunition to the beleaguered paratroopers. He also ordered that the Fifth Mountain Division prepare elements of its One Hundredth Regiment to fly to Crete at dawn.

Then, turning to General Ringel, he added, "General, you will be flown to Crete tomorrow to take over the field command!" [21]

With nightfall the sound of battle diminished around Hill 107.

The Germans around the hill were scattered, alone or in small groups. They made no movement, glued to the ground under the olive trees and vines, waiting for whatever the night might bring. They were hungry, thirsty, and tired, but not a single one dared close his eyes. The atmosphere was tense and uneasy.

Like Colonel Heidrich in Prison Valley, the wounded General Meindl at Maleme was equally apprehensive about the expected

New Zealand counterattack that could come at any moment during the night.

"What are the [English] waiting for?" he asked of his aide over and over again in a voice so racked with pain that it was difficult for him to speak. Meindl had less than fifty paratroopers holding the lower portion of the western slope of Hill 107.[22]

At brigade headquarters in the village of Platanias, Brigadier Hargest had had second thoughts about Andrew's latest appeal for aid. At last he decided to send reinforcements.

He instructed Colonel Leckie of the Twenty-third Battalion to dispatch one company of infantry to assist Andrew on Hill 107. He was sending a single company on a maneuver originally scheduled for a whole battalion. To bolster the force from the Twenty-third Battalion, Hargest ordered a company from the Twenty-eighth Maori Battalion to proceed to Maleme. These famous New Zealand fighters had been retained at Platanias as brigade reserve.

When Colonel Andrew was informed of Hargest's belated decision, he could not understand the logic of dispatching the Maori all the way from Platanias—a twelve-mile hike in total darkness—while other companies were available from the nearby Twenty-first and Twenty-third Battalions. Nevertheless he was pleased that his daylong appeals for assistance had finally received a positive response although he now feared that it was too late.

By 9:00 P.M. the promised reinforcements had not arrived at Maleme. Andrew ordered A Company to withdraw from its entrenchments on the highest point of Hill 107 and to descend to the lower ridge positions held by Company B. Finally, a half-hour later, the reinforcing company from the Twenty-third Battalion arrived. Colonel Andrew sent Captain C. N. Watson and the new arrivals up to man the positions at the crest of the hill formerly held by A Company.

Hargest never bothered to inform General Puttick, his division commander, that he was sending reinforcements to help Andrew. All day he reported confidently that his brigade was doing well at Maleme. Suddenly, at 11:15 P.M., he requested Puttick's permission to send the Twenty-eighth Battalion together with another battalion to assist the defenders of Hill 107. For the first time, Puttick realized that all was not going well at the airfield.

A little after midnight, the Twenty-second Battalion commander ordered both A and B Companies to leave their positions on the lower slopes of Hill 107. Captain Watson's relief company was to act as rear guard during the withdrawal.

At 0130 hours—an hour-and-a-half past midnight—the Maori company from the Twenty-eighth Battalion finally arrived at Maleme. They had been on the road for six hectic and eventful hours, having left Platanias at 7:00 P.M.

Their twelve-mile march included a brief but hotly contested skirmish with a group of paratroopers. Resolved only by a bayonet charge in the dark, the encounter cost the Maori two of their men. When Hill 107 loomed out of the darkness, Captain Rangi Royal, the company commander of the Maori, sent a scouting party to contact B Company of Andrew's battalion. The scouts found only empty entrenchments, for B Company had already withdrawn.

Captain Royal then took his company south along Xamoudokori Road, where he accidentally encountered Colonel Andrew and his two retreating companies heading eastward toward the defense positions of the Twenty-first and Twenty-third Battalions.

"You are too late, Captain," Andrew remarked dejectedly. "The situation has deteriorated to the point that I have to pull out."[23]

Colonel Andrew never asked Royal if he had encountered the isolated survivors of his headquarters company during the passage through Pirgos. To Royal's report of the bayonet charge, his only comment was, "You are damned lucky to be alive."[24]

At this moment in the battle, Andrew had the opportunity of saving the day at Maleme. He still had 300 unwounded men from his original battalion available for the defense of Hill 107. Captain Watson's company from the Twenty-third Battalion augmented this to approximately 450 men. Captain Royal and the Maori started out with 114 men, but in picking up many stragglers during the march westward, their strength increased to 180 troopers. With their arrival, the Twenty-second Battalion had a total of 630 men available to defend Hill 107—almost as many as had been available at the onset of battle. But instead of leading the Maori Company, together with his own two companies, back up to the entrenchments on the hill to join Watson's men, Colonel Andrew followed the opposite course.

"It is no use, Captain Royal," he said adamantly. "It's too late. I suggest you take all your men back to Platanias."[25]

The decision to withdraw from Hill 107 was final.

At 2:00 A.M. Captain Watson and his relief company also left Hill 107 and followed Andrew's men back to the defense positions of the Twenty-third Battalion. At this time two runners from Captain Beaven's isolated headquarters company at Pirgos finally broke through to the Command Post of the Twenty-second Battalion, only to find it empty. Surprised, they retraced their steps to Pirgos. Captain Beavan had, however, gone on a personal reconnaissance and, approaching the defense positions of Company B, also found them empty. When he returned to his own command post at Pirgos at about 3:00 A.M., he thought it wise to follow in Andrew's footsteps and withdraw. Taking all the survivors of his company, including the stretcher cases, he withdrew eastward.

Captain Johnson had watched as one section of his C Company was wiped out in the fruitless counterattack late that afternoon. He had also lost the Fifteenth Platoon under Lieutenant R. B. Sinclair earlier in the day's battle on the airfield's perimeter. Yet, in spite of these heavy losses, Johnson was proud of the fifty surviving members of his company. He felt that they "were in excellent heart, in spite of our losses . . . they had not had enough . . . they were first rate . . . and were as aggressive" as when the battle first began.[26]

At 0420 hours, he too ordered withdrawal, sending a runner to inform the Thirteenth Platoon at the northeast perimeter of the airfield of his decision. Ten minutes later, his men moved out in single file. They had been ordered to take off their boots and hang them around their necks—the success of their withdrawal depended on complete silence. The wounded went with them, each man taking his turn carrying the litters in the line of march. As they struggled quietly over the rocky, cratered ground, they could hear the snores of the sleeping Germans on their right flank. They met no opposition and were subsequently allowed to put their boots back on. Along the route of their withdrawal, they came across three men from the Twenty-second Battalion still asleep in their foxholes, unaware that their units had pulled out.

Slowly, quietly, the New Zealand defenders of Hill 107 withdrew. Although ordered off the hill, they were reluctant to leave. These gallant men absorbed severe punishment all day against great odds and proved themselves equal to the task. They felt they had been successful in their defense, and they resented the ill-conceived orders to withdraw. They wanted to stay and fight it out. Most of all, they resented the idea of leaving many of their comrades behind.

By 0500 hours on the morning of May 21, the withdrawal was complete.

As Captain Campbell and his sergeant major stopped momentarily crossing the summit of Hill 107, they, too, heard the grating sounds of Germans snoring—the deep sleep of exhausted men.

"Sleep, would you, you bloody bastards?" muttered Campbell's sergeant major. In one final heave of frustration, he threw a hand grenade into the darkness. The subsequent explosion brought screams of pain from the German positions followed by bursts of machine-gun fire. Campbell and his sergeant major beat a hasty retreat down the opposite slope of the hill.[27]

The Germans were surprised that there was no response to their machine-gun fire; they looked at each other questioningly. A small patrol went out to infiltrate the New Zealand positions. They returned in a short while with the surprising news that the New Zealand trenches appeared empty.

Oberstabsartzt Dr. Heinrich Neumann, the Assault Regiment's physician and the senior officer of the paratroopers at the base of the hill, quickly appreciated the possible meaning of the silence. The New Zealanders had withdrawn. Exhilarated at this possibility, he led a small group of men up the western slope of Hill 107 to its summit. There he was met by First Lieutenant Horst Trebes, who led a platoon from Stentzler's Second Assault Battalion, approaching the crest from the southern slopes. At the crest of the hill, the two parties quickly consolidated their unexpected windfall.

As the first light of dawn heralded the approach of the second day of the invasion, the strategic Hill 107 had fallen to the Germans. With its capture, the control of the airfield also passed into German hands. What they were unable to capture in daylight through feats of arms, was given to them as a gift during the hours of darkness.

# THE
# AFTERMATH

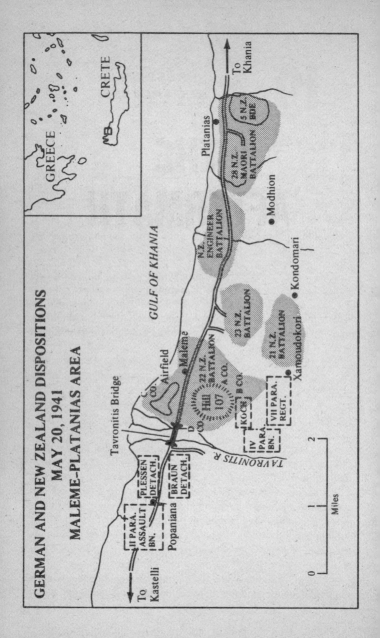

GERMAN AND NEW ZEALAND DISPOSITIONS
MAY 20, 1941
MALEME-PLATANIAS AREA

# 19 / "PRESS ON REGARDLESS"

**MAY 21, 1941**

In the first twenty-four hours of this historic and dramatic battle, Crete had been won and lost. It had been won by the heroic and determined resistance of the British, New Zealand, and Australian battalions; by the ill-armed and badly trained Greek regiments; and by the proud and hardy Cretan civilians. It had been lost by the vacillating hesitation of the senior commanders in the Khaniá-Maleme area.

It was a day on which no senior officer in those sectors seemed to take the initiative expected of a military commander—to order a counterthrust against the embattled invaders. It was a day on which the commanders followed the safest path—to avoid the onus of responsibility. They passed the buck to the next-higher echelon.

The buck finally reached General Freyberg. Twice in a two day period, he had been presented with a captured outline of the German plan of attack—and twice he ignored it. The first time he believed it to be a fabrication, a plant, and in light of the influential thinking emanating from the Cairo headquarters of General Wavell, the supreme commander in the Mediterranean, his reaction was acceptable. However, the second rebuff was inexcusable. A closer appreciation of the German operational plan indicated that the invader had failed to achieve his immediate objectives. Furthermore, it showed that the Germans were militarily off balance and outnumbered. A swift, well-supported counterthrust that first night would have overcome the Germans.

*That is how close the defenders of Crete came to inflicting upon the German military juggernaut its first land defeat in World War II!*

Although the exhausted, outnumbered paratroopers waited anxiously for the anticipated counterattack, it never came. Freyberg hesitated, as did his junior commanders. Instead of issuing immediate orders, Freyberg *invited* his sector commanders to meet him the next afternoon in order to *discuss* plans for a belated counterattack.

On that crucial first night of the invasion, the decision to delay any attack irretrievably lost the immediate opportunity for victory in Crete. After the abandonment of the prized Hill 107 and Maleme airfield, the Germans consolidated their windfall. Using Maleme as a base for men and matériel, they would eventually sweep eastward to inundate the rest of Crete.

Yet the Battle of Crete would last another nine hard-fought days, staining each square yard of Cretan soil with the blood of the attackers and defenders alike. There, under the twisted olive trees, amid the fruit orchards and the verdant fields, and on the rocky, sloping foothills of the White Mountains, a life-and-death drama was to take place that would remain a monument to all men who had ever fought to remain free.


The silence of the night was broken by a challenge: "Halt!" There was a mumbled sound as passwords were exchanged and acknowledged. Then in twos, threes, in fives, followed by larger groups, Andrew's retreating men from Hill 107 passed through the defense perimeter of the Twenty-third Battalion.

The men of the Twenty-third were taken totally by surprise. They were thunderstruck to see their friendly rivals from the Twenty-second struggle through their lines. Even in the darkness of night, they could feel the ordeal that the men of Andrew's battalion had sustained during the previous day's battle. Once the surprise had passed, they greeted them cordially and offered them whatever menial hospitality they could afford.

However, somewhere in the background, a raised voice was heard to ask: "What the bloody hell you doing here—who's guarding Hill 107?"[1]

Colonel Leckie of the Twenty-third Battalion suggested convening a battalion commanders' meeting, and he sent a runner to the headquarters of the Twenty-first to summon Colonel John Allen.

An hour later the meeting began, with Colonel Leckie presiding. Throughout the short conference, Andrew sat slumped dejectedly in a chair. With half-closed eyes he listened to the discussion, nodding his concurrence that the battalions "should hold their positions next day."[2]

Strangely enough, Colonel Leckie made no proposal that he take his Twenty-third Battalion forward, with the Twenty-first in support, to reoccupy Hill 107 and the airfield. Captain Watson's relief company had returned to the Twenty-third's area a few hours after the men of the Twenty-second entered Leckie's defense perimeter. Yet Leckie did not entertain the slightest thought of returning in force and reoccupying the vital hill, nor did he suggest this to General Hargest. Did Leckie derive an inner joy from Andrew's dilemma because of their own personal rivalry? In any event, nothing substantial came out of the meeting except the decision to hold their present positions—a decision that left the airfield open to the Germans.

And Colonel Andrew was too tired to care.

At the airfields in Greece, two companies of paratroopers, approximately 400 men representing Student's reserve, emplaned for the flight to Crete. Colonel Bernhard Ramcke was assigned the overall command of these reinforcements.

A second group of 350 men was also ordered to fly to Crete. These were the "leftovers" who had been stranded by lack of transport to carry them to the attack on Iráklion the previous afternoon.

Kurt Student had decided to drop Ramcke's 400 men in the area west of the Tavronitis River. Once landed, they would reinforce the men of the Stentzler and Gericke assault battalions and attack eastward. Student assumed that the New Zealanders' failure to counterattack the first night, and their subsequent withdrawal from Hill 107, meant they had no reserves available. To capitalize on that weakness, he ordered that the 350 leftover paratroopers be dropped in the Maleme-Pirgos area, where they would secure their positions and wait until the attacking assault troops reached them from the west.

Simultaneously, six JU-52 transports loaded to capacity with ammunition, rations, and medical supplies were to land at Maleme airfield. Right behind them, a task force comprising forty additional transports would ferry about 800 men of the Fifth Mountain Division to Crete. They would represent the first reinforcements that were not part of the original parachute assault force.

This phase of the invasion of Crete began with the floodgate—the abandoned airfield at Maleme—wide open for the Germans to enter.

While the 400 paratroopers under Colonel Bernard Ramcke's command were dropping safely west of the Tavronites River, the second, leftover group of 350 paratroopers was bailing out over the village of Pirgos. Unfortunately for them, they did not have the same peaceful descent as their comrades. What followed was a reenactment of the previous day's slaughter. It was to become the death knell for the Fallschirmjäger in Crete.

This wave of paratroopers was released along the northern coast road, strung out from Pirgos all the way to Platanias. They fell amid the men of the New Zealand Engineer Battalion attached to General Hargest's Fifth Brigade, and among the tough Twenty-eighth Maori Battalion.[3]

No sooner had the "sticks" of paratroopers left their transports than a cascade of rifle and machine-gun fire greeted them. The sporadic firing that had marked the earlier hours of this second day of the invasion now rose to a crescendo.

Captain J. N. Anderson of the Engineer Battalion scanned the sky, watching the paratroopers during their descent. Seemingly out of nowhere, one landed not more than ten feet in front of him. Anderson fired at him point-blank, while the trooper still lay beneath the canopy of his chute. Satisfied that he had disposed of the German, he looked up just in time to duck the feet of another paratrooper dropping right on top of him. At close quarters, Anderson fired the remaining bullets in his pistol into the paratrooper's body.

The New Zealander shook his head in distaste; he had killed the German without giving him a chance to defend himself. "Not cricket," he thought to himself, "but there it is!" With that, he ducked behind an olive tree to reload his pistol.[4]

All along the northern road, parachutes could be seen draped from the branches of olive trees or dangling from the telegraph wires that paralleled the road. From each parachute hung a dead body.

One paratrooper descended slowly, almost majestically, to earth, the path below him seemingly clear and quiet. Suddenly, out of their entrenchments, seven New Zealanders rose with fixed bayonets. When the paratrooper looked down again, what he saw struck terror in his heart. It was the first time that Captain Anderson ever heard a man scream with fear.[5]

Major H. G. Dyer, an officer in the Twenty-eighth New Zealand Battalion, led a group of Maori against the paratroopers.

Racing through a field, Dyer spotted a paratrooper firing at them from a partially filled-in well. He ordered Private Jim Tuwahi to pin the German down with his rifle while Dyer and another soldier approached him from the flank. When the German noted the flanking movement, he feigned death. Taking no chances, Dyer signaled the soldier to bayonet him. The young Maori rushed the well and, as his blade dug into the German's body, he turned his head the other way.

With that obstacle removed, Dyer led the rest of the Maori across the field. Germans were everywhere, clustered at fifteen-to-twenty-yard intervals. One German watched Dyer running toward him and lay down in order to take better aim with his tommy gun. The New Zealander fired a shot at him from the hip, the bullet grazing the paratrooper's buttocks and passing through his open legs. The German took careful aim at Dyer, who now appeared as a perfect target. But before he could squeeze the trigger of his machine pistol, another Maori speared the German with a bayonet. Such hand-to-hand encounters were common during the morning. Dyer continued his sortie against the Germans, many of the scattered paratroopers withdrawing in the face of the fierce Maori bayonet charge. Those Germans who remained behind were either dead or severely wounded.[6]

On the banks of the Platanias River, west of Platanias village, Manoli Paterakis and five other guerrillas had spent all morning hunting Germans. When additional paratroopers fell in their area, Paterakis and his men had a field day shooting them down.

Now a momentary silence fell over this section of the battlefield. Paterakis and the other Cretans stood ankle deep in the shallow waters of the river catching their breath and refreshing themselves from the heat of the day. The braying of a nearby frightened donkey echoed across the fields. For the moment, the area was empty of Germans.

Suddenly Gianni, one of the Cretans, acting as a lookout, gestured toward the road. Paterakis and the others crept carefully to the riverbank, following the lookout's motion. There, coming down the road, was a German officer with a squad of paratroopers behind him.

Major Franz Braun had collected the survivors of a company and was leading them down the road toward the village of Pirgos. When they reached the narrow, stone-arched Platanias Bridge, Braun spotted the braying donkey and decided to take it with him.

He left the road and crossed the small field to where the donkey stood, passing right in front of Paterakis and Gianni. Unaware of their presence, Braun nonchalantly leaned over and loosened the rope that kept the animal tethered to a stake. At that moment, Gianni pulled the trigger of his rifle.

Nothing happened except for a loud click.

Braun heard the sound, turned, and unholstered his Luger. Before he had a chance to shoot, Manoli Paterakis fired two bullets into his chest, killing him instantly. The shots alerted the squad of paratroopers, who stood idly in the middle of the road waiting for the major. Before they could scatter for cover, the other three guerrillas opened fire with their captured German tommy guns. In a matter of minutes, the paratroop squad was wiped out. No mercy was asked and none was given. The Cretans were not going to allow a single paratrooper to survive to fight them another day.[7]

Of the two companies that had been dropped between the village of Pirgos and Platanias, all the officers and noncoms, together with most of the lower ranks, of one had been killed; from the other, only one officer and eighty men survived the assault. These survivors retreated westward to Pirgos, holing up in stone houses until relief or darkness reached them, whichever came first.

At 1500 hours—3:00 P.M.—Captain Gericke's request for an airstrike against the villages of Maleme and Pirgos was finally fulfilled.

For almost an hour, the demonic Stukas subjected the two villages to a blistering bombing. Throughout those endless moments, the air was rent by the shriek of diving Stukas and by the shattering blast of their bombs. When the last plane left, a huge dust cloud hung low over the whole area.

Out of the dust, Gericke's men emerged. They advanced slowly on each side of the main road, moving from the southern edge of the airfield under the shadow of Hill 107, eastward toward Pirgos.

The men felt the rising excitement of victory. However, it was a short-lived exultation. Despite the ferocity of the bombing, there were still pockets of resistance by stubborn Cretans and isolated stragglers from the Twenty-second Battalion. From behind tombstones in Pirgos cemetery, from within the blasted piles of bombed stone houses, from behind walls and trees, armed Cretan civilians, using captured German machine guns and rifles, together with isolated New Zealanders, kept up continuous fire. This harassment slowed the German advance and gradually diminished their thoughts of an easy victory.

The paratroopers continued slowly across the open fields, waded the shallow Sfakoriako River, crossed a narrow valley, and started up the opposite slope—right into the defense positions of the Twenty-third New Zealand Battalion. The New Zealanders spotted them across the fields, their open formation making them perfect targets. They let them advance slowly, silently, into the trap.

At 150 yards, the New Zealanders opened fire.

It did not last long. The crack of rifles and the chatter of Bren machine guns echoed across the fields and valleys as the bullets tore into the ranks of the paratroopers. Occasionally the harsh crump of a mortar shell punctuated the din of battle. What was even more demoralizing for the Germans was the familiar sound of the more rapid-firing Schmeiser machine pistol being used against them.

When the firing finally stopped and the smoke cleared, the slope of the hill was covered with the bodies of German paratroopers. The survivors withdrew to the village of Pirgos, leaving behind them approximately 200 casualties. The advance had been stopped.

While the Germans were licking their wounds in the village of Pirgos, General Freyberg was convening a conference with his brigade commanders in Creforce Headquarters on Akrotiri Peninsula. This was the conference that was to crystallize a plan to recapture Maleme airfield.

In the dimly lit cavernous dugout that served as Freyberg's war room, the officers assembled around a table, some standing, and others sitting on crates.

At the outset of the conference, Freyberg suggested to his subordinates that the Eighteenth, Twentieth, and Twenty-eighth Maori and the Welsh Battalions be used as the major strike force in the counterattack, and that they in turn be supported by follow-

up units. His brigadiers strongly objected to this plan; to accept
it at face value meant that each area commander would have to
transfer units to Puttick's command. Their personal military pride
did not allow them to relinquish control of any unit to another
commander. They found innumerable lame excuses with which
to circumvent Freyberg's suggestion.

"We must guard against a sea invasion," argued General Weston.[8]

"Let us not dismiss the necessity of guarding our communications from the many isolated enemy in the rear," added General
G. A. Vasey of the Australian Brigade.[9] Finally, Freyberg acceded
to the suggestions by his subordinates and a compromise plan for
a counterattack was formulated.

Receiving no further dictates from his subordinates, Freyberg
was pleased to adjourn the conference. He optimistically added
that the counterattack would begin sometime between 10:00 and
11:00 P.M. that night.

Kurt Meyer was a German war correspondent who had been assigned to cover the landings of the mountain division in Crete.

As the transport in which he was a passenger approached the
coast of Crete, both side hatches were opened and the crew members stood trying to locate a clearing in which to land. The blast
of cold air hit Meyer fully, nearly throwing him out of his seat.
Through the open hatches, he could see the rooftops of villages
and the surrounding green fields. He also observed apprehensively the arcs of tracer bullets coming up at them. The pilot
zigzagged the aircraft to avoid enemy fire, all of which made
Meyer hold on for dear life.

The transport flew low over the airfield, and the pilot circled
and made a second pass. Not a single clear lane was visible; the
airfield looked as if a hurricane had struck it. With Junker transports all over the field, settled at various angles and facing in all
directions, it resembled a huge parking lot. Some transports were
smashed. Many had collided with other transports during the
landings. Interspersed between them were a few smoldering hulks
of aircraft that had caught fire.

The pilot of the transport carrying Kurt Meyer finally gave up
the idea of landing on the airfield itself and swung wide over the
water again. He circled and decided to bring the aircraft down
along a strip of land near the shore. Slowly the Junker dropped

lower to the ground. As it lumbered to touch down, the pilot noticed that the appearance of the strip had deceived him—it was not smooth at all, but interspersed with little rivulets, hollows, and rocks. It was too late to turn back; he had to land.

Just then a blast of machine-gun fire ripped into the right wing. With a last exasperated yell, the pilot warned everyone to hold on. The transport bounced heavily over the uneven ground. Its right wheel struck a rock, and the huge aircraft tilted offbalance to the left. The left wingtip clipped a low cactus and then dug itself into the sandy soil, spinning the aircraft into a half-circle, flinging men and cargo forward into a heap. The huge aircraft came to a sudden stop with one wing dug into the ground and the fuselage half-raised in the air.

Slowly the crew and the troopers separated themselves from the mixed pile of bodies and cargo. Though badly shaken and with some bad bruises, no one was seriously injured. Kurt Meyer's arrival in Crete had a brusque beginning.[10]

George Psychoundakis, the young, dark-eyed Cretan from the village of Asi Gonia, was stationed with ten other Cretans on the sandy shores near the village of Platanias. They had positioned themselves behind a half-fallen stone wall, from where they had a clear view of the shore and the narrow channel that separated the small isle of St. Theodore from the main island. Their assignment had been to protect this sector from a possible German sea invasion.

During the earlier hours of the twenty-first, Psychoundakis and his fellow Cretans had taken a good toll of paratroopers who had dropped nearby. The later hours of the afternoon had been quiet except for the sounds of battle from the west. Now, as late afternoon passed into early evening, six Junker transports began circling overhead. Some disappeared low over the hills, while one of them seemed to land by the shore further west, just out of sight.

Another transport came in low over the water and settled on the sandy strip near the pounding waves. No sooner had it rolled to a stop than the Cretans left the protection of the wall and dashed out to its landing site. Approaching the aircraft from all directions, they fired their machine guns until the barrels turned red. No one emerged from the transport. Finally the aircraft burst into flames.

Psychoundakis looked at the fiery pyre and shook his head, while his comrades danced a jig over their latest success.[11]

Of the six transports from this flight that had decided to land by the shore near Platanias village, not a single one survived the landing. Not a single trooper left his aircraft alive.[12]

All in all, the Germans had lost twelve Junker transports during this operation, but they did safely land 650 mountain troops out of a total of 800 men flown to Crete.

Within an hour after the first group of transports landed on Maleme airfield, Oberstleutnant Snowadzki and his Airfield Service Company were at work clearing the airstrip of wrecked aircraft. Using a captured Bren carrier and one of the abandoned Matilda infantry tanks, Snowadzki and his men pulled and pushed the derelicts to the side of the airfield, thus clearing the path for the arrival of additional reinforcements.

By 7:00 P.M., May 21, Colonel Ramcke arrived in Crete to assume command of all the paratroopers in the Maleme sector. He succeeded the wounded General Meindl, who had been flown out on a transport earlier in the day.

The hard-driving, aggressive Ramcke was not impressed with the difficulties the paratroopers had encountered earlier and that had halted their advance. As nightfall ended the second day of the battle, he issued sharp and succinct orders to Gericke and to the other commanders in his sector:

PRESS ON REGARDLESS . . . KEEP GOING INTO THE DARKNESS . . . ENSURE THAT THE ENEMY CAN NO LONGER REACH THE AIRFIELD.[13]

By nightfall on the second day of battle, the scales of battle were still evenly balanced.

# 20 / "IT HAS BEEN A GREAT RESPONSIBILITY"

## MAY 21, 1941

The news of the German invasion of Crete reached Prime Minister Winston Churchill before noon on May 20. During the early session of the House of Commons, Churchill rose to interrupt a heated debate. The members were somewhat crowded in their temporary meeting hall, having been dispossessed from the Commons chamber by the night bombings of May 10, which had wrecked the Parliament building and Westminster Abbey. In the slow, halting speech so typical of Churchill, particularly when the news bore the urgency of alarm, he addressed the hushed M.P.s.

"I hold in my hand an urgent signal from General Wavell . . . a serious battle has begun in Crete." A murmur ran through the chamber, and when it diminished, Churchill gave a brief resumé based on dispatches. Finally he concluded, "I am confident that the most stern and resolute resistance would be offered to the enemy."[1]

Toward late afternoon he read another report: "After a good deal of intense bombing, enemy troops have landed by gliders, parachutes, and troop-carriers in the Khaniá-Maleme area . . . there is a continuous enemy reconnaissance, accompanied by sporadic bombing and machine gunning, chiefly against antiaircraft defenses. . . . It is thought that the enemy were attempting to capture the aerodrome at Maleme. . . . so far this has failed . . . the military hospital between Khaniá and Maleme, captured by the enemy, has now been recaptured.

"It appears," concluded Churchill, "that for the present the military situation is in hand."[2]

The late editions of the *Daily Telegraph* and the London *Times* carried banner headlines of the German attack on Crete. All over Britain people listened to the BBC for news of the invasion. They listened intently, hoping for any word that might forecast a defeat for the Germans.

* * *

What surprised Major Karl Lothar Schulz, the commander of the Third Paratroop Battalion at Iráklion, was that the resistance he encountered came not only from British and Greek troops, but also from armed Cretan civilians. Old men, young boys, women, and girls vented their hate on the intruders. The girls threw stones at the paratroopers, while the women collected weapons and ammunition from German dead. The old men fought like youths and the young boys fought like men. From every vantage point, they fired captured German weapons. "They have no right to fight us," protested Major Schulz, "they are not soldiers—they are civilians!"

Oberleutnant von der Schulenberg, an officer in Schulz's battalion, captured one such youthful Cretan and brought him before Major Schulz. Schulenberg remarked that the captive had held one of the platoons pinned down for almost an hour until he had at last run out of ammunition.

The tall battalion commander could not help but admire the youth's courage.

"Why are you fighting us?" he asked him.

The young Cretan did not understand the question, but he must have sensed its meaning. He glared at the German major with hate; in a final display of contempt, he threw his head back, pursed his lips, and spit at Schulz.

Shocked at this disrespect to his rank, Schulz wiped the spittle from his face and walked away—half-angry, half-embarrassed. A short burst from a machine gun denoted the brave young Cretan's fate.[3]

For the remainder of this second day of battle, Schulz's advance had been checked; the resistance had become so stubborn that those little gains were measured in yards. The heat of the day was exhausting, but what was even more alarming was that his paratroopers were running low on ammunition.

Major Schulz had not slept since the night before the invasion. From the moment he landed in Crete, he was constantly in motion—running, shooting, barking orders. Suddenly he felt his strength ebb and decided to rest a few minutes in the cool shade of a stone wall. One of his company commanders, Oberleutnant Kerfin, approached him for orders: "Herr Major?" Schulz shook his head dejectedly.

"If something doesn't happen soon," the battalion commander remarked in a tired voice, "we'll have to evacuate the town."[4]

Kerfin looked at him in disbelief, surprised at his commander's remark. But Kerfin realized what he meant; he knew only too well that if the battalion did not receive a supply of ammunition soon, they might be forced to surrender.

The two men sat in tired silence.

At that moment, a perspiration-soaked Feldwebel snapped to attention in front of the two officers.

"What's up, sergeant?" Kerfin growled, still annoyed at the very suggestion of surrender.

Behind the sergeant were three civilians—a portly elderly man wearing a straw hat, a dark-haired girl, and behind these two a short, dark man dressed in the uniform of a Greek army officer with the rank of major.

"These people want to surrender Iráklion to us," replied the paratroop noncom.[5]

Major Schulz jumped excitedly to his feet; the statement brought a surge of energy to his fatigued body.

The dark-haired girl was the first of the group to speak. In German, she said, "Major Bock!"

Schulz immediately recognized the code word that introduced a German sympathizer.

"Are these gentlemen empowered to make this offer?" he asked the girl directly. She nodded affirmatively.

"The civilian is the mayor of the city and the officer is the Greek commandant of Iráklion. They have come to offer you its surrender."[6]

Satisfied that the two emissaries were officially authorized to act, Schulz immediately dictated the terms of the surrender. Kerfin scribbled hastily on a page taken from a field notebook. With the girl acting as an interpreter, the mayor and the commandant accepted the terms and signed the paper. Major Schulz then added his signature to the surrender document, making it official.

A new strength raced through Schulz—a strength derived from the knowledge that he had achieved the regimental objective—the capture of Iráklion.

He barked orders to his company commanders. Von der Schulenberg and Kerfin ran to lead their respective companies into the city. Lieutenant Becker was assigned the takeover of the Citadel—a fortresslike, elevated structure in the center of town.

Suddenly the momentary silence was broken by the characteristically slow-firing rattle of a British machine gun. It was fol-

lowed by a rising crackle of small-arms fire, all coming from the
direction of the Citadel. Schulz hastened after Becker.

"What's up?" he asked, angered by this breach of the surrender agreement.

"The British have fired on us," complained Becker, pointing
at the bastionlike walls of the Citadel. "They don't accept the
surrender agreement!'"

Schulz muttered a curse. Just beyond, in the open, he could
see the bodies of dead paratroopers from Kerfin's company. The
British did not plan to surrender. In fact, the Australians and the
British infantry unit defending the town pursued the Germans in
a spirited counterattack. Infantrymen from a platoon of the
Leicesters Regiment, aided by a platoon from the Yorks and
Lancs, drove the Germans back foot by foot.

Taking heavy casualties and running dangerously low in ammunition, Major Schulz had no recourse but to withdraw his men.
Leaving a few paratroopers as a rear guard, he took the remnants
of his battalion back to the wall at the western gate of the city.
All the hard-fought gains of the previous night and early morning
had been for naught.

Schulz's retreat left the city of Iráklion firmly in the hands of the
Greek and British defenders.

East of Iráklion, Major Schulz's regimental commander was not
faring any better. Oberst Bruno Brauer, still in his resplendent dress
uniform, ordered several desperate attacks to capture the Iráklion
airfield—all of which proved fruitless. During the predawn hours of
May 21, Colonel Brauer sent a platoon of paratroopers, led by Oberleutnant Wolfgang von Blücher, to occupy a hillock on the eastern
fringe of the airfield. He planned to use that high ground as a base
for an all-out attempt to seize the landing strip.

No sooner had this platoon of paratroopers dug themselves into
the side of the hill than they were surrounded and isolated by British
infantry. Brauer was alert to the platoon's predicament and ordered
whatever units were available to break through to the beleaguered
paratroopers on the hill. But the German thrusts were piecemeal and
easily repulsed by the gallant men of the famous Black Watch Battalion.

Later in the day, the infantrymen of the Black Watch launched
a vicious counterattack against the hill. They raced up the slopes
with the steel of their bayonets glittering in the afternoon sun.

Not even the wall of fire that greeted them could stem their charge. One German position after another fell in rapid succession until the hill was completely overrun. There were few German survivors and even fewer prisoners.

The reverses suffered by the Germans at Iráklion were similarly dealt to their countrymen at Rethimnon.

Lieutenant Colonel Ian Campbell, whose task it was to defend the airstrip east of Rethimnon, was being hard pressed by the Germans. By nightfall of May 20, the troopers of the Second Parachute Regiment had seized control of a strategic piece of high ground designated as Hill A. This hill was to Rethimnon what Hill 107 was to the airfield at Maleme; whoever possessed it controlled the airfield—the little clearing that served as Rethimnon's airport.

Campbell knew very well that if he were to hold the airfield, he had to regain possession of Hill A. What bothered him was that he had to do it with only the few men available, for there was no possibility of assistance from any quarter. But Campbell was an experienced officer who was not fettered by the stagnant military dogmas of World War I as were Generals Hargest and Puttick. Campbell believed in the military philosophy of maneuver and attack, shortly to be exemplified by General Rommel in North Africa. It was this belief that drove him to do what had to be done: attack with his few men and take the hill.

At dawn of May 21, Campbell sent one company of Australians, commanded by Captain D. R. Channell, against the Germans on Hill A. In the face of heavy small-arms and machine gun fire supported by a deluge of mortar fire, the Australians had to break off the attack. There were many casualties, which included the company commander among the wounded.

Campbell was not disheartened by this failure. His determination and fighting spirit drove him to a second attack. He ordered Captain O. Moriarty and the reserve company to take the hill.

The Australians charged up Hill A with Captain Moriarty in the lead, firing from the hip and yelling wildly over the din of small-arms fire. These sons of soldiers who had fought at Gallipoli showed the same spirit and determination as their commander in the sweep to seize the hill. When the Germans saw the naked steel of the Australian bayonets, they broke and fled—with the attackers in hot pursuit. The charge carried Moriarty's men to the crest and down the other side. The hill was taken and the airfield returned to Colonel Campbell's control.

The eastern half of the isolated paratroopers were soon joined by the German survivors retreating from Hill A. Together they were led by Major Kroh in a withdrawal further east to the village of Stavromenos, where they took shelter within the thick walls of an olive oil factory. Captain Moriarty's men of the First Australian Battalion were close on their heels.

Perhaps the greatest victory of the day for Colonel Campbell's brave Australians was the capture of the commanding officer of the Second Parachute Regiment.

Colonel Sturm had never achieved full command of his paratroopers in Crete. From the first hour of the landing in the Rethimnon area, the command remained separated into two sectors with Wiedemann commanding in the west while Kroh led in the east. Communications failure kept the two regimental forces isolated. It was a situation that did not sit well with the arrogant and aloof Colonel Sturm.

Colonel Campbell's determined series of attacks and tactical maneuvers succeeded in keeping the Germans apart. Unaware of Campbell's rapid advance northward, Sturm found himself suddenly surrounded in his headquarters by the attacking Australians, and was subsequently captured together with his whole regimental staff.

By late afternoon on the twenty-first, Colonel Heidrich in Prison Valley ordered Major Derpa's Second Parachute Battalion to attack Galatas heights again. Derpa grimaced at the order; it seemed to him that his battalion was doing all the attacking. His command was down to a strength of a little less than two companies, and his men were fatigued, thirsty, and hungry. Yet, disciplined as he was to follow orders, he gathered his surviving company commanders for yet another attack.

Major Derpa ordered two platoons from the paratroop company on his right flank to assault Cemetery Hill once again. He reasoned that if he succeeded in seizing Cemetery Hill, he could enfilade the adjacent Pink Hill—held by the New Zealand Petrol Company—neutralize it, and then coordinate an advance on Galatas village.

Captain Emorfopoulos and his executive officer, Lieutenant Kritakis, watched the paratroopers gathering in the protective shadows of a line of olive trees across the meadow that separated the Germans from Cemetery Hill. The veteran commander of the Sixth Greek Company correctly assumed that his men would soon bear the brunt of an assault. Runners bellied out to Lieutenants Piperis and Koulakis, the platoon commanders on the flanks of the company's defense position, with the captain's orders: "Tell them to hold their fire until the Germans get close—and make each shot count."[8]

The Greeks watched anxiously as the paratroopers left the line of trees and crossed the open meadow. They were approaching in almost parade-ground precision, their officers in the lead, noncoms shouting orders. Captain E noted admiringly the coolness of the attackers.

"Those men are real professionals," he commented to Kritakis.[9]

Halfway across the meadow, the paratroopers broke into a trot that quickly brought them up the slopes of Cemetery Hill. The Greeks opened fire.

One squad of Germans led by a big, heavyset sergeant charged toward Captain E and his headquarters staff. Lieutenant Kritakis, positioned behind a tree, aimed and fired his pistol—but not a single one of his targets fell. Captain E was in a prone position, taking unhurried aim with a rifle. He had earlier discarded his pistol as ineffective and had borrowed the rifle from a wounded soldier. He sighted carefully and fired; he ejected the shell, slammed the bolt forward, and fired again. With each shot, a German fell in his tracks.

Kritakis gleefully shouted congratulations to him. The company commander cast him an annoyed glance. The rest of his men followed their commander's example and set up a strong and effective field of fire that finally stopped the German squad. The big paratroop sergeant was the last to fall.

But the German assault on the flanks of the Sixth Company was more successful, forcing Lieutenants Piperis and Koulakos to withdraw their platoons behind the stone wall that separated the cemetery from the road to Galatas. This withdrawal left Captain E and his men exposed. The brave Greek company commander realized his predicament but held stubbornly to his position. He was virtually surrounded, and the German fire was cutting his men down all around him.

"We shall fight to the last man!" he shouted stubbornly to Lieutenant Kritakis, loudly enough for all his men to hear. Private George Katosis, the company runner, dug his hand deep into the side pocket of his tunic. When he opened it, he found that he had only five bullets left. The other men fared no better.[10]

For minutes that seemed like hours, the struggle continued amid the tombstones of the village cemetery.

Suddenly there rose a thunderous shout from beyond the cemetery wall. Everyone heard it over the din of battle; even the paratroopers were momentarily distracted.

In one lusty yell came the cry of "Aera!"

Captain E smiled with relief as did the survivors of his surrounded company. All Greeks knew what that shout meant—the battle cry of the kilted Greek evzones, those specially selected warriors known for their great valor and heroism in Greece's fight for independence. The Greeks were counterattacking.

Like water that bursts from a ruptured dam, so did 200 Greeks of the Sixth Greek Regiment burst over the wall with bayonets held high, shouting over and over again the bloodcurdling battle cry of "Aera!"[11]

In their lead was a tall, fair-complexioned British officer!

Captain Michael Forrester from the Queen's Regiment had reported to Colonel Kippenberger on official business on May 20. The German invasion delayed his return to Creforce Headquarters. All that day he remained at Galatas, finally attaching himself to the Sixth Greek Regiment as its advisor. When the green troops from some of its companies fled in the face of the German assault earlier on the first day of the invasion, Captain Forrester rallied them, scrounged ammunition for them, and planned to use them as a mobile reserve force.

As it became apparent on this hot afternoon of May 21 that the Germans might succeed in capturing Cemetery Hill, he led his 200 Greeks in a stirring bayonet charge that surprised even Forrester by its spirited success.

The charging Greeks raced over the crest of the hill and down its slopes with a passionate determination to avenge themselves for the previous day's retreat. In one continuous rush, like a wind blowing across a field, the Greeks swept from tombstone to tombstone, slashing and killing Germans, and dying in turn while avenging their honor. Not one single German survived the Greek counterattack; not one was taken prisoner.

The German assault against Cemetery Hill failed—as had all the previous attacks against the Galatas heights.[12]

* * *

By sunset on May 21, the situation in Crete still remained critical for the Germans. Everywhere throughout the island, the German troopers settled their fatigued, thirsty bodies uncomfortably for the night amid their hundreds of wounded and thousands of dead comrades.

Back in Berlin, Adolf Hitler kept a close watch on the events in Crete. He still had not permitted a single item about the assault to appear in the newspapers or to be broadcast over Radio Berlin. This continued restriction somehow gave the impression that Hitler felt the Cretan operation to be a lost cause, and that he wanted to hide the disastrous facts of this side venture from the German people. Hitler's thoughts were centered on *the* major military operation in the east—Operation Barbarossa—the invasion of Russia. Hundreds of thousands of troops were already positioned on the Russian border, waiting for the word to attack. But this assault on Crete caused a delay in his scheduled invasion of Russia. Spring had come and gone and summer was approaching.

General Kurt Student was very much aware of this increasing anxiety, and of the diminishing faith in his operation. But he still clung to the desperate last hope that the arrival of the Mountain Division in Crete would tip the scales in favor of a German victory.

Toward evening Brigadier Hargest summoned the battalion commanders who would be directly involved in the counterattack to meet with him at brigade headquarters in Platanias. When Colonel George Dittmer, the commanding officer of the Twenty-eighth Maori Battalion, entered the main room of the farmhouse that served as Hargest's headquarters, he was surprised to find one other battalion commander present—Major John Burrows of the Twentieth New Zealand Battalion.

Dittmer frowned, for he knew that the attachment of the Twentieth Battalion brought the Fifth Brigade's strength up to five battalions—a formidable force with which to counterattack. Yet the only other officer present at the conference was General Puttick's staff representative, Lieutenant Colonel W. G. Gentry. Why had Hargest not invited Colonels Andrew, Allen, or Leckie? As the brigade commander reviewed the tactical details of the operation, Dittmer realized why the three other battalion commanders were not present. Hargest had not included their battalions in his plans. The whole burden of the counterattack would rest solely upon the arms of his Maori and upon Burrows's men. Dittmer did not like the plan.

Hargest continued. The operation dictated that the two attacking battalions be at their starting line—a point just west of the Platanias River—by 1:00 A.M. Under the protective cover of darkness, the Twentieth Battalion would advance north of the road, while the Twenty-eighth would cross the territory south of the main highway. Three tanks would advance simultaneously along the highway and give support to the two battalions as required.

Starting time for the advance would be 1:00 A.M. The attack on the first major objective—the village of Pirgos—would begin at 4:00 A.M. Once that village had fallen to the New Zealanders, they would rest for thirty minutes and then advance to clear the airfield and capture Hill 107. Burrows's men would take the airfield while Dittmer's Maori seized Hill 107.

"There it is, gentlemen," Hargest concluded in an optimistic tone of voice.[13]

Dittmer was not as optimistic as Hargest. This operation *might* succeed in peacetime night maneuvers, he thought to himself, but an advance requiring speed and the cover of darkness for success—with one of the battalions waiting to be relieved before it can be brought up to the starting line—all against a determined enemy . . . ! He raised the obvious question: "What if enemy pockets in the territory between the starting line of the advance and Pirgos delay our timetable?"

Before Hargest could reply, Dittmer added: "May I suggest that the detachment of engineers from the Twenty-third Battalion be sent down to clear the path in advance of the main body . . . ?"

Hargest brushed off Dittmer's suggestion with a curt, "It is too late for any clearing up activity!"

It was Burrows's turn to clarify an obvious omission: "Can we expect assistance from the Twenty-third, Twenty-first, or Twenty-second Battalions once we have reached our objectives or if we run into difficulty?"

Hargest looked at Burrows for a few moments before answering. "Oh, I suppose I could send Allen around the left flank . . . and I might send the Twenty-Third in for a 'mopping-up' role."[14]

Dittmer wanted a more definitive answer: "Could we depend on their assistance . . . ?" But a frown from Hargest cut his question short.

"By the way, Dittmer," added Hargest as an afterthought, "as soon as the operation has been completed, you are to withdraw your Maoris and bring them back here to Platanias . . . you will entrust the defense of Hill 107 . . . to the Twentieth Battalion alone!"[15]

Burrows and Dittmer looked at each other incredulously. Instead of sending the three other battalions forward to consolidate the gains, Hargest was weakening the attack by *withdrawing* one of the attacking battalions! How could a strategy that had failed on the first day with a single battalion on line be expected to succeed two days later with another lone battalion composed of men tired from an all-night attack against a stronger enemy?

Dittmer closed his note pad angrily at the idiocy of the order.

Colonel P. G. Walker, the commanding officer of the Seventh Australian Battalion, had no trucks available to transport his men to Khaniá in order to relieve Burrows's Twentieth New Zealanders. His trucks were to arrive from the motor pool at Suda. Walker, still smarting from Brigadier Inglis's sarcasm that "a well-trained battalion could carry out such a relief in an hour"[16] wondered if his commander appreciated how many factors could affect the successful completion of such a maneuver. Walker felt that the order was ill conceived and open to many obstacles that might disrupt the whole operation. Disregarding, for the moment, a sky filled with Stukas and Messerschmitts searching for targets, his trucks had to travel some five miles east to his headquarters at Georgeopolis, pick up the troops, then backtrack over the same road (now going westward) to Khaniá in time to relieve the Twentieth Battalion—all this to be accomplished before nightfall.

Walker looked anxiously at his watch as the first trucks arrived in dribs and drabs. He left his executive officer, Major H. C. D. Marshall, to see that the companies got started properly, and he departed for the advance position at Khaniá.

It was well after 5:00 P.M. before the first contingent of Australians was ready for the truck ride to Khaniá. Leaving Lieutenant Halliday to look after D Company, which was still waiting for trucks, Major Marshall led the truck convoy on its eighteen-mile trip eastward.

The sky above was filled with marauding Messerschmitts; once the trucks began to move along the narrow, curving tarmac, the game of tag began.

Aware of the danger, Marshall remembered a trick he had learned during the Battle of Greece. Aircraft require a straight stretch of ground in order to strafe troops. A long, straight road or an open field gave the pilots a perfect run to shoot up their targets. If a target kept zigzagging, however, it often proved difficult to hit. That knowledge could help his convoy get through.

Marshall ordered the drivers to race the trucks at maximum speed along the straight stretches of road, maintaining a safe distance between. He instructed them to keep close to the shoulder of the road and against the walls of the overhanging cliffs wherever possible. At curves in the road, Marshall would stop the convoy and wait for the other trucks to catch up. Above them the aircraft circled, unwilling to chance a run on a curve, with those perilous cliffs rising on one side like a gray wall. Once the convoy started again, the pilots would be waiting patiently for them over the straight sections of the road ahead. Thus the game of tag would resume.

It was an unnerving trip for the drivers, but Marshall—proud of bringing the convoy through without losing a single man or truck to a strafing Messerschmitt—found it an exhilarating experience.[17]

Darkness had fallen by the time the convoy reached the eastern outskirts of Khaniá. Fires were still burning fiercely from daytime air raids, and the debris from the blasted buildings made passage through the streets impossible. To cross to the western gate of the city, the convoy had to make detours that caused additional delays. It was midnight before Major Marshall brought the trucks carrying Companies A and B to the positions of the waiting Twentieth Battalion. Company C was further delayed, for it had lost its way in the darkness of the blackout. No one knew when D Company would arrive.

Night settled over the battlefields of Crete, bringing with it the darkness of a moonless sky. Even the stars seemed dimmer than usual. At 23:30 hours—half an hour before the end of the second day of battle—the black northern sky was ruptured by intermittent waves of light followed by the distant rumble of thunder. The sound grew louder; the light grew brighter. Searchlights stretched white fingers into the darkness, and bright flares turned night into day. Rockets arched into the sky trailing a fuzzy light in their wake. The roll of thunder now became the more distinct sound of shells detonating on target, over and over again. At the center of this spectacular display was a constant glow of flame.

Everyone everywhere in the Khaniá-Maleme area stopped to watch; they all knew what it meant—a sea battle was in progress. For thirty minutes it continued. Then, with one last flicker of light and one last roar of thunder, it ended. The lights disappeared and darkness prevailed once again.

High up on the heights of Akrotiri Peninsula, General Freyberg and his staff members watched the events taking place in the waters north of Crete. Smiles of elation were shared by Freyberg, his chief of staff, Colonel Stewart, and Lieutenant Geoffrey Cox. The fear that had gnawed at Freyberg from the first day he assumed command of the Cretan garrison was finally dispelled. The Royal Navy had saved Crete this night from a seaborne invasion, and at that same hour the New Zealand counterattack should be in progress. By morning, Maleme airfield would be recaptured and the Germans pushed back beyond the Tavronites River. Satisfied with this thought, and breathing a sigh of relief, he turned to his chief of staff: "Well, Jock, it has been a great responsibility."[18]

Captain von der Heydte, commanding officer of the First Parachute Battalion, had watched the same fiery display from a hill south of Galatas.

Although von der Heydte's parachutists had incurred many casualties during the first two days of battle, he was still able to field a battleworthy battalion. He knew that the Third Parachute Battalion had ceased to exist as a fighting force and that Major Derpa's Second Battalion had suffered such heavy losses from its repeated and fruitless attacks on Galatas heights that it was down to less than two companies.

Colonel Heidrich, the commanding officer of the parachute regiment in the Prison Valley area, had ordered von der Heydte to turn over all his available ammunition to Derpa's battalion. Heidrich wanted Derpa to renew his attack on Galatas heights the next day. If Derpa were to fail again, the whole regiment would have to withdraw into a tight defensive position: There would be no ammunition with which to attack.

The successful arrival of the naval convoy in the Maleme area would offer a solution to the supply problem.

When the bright lights and deep roars of battle diminished in the waters north of Crete, von der Heydte shook his head dejectedly, descending the hill to return to his headquarters. The German hopes for reinforcement and resupply by sea had been unsuccessful. The convoy had been obviously intercepted by the Royal Navy. Tomorrow would be a difficult day for his paratroopers.[19]

# 21 / "THE WHOLE WORLD IS WATCHING YOUR SPLENDID BATTLE"

## MAY 22–23, 1941

The major counterattack that was to wrest Maleme airfield and Hill 107 back from the Germans had not yet begun. General Freyberg had envisaged it as starting sometime between 10:00 and 11:00 P.M. on the night of May 21. Now it was approaching 1:00 A.M.—with the third day of battle soon to dawn—and the order to begin the attack had not been given.

Colonel Dittmer, commanding officer of the Twenty-eighth Maori Battalion, moved his men to the starting line as early as 11:30 P.M. on the night of the twenty-first. There they sat for three frustrating hours awaiting the arrival of the Twentieth New Zealand Battalion.

A little before midnight, Colonel Dittmer asked Brigadier Hargest to allow Major Burrow's Twentieth Battalion to move up to the attack line without waiting for the arrival of the tardy Australians. Dittmer realized that each moment's delay during the hours of darkness lessened the counterattack's chances of success. The commander of the Maori Battalion believed the attack should begin as soon as possible, but Hargest could not decide for himself and referred Dittmer's request to the divisional commander, General Puttick. Puttick refused, replying that the Twentieth Battalion must hold its defense position until the arrival of the *full* Australian battalion to complete the relief. He explained that the Twentieth's position protected that sector from sea invasion, despite the fact that he—like everyone else in the Maleme-Khaniá area—had just witnessed the interception of the German convoy at sea.

Major Burrows, commanding officer of the Twentieth Battalion, shared Dittmer's opinion regarding the need for haste. He decided to skip the chain of command and make the same request—directly to General Puttick. Puttick's refusal was equally direct. To avoid further delay, Burrows decided to sidestep divisional orders. On his own initiative, he ordered the companies of his battalion to move forward to the line of attack as they were relieved, instead of waiting for Walker's entire battalion to arrive.

At 2:00 A.M. Burrows arrived at Platanias with the first two of his relieved companies. He went immediately to see Hargest at brigade headquarters.

He found the old farmhouse that served as Hargest's headquarters on the road ascending toward the church of St. Demetrios. In the main room, he met Lieutenant Colonel W. Gentry, the staff officer from Puttick's headquarters who had been present all evening, and Lieutenant Roy Farran, who was to command the three tanks that would participate in the planned counterattack.

To Burrows, studying the portly, red-faced brigadier who looked more like a country farmer than a brigade commander, it was apparent that Hargest was very tired. His words were uttered slowly and he hardly completed a sentence; the strain of the attack must have weighed heavily on him. Burrows thought it best not to mention the fact that he had arrived in Platanias with only two of his companies.

In the middle of the conference, Hargest abruptly stopped, looked at the three men, and asked, "Must the attack go on?"[1]

Burrows, Gentry, and Farran looked at each other in complete surprise. It seemed that the brigade commander had lost his zeal for the attack. Hargest mechanically picked up the telephone to call Puttick.

Puttick's reply was brief and to the point: "The attack must go on!"[2]

Hargest put down the phone and stared at it for a few minutes, while the three men watched him in silence. Then he turned to them and asked them to wait for half an hour while he had some sleep.[3]

At 3:30 A.M., some three hours delayed, the counterattack finally began.

Through the waning darkness the New Zealanders picked their way across ditches, into ravines, through bushes, past olive trees, and over walls, moving slowly but surely forward.

A stone house near the beach had been converted by the paratroopers into a strong point. When D Company, on the right flank of the Twentieth Battalion, approached the house, the Germans loosed a withering fire that pinned the New Zealanders down and brought the whole company to a halt. Lieutenant P. Maxwell ordered the platoon to work themselves around the house. Dashing in short spurts toward the flanks, many of the men fell victim to the persistent German fire. With great effort, the New Zealanders finally maneuvered themselves into positions from which they set up a heavy concentration of rifle fire on the house from all directions. It was only a skirmish, but the continuous din of rifle and machine-gun fire gave it the sound of a major battle.

With the first crack of dawn streaking the eastern sky, a handful of paratroopers emerged to give themselves up. As a squad of Maxwell's men went forward to accept the surrender, a few diehard Germans opened fire on them from behind a wall. Angered by this breach of military etiquette, the New Zealanders charged the house. The surviving paratroopers threw down their weapons to spare themselves the fury of the New Zealand bayonets.

This lone stronghold was taken at great expense in time and men. This was one obstacle of many in the path of the major objective ahead, and each would prove to be as strongly fortified. Even worse, the necessary cover of darkness was rapidly disappearing as May 22 dawned.

The din of battle rudely awakened the tired, sleeping Germans. Caught unprepared by the attack, in the confusion some of them rushed out of the houses without their pants while others forgot to put on their boots. But not a single one of them forgot his weapon.[4]

While D Company was clearing its first major objective, its sister company on the left flank was running into even heavier resistance.

From every ditch and from behind every obstacle, rifle and machine-gun fire increased into a heavy concentration against the New Zealanders of C Company. Tracers rained down on them from all directions.

South of the main road, Colonel Dittmer's Maoris advanced steadily against light resistance. Dittmer was surprised to encounter only scattered opposition. The heavy and continuous firing that echoed from the direction of Burrows's two companies, across the road to the north, told him that the advance was not unopposed. Dittmer did not know that in order to avoid the annoying fire from the entrenchments of the Twenty-third Battalion, many paratroopers had shifted their positions to the north of the main road the previous day. Now these paratroopers found themselves deployed in depth before the advancing companies of the Twentieth Battalion. Burrows's earlier suggestion that a reconnaissance patrol precede the counterattack might have pinpointed these emplacements.

Nevertheless, the Maoris did find scattered pockets of resistance in their path, which they quickly eliminated with grenades and handy use of the bayonet.

When the men of Dittmer's battalion crossed the Sfakoriano River, they were joined by Manoli Paterakis and his fellow Cretans—now fighting their own war against the German invaders. They were not the only Cretans to join the attack. As the New Zealanders advanced, other Cretans slipped like ephemeral shadows from their hiding places and, with captured German weapons, took their own toll of the paratroopers.[5]

Paterakis and his men preferred to follow in the wake of the advancing troops, applying their natural skills in stalking the isolated groups of paratroopers who now found themselves behind the New Zealand lines. These fearless Cretans, who had come from all over Crete to help fight the Germans, were proficient at this game of hide-and-seek. They had spent all their lives in the fields hunting game for sustenance. Now they were ferreting out a new species for their survival, and they were taking no prisoners.

The Maoris continued their advance. A platoon from the company on the right flank entered the southern outskirts of Pirgos against heavy opposition. The fighting had become so fierce that even these brave New Zealanders were brought to a standstill.

On the opposite end of the Maoris advance, the company carrying the left flank crossed the Xamoudokori road and captured that village. This brought them to the base of their major objective—Hill 107.

By now it was broad daylight. The paratroopers on Hill 107 could observe the movements of the Maoris and, from their defense positions, could rain mortar and machine-gun fire on them. With daylight came the Messerschmitt 109s, bombing and strafing anything that moved in the fields. The Maoris had no choice but to dig in and hold.

All along the line, the advance had been stopped.

* * *

Lieutenant Roy Farran halted his three Vickers light tanks outside Pirgos and deployed them under some trees for protection from air attack. There he awaited further orders. He dared not advance alone into the village, for he heard that the Germans were using captured Bofors guns as effective field artillery. One shot from a depressed Bofors gun at his thin-skinned vehicles and he would be a tank commander without tanks.[6]

Farran was resting momentarily under the shade of a tree when an angry voice aroused him. It was Captain R. Dawson, Hargest's brigade major. Hargest never left headquarters to visit his forward units, but he relied heavily on his field representatives. Unlike Hargest, Captain Dawson was spirited, vigorous, and aggressive in battle. When the attack faltered, he rushed forward to get it moving again. The first targets of his ire were Farran and his tanks.

Dawson stopped in front of the lead tank and urged the sergeant to move on into the village.

"Get moving . . . there is nothing to worry about except perhaps small-arms fire!"[7]

The sergeant looked back at his troop commander, just then climbing into the second tank. Farran waved him forward. The lieutenant shook his head disapprovingly, knowing that it would be suicide for any tank to venture into that hornet's nest without infantry support.

"I know," he muttered to his driver, "that the first tank will get it!"[8]

The sergeant rode the lead tank down the highway into the village of Pirgos. As he approached an intersection, a Borfors gun roared from behind the cemetery wall. The shell struck the tank just below the turret, wounding the gunner. The driver spun the tank around, and the wounded gunner sprayed the German gun crew with its machine guns. Then a second Bofors barked, hitting the tank broadside, killing the crew and setting it afire.

The tank column was observed by a passing flight of ME 109s. No sooner had the first tank burst into flames than the Messerschmitts dived to strafe them. Their bullets hit the light-armored tanks like molten rivets. The crew members covered their faces to protect themselves from the hot flakes of burning metal flying off inside.

Farran halted his vehicle beneath a tall tree for protection, but to no avail. The bullets ripped through the branches, striking the metallic hull in a persistent patter. Like a huge animal trying to avoid repeated bee stings, Farran spun, turned, and backed his tank, finally crashing into a field of bamboo.[9]

One of the tank's bogey wheels was broken, and the frustrated lieutenant inspected the damage that, for the moment, had put him out of action. He ordered the third tank not to proceed, for he feared that it would meet the same fate that had greeted the luckless lead tank.

Long before Burrows's messenger contacted D Company of his battalion with orders to resume the attack, Lieutenant Maxwell and his men had reached the eastern perimeter of the airfield. They had suffered many casualties during their advance along the coastal strip; most of the officers had been killed or wounded. Maxwell considered himself lucky, for he was the only officer to remain unhurt.

When he and the remainder of the company reached the edge of the airfield, they were amazed at what they saw. From their hiding places in bushes and behind trees, they watched in awe as transport after transport circled and landed on the congested airstrip. Disabled Junkers were pushed aside by what looked like a tank. It was in fact an abandoned Matilda—one of the ill-fated infantry tanks from Colonel Andrew's unsuccessful attack on the twentieth—used as a bulldozer to make landing space available for the arriving transports.

No sooner did a transport come to a halt than the hatches on either side opened, twenty-five to forty troopers jumping out. Officers and noncoms in the field guided the new arrivals directly into the battle line. Junker 52s landed, unloaded, and departed, making room for others. The roar of motors was a continuous din that easily drowned out the sounds of battle.

Private Amos knelt next to Lieutenant Maxwell and looked on in frustration. "Sir," he said, "I've carried this antitank rifle all this way and I now am going to have a shot!"[10] With that he loaded the rifle and fired two shots at a transport just as it rolled to a stop. Both shots hit the aircraft: The first one caused it to smoke and the second blew it up. Private Amos smiled proudly.

Now fully aware of their presence so dangerously close to the airfield, the Germans on Hill 107 showered D Company with heavy mortar and machine-gun fire. The concentration was so intense that D Company had to withdraw to less exposed positions away from the airfield perimeter. Lieutenant Maxwell realized that if crossing the airfield in the daylight would be difficult, capturing it would be impossible.[11]

Coming up south of Pirgos, the Maoris Company nearest the highway pressed forward in its own attack on the village. The men from Burrows's C Company had been brought to a standstill in the center, and the Maoris were having an equally difficult time on the outskirts.

Not only were they receiving frontal fire from the houses south of the village, but mortar and machine-gun fire rained down onto their flank from the lower slopes of Hill 107. Nevertheless the hardy Maoris pressed on, disregarding the storm of bullets. It was an indescribable feat of heroism and perseverance in the face of such deadly opposition.

Major H. G. Dyer, the executive officer of the Twenty-eighth Battalion, marveled at the Maoris' drive. He kept repeating to the battalion sergeant major, "We must get forward and get above and around the Germans." Sergeant A. C. Wood nodded his head in agreement as he took aim and fired at a German running between the trees.[12]

Germans were firing their tommy guns from behind every tree, dodging from tree to tree as the Maoris approached. Dyer led his men in small groups against each position, wiping out one only to have two others open fire from another position farther ahead.

Wood, the redoubtable sergeant major, led a shouting group of Maoris in a bayonet charge against a platoon of paratroopers who had set up a strong point in a stone house. It was a wild melee, and when the yells and screams subsided, the Maoris held the stone house. All the paratroopers had been shot or speared by bayonets.

The energetic commander of the Maoris hustled through the field to his battalion's left flank. Colonel Dittmer wanted to know why his advance company—which had already captured Xamoudokori village and reached the southern base of Hill 107—had not seized the hill. Its capture would eliminate the harassing fire that was tearing into the company on the right flank and hindering its advance on Pirgos.

When he reached the company's forward positions, he found the men dug in or under cover. Standing before them with his hands on his hips, in full view of the watchful Germans on the hill, he shouted angrily at his men: "Call yourselves bloody soldiers?'' His face got red as he pointed up the hill with his swagger stick. ''Let's move!''[13]

With that command, he plunged forward into a storm of bullets and mortar shells, his men following close at his heels.

It did not take long for Dittmer to realize why his brave Maoris had sought cover. The fiery wall of machine-gun and mortar fire was an obstacle too formidable even for them to overcome.[14]

By midday Major Burrows had finally been reinforced by the arrival of his other company, but it was too late. His two attacking companies had taken heavy casualties during the day, and the survivors were dropping from sheer exhaustion. Added to this was the sad fact that the day's battle had depleted the battalion's supply of ammunition, hand grenades, and mortar shells. What might have succeeded earlier with a force of four fresh attacking companies could fail now in the face of increasing German resistance.

Burrows decided to alter his phase of the attack plan. He would bring all his companies south of the road and help Dittmer in an assault that would capture Hill 107. With this idea in mind, he dispatched Lieutenant C. H. Upham to carry the withdrawal order to D Company.

Upham took his batman, Sergeant Kirk, with him. When he reached the D Company positions, he saw the same spectacle on the airfield that had awed Maxwell and his men. When Upham finally returned with D Company behind him, he commented to Burrows, ''The mortar and machine-gun fire on the open ground was very heavy, and we were lucky to get back alive.'' Adding, ''With another hour of darkness, we could have reached the far side of the 'drome.' ''[15] Now, in broad daylight, it was too late.

Burrows conferred with Dittmer again in the shade of a grape arbor. He was dismayed to learn that the Maoris' advance had been stalled by superior German fire power and by those accursed Messerschmitts. With the Maoris at a standstill, Burrows's revised plan of attack had no purpose. The counterattack was failing, but the diehard Dittmer would not accept defeat.

''No!'' he said with determination. ''There is a way . . . we need help, and I'm going to get it!''[16]

General Hargest had finally awakened from his severe case of nerves which, the night before, had caused him to request cancellation of the counterattack. Now, with the dawn of a new day, he took a different view of the attack and of its result. He wired his division commander:

> STEADY FLOW OF ENEMY PLANES LANDING AND TAKING OFF.
> MAY BE TRYING TO TAKE TROOPS OFF.[17]

When Lieutenant Farran returned to get the fitters to repair his tank, he reported what happened to his lead tank and the stiff resistance encountered by the attacking battalions.

Other reports indicated that the Germans were landing men in droves and were being supplied artillery and motorcycles from the arriving transports. In spite of these frontline reports, Hargest sent another wire still filled with misguided optimism:

> BECAUSE ELEVEN FIRES HAVE BEEN LIT ON 'DROME, IT APPEARS
> AS THOUGH ENEMY MIGHT BE PREPARING EVACUATION.[18]

Colonel Dittmer quickly covered the three-quarter mile back to the headquarters of the Twenty-third Battalion. If he was going to get help to resume the attack, it would have to come from Leckie's battalion. After all, he thought to himself as he wiped the dust and perspiration from his face, the Twenty-third has not seen action since the first day of the invasion. Leckie's men are rested and fit for combat. He felt certain that their assistance would turn the tide.

He found Colonel Leckie in his headquarters having lunch with Colonel Andrew of the Twenty-second Battalion. Good! he muttered to himself at the sight of Andrew. He knew that Andrew had three companies intact, and they could hold down the fort while the Twenty-third Battalion followed him back to Hill 107.

Colonel Leckie did not share the enthusiasm or aggressive leadership that inspired Dittmer. He was surprised by the request, because he was under the impression—based on incorrect information received from stragglers—that the Twentieth Battalion had withdrawn from the attack.

"My dear Dittmer," he replied, sipping a cup of tea, "I really feel that you chaps cannot make any more progress without more infantry and artillery."

Colonel Andrew muttered concurrence. Dittmer looked at them, incredulous at their lack of enthusiasm. "That's why I am here—for more infantry!"

Leckie turned a deaf ear: "I think the best course would be to hold what ground you have and stop the enemy infiltration that is constantly going on."[19]

Dittmer left Leckie's headquarters angered by this shortsighted refusal. Without the assistance he sought, the counterattack was doomed to failure.

By early afternoon Hargest's optimism began to wane. All reports indicated that Maleme airfield was the door through which the Germans gained strength in arms and men. At 1325 hours he wired Puttick and admitted that the "situation was confused." He added:

TROOPS *NOT* AS FORWARD ON LEFT AS BELIEVED. OFFICERS ON GROUND BELIEVE ENEMY PREPARING FOR ATTACK AND TAKING SERIOUS VIEW.

Yet in spite of all the on-the-spot information reaching him from the men in the front lines of battle, he went on:

I DISAGREE, OF COURSE.

And instead of hurrying to get a clearer view of the battle situation, he went in the opposite direction, informing Puttick:

[I] WILL VISIT YOUR H.Q. WHEN BRIGADE MAJOR RETURNS.[20]

Colonel Dittmer returned to his battalion still seething over Leckie's refusal. He informed Burrows of the situation and then gave orders that his battalion withdraw to the safety of a valley southeast of Pirgos. The counterattack was over.

As dusk began to fall over the hills and valleys, Colonel Bernhard Ramcke, the new German field commander who had relieved the wounded General Meindl, mustered the newly arrived mountain troops for an attack.

Three companies from the Second Battalion of the Eighty-fifth Mountain Regiment were ordered to counterattack the New Zealanders and smash their forward line. Ramcke felt that the time was ripe and that the exhausted, depleted ranks of the Maoris would scatter before these newly arrived mountain troops.

The Maoris watched the German preparations from behind the twisted olive trees of an orchard on the reverse slope of a hill. Slowly the Germans advanced through the fields. Major Dyer watched them as they crossed the valley carrying a huge flag with a black swastika in its center, suspended from two poles. Dyer reflected that it looked more like a military procession than men preparing for an attack.[21]

Through the fields, the valley, and up the hill the excited Germans advanced, some singing, some shouting, some firing.

At the crest of the hill, they threw hand grenades and then charged over the top.

The Maoris were waiting for them. Slowly the gallant New Zealanders, who had already suffered so much that day, opened fire on the Germans. Then, singly or in groups, with knees bent and firing from the hip, they moved forward to meet the charging enemy. Major Dyer watched as force met force on the reverse slope of the hill.

When the Maoris had spent their ammunition, they broke into a run with bayonets held level. From their throats came the Maoris' battle cry, "Ah! Ah! Ah!"

The advance rank of Germans went down to Maori fire, the second and third ranks watching stupefied as the short, shouting men came at them with bayonets held high. Bullets whined into the Maoris' ranks and many fell dead or wounded, but they kept on coming. The Germans could take no more: They turned and fled down the hill and through the valley back to their starting point, with the pursuing Maoris hot on their heels. Dyer, laughing at what he described as the "Huns with their fat behinds to us running for their lives," raced after the Maoris to keep them from going too far.[22]

It had also been a weary, daylong ordeal for the men and ships of the Mediterranean Fleet. The score indicated that the Germans, after an all-out effort, lost only two planes as definites, with six probably lost and five damaged—a mere pittance compared with the Royal Navy's loss of two cruisers and one destroyer, with severe damage to two mighty battleships and swift cruisers. It was *not* an even exchange! When Admiral Sir Andrew Cunningham heard the tragic news of the day's losses, he ordered the

whole squadron back to Alexandria. The time had come to take
stock, and to review the disastrous results of this day.[23]

Captain Lord Louis Mountbatten, cousin to King George VI of
England, left the beleaguered island of Malta on Wednesday night,
May 21, planning to join Admiral Rawlings's force by 10:00 A.M.
the next day. However, though they had an uneventful trip,
Mountbatten's flotilla of five destroyers—comprising the flagship
*Kelly*, and the *Kashmir*, the *Kelvin*, the *Kipling*, and the *Jackal*—
did not join Rawlings's squadron until 4:00 P.M. on May 22.
They were just in time to take defensive positions against the
German air attacks that had been in progress all day.

Later that night, Rawlings ordered Mountbatten to take the
*Kelly, Kashmir,* and *Kipling* north in search of survivors from the
*Fiji* sinking. The destroyers *Kelvin* and *Jackal* were dispatched
on a similar mission, to seek out survivors of the cruiser *Gloucester.* (The British did not know that a German air-sea rescue operation had picked up as many as 500 of the *Gloucester* survivors.)

After the rescue mission was recalled, Mountbatten regrouped
his ships—with the exception of the destroyers *Kelvin* and *Jackal,*
which had left earlier on their own to rejoin Rawlings's group—
and pursued an active evening against the Germans.

As May 23 dawned, the *Kelly* became the next target, as 24
dive-bombers now concentrated on the two destroyers. Speeding
and maneuvering at thirty knots, Mountbatten's flagship was
struck by a huge bomb on the rear turret. She stopped dead in the
water, listing heavily to port. Mountbatten watched the launching
of all available rafts and boats before giving the order to abandon
ship. The *Kelly* slowly turned turtle and floated in that position a
half-hour before sinking, giving her survivors ample time to get
clear of the ship.[24]

Now the only remaining destroyer came to the rescue. Commander A. St. Clare-Ford of the *Kipling* lowered all her lifeboats
and rafts, still fighting off the ever-present dive-bombers. During
a lull in the attack, she would sweep in to rescue the *Kelly* survivors, including Mountbatten. When the German divebombers
returned, the *Kipling* maneuvered quickly away, dodging bombs
as she sped across the water. At the next lull, the plucky destroyer
returned to pick up the *Kashmir* survivors. Satisfied that she had
done all she could, she turned and headed for the safety of Alexandria. From 8:20 A.M., when she stood alone after the *Kelly* and
*Kashmir* had been sunk, until she departed those perilous waters

at 1:00 P.M., the *Kipling* had warded off at least forty individual attacks and avoided some eighty-three bombs. It was a miracle that she survived unscathed.[25]

Back in Athens, in the second floor war room of General Student's headquarters in the Grande Bretagne Hotel, details of the New Zealand counterattack were coming in hourly.

Student followed the reports closely. By late evening on May 22, the commander of the Eleventh Air Corps received the satisfying news that a total of three battalions from the Fifth Mountain Division, together with artillery and a field hospital, had landed safely in the course of the day. Student smiled with relief. To all appearances, the airfield at Maleme was securely controlled by the Germans. Always confident that his plan would work against any adversity if given the chance, he now felt that the danger was over.

Since the evening of May 19, when the invasion of Crete began, Student had taken his meals at his desk in the war room. Now he left to go to dinner.

Seated at his private table in the headquarters dining room with his chief of staff, Student remarked that the scale of battle seemed to be swinging in their favor.

"If the enemy," he added in retrospect, "had made a united all-out effort in counterattacking during the night from the 20th to the 21st, or in the morning of the 21st, then the very tired remnants of the Sturm Regiment . . . could have been wiped out."[26]

In London, Churchill followed the battle closely through dispatches. He was aware that this had been a hard day both for the New Zealanders in Crete and for Admiral Cunningham's Mediterranean Fleet.

At first, he was elated to hear that the German convoy had been intercepted and destroyed. But his elation was shortlived, for in the course of the day, he was informed of the loss of the destroyer *Greyhound* and of the two heavy cruisers *Gloucester* and *Fiji*. He realized that without an airfield in effective range, he could not order the Royal Air Force into action either to help the New Zealand defense or to fly protective cover for the Mediterranean Fleet.

Deeply concerned that Crete's strategic position be maintained

at all costs, his words were emphatic when he wired General
Wavell in North Africa:

CRETE BATTLE MUST BE WON.[27]

Anticipating Churchill's concern, Wavell had already ordered that
900 men from the Queen's Royal Regiment, together with the
headquarters staff of the Sixteenth Infantry Brigade and some
eighteen vehicles, set sail for Crete. In the late afternoon of this
third day of battle, the special service ship *Glenroy* left Alexandria for Tymbaki, a fishing village on the southern coast of the
island.

While Wavell was at last awakening to the fact that Crete
needed reinforcements, Churchill sent off another message to his
dear friend General Freyberg:

THE WHOLE WORLD IS WATCHING YOUR SPLENDID BATTLE, ON
WHICH GREAT EVENTS TURN.[28]

# 22 / "MALTA WOULD CONTROL THE MEDITERRANEAN"

## MAY 23–24, 1941

General Freyberg was disheartened when he heard the counterattack had failed.

Later in the afternoon on May 22, Freyberg summoned Puttick to his headquarters for a conference. The New Zealand divisional commander arrived at 5:00 P.M., at which time Freyberg expressed his wishes for a new counterattack. "I want the Fifth Brigade to attack en bloc!"[1]

The lean-faced Puttick seemed skeptical. Freyberg noticed the hesitation and, to make the idea more acceptable, added: "I shall release to you the Eighth Australians and the Eighteenth New Zealanders from the Fourth Brigade."

Puttick's expression did not change, nor did he appear enthusiastic about the whole idea. The Creforce commander stared at him and, in a firm if not stern voice, intoned: "By my order!"[2]

For the first time since the battle for the island had begun, Freyberg was not diffident in interfering with his subordinate commanders. For the first time, he *ordered* an attack.

Brigadier Hargest listened quietly, but with increasing irritation, as his division commander forwarded Freyberg's order. Puttick's unenthusiastic mood must have been contagious. After a few minutes of silence, Hargest reacted with a flurry of pessimistic protests.

"My men are not fit for further attack," his tired voice rasped over the phone. It was a remark that would have angered the gallant Dittmer and his brave Maori or the intrepid Burrows and the determined men of the Twentieth Battalion. "Besides," he added, "they are exhausted!"[3]

When Puttick catalogued this report with Hargest's glum picture of the situation, he decided to contact Freyberg and request a reversal of the earlier order to counterattack.

"I do not like the suggestion of a withdrawal, Puttick,"[4] replied the Creforce commander, annoyed at Puttick's suggestion that the Fifth Brigade be withdrawn from its present position. "Why not relieve Hargest's men with the two battalions I released to you and let Hargest pull his men back to reorganize?"

Once again the Creforce commander reverted to his earlier habit of suggesting rather than ordering.

"How could we expect two battalions to hold what five could not?"[5] was Puttick's response. Puttick did not know that Hargest had never utilized the full strength of all his battalions in a concerted effort.[5]

"Very well," Freyberg acceded, dismay evident in the tone of his voice. "I'll send Stewart down to your headquarters, and you can draw up the details for the withdrawal."[6]

Freyberg replaced the phone and slowly resigned himself to the idea that his original order to counterattack had somehow been converted to an order for withdrawal. He realized that with this decision, all hope of recapturing Maleme airfield had to be abandoned.

On the same night that Puttick, Hargest, and Stewart were planning the withdrawal of their forces, Major General Julius Ringel, the commanding general of the Fifth Mountain Division, landed at Maleme airfield. He immediately assumed the command of all German troops in western Crete.

The goateed, nattily dressed former head of the Austrian army's Nazi party, carried with him revised orders from the Fourth Air Fleet. He was instructed to secure Maleme airfield, advance and clear Suda Bay, relieve the surrounded paratroopers at Rethimnon, make contact with Iráklion, and last but not least, occupy the whole island. Ringel planned to fulfill each part of the order exactly as prescribed in his written orders.

Ringel's arrival marked a change in the field command of the whole operation—it was no longer an all-Luftwaffe affair. Ringel was a Wehrmacht officer who carried with him into Crete the support and professionalism of the militarists of the German army. "Now we will see results!" opined the Wehrmacht staff officers of the German Army High Command.[7]

The new commanding general let it be understood that he was in complete control. He sent a radio message to Colonel Heidrich in Prison Valley informing him that effective immediately Group

Center and Group West were to be combined into a single force referred to as Ringel Group. All paratroop survivors in the Maleme area were placed into a single group under the command of Colonel Ramcke. Once Ringle's command had been asserted, he sat down to plan the operation that would end the battle of Crete in a decisive German victory.

Ringel explained to his staff that by next morning, he wanted Maleme airfield to be fully operational. That same afternoon ME-109s would use the airfield as a forward base, thus offering continuous air support to the attacking German columns. During the course of day, he expected the arrival of two batteries of the Ninety-fifth Mountain Artillery Regiment, the Ninety-fifth Anti-tank Battalion with 50-mm antitank guns, the Fifty-fifth Motorcycle Battalion, and the first battalions of the One Hundred Forty-first Mountain Regiment. Within twenty-four hours, he stated that the full strength of the mountain division would be in the battle.[8]

All this would be happening at Maleme airfield, a door that Hargest had left open to the Germans.

It was 10:00 P.M. before General Puttick and Freyberg's chief of staff, Colonel Stewart, completed the details of the withdrawal.

In a series of continuous movements, the whole of the Fifth Brigade would be pulled back to a point east of Platanias, where its left flank would link up with the Tenth Brigade in the Prison Valley—Galatas area. The disorganized Twenty-second Battalion would go in reserve within the ranks of Brigadier Inglis's Fourth Brigade. The Seventh Australian Battalion, which relieved Major Burrows's Twentieth New Zealanders east of Khaniá the night before, would join its sister unit—the Eighth Australians—and protect the New Zealand left flank at the village of Perivolia. Colonel Dittmer's Twenty-eighth Maori Battalion, deployed in the hard-fought positions east of Pirgos and situated closest to the Germans, would be the last to depart. They would fight as the rear guard, protecting the brigade's retreat.

Puttick called the commander of the Fifth Brigade with the news, andrelated the withdrawal plan to him. Hargest received the new orders with a sigh of relief, and immediately dispatched his brigade major to relay the order to the line battalions.

The first men to hear the news were the medics of the brigade's field ambulance, located on a low hill near Modhion village. Captain Palmer and most of the other off-duty medics awakened to the disappointing orders to pull out. What surprised the sleepy men most was that they thought everything was going well.[9]

Quickly the men transferred the movable wounded to stretchers and then carefully and silently began the long trip. They moved down the hilly slope until they reached the main road and then, turning eastward, headed for Platanias. The wounded who could not be moved were left behind with medical personnel who volunteered to stay and care for them.

When Colonel Dittmer was told that his Maoris had to forsake all the ground they gained through such bitter fighting, his face turned crimson with anger. And when Dawson informed him that his battalion had been delegated to act as the rear guard, the brave colonel became furious.

"My men have fought hard for this ground, and to have to leave it—" Dittmer protested, pointing out the many casualties his unit had suffered. "Now you tell me that I am to be the rear guard!" He continued in a rude vein, expressing himself in well-chosen words that made his sergeant major smile with pride. Dittmer knew that once the Germans discovered the retreat, the full fury of their fire would fall on the rear-guard unit—his Maoris.[10]

The movement began after midnight. The units withdrew slowly, climbing down the steep sides of cliffs, marching through ravines and over hills, past glades of bamboo, through wheatfields, arbors, and olive groves. The men trekked through terrain that had been painfully won in battle.

They were resentful, but sworn to follow orders, not a single man disobeyed. They trudged eastward mile after mile with a discipline that made their officers proud. The wounded were carried on makeshift stretchers, while the stronger carried the weapons of the fatigued.

The last to receive the order were the men of the artillery units, who were not contacted until 4:00 A.M. It was too late for them to hitch up their guns and move within the protective line of the rear guard, so gun after gun was destroyed before being abandoned. Two 3.7-inch howitzers and three 75-mm fieldpieces were included—guns that might have been useful later. A truck with its cannon in tow slipped off the edge of the road and spilled down a ravine. Left without their cannon, the crews joined the Twenty-eighth Maori as infantrymen to help in the rear-guard action.

* * *

It was daylight before Captain Dawson, the brigade major, reached the headquarters of the Twenty-third Battalion. The battalion commander took one look at him and saw fatigue written all over his face. Dawson slumped heavily into a field chair, and in a slow, tired voice said, "I have some very surprising news for you."

"What, have they tossed it in?" asked Colonel Leckie, who, seeing the new day dawn peacefully, assumed the Germans had departed during the night.

"You are to return to the Platanias River line," was Dawson's answer. Then he added, with half-closed eyes, "The withdrawal of your battalion was supposed to have started half an hour ago."

Leckie masked his surprise, but before issuing orders for the movement, he gave the sleepy Dawson a blanket, comforting him with, "Here, have a sleep . . . I will awaken you in good time."[11]

By first light the aggressive Colonel Ramcke found the morning stillness unusual, and sensed something afoot. A reconnaissance patrol reported that they had not encountered any opposition—not a shot fired at them and not a New Zealander in sight.

Ramcke slapped his fist down triumphantly. "They have retreated," he declared with finality.[12]

The word that the New Zealanders were retreating raced through the German lines. Kurt Meyer, the war correspondent, had now attached himself to a battalion of mountain troops. He could not believe that the New Zealanders were retreating; he felt that they must have misunderstood the situation.

"Either they overestimated our forces," he noted, "or they supposed that we could go into an attack with only a handful of mountain troops."[13]

"Nonsense," replied Colonel August Wittmann, the commanding officer of the One Hundred Eleventh Mountain Artillery Regiment, newly arrived and unscarred by battle. "They have lost their nerve!"[14]

With the sun rising higher each passing hour, the paratroopers moved slowly and carefully forward through the grim landscape of the battlefield. Wherever they looked, trees were bullet-torn or splintered, fields were scarred by discolored earth churned up by exploding shells, shattered vehicles and dead mules lay all around, the blackened walls of some cottages still smoldered, and worst of all were the hundreds of dead paratroopers.

Captain Gericke, the battalion commander of the Fourth Parachute Assault Battalion, led his paratroopers into an area east of Pirgos and into the fields and groves beyond, and there he solved the mystery of what had happened to Major Scherber and the Third Assault Battalion of the Storm Regiment. The scene was frightful to behold; it was a field of carnage.

It was painful even for an experienced soldier like Gericke to accept the nightmarish vista before him. The green fields had turned blue-gray, carpeted with the uniforms of dead paratroopers. The olive trees were covered with the silk of parachutes from which hung paratroopers suspended from their harnesses, swinging in the breeze. Others lay in the fields where they had fallen, their parachutes half covering them like shrouds. There were still other paratroopers, dead in the grass, singly or in groups, amidst the debris of helmets, ammunition boxes, weapons, grenades, and bandages. All over the corpses, big, fat, blue flies clustered like vultures.

Hardened as they were, many of Gericke's men vomited at the sight.[15]

Ringel's mountain troops in the center were held back by brief and bitter skirmishes with the stubborn Maoris of the Twenty-eighth Battalion. But the Germans were persistent, following close behind the retreating rear guard. Messerschmitts were out in full force, flying overhead in support of their comrades on the ground, but the fluid battle lines made it difficult for them to pick out targets. The Maoris were aided by this close-quarter fighting.

Three times the Maoris had to stop and fight off their pursuers. The Germans towed several captured Bofors guns and manhandled them into line, firing at the Maoris from a range of 300 yards.

Major Dyer, the battalion's executive officer, led his men up to a wooded creek just west of Platanias village, reaching it by midday. Safety was just a few hundred yards away—a dash through a field and up the face of a ridge. Dyer turned to his men: "We must get up that hill—let's move!"

They dashed for the ridge, every man for himself.

The Germans kept up a steady fire, and the captured Bofors barked repeatedly, slamming shell after shell at the Maoris. A shell exploded on Dyers's left, and when he looked, he saw that his sergeant had been decapitated.

In one last rush, the men of the rear guard reached the safety of the new defense perimeter, leaving many of their friends lying in the fields behind them. It was now 2:00 P.M. on the fourth day of battle.[16]

By the side of the road beyond Platanias, where it curves toward Galatas, Colonel Kippenberger, the commanding officer of the Tenth Brigade, stood watching a group of men marching past. When Major Burrows walked by, Kippenberger realized that these men represented the depleted ranks of the Twentieth Battalion—the unit Kippenberger had commanded in Greece.

He saw their torn and dirty uniforms, observed the tired, listless way they marched, and, *for the first time in Crete, recognized the painful signs of defeat.*[17]

If Captain Walter Gericke's advance through the fields east of Pirgos solved the mystery of what happened to Major Sherber's Third Assault Battalion during the first day of the invasion, there now remained a second mystery: Where was Oberleutnant Peter Muerbe and his detachment of seventy-two paratroopers?

When General Ringel completed the deployment of the troops under his new command, he ordered that one Kampfgruppe advance westward toward the village of Kastelli at the base of Kisamos Bay. He ordered Major Schaette and his Ninety-fifth Engineer Battalion to secure those positions.

Schaette's men advanced robustly at first until they came within a few miles of the eastern approach to Kastelli. At that point, their attitude changed, as they crossed the fields where Lieutenant Muerbe and his paratroopers had met the men of the First Greek Regiment.

The grim scene that greeted Captain Gericke east of Pirgos now reappeared in all its horror before Major Schaette and his soldiers. The fields were strewn with the blackened, bloated corpses of Muerbe's men. What shocked the Germans most of all was that many of them had apparently met their deaths not by bullets but by the distinct slashes and punctures of knives and swords—or by having their skulls bashed in. To an impeccable officer like Schaette, this was not warfare but an act of atrocity.

"Obviously," he surmised incorrectly, "these men had been executed after their surrender."[18]

The thought never occurred to him that the defenders had no bullets with which to repel the invaders and had resorted to the age-old weaponry of knife and club.

As the Germans advanced toward Kastelli, they were exposed to sporadic fire from the outlying positions of Battalion A of the First Greek Regiment. It was getting dark, and Schaette did not relish the thought of continuing with his troops into unreconnoitered territory where hidden Cretan snipers could ambush them. He decided to halt his advance for the night. When he reported his position to General Ringel, he made certain to mention the "atrocities."

For three days after Muerbe's attack, the men of the First Greek Regiment rested in the peaceful countryside. They could hear the roar of battle far to the east at Maleme, but there was not a single German near them to disturb the uneasy tranquility; the only Germans around were the seventeen parachutists still detained in the town's jailhouse.

When the outposts reported on May 23 that the Germans were approaching in force, the men of the First Greek Regiment realized their temporary respite had ended.

The next morning the terrors of the sky—the dreaded Stukas and the feared Messerschmitts—appeared over Kastelli. They represented the first blow that General Ringel would use to destroy "those bestial hordes" at Kastelli.

For more than an hour, the Stuka dive-bombers ranged over the town, diving from heights of 4,000 feet to almost treetop level before releasing their bombs. At such low altitudes, they could not miss. Some squadrons carried 110-pound bombs, which they dropped in clusters of four. Other Stukas came down with 1,100-pound high-explosive bombs, aimed at the buildings in the town.

The men in Battalion A on the eastern perimeter of the town listened to the heavy bombardment and feared for the lives of their wives and children. Some of these men, still considering themselves civilians rather than soldiers, left their positions to seek out their families.

The ferocity of the Stuka attack suggested to Major Thomas Bedding, the New Zealand military advisor to the Greek Regiment, that it was a softening-up process before the renewal of the German ground attack. Just as he turned to give Lieutenant Baigent new orders for the Greek regimental staff, a 1,000-pound bomb exploded outside the coffeehouse, showering the occupants with pieces of masonry and wood and choking them with dust.

At the same time, another bomb hit the jailhouse, knocking out its front wall. The prisoners rushed through the opening, attacking and taking weapons from the surprised guards. Picking up additional rifles along the way, they headed for Bedding's headquarters.

No sooner had Lieutenant Baigent dusted himself off than he left to carry out Bedding's orders. He did not get far beyond the front door when heavy rifle fire forced him to return. Bedding grasped the situation in a moment and led the young lieutenant out the rear door into a narrow alley. One end of the alley was blocked with debris; when they turned in the other direction, they ran into Germans coming at them through the heavy clouds of dust that still filled the air. They ran back into the *kafenion,* or coffeehouse, only to come face to face with the muzzles of rifles held by paratroopers who had entered through the front door. They were prisoners; the captors had become the captives.

Lieutenants Campbell and York from Bedding's staff learned of their commanding officer's capture and planned to rescue him. They rounded up some Greeks led by a Sergeant Argyropoulos, and together with a few others, rushed the coffeehouse. The Germans, who were enjoying their newly found freedom, had armed themselves with a Bren gun, in addition to Enfields and grenades, and had taken good defense positions amidst the broken walls of the *kafenion.* The Greek sergeant led his men in a wild charge against heavy fire. His men were easily cut down, but Sergeant Argyropoulos managed to get into the house before the Germans killed him. Lieutenant Campbell was also killed in the skirmish, leaving Lieutenant York no alternative but to withdraw with the survivors. Major Bedding remained a prisoner of the Germans.

Major Schaette's advance from the east resumed as soon as the Stukas completed their devastating work. The men from Battalion A resisted as long as their ammunition held out, resorting to the use of the bayonet once it was spent. Major Nicholas Skordilis, the commanding officer of the battalion, led his men in countless bayonet charges against the well-armed engineers of the mountain division, but they always fell short of the German line. It was a heroic but fruitless effort that left over 200 Greeks, together with their battalion commander, dead in front of the German guns.

By noon, Schaette and his engineers had reached the center of Kastelli.

Major Emmanuel Kourkoutis, who had deployed his men from Battalion B on the western side of the town and around the harbor, continued the resistance for another three days. Making good use of the weapons captured from the ill-fated Muerbe detachment, they made Schaette's men pay in blood for each yard of their advance. But the captured rifles and machine guns used by the Greeks were no match for the artillery brought up by the engineers. What subsequently developed into a house-by-house resistance was methodically crushed by Schaette's men. Shells from antitank guns blasted the houses, which the gallant Greeks had turned into strong points. It was a bitter resistance to the death; the Germans took no prisoners. Those few Greeks who did survive the onslaught slipped off into the southern hills under the cover of darkness.

By May 27 all of Kastelli, including the harbor, had been secured by the engineers of the Ninety-fifth Pioneer Battalion.

In that final attack, which had begun on May 23, Schaette utilized the power of the Stukas and Messerschmitts from above and the massive firepower of machine guns and artillery on the ground against the rifles and bayonets of the outnumbered men from the First Greek Regiment. Yet it still took the Germans four days to secure their objective.

Now that Major Schaette had completed the capture of Kastelli, he turned his attention to the unfinished business of finding a scapegoat upon whom to vent his wrath for the "execution" of the paratroopers from the Muerbe detachment.

The circumstances of their death suggested to him an "atrocity" committed by the local inhabitants. "They must be punished!" he repeated in his report to the commanding general of the mountain division.

From the first hour that Julius Ringel assumed command in Crete, he was informed about the surprising opposition of the civilian population. (Admiral Canaris's Bureau of Military Intelligence—the Abwehr—had reported that the Cretans were Germanophiles who would greet them with open arms.)

The Abwehr's intelligence staff had failed to evaluate the history of Crete in their bitter struggle against another oppressor—the Turk. All that an Abwehr agent had to do was step into a

Cretan home—simple and austere as it was—and observe the family photographs that adorned the walls. Portraits of grandfathers, fathers, husbands, and sons—the Kapetans of Cretan tradition—dressed in their native costume, rifle in hand, pistol and knife at the belt, and bandoleers across the chest, would have given him an indication of what to expect.

Though there were international regulations governing the treatment of enemy soldiers in uniform, not a single word referred to civilians—whether men, women, or children—fighting as soldiers without uniforms. When Major Schaette's report about Muerbe at Kastelli arrived, Ringel decided that he had heard enough.

With the finality of a judge rendering a verdict, he concurred that "they must be punished!"[19]

On May 23 a memorandum was issued at the headquarters of the Fifth Mountain Division:

THE GREEK POPULATION, IN CIVILIAN OR GERMAN UNIFORMS, IS TAKING PART IN THE FIGHTING. THEY ARE . . . MUTILATING AND ROBBING CORPSES . . . ANY GREEK CIVILIAN TAKEN WITH A FIREARM IN HIS HANDS IS TO BE SHOT IMMEDIATELY.

And, finally, the words that would begin a pogrom of senseless executions, first in Crete and later in other occupied countries:

HOSTAGES (MEN BETWEEN 18 AND 55) ARE TO BE TAKEN FROM THE VILLAGES . . . AND IF ACTS OF HOSTILITY AGAINST THE GERMAN ARMY TAKE PLACE . . . WILL BE SHOT IMMEDIATELY . . . 10 GREEKS WILL DIE FOR EVERY GERMAN![20]

On the airfield at Maleme, a group of fifteen Cretan civilians had been ordered to help unload the Junker transports that were bringing supplies for the mountain troops. The captives refused the order, and a delegation of three approached an officer at the end of the runway contending that they could not in good conscience obey an order that would aid the Germans against their own people. The German lieutenant turned his back on them and walked away, openly ignoring their persistent protests. The Cretans followed him.

Suddenly the German spun around angrily, pistol in hand. His Luger coughed three times in rapid succession. Although the sound was smothered by the roar of transport motors, the horror of the scene would be long remembered by the other prisoners. Stepping over the three sprawled bodies, the German motioned the other Cretans back to work.[21]

At Kastelli, Ringel's memorandum was all Major Schaette required to enable him to satisfy his lust for revenge. He was still fuming at the bitter resistance that delayed his capture of Kastelli, an anger compounded by his false impression that atrocities had been perpetrated on the paratroopers of the Muerbe detachment.

Squads of soldiers from his Ninety-fifth Engineer Battalion were ordered to round up all Cretan males in the surrounding countryside and to bring them to his command post in the center of town. Within a few hours, 200 villagers were herded in front of Schaette's headquarters and made to stand in ranks in the dusty, debris-filled town square. Many of them bore the wounds of the recent battle, yet they stood proud and disdainful in the hot sun. They did not know that Schaette had given orders for their execution.

When Major Bedding heard of the order, he protested vehemently. "There is no justifiable reason for these people to be executed," he argued. "Your soldiers were killed in the course of the battle!" The seventeen paratroopers who had been held prisoners in the jailhouse added assurances that they had been properly treated by their captors. Nevertheless, in spite of these protests and assurances, Schaette wanted his revenge. He ordered the executions to begin.[22]

Stavros Beroukakis, a villager who looked older than his years, approached Major Bedding, imploring him to intercede in his behalf. His fourteen-year-old son, John, was among the 200 condemned hostages. Beroukakis was offering himself as hostage in place of John. Would the Germans accept him and reprieve his son?

The German captain to whom Major Schaette delegated the duty of carrying out the executions studied the pleading father who stood before him, hat in hand, tears in his eyes.

"So the Cretans can cry after all," he sneered contemptuously. Then, turning to his sergeant, he snapped, "Shoot them both!"[23]

In groups of ten, the boys and men were marched out into a field, and with short bursts of machine-gun fire, all 201 were slaughtered in order "to teach the rest a lesson."

* * *

Word of the New Zealand withdrawal spread rapidly among the Cretan civilian population.

From the villages of Spilia, Voukoules, Gerani, Modhion, Vryses, Fournes, Vatolakos, and Platanias, the message raced through the grapevine faster than any radio: "The New Zealanders are retreating to Galatas."

In Fournes, a village located south of the battlefield, thirteen-year-old Tasso Minarakis heard his father advising the men of the village that the fighting was centering around Galatas, and that all Cretans should go there to fight the enemy.[24]

From the nearby village of Vatolakos, Nicholas Daskalakis took his teenage son, Theodore, with him to help fight the Germans. In his left hand he held an old vintage rifle for which he had only three bullets, while in his right, he carried a heavy bag filled with stones. His son carried two such burlap bags, also filled with stones. These stones were the weapons with which these two Cretans were going to fight the enemy. With knives in their belts, father and son set off for Galatas.[25]

George Christoudakis was a combat veteran of the Albanian front against Italy; his wounds had caused the loss of his left arm. Officially discharged from the Greek army and living in his native village of Vryses, south of Modhion, the embers of a Cretan warrior still glowed in his heart. When word reached him that all men were needed at Galatas, those embers rekindled into a flame.

Christoudakis did not consider the loss of his left arm a handicap, for he still had his right arm. Taping a long knife to the end of a broomstick, he improvised a spear. Holding this primitive weapon under the stump of his left arm and with a revolver in his belt, he departed for Galatas. The crippled Cretan warrior was off to war again.[26]

Manoli Paterakis had spent the last two days ambushing Germans. Following the New Zealand counterattack, Paterakis and the fellow Cretans who made up the band accounted for some two-score Germans in their personal war against the invaders.

Many of these ambushes became hotly fought skirmishes. On one occasion, Paterakis and his group were almost surrounded in a wheat-field. By setting fire to the wheat, they were able to escape under cover of the dense smoke.

Much later, while crossing a field, a passing Messerschmitt spotted them and came down to strafe. The men lay flat in the field. Paterakis dared not move from his place behind a stone wall, changing his position only to avoid the strafer's line of fire.

The day before, Paterakis had taken a pistol from a dead German. What caught his eye was the pistol's unfamiliar shape: It had a short, stubby nose with a wide-cylindered barrel in which was a missile that looked like a shell. Paterakis assumed that it was a specialized antiaircraft pistol; he had never seen or heard of a flare gun.

When the ME-109 came down for another pass, Paterakis fired at it with his new acquisition. His eyes opened in surprise when he saw a green flare shoot up into the air.

"Now you've done it," admonished his friend Gianni. "You've given away our position. He has spotted us!"

The Messerschmitt made a wide circle and came down again, but this time, instead of firing, he dipped his wings. The pilot assumed that the signal had come from a German whom he had mistaken for Cretan. To make amends for the error, he dropped a package of caramels.

As soon as the aircraft disappeared beyond the trees, Paterakis retrieved the package and shared the contents with his friends, after which they resumed their trek toward Galatas.[27]

As the battle progressed into the third day, Freyberg still had no inkling of King George's whereabouts. Considering Freyberg's tactless comment that he would rather the king were wounded or killed fighting for Greece than be taken prisoner, he now faced a frantic period of concerned waiting that added to his considerable troubles.

The members of the royal party continued their flight from the Germans. Struggling upward in the continuous climb toward the near-alpine heights of the White Mountains, the king, Prime Minister Tsouderos, and the whole entourage, buttoned their collars to keep warm as they crossed those peaks on mules.

Once they left the village of Therison, the royal escort of gendarmes was ordered to return north to the battle area. They were replaced by villagers from the mountains who volunteered to become the king's bodyguard.

At one point, villagers brought the king some boiled lamb to eat. There, upon the cold rocks amid the snow, the king and his party sat down and ate the lamb together with freshly baked bread and feta cheese dripping with brine. There was no water available to drink, but that problem was easily solved by melting snow.

From the hour that they had left Therison, the royal party encountered innumerable villagers—old men, old women, and boys and girls—all heading north to fight the invader. The patriotic spirit that compelled them to defend the soil of Crete, instead of staying in the safety of their mountain homes, touched the king and the prime minister to the point of tears.

The trail continued in a southwesterly direction, and as the lower altitudes were reached, the snow gradually disappeared. They had finally crossed the spine of the White Mountain range.

Then began the slow descent over narrow, almost impassable goat trails, until they reached the canyon of Samaria. During the passage through the high-walled, narrow gorge, the king stopped many times to admire the unsurpassed beauty of the flowers amidst the ruggedness of this natural wilderness.

It took several hours before they reached the village of Samaria, located deep in the shadows of the canyon. After a short stay, during which King George and the prime minister prepared a final proclamation for the people of Greece and Crete, they resumed the trip south until the narrow walls of the canyon opened like a huge door on the vast expanse of the Mediterranean beyond.

At 6:00 P.M. on the evening of Thursday, May 22, the king and his party reached the end of their long trip—the village of Aghia Roumeli on the southern coast. There, waiting for the king to arrive, was an advance party that included a British admiral and his staff. Ahead lay the crossing of the Mediterranean and the safety of Egypt.[28]

Late the same day, Admiral Cunningham, in Alexandria, forwarded a message to the commanding officer of Task Force A1, ordering him to send two destroyers to pick up King George and his party. Admiral H. G. Rawlings immediately dispatched the destroyers *Decoy* and *Hero* to Aghia Roumeli.

It was not until 1:00 A.M. on Friday, May 23, that the king set foot on the deck of the British destroyer. Once the whole royal party had embarked, the two warships sped off to rejoin Rawlings's naval squadron.[29]

General Freyberg, back in Crete, knew nothing of this. It was not until May 26 that General Wavell thought of informing him that the king of Greece had finally completed his flight from the Germans.[30]

Four hundred miles to the south, across the Mediterranean and the scorching sands of North Africa, a German general followed the battle of Crete with utmost concern.

Bardia, situated high on the precipitous cliffs overlooking the sea, was a hot and weatherbeaten array of stone houses. Too small to be considered a town and too large to be a village, Bardia first emerged from obscurity as the site of an early British victory against Mussolini's African army. Now it housed the advance headquarters of the German Afrika Korps.

The general who took such intense interest in the events in Crete was in Bardia as the commanding officer of the Afrika Korps, and he knew that whoever controlled the Mediterranean would ultimately win North Africa; his mission in that northern desert was to conquer Egypt and seize the Suez Canal. From the day he assumed command, he wasted no time in exhibiting the military talent that would make his name a household word that would strike fear into the hearts of his enemy.

Through a series of rapid and daring maneuvers, his panzer army won several outstanding victories in North Africa. These feats rapidly transformed him into a hero and earned him the sobriquet of Desert Fox. This corps commander was none other than General Erwin Rommel.

On the evening of May 23, General Rommel joined his staff for the evening meal in the main room of the huge stone house that served as his headquarters in Bardia. His staff felt honored to be eating with their general, whom they respected not only for his military skill and leadership, but also for his spartan traits. Rommel was modest in his taste for food, usually eating the same rations as the men in the ranks. Once in a while, but only on special occasions, he took wine. Tonight he requested some and toasted the ultimate success of his plan to seize the Suez Canal. After meals it was Rommel's habit to retire to the privacy of his quarters and attend to his mail. This night was no exception, and as he left the table, he beckoned his aide to accompany him.

As Rommel's aide, it was Leutnant Heinz Werner Schmidt's duty to make all the necessary preparations for the next day's tour of the front lines, and to make certain that the appropriate memoranda and orders had been issued to the various field commanders. In the evenings, Schmidt had the additional assignment of acting as the general's private secretary.

Schmidt noticed Rommel looking at a recently received communication. Its content must have been of a serious nature, for the general's strong chin was set in apparent disgust as he dropped the paper in the out box. The young aide stood silently in the shadows, watching him.

"Well," said Rommel, acknowledging Schmidt's presence for the first time. "It looks like the Reichsmarshall's paratroopers have attacked Crete."

"Yes, Herr General, I have heard reports about the landings from intelligence."

The general nodded, adding in an almost inaudible mutter, "I suppose that the seizure of Crete could provide a favorable base for operations against the enemy in the desert and in the Middle East . . ."

As his voice trailed off, he rose from his desk and slowly walked over to a huge map of the Mediterranean area hanging on the wall, Schmidt's eyes following him. After a few minutes of silent study, Rommel placed a finger on a speck south of Sicily.

"I tell you, Schmidt, that the occupation of *this* island would be of greater value to us than Crete!"

Schmidt looked hard, trying to determine to what island he was referring.

"*This* island," continued Rommel, now speaking in a loud, emphatic voice, "lies there like a thorn in our side . . . a constant menace to our lifeline of supply here in North Africa!"

Then, repeatedly tapping the little speck with his forefinger, he concluded: "It is *Malta* and *not* Crete that would control the Mediterranean. That's where Goering should have sent his Fallschirmjägers!"[31]

# 23 / "STAND FOR NEW ZEALAND"

## MAY 24–25, 1941

With his headquarters less than a mile from the newly formed defense line, General Hargest was able for the first time to see the rising smoke of gunfire. Paradoxically enough, not since the beginning of the invasion had Hargest ventured from his headquarters to visit his forward positions. Now his forward positions had retreated to within a stone's throw of his headquarters. For Hargest, this was too close for comfort.

His most recent apprehensions centered upon the strain under which his men had been fighting since the first day of battle and upon the severity of their estimated losses. In a report he dispatched to the New Zealand Division Headquarters on the night of the withdrawal, Hargest had estimated that the Twenty-second had been depleted to 110 men, while the Twenty-third was only able to muster 250. *In each case he overestimated his losses.*[1]

These erroneous figures were the basis for Hargest's contention that he did not have the capacity to hold the new defense line. By 2:50 P.M. the next afternoon, May 25, he was quite emphatic in his doubts, and the question was raised as to whether he should abandon the Platanias River line. Puttick, his division commanding general, listened to Hargest's argument, but had no fear about his New Zealanders' ability to hold the line against a German frontal assault. His only fear was for the defense line's left flank, which ended in midair, unsupported and indefensible. It was that factor alone that forced Puttick to agree with Hargest that the Fifth Brigade should abandon its new position and move farther east.[2] So it was that when darkness arrived, the plucky but disgruntled New Zealanders of the Fifth Brigade once again began a withdrawal.

This new withdrawal eastward toward Galatas left a void quickly entered by the newly arrived German troopers of the Fifth

Mountain Division. In a matter of hours, the larger villages of Fournes, Gerani, Modhion, Vatolakos, Vryses, and Platanias fell to the Germans. With the exception of innumerable New Zealand stragglers and Cretan marksmen—who still harassed the Germans with sniper fire—organized resistance west of Galatas had been virtually eliminated.

As May 24, the fifth day of battle, dawned, the opposing forces faced each other like two gladiators ready for a life-or-death struggle among the hills that ringed the walled village of Galatas.

If Maleme, with its airfield, was the door through which the Germans entered Crete, Galatas would be the gateway for the seizure of the Cretan capital of Khaniá, and thence the remainder of the island.

Galatas was a small village of some twelve whitewashed stone buildings—that had lain in peace for decades amidst its hilltop splendor. Its white houses reflected the sun's rays with the sparkle of jewels, sharply contrasted against the surrounding backdrop of green hills. A natural string of shallow eminences that offered the defenders a favorable position from which to protect Galatas and the roads beyond leading to the capital of Crete, these hills were destined to play a major role in the forthcoming battle.

There were five prominent hills west of Galatas, none of them exceeding a height of 400 feet. They lay in a semicircle whose arc bellied westward. The northern point of the arc began less than a mile south of the main coast road, where the ground rose abruptly to the summit of the first hill—Red Hill—so named for the preponderance of bougainvillea that gave the terrain its color. From Red Hill the arc curved south and east to include Wheat Hill, named for its waist-high crop of wheat, and Pink Hill, with its varicolored flora, finally terminating at its southern tip in the village's Cemetery Hill. Bisecting this arc of hills at its center was a long, low ridge called Ruin Ridge. It extended westward for a quarter of a mile and ended in an abrupt peak—the highest hill of the five. Nestled within the open end of this arc of hills lay the village of Galatas; the surrounding eminences were known as Galatas heights.

The Third Parachute Regiment in Prison Valley was already familiar with these heights and with the men defending them. Now the men of Julius Ringel's Mountain Division were to taste the same bitter fruit.

With his first objective—Maleme airfield—taken, the time had arrived for Ringel to begin the second phase of his operation.

The northern sector of the German attack force would be led by Colonel Ramcke, commanding the remnants of parachutists. From the area immediately above the main northern coast road to a point south of Red Hill, the survivors of Captain Gericke's and Major Stentzler's paratroop battalions took up their positions for the attack.

Exhausted after a continuous five-day battle against a stubborn army under a searing hot sun, these survivors of the original assault regiment now hoped for victory.

In the center of the line, General Julius Ringel placed the fresh troops of Colonel Utz's One-hundredth Mountain Regiment. The regiment's Second Battalion, commanded by Major Schury, took up a position opposite Ruin Hill, while on its right flank, the First Battalion, under Major Schrank, posed itself before Pink Hill in the center and Cemetery Hill on the right.

Far to the south, an enveloping column, using the First and Third Battalions of the Eighty-fifth Mountain Regiment under Colonel Krakau, was to swing wide, capture Alikianou village, join forces with the Third Parachute Regiment in Prison Valley, and break into the rear of the New Zealand defense line.[3]

As ambitious as the attack plan looked on paper, it had one drawback: The attack was to be a series of separate assaults, starting in the northern sector and continuing down the line, instead of a simultaneous all-out mass attack. It would start with Ramcke's force in the north, be continued by Utz's regiment in the center, and be followed up by Heidrich's parachute regiment in the south later in the day. The main stroke would be borne by Colonel Utz and his battalions in the center of the line. With Krakau's men of the Eighty-fifth Regiment coming up on the Zealanders' rear, it was felt that the defense line would crumble between the jaws of these two factors.[4]

From the Galatas heights, the New Zealand defenders watched these fresh German troops move into position. Wherever they looked, groups of men were digging entrenchments for mortars and machine guns. The Germans were only two miles away, but the New Zealanders were so low on mortar and machine-gun ammunition that they held their fire for the moment when the mountain troops would begin the attack.

When the sun rose on May 24, the Eighteenth Battalion held

the high ground from Red Hill south to Wheat Hill. The withdrawn Composite Battalion occupied positions in the rear of the Eighteenth Battalion on Ruin Ridge. The Divisional Petrol Company and the Divisional Cavalry Detachment were all that remained of Kippenberger's original Tenth Brigade on the firing line; both units were combined under the command of Major John Russell and were subsequently referred to as Task Force Russell.

The Petrol Company was dug in on the right of Pink Hill, linking with the Eighteenth Battalion's left flank at Wheat Hill. The Cavalry Detachment held the left forward slope of Pink Hill, where its left flank joined the Fourth Brigade's Nineteenth New Zealand Battalion.

General Hargest's Fifth Brigade was withdrawn far to the rear of the Galatas defense line. The brigade's Twentieth, Twenty-third, and Twenty-eighth Battalions were repositioned near the Galatas turn, just south of the promontory housing the Seventh General Hospital. The Twenty-second and Twenty-first Battalions were held farther east, straddling the coast road and well out of the immediate battle zone.

To protect the extreme left flank, well east of Cemetery Hill where the survivors of the Sixth Greek Regiment had dug in, Puttick placed the Seventh and Eighth Australian Battalions in line on the left flank of the New Zealand Nineteenth Battalion.[5]

On May 23 Colonel Heidrich summoned Von der Heydte and Major Wulf Derpa, the CO of the Second Parachute Battalion, to his headquarters tent. The previous day, the regimental commander had ordered Von der Heydte to give all his ammunition to the Second Battalion and told Derpa to resume his attacks against both Pink and Cemetery Hills. Derpa's battalion subsequently made several spirited assaults on both hills, which ended in failure with heavy losses. As a result, the Second Battalion had been reduced to a strength of only two companies.

On this morning of the twenty-third, Heidrich ordered Derpa to continue his attack on Cemetery Hill, and Major Derpa finally protested.

"Herr Oberst, I question the practicability of these incessant frontal attacks."

Colonel Heidrich glared at the battalion commander, a surge of fury rising within him. The regimental commander's nerves strained to breaking point by the repeated defeats suffered at the hands of the Greeks and New Zealanders, he was in no mood to have his orders questioned.

"You will do as I say, Major," he shouted at Derpa. "Have you no more stomach for fighting—are you afraid to die?"

There was silence in the tent, everyone stiffening at this harsh accusation.

The sensitive, courageous battalion commander paled at the unwarranted insult to his courage. He clicked his heels and through tightly compressed lips, he replied, "It is not a question of my own life, sir; I am considering the lives of the soldiers for whom I am responsible." After a pause Derpa added, "My own life, I would gladly give!"

Colonel Heidrich ordered Derpa to resume the attack.[6]

From the far side of Prison Valley, Captain Von der Heydte sadly watched his colleague and friend leading the remnants of the Second Battalion in a renewed attack against the right slope of Cemetery Hill.

Smoke covered the crest of the hill as the Germans approached the positions held by the right flank of the Nineteenth New Zealand Battalion. The crack of rifles and the deadly rattle of machine guns echoed across the valley. Von der Heydte could see the paratroopers of the Second Battalion charging up the steep hill, where the smoke of gunfire enveloped them. Soon the roar of firing diminished and finally stopped. When the smoke lifted, the hillside was covered by the blue-gray uniforms of dead and wounded paratroopers. The survivors trickled back down the hill; once again the attack had been repulsed.

Still smarting from Colonel Heidrich's insult—which reflected on his men—Major Derpa ordered the survivors to join the remnants of his battalion for a renewed attack. Derpa was very proud of his paratroopers, but they were tired, hungry, and thirsty. The heat of the Cretan sun had taken a heavy toll; most of them had no water left in their canteens and they were still wearing the heavy woolen paratroop uniform. Many of his men had discarded their outer smocks, opened their tunics, and rolled up their sleeves for relief. Others had even cut the legs from their trousers, hoping for some cooling comfort. Their uniforms saturated with perspiration, many of his men had fallen victim to heat prostration.

Derpa requested a few hours of rest for his men, but Heidrich insisted that the attacks continue.[7]

Captain H. M. Smith, whose men had just repulsed the first assault, warned his men to remain on the alert, his intuition telling him that the Germans would attack again. If they attacked on his front, he held no fears: The earlier attack had cost him only a few casualties, and the rest were in good spirits. But Smith did have one concern—his right flank.

That section of the hill defense was protected by the remnants of the Sixth Greek Regiment. Many of the Greeks had been scattered by the earlier German attacks, but the Sixth Greek Company was still holding its own on the rise of ground to the right of Smith's Nineteenth Battalion. If the Germans pressed their attack on the Greek position and succeeded in penetrating their defenses, the New Zealand flank would be turned and the whole hill defense could be lost.

When Derpa's men aimed the thrust of their second attack at the Greek positions, Smith's worst fears were realized. He had no men to spare, and the New Zealand ammunition did not fit the Greeks' prewar Styr guns. But he did send an officer to the commander of the Sixth Greek Company beseeching him to "hold the line at all costs."

"We shall!" replied Captain E.[8]

From behind the olive trees, the Germans emerged at a trot, charging directly up the slope toward the positions of the Sixth Greek Company. Captain Smith ordered his men to commence firing into the attackers' flank, but—realizing that the undulating terrain sent the New Zealand fire well over the heads of the charging paratroopers—he had to rescind the order.

The Germans gathered momentum as they charged up and over the crest of Cemetery Hill, pressing the attack as they approached the village cemetery wall at the top of the rise.

Above the crack of rifles and the rattle of machine guns, there now rose a new sound from the Greek positions—a heart-stopping human cry echoing over the defense positions as it passed from man to man, each Greek in turn repeating it louder and louder until it crescendoed over the hillside, smothering the roar of the German attack. The New Zealanders had heard that call before. It was "Aera!"—the rallying battle cry of the immortal Evzones— and to the Greeks, it had one meaning: "Attack!"

The New Zealanders watched in awe, and Captain Smith uttered to no one in particular, "Why, those bloody crazy Greeks!"[9]

Over the top of the cemetery wall came the madmen. They

had no more bullets, but they still had their bayonets, and down the hill they charged, screaming "Aera!" at the top of their lungs, the gleam of their bayonets reflecting the midday sun.

For a moment, the Germans stood in disbelief.

With snarling fury, the Greeks met the Germans head-on, halfway down the rise. They slashed, they butted, and they bayonetted, German after German falling to their piercing stabs. In the lead was Captain E, with Lieutenant Kritakis at his side.[10]

There was a brief moment when the two forces swayed in furious hand-to-hand combat. Then the Germans broke, turned, and ran down the hill, the Greeks in close pursuit.

Captain Smith shook his head, admiring the heroism with which these gallant Greek soldiers had shattered the German attack.[11] The Second Paratroop Battalion had ceased to exist as a fighting force. Severely wounded by a bayonet thrust in the stomach, its commanding officer, Major Derpa, was later to die in the Regimental Field Hospital. He had proved his courage with his life.

But by midday on May 24, the German advance was succeeding. The radio broadcast from Berlin, which finally told the German people that Crete had been invaded, was a good sign. The Fuehrer's public acknowledgement of the battle for Crete meant that victory was at hand. To the embattled, exhausted paratroopers in Prison Valley, this announcement was a shot in the arm.

When Lieutenant Colonel J. R. Gray and his Eighteenth Battalion took over the defense perimeter previously held by the Composite Battalion, they found that this newly assigned position covered a much greater area than a half-strength battalion could properly defend. Gray positioned his men carefully over the mile-and-a-half stretch of hilly terrain that extended from Wheat Hill north to Red Hill, finding the defense line so overextended that he did not have sufficient men to hold its highest point. He decided not to defend Ruin Hill, even though its capture by the Germans would have them breathing down his neck. It was a tactical error, for the hill was to become the weakest link in a relatively weak defense line.

On the morning of May 24, Colonel Utz sent a patrol on a reconnaissance of the New Zealand positions. They found Ruin Hill undefended and immediately brought up mortars. With these entrenched on the reverse side of the hill, the Germans could bring flanking fire to bear on Red Hill to their left front and Wheat Hill to their right. This firing position could make those hilly bastions in the New Zealand defense line almost untenable.

When Utz was informed that Ruin Hill had been seized, he ordered Major Schury of the Second Mountain Battalion to send out a company-strength combat patrol to pierce the line, advancing slowly and unopposed until it reached the far edge of an olive grove leading into the valley between Red and Wheat Hills. Once it left the protection of the trees, the patrol was caught in a crossfire from the New Zealand defense positions. Pinned down for hours, they finally withdrew, leaving more than half of their number behind. The episode was evidence enough for Colonel Utz to postpone any further attacks until he received proper air support.[12]

That support was already evident in the clear blue skies farther east. However, the Luftwaffe's targets were not the New Zealand hill positions before Galatas, but Khaniá.

From a little past noon until 8:00 P.M., Stukas, Dorniers, and Heinkels, interspersed by marauding ME-109s, kept up a constant bombing of that hapless city. By dusk, flames rose hundreds of feet into the sky, turning the advent of darkness into daylight, and outlining the devastation wrought on that once beautiful capital of Crete.

In the wake of the torrential rain of death that had drenched the city for an eight-hour period, there remained the scars of uprooted trees, shattered buildings, torn walls, and debris-filled streets, fogged by clouds of pulverized stone eerily reflecting leaping tongues of flame. Amid the rubble lay hundreds of dead civilians, innocent victims of man's ability to wield death from the sky.[13]

On the next day, May 25, General Kurt Student, the overall commander, finally set foot upon Crete. No longer tethered to the stake, he was "off the hook."

Student was greeted at Maleme airfield by General Ringel. The goateed, immaculately dressed commander of the mountain division personally conducted him on a tour of the battlefield. The whole day was spent visiting the regimental headquarters at the forward positions. Student talked and ate with the troops. He listened and observed, finally satisfied that the operation was progressing well, albeit delayed.

There was, however, one aspect of the tour that bothered him.

The sight of thousands of corpses of his beloved paratroopers scattered over the fields of Crete shocked him. He had always considered his elite Falschirmjägers to be invincible. Their stinking, bloated corpses lying on soil reddened with their blood would stay with Kurt Student for the rest of his days.[14]

When Captain E, CO of the Sixth Greek Company of the Sixth Greek Regiment, returned to his original position after the counterattack that shattered the German assault of the Second Battalion in which Derpa was killed, he gathered the survivors of his company and reestablished a more concentrated defense line behind the stone wall atop Cemetery Hill. There were not that many of his men left, and that worried him, for if the Germans were to attack again, it would be almost impossible to hold the line.

Nearby, a wounded German paratrooper lay beside a shattered tombstone, feigning death. As Captain E stood in the open, positioning his men, the German slowly and deliberately raised his Luger, carefully aiming at the Greek captain. Kritakis spotted the movement and shouted, pushing the captain out of the line of fire just as the Luger barked. The bullet missed the captain but nicked Kritakis in the arm; at the same instant, Captain E's aide dispatched the German with a quick thrust of his bayonet.

There was no time to thank Kritakis for his alertness, for before any appreciation could be expressed, a flight of Messerschmitts raced past, sprewing bullets all over Cemetery Hill, scattering the men to cover. When the strafing attack passed, Captain E noticed blood on Kritakis' sleeve. He examined the wound, grateful that his life had been saved, and suggested that Kritakis go to the dressing station in Galatas, Kritakis refused. "My place is here with you," he replied.

"My friend, must I *order* you to the dressing station? Go, get away from this hell!" Kritakis reluctantly left the hill position.[15]

A squad of German machine gunners had been ordered out of Schrank's battalion to set up a machine-gun position on a small hillock between Wheat and Pink Hills. The Germans worked their way along the protective edge of an olive grove, crossed a small depression, and reached their objective unobserved by the New Zealanders. But a Cretan civilian noticed them and raced off to report their position.

When the German squad reached the hillock, they immediately

went to work digging entrenchments, the squad's two heavy machine guns lying nearby. The guns were to be placed so as to face the flank of Wheat Hill, thus giving protective cover to any German advance in the valley between Wheat and Pink hills. The olive grove, through which they passed, protected their rear. As they dug their positions, the Germans became aware of a clamoring noise arising from the edge of the olive grove through which they just hiked. The babble of voices was loud enough to distract them and, pausing in their digging, they watched with interest and bewilderment as a motley collection of old men, old women, children, and a few dogs came into view. Some of the men carried what appeared to be long-barreled, muzzle-loading muskets; others carried swords and hoes, while the women bore sickles and sticks. Not to be outdone, the children carried bags of stones and the dogs raced about yipping and sniffing.

The Germans looked at each other, amused; until they saw the leader of this ragged group. His appearance gave them cause for alarm.

He was tall and thin-faced—from his bearing obviously a British officer—dressed as strangely as the people he led. Clad in shorts and wearing a long buff-colored army jacket that reached almost to his knees, he had a yellow bandanna around his forehead. With a service revolver in each hand, he formed the Cretans into a single rank.

He was Captain Michael Forrester, the same officer from Freyberg's headquarters who had attached himself to the Sixth Greek Regiment after the first day of the invasion and two days later led 200 shouting Greeks in a charge that broke up a German attack. Now he was back with this odd collection of civilians.

Here was George Christoudakis, the one-armed veteran of the Albanian War, his spearlike weapon under the stump of his left arm, while his right held the shaft. Here also was the octogenarian from the village of Daratsos, Spiro Gregorakis, bearing an ancient, rusty rifle from the Turkish campaigns.

Forrester turned to the Cretans and, pointing up the hill, waved his arm forward. Before the Germans realized what was happening, these bedraggled civilians charged with the screams of warriors going into battle.

The German machine guns were now in position, but facing the wrong direction, and the ammunition belts had not been passed through the breach. Before the Germans could raise their pistols or rifles, the Cretans were on top of them. It was a costly hesitation based on the belief that such civilians would never dare attack a trained, armed German squad.

Forrester leaped over the trench firing his pistols at the Germans. Christoudakis felt the blade of his spear snap as he drove it into the body of a startled German. Gregorakis came face to face with another German, raised his ancient rifle, and pulled the trigger. The gun's blast tore the German apart, but its kick was enough to topple the eighty-year-old Cretan over the parapet and down the hill.

The women pounded the Germans with their sickles and sticks, while Forrester shouted encouragement. When the bewildered German survivors broke and ran, the children followed them down the hillock, throwing stones in their wake. Even the dogs chased at the Germans, nipping at their heels.

Later that day, eighty-year-old Spiro Gregorakis returned to his village of Daratsos. As he walked up the path to his house, he shouted to his wife Maria and daughter Eleni. When they greeted him, he raised his right arm high, holding before them a captured German tommy gun. He smiled proudly at them with a twinkle in his eye as he stated: "I blew his head off!"[16]

Throughout the night of the twenty-fourth, sporadic firing continued along the whole defense perimeter before Galatas, enough to keep everyone alert and on edge.

Bright and early the morning of May 25, Ramcke formed his paratroopers for the attack. Their movements were readily observed from Red Hill, and word was passed back to Colonel Gray, who ordered an immediate mortar attack on Ramcke's positions. The sudden mortar deluge scattered the paratroopers, causing them many casualties. But this liberal use of mortar shells created a new problem for the men of the Eighteenth Battalion, for it depleted their supply to ten shells. Colonel Gray's request for replenishment was answered with thirty more and a note stating that these were the last shells available in the whole brigade.

The men of the Eighteenth Battalion knew they were sitting on a powder keg. Mortar shells were in short supply; so was their rifle and machine-gun ammunition. A reconnaissance patrol during the previous night had found as many as seventeen German machine guns in one sector alone—more machine guns than the entire Eighteenth Battalion had in the whole one-and-a-half-mile stretch of their defense line.

Colonel Utz had been persistently inquiring about air cover. "When do we get Stuka support?" was the question that he repeatedly asked of General Ringel. He was finally told to expect an air strike by 4:30 that afternoon.

Following Colonel Utz's earlier instructions, Major Schury ordered his Second Mountain Battalion forward without air cover. But a continuous wall of fire from the New Zealanders made an advance almost impossible, and the German need for air support became even more apparent. Thus, for the major part of this day —like the day before—the New Zealand line held the Germans at bay, but they knew the fuse to the powder keg had been lit.

At 4:30 in the afternoon, it exploded.

The sky above the New Zealand forward positions filled with Messerschmitts and Stukas. Even Dorniers joined in the attack, and for half an hour the rain of death continued. In the north, Colonel Ramcke's paratroopers attacked first, driving south between the coast road and Red Hill. To support them Ramcke unleashed a heavy concentration of high explosives from 55-mm antitank guns and some captured Bofors, all firing over open sights. The New Zealanders were taking heavy losses from this direct fire, with no chance for retaliation. The commanding officer of the New Zealand unit on the right flank had been severely wounded and his successor killed, leaving the leadership of the company in the hands of sergeants and corporals. The persistence of the paratroop attack was such that it succeeded in surrounding and cutting off Red Hill, causing a breach in the northern end of the New Zealand defense line. The road to Khaniá lay momentarily open.[17]

Colonel Gray, with rifle in hand, rushed forward with a small collection of cooks and clerks from the Composite Battalion, including the battalion chaplain. He ran into the midst of the fight, yelling, "No surrender! No surrender!"[18] But the paratroop attack, with its devastating mortar and antitank fire, was so intense that Gray had to withdraw the twelve survivors of the forward company, leaving Red Hill securely in German hands.

Now, the second phase of Colonel Utz's tactical plan went into effect. Major Schury, who had been repulsed earlier in the day, sent his men back against Wheat Hill in the center. For the New Zealanders, defending the slopes of the hill, it became a hell on earth. Heavy mortar and artillery shells fell on them in a crossfire from the abandoned Ruin Hill position before them and from the newly captured Red Hill on their right. The whole of Wheat Hill was hidden in a cloud of smoke, as shell after shell burst upon it. Kippenberger watched the devastating fire through his field glasses, yet twice refused requests for withdrawal.[19]

At the end of this fiery two-hour pounding, the men of C Company could take no more. The few survivors pulled out, led by Major R. J. Lynch. Wheat Hill—the third bastion in the New Zealand defense line—had fallen to the Germans.

Further down the line, the third phase of the plan—the attack on the southern part of the position—began.

Even though it was now early evening, Utz felt that to call a halt to the attack because of pending darkness might give the New Zealanders an opportunity to regain their balance and bring in men to reinforce the line. To prevent this, he ordered Major Schrank's First Mountain Battalion to attack and seize Pink and Cemetery Hills, while Schury's Second Battalion would continue the advance in order to capture the village of Galatas.

Major Schrank's men rushed forward to attack the two hills, carrying with them the additional strength of the Engineer Detachment from the Third Mountain Battalion, which had been held in reserve by Utz. The firepower from this reinforced battalion was too much for the depleted and exhausted ranks of the Cavalry Detachment and for the survivors of the decimated Sixth Greek Regiment. As the sun dipped behind the Rodopos Peninsula in the western part of Crete, the mountain troops of Schrank's First Battalion finally captured Cemetery Hill.

But Pink Hill still held.

The gallant Petrol Company struggled desperately to hold this last hill in the New Zealand defense perimeter. This heroic assortment of truckers and supply men had fought for days as bravely as any first-class infantry unit. Now, with Cemetery Hill captured, the mountain troops turned their efforts toward Pink Hill.

Captain H. A. Rowe, the brigade supply officer commanding this gallant company, received some reinforcements to bolster his dwindling ranks. Two platoons arrived from the Nineteenth Battalion, located far on the left flank beyond Cemetery Hill. Lieutenant W. N. Carson joined him with several drivers, and Lieutenant J. P. Dill brought a platoon of gunners.[20]

The deadly deluge of bombs continued to pound them. From the sky ME-109s and Stukas strafed and bombed the hill continuously; from the ground German rifle and machine-gun fire arched into the New Zealand emplacements together with the murderous crash of mortar shells. Their position soon became untenable. When machine-gun fire from Wheat Hill struck them in the rear, Captain Rowe ordered the survivors of the Petrol Company to withdraw to the safety of buildings in Galatas. The men of the Petrol Company fought as they went, even in retreat.

While Lieutenant Kritakis, the executive officer of the Sixth Greek Company, was having his wound treated, two disheveled Greek soldiers brought in a wounded man. Kritakis recognized one of the litter bearers as a man from his own company. When he walked over to see the wounded man, he was shocked to discover that lying on a makeshift stretcher was his commanding officer. Captain E was semiconscious, with a wound in his chest.

One of the Greeks carrying Captain E turned to Kritakis with tears in his eyes, repeating over and over again, "The Germans have overrun our positions!"[21]

The heavy German bombardment of the New Zealand line in the Wheat Hill area had killed more than 100 of Colonel Gray's men, almost decimating the Eighteenth Battalion. The whole western part of the defense line had lost all semblance of cohesion. It had been pierced at many points, and most of the New Zealanders lay in their trenches, completely surrounded, fighting to the death.

But the fiery onslaught was too much for many of them, and they finally broke.

Colonel Kippenberger watched with increasing alarm as the men of his brigade stumbled back. They were wild-eyed, some without helmets and others without weapons. When Colonel Gray emerged from the cloud of smoke looking "twenty years older than three hours before,"[22] Kippenberger recognized the symptoms.

As more of his men came over the hill, he rushed into their midst, waving his arms and shouting over and over again: "Stand for New Zealand!"[23]

Electrified, the men awakened from their momentary lapse. The retreat was stopped before it became a rout.

The Germans continued their advance into Galatas. Maddened with the fury of battle and enraged by the stout resistance of the defenders, the mountain troops fought mercilessly. In the ensuing struggle, furious charge and counter-charge left New Zealand, Greek, and German bodies piled up in the streets of the village. The attackers gave no quarter and none was given in return; captured soldiers were slain on the spot. A group of surrounded New Zealanders raised their hands to surrender, but the Germans burned them alive with flamethrowers. One survivor tried to escape, only to be caught and thrown back into the flames. The street-by-street battle developed into a carnage.

Galatas finally fell to the Germans.

The loss of the village of Galatas was a terrible blow for the New Zealanders. However, the diminutive but aggressive commander of the Tenth Brigade, Colonel Kippenberger, was determined to take Galatas back from the Germans.[24]

Just before dusk Lieutenant Roy Farran appeared out of nowhere with his two light tanks. Kippenberger looked upon them as a gift from heaven. These were the same tanks that had survived the fruitless counterattack on May 22 at Pirgos. When Brigadier Inglis of the Fourth Brigade heard that Wheat Hill had fallen and that the New Zealand line had been breached, he sent Farran forward to see if he could help.

Kippenberger lost no time in putting the tanks to good use. He immediately ordered Farran to take them into the village on a reconnaissance patrol. The two tanks clattered down the dusty road and soon disappeared into the smoke that hung low over the village.[25]

While Kippenberger waited for Farran's return, the remaining two companies of the Twenty-third Battalion appeared over the crest. They also had been sent forward by Inglis to reinforce the New Zealand line.

About 100 yards from the edge of the village, they came upon Colonel Kippenberger, standing in the middle of the road, a pipe in his mouth, waiting for Farran's tanks to return. He lost no time telling them what he had planned for them: "You have to take Galatas with the help of the two tanks. There is no time for reconnaissance," he continued. "You must move straight in up the road and . . . and take everything with you!"[26] Farran's two tanks reappeared.

Farran lifted the lid of his turret and reported to Kippenberger,

"The place is stiff with Jerries!" He added, as he hauled himself out of the tank, "They are everywhere in the village!"[27]

"I have two companies of infantry," interrupted Kippenberger. "Would you go in again with them?"[28]

Farran nodded. The infantrymen of the Twenty-third Battalion waited nervously.

Major Thomason of the Twenty-third replacing the wounded Leckie now took his turn to pass instructions to the men of his two companies: "D Company will be attacking on the left side of the road. We have two tanks for support," he added, but cautioned that "the whole show is stiff with Huns . . . it is going to be a bloody affair, but we have just got to succeed." Then he added with a wave of his hand, "Now, for Christ's sake—get cracking!"[29]

There it was—the order to attack!

No sooner had the advance begun than stragglers from other units joined them. Men separated from the remnants of the Petrol and Cavalry Detachments, together with the survivors from the Composite, the Twentieth, and the Eighteenth Battalions, fell in at the rear of the column. More than 250 men had been collected for this do-or-die effort to dislodge the Germans from Galatas.

At first, the infantrymen moved forward at a normal walking pace, but as the tanks increased their speed, the New Zealanders broke into a trot. At that precise moment, a spontaneous shout rose from their ranks. It echoed across the hills and fields like the bloodcurdling scream of a banshee.

Lieutenant Colonel Gray, standing on the eastern outskirts of the village with some survivors from his battalion, heard the shout and thought it was the cry of a wild beast. Lieutenant Farran heard it above the noise of the tank's motors. It even reached Von der Heydte's ears in Prison Valley, and it made his flesh crawl.

It was the shout of New Zealanders on the attack. It was the battle cry of men who were returning with a vengeful wrath.[30]

The Germans were caught off guard by this new attack at twilight. When Farran retreated with his two tanks earlier, the Germans assumed that the battle was over for the night. No sooner did they hear the chorus of shouts than the two tanks were back, this time supported by a flood of wildly charging men.

The slaughter began all over again as the New Zealanders tore into the Germans.

Firing came from all directions—from windows, from rooftops, and from behind trees, chimneys, and walls. Those Germans caught in houses were quickly killed with grenades thrown through windows. Others raced into the streets only to be cut down by New Zealand bullets. Soon the streets were filled with struggling men fighting savagely with bayonets, pistols, rifle butts, and even with bare hands.[31]

A mortar blast crippled Lieutenant Farran's tank, wounding him and killing his driver. As Farran emerged from his tank, he was hit a second time, and now he lay in the gutter next to his disabled vehicle, on the village's main street just off the town square.

A squad of New Zealanders trotted past Farran with Lieutenant Thomas of the Twenty-third in the lead. When they reached the main square, they ran into a group of Germans less than fifty yards away. The New Zealanders opened fire on them, cutting some of them down, but the rest turned and charged.

Lieutenant W. B. Thomas aimed his pistol at a German less than three yards away, whose youthful face had been contorted into a snarl. Thomas fired point-blank at him and, through the flash, saw the youth shudder with surprise as he lunged forward. The German fell dead at Thomas's feet, but not before his bayonet had pierced Thomas's thigh. Thomas now lay wounded, bleeding badly, amid other bodies of Germans and New Zealanders—some groaning in pain, others silent in death.[32]

Through the wild melee and the shouts, he heard a distinct English voice from across the square shouting to the New Zealanders, "Good show, New Zealand—jolly good show—come on, New Zealand!"[33]

The vicious battle continued. It was a bitter struggle that was fought street by street, house by house, room by room, until, in time, the whole village was littered with the bodies of the dead, the dying, and the wounded. Little by little, the Germans were pushed out of Galatas. As twilight lapsed into darkness, Galatas was once more in the hands of the New Zealanders.

# 24 / "WHY IS CRETE STILL RESISTING?"

**MAY 26–28, 1941**

Stillness finally reigned over the battlefield of Galatas. The streets of the village presented a grim crimson tableau. The dead—the New Zealanders, the Greeks, the Cretan irregulars, and the Germans—were lying one on top of the other. New Zealand medics tended to the fallen, treating friend and foe alike. Volunteering assistance were a handful of Cretan women who offered water and bread to the wounded.

A little after 10:00 P.M., a messenger brought Kippenberger a dispatch from the area brigade commander, General Inglis, summoning him and the brigade's battalion commanders to meet. Ignoring his fatigue, he departed for Inglis's headquarters.[1]

Kippenberger groped through the darkness, stumbling over the rocky terrain past vineyards and ravines, looking for Inglis's command post. He finally found it in a deep hollow, covered by a huge tarpaulin. Inside, Inglis was sitting at a small table, straining his eyes to read a map by the flickering glow of a single candle. In the shadows cast by the dim light, Kippenberger was able to distinguish Burrows of the Twentieth, Blackburn of the Nineteenth, and Major Sanders. Colonel Dittmer of the Twenty-eighth Maori Battalion was the last to arrive, entering on Kippenberger's heels.

General Inglis glanced at his watch. He had also invited his division commander, General Puttick, to be present. Annoyance appeared on his face, for time was of the utmost importance, and the hours of night would wait for no man.

"Gentlemen," he began, "you realize that if a counterattack is to have any chance of restoring the position, it must be delivered tonight and in as great strength as possible."[2]

The officers wearily nodded their agreement.

"The attack must be carried forth by a fresh force," he continued. "When General Puttick arrives, he could well decide what units to put in to restore the situation."[3]

Kippenberger and the battalion officers knew very well that by a "fresh force," Inglis referred to the use of units from the reserve force located at Suda Bay. To have those units released to Inglis's command, General Puttick would have to ask Freyberg. That would take time, and daylight was only six hours off. Yet Puttick, the only man who could properly make this request of Freyberg, had not arrived, and the hours slipped silently away.

While the men waited for Puttick, the fate of the battle for Galatas hung by a thin thread, and on that flimsy link depended the outcome of the battle for Crete.

Inglis was growing apprehensive about Puttick's absence. Could it mean that there was no possibility of help? If that was the case, then he would have to use any available force at his command. His attention turned to the Twenty-eighth Maori Battalion.

The Maoris had been in reserve during the battle of Galatas. Their ranks had been reduced to 477 men by their unsuccessful counterattack two days earlier at Pirgos, but their morale remained high. Inglis felt that if any unit could attack and restore the situation, it would be the brave Maori, even in their depleted state.

"What do you think?" Inglis inquired, turning to Colonel Dittmer, the Maori battalion commander.[4]

Kippenberger interrupted: "It cannot be done. The terrain is crisscrossed by vineyards and ravines cut at angles to the line of advance. They don't know the ground," he continued, speaking from experience, having just groped his way over the same terrain, "and in the darkness, they will get lost and cut off."[5]

"What choice do I have, Howard?" Inglis replied to Kippenberger's objection. "We are done if it does not come off!"[6]

Then Inglis once again turned to Dittmer. "Can you do it, George?"

"I'll give it a go," replied the plucky Maori commander.[7]

At that moment there was a movement at the entrance to the headquarters tent. The tarpaulin parted and an officer entered. Kippenberger and the others peered through the dim light, hoping to see Puttick. Instead, they recognized Colonel W. G. Gentry, Puttick's staff officer.[8]

When Gentry heard of the plan to use the Maori battalion in a counterattack, he replied with a very emphatic no.[9]

"That is it, then, gentlemen," Inglis remarked, relieved that the weight of responsibility had been taken from his shoulders, yet irked that Gentry's decision meant no counterattack. "Galatas will have to be abandoned!"[10]

Kippenberger stalked out of the meeting, his fatigue forgotten in the heat of his anger. The aggressive young colonel was furious at the thought that no effort would be made to restore the line at Galatas. "After all that fighting—after all that bloodshed!" he murmured to himself. With that thought, he set out to order his men to withdraw to a line east of the village of Daratsos.

From the day that preceded the battle of Galatas, Freyberg had come to the conclusion that Crete could no longer be held. He felt that it was just a matter of time, that no matter how bravely and stubbornly his men fought, it was of no avail against the increasing strength of the mountain troops arriving hourly at Maleme airfield. Nor could they sustain a proper ground defense while the Luftwaffe terrorized them from the sky. Freyberg felt that "at this stage, [it] was quite clear . . . that the troops would not be able to last much longer against a continuation of the air attacks."[11] All reports received from the forward battalions at Galatas forced Freyberg to conclude that the end was rapidly approaching. It was gradually becoming a situation that offered only "two alternatives, defeat in the field and capture, or withdrawal."

He sat down to write these thoughts to his commander-in-chief in Cairo, yet he hesitated to mention the dreaded word "evacuation."

TODAY HAS BEEN ONE OF GREAT ANXIETY TO ME HERE . . . THIS EVENING AT 1700 HOURS, BOMBERS, DIVE BOMBERS AND GROUND STRAFERS CAME OVER AND BOMBED OUR FORWARD TROOPS AND THEN HIS GROUND TROOPS LAUNCHED AN ATTACK. IT IS STILL IN PROGRESS AND I AM AWAITING NEWS.[12]

Freyberg ended his message with the hopeful words:

IF WE CAN GIVE HIM A REALLY GOOD KNOCK, IT WILL HAVE A VERY FAR-REACHING EFFECT.[13]

No sooner had he completed this message to Wavell than Frey-berg received news from Puttick:

THE ENEMY IS THROUGH AT GALATAS AND MOVING TOWARD KARATSOS![14]*

Puttick's report alarmed Freyberg, forcing him to erase the last sentence from his message. In its place, he penciled:

I HAVE HEARD FROM PUTTICK THAT THE LINE HAS GONE AND WE ARE TRYING TO STABILIZE. I DON'T KNOW IF THEY WILL BE ABLE TO. I AM APPREHENSIVE.[15]

Once again the men of the New Zealand division were ordered to withdraw. Kippenberger glared icily at a junior officer who, when given the order, replied flippantly, "This is becoming a bloody habit!"[16]

General Freyberg had by now interceded personally in the plan for the withdrawal from Galatas. The Creforce commander or-dered that a new defense line be established at the Kladiso River, which ran a few miles west of the Cretan capital. He was deter-mined to hold a line west of Khaniá and Suda until such time as enough food supplies had been received at Suda to enable the quartermaster to set up a series of supply dumps on the road south to Sfakia. This would be the first preparatory step in the with-drawal to the southern beaches for evacuation.

The New Zealander order of battle facing the Germans on the morning of May 26 found half the Fifth Brigade back in the line in the northern sector, with the Twenty-first Battalion holding the right flank, the Nineteenth Battalion in the center, and the Twenty-eighth Maori on the left. Farther south of the Fifth Brigade, Brig-adier Vasey's Seventh and Eighth Battalions of his Australian brigade were holding the extreme left of the line.

Far to the rear, the survivors of the Eighteenth and the Com-posite Battalions, who had fought so desperately the previous day at Galatas, were scattered in isolated groups, unfit to fight as a cohesive force. Most of their comrades had been left behind in the narrow dirt streets of Galatas, either wounded or dead.

*The British referred to Daratsos as Karatsos.

Puttick was told by Freyberg that General Weston, the Suda base commander, was to assume command of the whole western defense perimeter. In so doing, Freyberg placed under Weston's control his own detachment of Royal Marines, the Australian brigade, and the Force Reserve. Weston's orders included putting Force Reserve in relief of the New Zealand division that same night. But Freyberg did not clarify what Puttick's status would be with regard to Weston's frontline command.

At 5:45 P.M. that afternoon of the twenty-sixth, General Weston arrived at the New Zealand Divisional Headquarters with his chief of staff, Lieutenant Colonel J. Wills.

In view of the events that were taking place in the front lines, Puttick felt it imperative that his men be withdrawn. When Weston appeared, Puttick greeted him with the news that his flanks were under great pressure and that his forward units would be totally unable "to hold their front after dark."

Weston disregarded Puttick's appraisal, replying only that *the line was to hold* and that Force Reserve would relieve the New Zealand division that night as planned. Lieutenant Colonel A. Duncan, the CO of the First Welsh Battalion, was present at the conference but remained silent during the heated debate that ensued.[17]

Brigadier Inglis, whom Freyberg earlier appointed as CO of Force Reserve, pressed for a withdrawal to a rear position that he had personally reconnoitered. Weston remained adamant that the forward line was to be held as instructed. In a rush of angry language, Weston was prophetically warned that "if he sent Force Reserve forward, he would never see them again."[18] Colonel Duncan did not appreciate the warning for his unit was part of Force Reserve.

When tempers returned to a calmer level and a momentary embarrassed silence prevailed, Weston picked up the phone and called Vasey to hear for himself how the Australians were faring on the left flank. The Australian brigade commander reported that it would not be possible for him to hold his present position for an additional day and that he "considered it necessary . . . in conjunction with the New Zealand division to withdraw to a shorter line east of Suda Bay."[19]

Weston replied that he could not make such a decision but that he would consult Freyberg. Weston departed in search of Freyberg, leaving behind him a command structure that was complex if not totally muddled.

Inglis was in command of Force Reserve, but Weston also controlled Force Reserve. Puttick was in command of the defense perimeter and so was Weston. Weston had been given control of Vasey's Australian brigade, but no one mentioned that to Puttick, who assumed that the Australians were still under his area command. And in a final stroke that was to add more confusion to an already unsettled situation, Weston informed Duncan, the CO of the First Welsh Battalion, that the Ranger and Northumberland Battalions were to come under Duncan's personal command during the relief operation—which brought everything back full circle to Brigadier Inglis's command of Force Reserve.

Weston finally found Freyberg at Suda sometime after 9:00 P.M.—more than two hours after leaving the New Zealand divisional headquarters. Puttick's requests for withdrawal made no impression upon the Creforce commander. He insisted that the line should be held *at all costs* in order to keep the Germans away from the Suda dock area.

Weston remembered to report Vasey's remarks about the Australian brigade's inability to hold for another day. On the basis of Weston's report, Freyberg hastened to issue a strongly worded message to Vasey that concluded with the order that "the Australians were to continue to hold their line at all costs."[20]

As the evening wore on, General Puttick waited at his divisional headquarters for orders from Weston. Each passing hour brought with it new levels of alarm as the roar of battle remained undiminished. If anything, the ferocity of the fighting seemed to increase, which conjured in Puttick's mind the nightmare of a German breakthrough with subsequent encirclement and destruction of his force.

From a little past 6:00 P.M., when Weston had left, until ten o'clock that night, there was no message from Weston. Those hours dragged slowly for Puttick. At 10:00 P.M. he was finally able to reach Creforce headquarters by radio, but still had made no contact with Weston's command post. To his request for orders, Puttick was reminded by the crackling radio voice from Creforce that he was under Weston's command and that General Weston would "issue orders."[21] But Weston was nowhere to be found. At last Puttick could wait no longer and decided to take matters into his own hands. At 10:30 P.M. he issued orders to his forward units to begin a withdrawal at 11:30 P.M. To cover his action, he dispatched Captain R. M. Bell of his staff with a hand-written message for Weston:

NEW ZEALAND DIVISION URGENTLY AWAITS YOUR ORDERS. CANNOT WAIT ANY LONGER AS BRIGADE COMMANDERS REPRE-SENT SITUATION ON THEIR FRONTS AS MOST URGENT. PROPOSE RETIRING WITH OR WITHOUT ORDERS BY 11:30 HOURS 26 MAY.[22]

No sooner had Bell left than Vasey called to inform Puttick of Freyberg's stern order that the Australians were to hold "at all costs." Vasey then asked Puttick for an explanation. "In view of Freyberg's order, how is it that you authorize us to withdraw?" Puttick hesitated, momentarily disconcerted by Vasey's question, then retorted gruffly, "I will take full responsibility for counter-manding General Freyberg's orders!"[23]

Captain Bell finally found General Weston's headquarters, lo-cated in a hollow not far from the Suda docks, an area referred to as Forty-second Street. It bore no relationship to New York City's famous or infamous thoroughfare, but was named after the 42nd Field Company, which had been stationed there before the invasion.

Much to Captain Bell's surprise, he found that General Weston was asleep and no one wished to disturb him. It was not until 1:00 A.M. that the duty officer, at Bell's insistent urgings, decided to disturb the general. Once awakened, Weston read the message, realized that the withdrawal—already in progress—left Force Re-serve in "a difficult position," and ordered that they be called back. With that matter taken care of, the seemingly unperturbed Weston went back to sleep![24]

The staff had difficulty finding dispatch riders to carry this all-important message to Force Reserve. Finally three couriers were located, and they raced off with the order. Sometime after 3:00 A. M. they returned, reporting that the message had been handed to officers of Force Reserve. *But Colonel Duncan, the acting CO of Force Reserve, never got the message.*

Weston's sleep was destined for further interruption. General Puttick arrived shortly thereafter with Colonel A. F. Hely of the Suda brigade and angrily inquired why no orders had been sent to him.

"No use sending orders," replied the irritated Weston, who

seemed more annoyed by the interruption to his sleep than by the question. Then he sarcastically added, "Your division command had made it very clear that the New Zealand division was retiring, whatever happened."[25]

Puttick and Hely exchanged glances. If Weston accepted the fact of the withdrawal come what may, *why had he waited until 1:00 A.M. to recall Force Reserve?*

By dawn of the twenty-seventh, Force Reserve moved into positions beyond the Kladiso River, with the Rangers and Northumberland Hussars taking up unprepared positions near the river, while the Welsh occupied the same trenches they had dug weeks before. When they were all in position, the battalions formed an arc facing westward, with one end resting on the sea and the other, a-mile-and-a-half south, across the Alikianou road.

At the crack of first light, Force Reserve was in position—all alone. During the night, the withdrawal of the New Zealand division had been completed, and with the New Zealanders went Vasey's Australians and Hely's Suda brigade. However, the men of Force Reserve did not know this and believed that their left flank was well protected. Worse yet, Brigadier Inglis, the *official* CO of Force Reserve, had retired with the New Zealand division, assuming that Force Reserve would also be withdrawn. After all, the command of Force Reserve was in Duncan's hands during the relief, thus his presence would not be required in the withdrawal. Such were the effects of a muddled command system. The end result was that Force Reserve not only stood isolated and alone, but it stood without its commanding officer.

By the time the early morning mist evaporated, 4,500 German troops were ready to launch an assault against the 1,000-odd men of Force Reserve.

General Ringel issued final orders to his unit commanders that they use mortars and machine guns and a maximum effort to break through the enemy's defense positions. He was not yet aware that the New Zealanders and Australians had withdrawn during the night and that the only force before him was an outnumbered combination of three depleted battalions with open flanks.

Once the German attack began, it took little time before Colonel Duncan of the Welsh battalion heard the sound of Spandau machine guns and Schmeisser tommy guns firing at him from his flanks. He was bewildered, for he still was under the impression that the Suda brigade was on his left. Patrols sent to contact the Suda brigade returned reporting no contact—only the presence of Germans. When firing of German tommy guns was heard to his rear, Duncan became alarmed and felt that General Weston should be told of the situation. He sent an officer with a brief but frantic note to Weston, but the messenger never got through the German lines.

The message would have made little difference, even if it had succeeded in reaching Weston's headquarters. At that very hour, General Weston and his staff were well on the road south to Sfakia, having left Force Reserve to fend for itself.

The German fire on Duncan and his men was becoming incessant, as the mountain troops began to close the ring on Force Reserve. Duncan realized that his battalions were completely surrounded and that his companies were being cut to pieces. He ordered that they break out and flee for the rear. Over the echoing roar from the heavy sound of battle, Duncan yelled to his executive officer, Major J. T. Gibson, to muster as many survivors as he could find from the three battalions and lead them back to Khaniá.

In small groups, the tired men of Force Reserve dragged themselves through the olive groves, splashed through the shallow waters of the Kladiso River, and headed through the outskirts of the debris-filled streets of Khaniá. Gibson hoped to reorganize them somewhere on the Suda road, but the Germans gave them little respite, following close behind. Colonel Duncan remained behind with about 200 men of his Welsh Battalion to prevent the withdrawal from becoming a debacle.

By midday the First Battalion of Colonel Jais's One Hundred Forty-first Mountain Regiment had advanced toward Suda, where they ran into the Australians of the Nineteenth Brigade and the New Zealanders of the Fifth Brigade, defending Forty-second Street. As the German column turned north toward the head of the bay, Australians from the Seventh Battalion and Maoris from the New Zealand Twenty-eighth Battalion attacked them on the right flank. There followed a savage and bitter encounter where once again the Maori and Australian bayonets did their deadly work. The Germans broke and fled to the west with the Maoris in close pursuit, bayoneting any German in their path.

In the half-mile retreat that followed, the Germans lost more than 300 men to the Maori and Australian counterattack. The First Battalion ceased to exist.[26]

The counterattack came as a shock to the Germans, but it allowed Duncan and his men to slip past the enemy and reach the Kladiso River bridge. The Germans followed them through the main streets of Khaniá and onto the rocky terrain of Akrotiri Peninsula beyond.

General Hargest of the Fifth Brigade followed the retreat with his field glasses from his position at Forty-second Street. He watched in dismay as Duncan and his Welsh survivors were annihilated in this, their final defense position. Hargest shook his head dejectedly, muttering caustically to his aide, "Whoever sent them forward should be shot!"[27]

Force Reserve had been totally destroyed.

By 3:00 P.M. Colonel Jais and the other battalions of his One Hundred Forty-first Regiment succeeded in reaching the western fringe of Suda Bay. About the same time, Captain von der Heydte led the paratroopers of his First Battalion into the burned-out outskirts of Khaniá from the south. It had taken him eight days to capture his first day's objective.

The capital of Crete had finally fallen to the Germans.

At his headquarters at the Grande Bretagne Hotel in Athens, General Kurt Student stared thoughtfully out the tall windows of his office overlooking Constitution Square. He was concerned. He had just returned from a personal inspection of the battle situation in Crete. It seemed that his field commander, Ringel, had things well under control. His forces were advancing steadily, but their progress was painstakingly slow. And that slowness concerned Student.

Again the paratroop commander pondered the same question that had tortured him during those dreadful first hours of the Cretan invasion, when events were going so badly. "How could our intelligence have been so faulty?" he muttered, reviewing the prebattle predictions made by the Abwehr. Admiral Canaris, the intelligence chief, had reported that the British garrison was ill prepared and too outnumbered, after the Greek fiasco, to offer any extended resistance to the airborne assault.

Student swept his eyes across Constitution Square to the Parliament building beyond and then back to the Tomb of the Unknown Soldier. He steadied his gaze upon the crowds of Athenians crossing Amalia Avenue with utter disdain for the presence of the German troops.

He could not erase from his mind the grim scene of thousands of dead paratroopers littering the island, and he paced nervously from the windows to his desk and back again, hands clasped behind him, his head bowed in deep reflection.

All this misinformation, this faulty intelligence, was the cause of delay in seizing Crete. It was a delay that ultimately reflected upon himself and embarrassed him before his Fuehrer.

Kurt Student had promised Adolf Hitler that he would capture Crete in five days. The attack had been postponed from the original date of May 15 to the seventeenth, and finally to the twentieth. Now, one week later, May 26, Crete was still in the hands of the British. Student was aware that time was most important in Hitler's plan for the scheduled attack on Russia. Even General Franz Halder, chief of staff of the German army, had written a memorandum that the delay in Crete might cause a postponement of Operation Barbarossa.[28] The very thought that all these circumstances prevented him from keeping his word to Hitler rankled.

Finally a voice interrupted Student's solitude. "Herr General!" It was his chief of staff, who handed the general a telegram. Student read it and paled:

FRANCE FELL IN EIGHT DAYS, WHY IS CRETE STILL RESISTING?[29]

It was signed by Adolf Hitler.

About the same time that Kurt Student was reading Hitler's telegram, General Freyberg sat down to write another message to his commander in chief in Cairo:

I REGRET TO HAVE TO REPORT THAT IN MY OPINION THE LIMIT OF ENDURANCE HAS BEEN REACHED BY THE TROOPS UNDER MY COMMAND HERE IN SUDA BAY . . . OUR POSITION IS HOPELESS. PROVIDED A DECISION IS REACHED AT ONCE, A CERTAIN PROPORTION OF THE FORCE MIGHT BE EMBARKED.[30]

But Wavell was not convinced by Freyberg's appeals; evacuation meant defeat, and that was out of the question. Instead he instructed Freyberg to reorganize his force, withdraw eastward toward Rethimnon, and set up a defense at that point. Freyberg was to make every effort to hold the eastern half of the island. Wavell remembered Churchill's earlier message that "Crete must be held."

While the battle in the western part of the island swept to its critical stage, the defenders at Rethimnon maintained a constant pressure on the Germans of the Second Parachute Regiment, caught in a continuous and isolated struggle.

Lieutenant Colonel Ian Campbell, the Rethimnon area commander, made every effort to ensure that the initiative remained with the Australian and Greek units at all times. The Rethimnon defense garrison now assumed the role of the attacker, while the Germans became the defenders. Campbell meant to keep it that way.

Unlike General Hargest of the Fifth Brigade, Campbell travelled from unit to unit, always appearing in the front line of battle to make certain there would be no letup against the Germans. His mode of transportation was a motorcycle, for he had early discovered that German aircraft ignored solitary cyclists traveling on the dusty roads below. This was a blessing for Campbell, and the intrepid, aggressive commander appeared wherever the action was.

By the fourth day of the battle, Campbell's leadership had succeeded in keeping the enemy force split into two separate elements, fighting for survival and unable to offer aid to each other. With the Germans kept apart, the airfield that was their major objective remained under Australian control. The other German objective—the city of Rethimnon—was well under the control of the Greek gendarmerie unit garrisoning the town.

On the western sector of the Rethimnon battle zone, some four miles west of the airfield and two miles east of the town itself, the Eleventh Australian Battalion was slowly forcing Captain Wiedemann's men back toward the eastern fringes of the village of Perivolia.

On the afternoon of May 21, Australian signalers had laid out some captured German markers that conveyed a request to the Luftwaffe to bomb the village.[31] At 5:00 P.M. Stuka divebombers fell for this ploy and bombed the village, raining their missiles on their own men and forcing them to withdraw further. The

Australians pursued the Germans into the village, but the paratroopers strengthened their position amid the rubble of the houses and subsequently held the attacking Australians at bay.

With each passing hour, the Germans strengthened their entrenchments, one flank resting in the village houses and the other around the solid granite, walled-in church of St. George, on a prominent rise beyond. From the church's bell tower, the Germans were able to observe the slightest movement by the Australians, making an advance almost impossible.

Lacking artillery, the Australians had no hope of dislodging the Germans. All they could do was to contain them in that line. Even a company of Rangers dispatched by Freyberg from Suda could not force the rear of the German defense line without artillery; the German roadblock set up between Rethimnon and Perivolia was too strong.

In the late afternoon of May 23, German Stukas returned to bomb the Australians for a five-hour session, causing many casualties among the men of the Eleventh Battalion. Then, with the sun to their backs, the German paratroopers left their defense line and rushed forward in a surprise attack. The Australians stood fast, meeting the assault with a stubborn wall of fire. Many of them climbed out of their trenches and, standing in the open, fired from the hip at the charging Germans.

The Germans were repulsed, with so many casualties that they requested a truce to bury their dead and tend their wounded. Campbell granted the truce, and it was strictly enforced, a chivalrous note in a battle that was characterized by so much brutality. Even Campbell's German prisoners were granted permission to collect the German dead, after which they returned to the Australian prisoner-of-war stockade. They were true to their word and their word was their honor.[32]

On the eastern sector of the Rethimnon battle zone approximately one-and-a-half miles east of the airfield, Major Kroh's paratroopers had withdrawn to an olive oil factory in the village of Stavromenos. Inside its thick walls, the Germans established a well-fortified bastion. All efforts by the Australians of the First Battalion to dislodge them had been futile.

On May 22 the aggressive and persistent Colonel Campbell had ordered another attack against the factory by a group of forty Australians led by Captain G. W. Mann. They were to be supported by a detachment of 200 Greeks from the Fifth Greek Regiment. However, a communications failure kept the Greeks back; when the Australians attacked alone and unsupported, they were quickly repulsed.

Colonel Campbell left the 200 Greeks to keep the factory under fire while he departed for the western sector of the battle zone to help his Australians of the Eleventh Battalion beat off the German attack of May 23.

Two days later Campbell returned to Stavromenos, this time *determined* to capture the olive oil factory. He brought with him a repaired infantry tank and three 75-mm guns. After a short period of point-blank shelling, the Germans indicated that they had had enough. As Captain F. J. Embrey and his men stormed the factory buildings, the Germans surrendered—eighty-two of them walking out with their arms raised. The position had finally been taken, and the eastern sector of the Rethimnon battle zone had been secured.

On the day that General Freyberg was wiring Wavell that the "limit of endurance has been reached by the troops under my command" the Australians of the Eleventh Battalion had broken into the German defense line on the *western* sector of the Rethimnon battle zone and finally captured the redoubts around the Church of St. George.

Colonel Campbell had mustered his men and all available 75-mm guns in order to capture the village of Perivolia and thus break through the German roadblock to the west.

While Freyberg appealed for an evacuation, Campbell was ordering the new attack! It was typical of the Rethimnon area commander. Besides his ground successes, Campbell could also boast of holding 500 German prisoners, including the commander of the Parachute Regiment, Colonel Sturm.

Even though General Freyberg had said before the invasion that he was unimpressed with Campbell, Campbell's fighting leadership caused Freyberg to reconsider his earlier evaluation. Campbell's successes impressed Freyberg enough for him to wire Campbell:

YOU HAVE BEEN MAGNIFICENT![33]

The Germans at Iráklion did not fare any better than their comrades at Rethimnon.

By the fifth day of the battle, the survivors of the First Parachute Regiment found themselves isolated in two groups, six miles apart, and suffering a humiliating existence. Having arrived as conquerors, they now cowered on the brink of defeat.

Colonel Brauer and his eighty survivors had to hide among the rocks and seek the soothing shade of caves while hoping for some miracle that might save them from this dire predicament.

In the western sector of Iráklion, the second isolated group of German paratroopers fared little better than Brauer's men.

The two major German objectives—the city of Iráklion and its airfield—remained in the hands of British and Greek units. Nor was there any possibility for the Germans to gain their objectives; the German attack on Iráklion had been a failure.

Unfortunately for the defending forces, the commander of the Iráklion garrison, Brigadier Chappel, was too indifferent to appreciate that he had the Germans reeling in defeat.

On May 24 Student sent the last of his "leftover" paratroopers to Crete. Four hundred men who had not made the initial drop on the twentieth because transport was lacking now descended in an area south of the Iráklion defense perimeter. They were quickly surrounded by units of the Argyll and Sutherland Highlanders and either killed or captured. Some survivors fled to join Major Schulz's battalion.

This was the last of any available reinforcements for the attackers at Iráklion. A few subsequent supply airdrops followed but they fell into the welcoming arms of British troops and Cretan irregulars, who thus replenished their own supplies. For the Germans—low on ammunition, food, and water—there would be no more airdrops, for the Luftwaffe aircraft were now needed to fight the Royal Navy at sea.

Unable from their precarious position to mount an attack against the British with any possibility of success, the frustrated Germans of Major Schulz's battalion vented their fury on the civilian population.

On May 22 the paratroopers of the Third Battalion had been forced to withdraw from Iráklion under pressure from the attacking British and the harassing Cretan irregulars. Even the monks from the monasteries took part, carrying water and food to the British. During the withdrawal, Schulz ordered the seizure of forty-two civilians as hostages. He planned to punish the Cretans for their folly of resisting the German conqueror.

He ordered that all forty-two hostages be shot.

On May 24, the hapless Cretans were lined up in ranks of ten for the execution, with little regard for age or sex. Among the hostages were an old man of ninety and a girl of fourteen; there was also a priest, who spent the last moments of his life praying; there were the Katsanevakis brothers and their friend Manoli Gavdiotis, who stood bravely against the wall, glaring unflinchingly at their executioners. And there was one man whose execution gave the Germans a particular delight. He was Rabbi Ben-Israel Sholub.

Raised in Germany, the middle-aged rabbi and his wife fled that country during the early days of the Nazi pogroms. He traveled to Greece to join his relatives in Salonika. When the Germans invaded Greece, he fled once again, boarding a refugee-filled boat for Egypt, but was transported instead to Iráklion. He thought for a while that he had found safety in Crete, but the Nazis followed in his wake. On May 24 his flight finally ended at the execution wall, at the hands of those he had tried so hard to escape.[34]

On May 25 the Luftwaffe returned to reduce the city of Iráklion to dust and rubble, leaving it a stark shambles of shattered buildings, debris-filled streets, and crushed bodies—like its sister city of Khaniá to the west.

At 11:00 A.M. on May 27, Winston Churchill gave a progress report to the House of Commons about the situation in Crete and about the search for the *Bismarck*. (The Commons had been meeting in the Church House ever since the Parliament building had been destroyed on May 10 during a severe German air raid.) No sooner had Churchill finished and taken his seat than he was handed a message. He rose once again and with a touch of dramatic finality in his voice, reported: "I have just received news that the *Bismarck* is sunk." Like their predecessors after the announcement that bore the news of Nelson's victory at Trafalgar, the members stood and cheered.

With the problem in the North Atlantic resolved, the prime minister now turned his undivided attention to Crete. If only the events there would come to an equally successful conclusion. Wasting no time, Churchill telegraphed General Freyberg on May 27, hoping that his words could inspire a victory in Crete:

YOUR GLORIOUS DEFENSE COMMANDS ADMIRATION IN EVERY LAND . . . ALL AID IN OUR POWER IS BEING SENT[35]

and General Wavell in Cairo:

VICTORY IN CRETE IS ESSENTIAL AT THIS TURNING POINT IN THE WAR. KEEP HURLING IN ALL AID YOU CAN.[36]

Wavell had made one last effort to reinforce Crete. On May 26, the day before he received Churchill's order to "keep hurling in all aid," Wavell ordered the Second Battalion of the Queen's Regiment to be ferried to Tymbaki aboard the transport *Glenroy*, with the destroyers *Jaguar, Stuart,* and *Coventry* as escorts. Colonel Laycock's commandos were already on their way, but a different fate awaited this convoy. Halfway to Crete the ships were attacked by a heavy concentration of torpedo- and dive-bombers, setting the *Glenroy* afire and forcing the convoy to return to Alexandria. There would be no more reinforcements for the defenders of Crete.

Fighter Command in Egypt dispatched ten Hurricanes to the airfield at Iráklion. Unfortunately, six of the ten were shot down by the trigger-happy defenders. When two other fighters observed their first six comrades shot down because of mistaken identity, they turned back over the sea. Too short of fuel to return to their home base in Egypt, they were never seen or heard of again. The remaining two Hurricanes, which succeeded in landing safely, were destroyed by German strafers the next day.

When the commander in chief returned to his desk, he found a personal message from Freyberg waiting for him. It was another despairing plea for the evacuation of the troops from Crete, couched in terms of hopelessness. To Wavell, these words were an indication of Freyberg's determined state of mind. He realized that he could not force a commander fighting an isolated battle 400 miles away and without hope of receiving reinforcements to continue a struggle he had already deemed lost.

Wavell therefore had no alternative but to accept Freyberg's view of the true state of affairs prevailing on Crete. Reluctantly, he dictated a four-point message to Winston Churchill:

1. FEAR THAT SITUATION IN CRETE MOST SERIOUS . . . THERE IS NO POSSIBILITY OF HURLING IN REINFORCEMENTS.

2. . . .CONTINUOUS AND UNOPPOSED AIR ATTACK MUST DRIVE STOUTEST TROOPS FROM POSITIONS . . . AND MAKES ADMINISTRATION PRACTICALLY IMPOSSIBLE.

3. TELEGRAM JUST RECEIVED FROM FREYBERG STATES ONLY CHANCE OF SURVIVAL OF FORCE IN SUDA AREA IS TO WITHDRAW TO BEACHES IN SOUTH OF ISLAND. . . .

4. FEAR WE MUST RECOGNIZE THAT CRETE IS NO LONGER TENABLE AND THAT TROOPS MUST BE WITHDRAWN AS FAR AS POSSIBLE. . . .[37]

Thus the heroic battle for the island of Crete reached its final stage. Wavell's message to Churchill was a request for permission to evacuate the island. With a heavy heart, Churchill, recognizing that all hope for victory in Crete was gone, authorized the evacuation.

With that authorization began another epic of heroism—by the men of the withdrawing force, by the officers and men of the Royal Navy who rushed to their rescue, and by the Cretans and Greeks who remained behind to continue the fight.

# 25 / "300 YEARS TO BUILD A NEW TRADITION"

## MAY 26–30, 1941

General Wavell did not wait for Churchill's acknowledgment that Crete must be abandoned. While the prime minister and his cabinet mulled over the hard-to-accept situation, Wavell authorized Freyberg to begin the evacuation as soon as possible, assuring him that the Royal Navy would be waiting to embark the troops.

The day before—May 26—General Wavell had met in Alexandria with the other two chiefs of services. Admiral Sir Andrew Cunningham and Air Marshal A. W. Tedder were joined by General Sir Thomas Blamey, the commanding general of the Australian forces in the Middle East, and Peter Fraser, the prime minister of New Zealand. Both Blamey and Fraser voiced deep concern for the Anzac troops that represented their two nations. The sole subject on the meeting's agenda was "the consideration for a possible evacuation from Crete."

A solemn mood filled the air of the conference room. Each man bore a heavy burden of responsibility in his representative position, but the heaviest lay painfully upon the shoulders of the Middle East commander, General Wavell.

Once the decision had been reached to abandon Crete, the question arose if the troops could be evacuated safely or would losses make surrender inevitable? Admiral Cunningham warned that incessant German air attacks could inflict terrible losses upon the men, "and to save lives, surrender might be more humane."[1] At these words Blamey and Fraser looked at each other and then at Wavell as if to remind him that the bulk of the troops on Crete were New Zealand and Australian. Wavell avoided their glance.

Cunningham then added somewhat proudly, "After all, gentlemen, the navy's duty was achieved and no enemy ship, whether warship or transport, succeeded in reaching Crete."[2]

"Does that mean," he was asked, "that the Royal Navy deems

it impossible to evacuate the troops in the face of the German air onslaught?"[3]

The Mediterranean Fleet commander hesitated thoughtfully for a moment before replying. On May 21 the destroyer *Juno* had been sunk; the next day the destroyer *Greyhound* and the cruisers *Gloucester* and *Fiji* went down, while the cruisers *Naiad* and *Carlisle* and the battleships *Warspite* and *Valiant* were heavily damaged by bombs. On the twenty-third the destroyers *Kashmir* and *Kelly* together with five motor-torpedo boats had been sunk by German aircraft, and on May 26 itself, the aircraft carrier *Formidable* was severely damaged while the destroyer *Nubian* had her stern blown off. Eleven ships had already been sunk as of May 26, with six of Cunningham's first-line men-of-war badly damaged. *Never before had the Royal Navy suffered such losses in any one single battle.* How many more ships would be lost during an evacuation?

He finally broke the silence: "Whatever the risks, whatever our losses, the remaining ships of the fleet will make an all-out effort to bring away the army."[4]

There was a sigh of relief from Blamey and Fraser, while Wavell forced a pained smile. The Royal Navy would be there once again to rescue the army as it had earlier at Dunkirk and later in Greece.

Cunningham shook his head sadly at the thought of what lay in store for his men and ships. In grave tones he reminded the conferees of the heavy losses suffered by his fleet in the waters around Crete. "This time we evacuate with fewer ships, far less resources, and with our men and ships worn to the point of exhaustion.

"But let us remember, gentlemen," Cunningham continued in a voice infused with the spirit of Nelson, "it takes the navy three years to build a new ship. It will take 300 years to build a new tradition."[5]

Once Freyberg received the authorization to abandon the island, he centered his attention on the business of disengaging the troops and sending them on an organized retreat to the southern beaches of Sfakia for evacuation. The release had not come any too soon, for even the island's Greek commander had seen the handwriting on the wall.

The order to withdraw to the south was quickly passed to the troops. Suddenly everyone—British, Australians, and New Zealanders—felt the urgent desire to leave this once beautiful and peaceful island that the flames of war had converted into a place of death and desolation. The dusty, dirty route south to Sfakia was soon choked with columns of ragged, tired soldiers.

The men moved forward in overheated exhaustion, stumbling over each other in their haste. Many of them discarded their helmets, their weapons, and their ammunition; others removed their tunics and cast them aside. The whole trail was soon littered with the accoutrements of an army in disorderly retreat. Blankets, gas masks, field packs, helmets, and ammo boxes were scattered with related castoffs along the side of the trail.[6]

During the day, trucks passed through the retreating column, bumping from side to side on the hard, rocky, rutted road, spewing dirt and dust on the perspiring, weary marchers. The men cursed the trucks for thus adding to their discomfort.

As the men struggled through the heat and dust, their attention was forever riveted to the sky. Fear of the marauding Luftwaffe was always uppermost in each man's mind. The slightest sound of an approaching aircraft was enough to raise the alarm of "Take cover, take cover," whereupon the men would scatter onto the rocky slopes on either side of the trail.

Today, however, the Luftwaffe was surprisingly absent. It was concentrating its efforts on the ships of the Royal Navy in the waters all around Crete. There were, however, a few strafings by Messerschmitts—enough to keep the retreating troops on the alert.

At night, even the flicker of a match was enough to raise angry shouts. So great was their fear of an air attack that some of the men even fired at the light, with complete disregard for order and discipline.

At dusk on the first night of the retreat, Colonel Kippenberger, at the head of his column of men from the Tenth Brigade, reached a fork in the road. Uncertain which of the two paths led south to Sfakia, he laid his map on the ground and shone his flashlight on it. Careful as he was to cover it, a slight glimmer of light was evident. Instantly there followed a series of curses and shouts from above the trail to "put out that bloody light!"

One outraged soldier rushed up and kicked the flashlight from Kippenberger's hand. Incensed at this gross breach of military discipline, Kippenberger grabbed the trooper and threw him to the ground. The furious brigade commander threatened that if there was any repetition of such discourtesy to an officer, he would shoot the offender.[7]

Throughout the night of May 27 and into the twenty-eighth, a continuous stream of men trudged down the long, rugged mountain trail that led to the southern coast. For most of the tired men, the retreat had become a test of endurance. There was little food left to relieve their hunger; their parched throats demanded water, but water was in even shorter supply than food. Nevertheless the men staggered silently onward, often weaving and ready to drop with fatigue. Their clothes were dusty, dirty, and torn; their boots had been slashed by sharp rocks; their feet were blistered and bleeding, but onward they marched. They had no choice.

Throughout the whole night of the withdrawal from Suda, Hargest and Vasey felt the dread of an ambush or a flanking German attack on the exhausted column. They could not know that it was a groundless fear, for the Germans were as yet unaware that the defenders were fleeing to the southern beaches.

General Ringel was still following the original order of priorities given him by General Alexander Löhr, the Fourth Air Fleet commander, when Ringel took over field command of the invading forces in Crete. He was to secure Maleme airfield, seize Khaniá and Suda Bay, and capture Rethimnon and Iráklion—in that sequence. In his anxiety to succor his beloved paratroopers at Rethimnon and Iráklion, General Student had never altered this order of priorities. Thus, while the defenders were withdrawing toward the south, Ringel reminded the Eighty-fifth Mountain Regiment of his Fifth Mountain Division that they were not to be "drawn away southward," and that they were still to take Rethimnon.[8]

The orders issued from Ringel's headquarters on May 28 emphasized that "the enemy was to be pursued eastward through Rethimnon to Iráklion without a pause." The first objective would be Rethimnon, followed by the relief of the paratroopers at Iráklion. He ordered Colonel August Wittmann, the former commanding officer of the One-hundred-eleventh Artillery Regiment and now commanding the Ninety-fifth Artillery Regiment, to lead a task force comprised of ancillary artillery units, engineers, and antitank gunners attached to the Ninety-fifth Motorcycle Battalion in the drive eastward.

Ringel's right-hand punch, led by Colonel Krakau's Eighty-fifth Mountain Regiment, was still stalemated by the Eighth Regiment in the shrubs and broken hills around Alikianou village. Krakau was following Ringel's edict not to be drawn to the south, but his battalions could not move eastward either. The Greeks of the Eighth Regiment, joined by the Cretans, continued their fierce resistance, keeping the Germans at bay. First it was the Engineer Battalion of Heidrich's Third Parachute Regiment that was kept in check; five days later, it was Krakau's battalions of the Eighty-fifth Mountain Regiment.

The Greeks and the Cretan irregulars repulsed the Germans over and over again, day in and day out. These were the men to whom Kippenberger had referred as "malaria-ridden little chaps." This was the unit that had been reported destroyed in the first day of battle, yet seven days later, it was still holding the Germans in the hills around Alikianou.

The British command was not to realize until much later that the courage of the Eighth Greek Regiment was another factor enabling the Commonwealth troops to withdraw to the south. If the Greeks and Cretans had fled on the first day of battle as incorrectly reported, there would have been no chance of a withdrawal—instead, the whole New Zealand command would have been surrounded and wiped out. For these two reasons—Ringel's adherence to his priority of orders and the resolute resistance of the Eighth Greek Regiment at Alikianou—the Commonwealth defenders were now able to move south for evacuation.[9]

Finally, on May 27, the depleted ranks of the Eighth Greek Regiment dispersed and fled to the hills to continue the fight as guerrillas in the resistance movement that was to follow during the German occupation. At last the three reinforced battalions of Krakau's regiment were able to advance eastward, breaking through to Stilos only to find Hargest's men already there. As a detachment of the Second Battalion climbed the slope of a hill west of Stilos, they were met by withering fire from the New Zealanders, who had arrived some hours earlier. Thanks to the gallant defense of the Eighth Greek Regiment, the Germans arrived at Stilos twenty-four hours too late. *That delay made the evacuation possible.*

At 10:00 P.M. that Tuesday, May 27, the Creforce skeleton staff abandoned their headquarters compound. The wireless station had been destroyed and the codes burned; the men wearily mounted the trucks and headed south.

When Freyberg finally arrived in Sfakia, he established his

headquarters in a cave high in the cliffs above the village. He immediately forwarded an urgent message to Alexandria for the evacuation to begin. At his first opportunity, he sat down and penned an assessment of his situation. He planned to have the message carried to Alexandria by his personal aide, Lieutenant John White:

> WE HAVE HAD A PRETTY ROUGH TIME. THE TROOPS WERE NOT BEATEN BY ORDINARY CONDITIONS, BUT BY THE GREAT AERIAL CONCENTRATION AGAINST US . . . WE WERE HANDICAPPED BY LACK OF TRANSPORT, COMMUNICATIONS, AND LACK OF STAFF. EVERYBODY TRIED HARD IN MOST DIFFICULT CIRCUMSTANCES. I AM SORRY CRETE COULD NOT BE HELD. [10]

Then, in a final sentence, he assumed complete responsibility for the debacle:

> IT WAS CERTAINLY NOT THE FAULT OF THE TROOPS. [11]

Everywhere the men of the retreating column saw the destruction wrought by the Luftwaffe. Fields were pitted with bomb craters, stone cottages lay shattered, and roads were littered with burned-out, strafed vehicles—many still filled with the corpses of fighting men. Corpses lay everywhere, at roadsides and in the fields; with them lay the badly wounded and those too exhausted to continue. The retreating men looked straight ahead, as if these horrible sights of defeat were invisible.

Strangely, this movement in broad daylight was unimpeded by a single German aircraft. Most of the Stukas and Messerschmitts were involved in attacks on the ships of the Royal Navy. Other Luftwaffe squadrons had already been withdrawn to the eastern front, for Hitler had at last decided that the invasion of Russia would begin on June 21, now that the campaign in Crete was nearing a successful conclusion.

Under a clear sky, Hargest rode up and down the column in his Bren carrier giving his men encouragement and admiring their unfailing spirit. The men hiked through the village of Babali Hani, six miles beyond Stilos, and then another six miles to Vrises. There they paused to rest in the cool shade of olive, oak, and plane trees and to quench their thirst with the cool waters that gave the village its name. [12]

From prisoners taken when isolated pockets of resistance were overrun, German intelligence finally learned that there was a mass movement of troops toward the southern coast of Crete. Still following Ringel's orders to advance eastward toward Rethimnon, Colonel Wittmann dispatched only the Third Battalion from his Eighty-fifth Mountain Regiment in pursuit.

Their heated, day-long skirmish with Commonwealth rearguard troops attracted German reinforcements. By nightfall, the whole of Wittmann's Kampfgruppe turned south to give battle.

It was time for the commandos to withdraw.

By 10:00 P.M. that night, Colonel Young of the commando battalion successfully disengaged his men from battle and turned to follow the retreating New Zealanders.

The advance group of the retreating mass of exhausted men burst through the massive barrier of the White Mountains and reached the southern coast. The rock-strewn mountain path terminated on an escarpment 500 feet above shore; from there a faint goat trail meandered down the steep side of the rugged cliff to the white stone houses that lay in its shadow.

This was the fishing village of Sfakia.

Off the narrow strip of sandy beach that touched the sparkling cool water of the inlet, the ships of the Royal Navy were soon to drop anchor and begin the evacuation. They would be a welcome sight to the men who had suffered the ordeal of battle this past week.

From his headquarters atop the cliffs, approximately a mile above the beach at Sfakia, General Freyberg made systematic plans for the evacuation. He decided that the troops should embark during the three hours after midnight. This would allow the ships a safety margin of darkness—four hours to reach Sfakia, three to embark the troops, and another four to steam beyond the reach of enemy aircraft—before dawn.

Freyberg ordered that all Creforce personnel from the Suda Bay area be evacuated from the beach at Sfakia, while Chappel's troops at Iráklion would be embarked from the city's harbor. Lieutenant Colonel Campbell's Australians at Rethimnon were to retire to the south and be evacuated from the tiny village of Plaka.[13] With typical indifference, there was no concern for the evacuation of the Greek regiments.

* * *

In the early predawn hours of Saturday, May 31, General Frey-berg, following Wavell's orders, left Crete with the naval liaison officer, Captain J. A. V. Morse, in a Sunderland flying boat. As the huge craft lifted off the waters off Sfakia, Freyberg looked back in dismay. His first and only senior command had ended in defeat. It was a bitter pill for this fine soldier who held so many honors; moreover he felt great concern for the men he was leaving behind.

That same day, having arrived safely in Alexandria, Freyberg with New Zealand Prime Minister Fraser went to plead that an additional effort be made to evacuate the rest of the men on Crete. He begged that the ships "take aboard at Sfakia every man [they] could pack."[14]

After consulting with his officers, Admiral Cunningham de-cided to send additional ships back to Crete in what was destined to be the last rescue mission.

With food and medical supplies transferred from the ships to the beaches of Sfakia, the embarkation began. In a matter of a few hours, as many as 3,710 men had been ferried out to the waiting ships. Well before dawn on Sunday, June 1, the last ship of the force left Sfakia for the final journey to Alexandria.[15]

When Prime Minister Churchill learned late on the thirty-first that the rescue operation was to be terminated while British troops still remained on Crete, he protested to the Navy vice-chief of staff. In turn, the Admiralty urged Cunningham to continue the evacuation, but the Mediterranean Fleet commander was adamant in his decision. His fear of what Luftwaffe air superiority could do to his ships made his decision final.

Cunningham was to describe the whole evacuation operation as one of "great tension and anxiety such as I have never expe-rienced before or since."[16]

His decision to end the evacuation sealed the fate of more than 11,000 men still on the southern beaches of Crete. For them, the fighting was over.

# 26 / "CRETE HAS BECOME THE GRAVEYARD OF THE GERMAN PARATROOPER"

**MAY 30–31, 1941**

The ships of Admiral Cunningham's Mediterranean Fleet succeeded in evacuating approximately 16,511 men from the beaches of southern Crete during those last days in May.[1] However, that those fortunate men were available for embarkation was due in large part to the resolute resistance of the rear guard in the ravines and rocky passes of the southern mountains above Sfakia.

As more troops were evacuated each night, the defense perimeter was gradually contracting. Despite the German flanking maneuvers, the stubborn rear-guard defense brought the German mountain troops to a standstill. Each day the crack of rifle and machine-gun fire echoed through the mountains as skirmishes turned into bitter battles. The Germans were unable to breach the defense line. Colonel Utz of the One hundredth Mountain Regiment concluded that he could not successfully press the attack without proper air cover and artillery support. While he waited for this help, he decided to postpone any renewed attacks for at least two more days. By June 2, he felt, his reinforcements would have arrived, and his flanking companies would reach the coast. All would be in readiness for the final assault to break the rear-guard defense and cast the defenders into the sea.

When General Freyberg was ordered to leave Crete on Saturday, May 31, he turned over the command of Crete's defense to General Weston. Weston's first act as commander was to wire Wavell that some 9,000 men remained on the island ready for evacuation. He optimistically added that he felt he would be able to hold Sfakia for at least two more days, enough time to get these men off the island. It was not until later that afternoon that Weston received word of Cunningham's decision to terminate the evacuation with the departure of Admiral King's ships later that night. The message included orders for Weston to leave Crete aboard a Sunderland flying boat that would arrive the same night. The final sentence in the message advised Weston to "authorize the capitulation of any troops who had to be left behind."[2] The end was near.

Weston summoned Colonel Laycock to his headquarters and informed the commando leader of the decision to end the evacuation. "I am ordered out tonight," he told Laycock, "and I have been instructed to pass the command to the next senior officer."

Laycock shifted his stance nervously and clasped his hands behind him. He had a premonition of what was to follow. "I am *offering* you the command of the remaining troops," continued Weston, "and am authorizing you to negotiate their surrender at your convenience anytime after tomorrow."

Colonel Laycock bowed his head momentarily in thought. After a silence that seemed eternal, he snapped to attention and looked into the general's eyes. "I respectfully decline the offer, sir!"

Weston understood. He had not *ordered* Laycock to take command, he had *offered* him the command.

"I did not come to Crete," explained Laycock, "to surrender to the Hun. I believe I can be of greater service with my Commando Brigade than as a prisoner of war."

"Very well, then, Laycock, *you* pick the officer who is to negotiate with the Germans."

This time, Weston's words were a command.[3]

Colonel Laycock passed the responsibility to an officer in his command. He ordered Lieutenant Colonel G. A. D. Young, whose brave leadership of D Battalion had kept the Germans at bay during the rear-guard action, to take command of the remaining troops when he and Weston departed. Unlike Laycock Young was not *offered* the command; he was *ordered* to assume it. Thus it was to fall to this unfortunate officer to surrender the island to the Germans.[4]

The hours passed quickly that last afternoon, and the ships of Admiral King's task force would soon arrive. General Weston made one last decision before turning the command over to Young. He ordered that the men who had been engaged in the fighting since the first day of the invasion should be given first evacuation priority.

He ordered Brigadier Hargest's Fifth Brigade of New Zealanders and Vasey's Australian brigade to prepare for departure. As the sun began to dip in the western sky, Hargest made his preparations. He gathered the 1,100 survivors of his brigade and gave specific orders to the officers. The only New Zealanders who were to be evacuated were those wearing helmets and carrying rifles; all others were to be considered stragglers. It was a painful but necessary decision.

Hargest sent Colonel Andrew and the Twenty-second Battalion—the defenders of Hill 107—down to the beach to clear a path for the rest of the brigade. "Have your men fix their bayonets if you have to," he instructed Andrew, "but keep the path to the beaches clear."[5]

The men were ordered to shave, bear rifles, and carry haversacks on their backs as if on parade. When darkness finally blanketed the island, the New Zealanders of the Fifth Brigade began the long descent down the trail to the beach and ultimate rescue by the ships that were already dropping their anchors in the waters beyond.

When Colonel Walker and his Seventh Australian Battalion reached the trail to the beach, he found confusion all around him, with large groups of noncombat soldiers sitting down on the trail, effectively blocking it. A self-appointed movement-control officer informed Walker that only a single file could pass at this point and that the Australians would have to wait in line.

Walker was furious and was almost tempted to order his men to draw their bayonets and force a passage to the beach. Instead he decided to take a detour.

For the next five hours, the men of his battalion, led by the second in command, Major H. C. D. Marshall, struggled in the darkness over the broken ravines and rugged mountain terrain seeking an alternative path to the beach.

The men staggered onward spent with fatigue; they had fought so many days, and now when rescue was within their grasp, they had to undergo this additional ordeal. They had to fight not only darkness and the mountains but, more important, they had to struggle against time.

One Australian fell, too exhausted to move, and pleaded to be left where he had fallen. Major Marshall picked him up and supported him for miles until they reached the beach. Throughout the arduous trek, Marshall also pushed and even threatened his men to keep up a "fast and proper pace."

When the battalion finally reached the beach, they lined up quietly in orderly ranks waiting to be evacuated, but it was too late. From the last departing barge, the officer aboard could see the Australians waiting on the beach for his return.[6]

Major Marshall found his CO, Colonel Walker, sitting dejectedly on the stone sea wall as the last ships in the bay weighed anchor for departure.

Realizing that it was all over for them, some of the noncombatant stragglers raised white flags. At the sight of this surrender signal, two of Walker's NCO's rushed over to him and angrily asked, "Shall we shoot the bastards?"

"No," he replied slowly, "we may not like it, but we might as well pack it in!"[7]

By 3:00 A.M. the last of Cunningham's ships had sailed for Egypt.

Lieutenant Colonel Young, designated by Laycock to assume command of the remaining troops, opened the sealed envelop that represented General Weston's final order before departure. It was addressed, "Senior Officer left on the Island."[8]

Young ran his eyes down the six paragraphs of the order. The fourth was brief and to the point: "No more evacuation is possible,"[9] and the sixth and final paragraph clearly indicated what he was expected to do: "You are ordered to make contact with the enemy and arrange capitulation."[10]

The colonel folded the order and put it in his breast pocket. With a heavy sigh at the distasteful task before him, he picked up a white flag and went out to meet a German officer.

The battle for Crete was finally over.

Although most senior officers reluctantly obeyed the order to capitulate to the Germans, there were many New Zealanders, Australians, and British troopers of all ranks whose fighting spirit would not allow them to surrender, to spend the rest of the war in a German prison camp. When it became evident that no more rescue ships would arrive, many men decided to seek their own means of escape.

In the early morning hours of the first day of the surrender, a group of stranded soldiers found an abandoned landing barge. The men knew little or nothing about handling the boat until Private Harry Richards, an Australian, offered to act as boat commander. A New Zealander, Private A. Taylor, volunteered to be the navigator. The rest of the group, made up of Australians, New Zealanders, and British, helped maneuver the barge into a huge cavern to keep it out of sight until nightfall. That night they set sail on what they hoped would be an easy and rapid trip to Egypt. It was destined to be neither.

The next morning the barge ran aground on Gavdos, an island south of Crete. Although repairs were made quickly, Private Richards, acting as skipper, realized that the boat was overloaded and asked for volunteers to remain behind.

The journey resumed early that evening, lighter by ten men. A day's journey later, the barge ran out of fuel. In desperation, an oar was rigged up as a mast, and a worn blanket as a sail. The trip became intolerably slow, with the danger of attack from the air ever present. What little rations and water they had were soon gone, leaving the men under the hot sun, hoping for the slightest breeze to billow the sail. They weakened, and often tempers flared in their misery. Finally, on June 8—one week later—with hope almost gone, they reached the rocky beach of Sidi Barrani in North Africa. The landing site proved to be near a British camp, from which the troopers rushed out to welcome them.[11]

While Richards's group of escapees struggled to cross the waters to North Africa, another group of 137 Royal Marines under Marine Major R. Garrett set forth on a similar journey. Garrett and his men had also found an abandoned barge and launched it for their escape. Paralleling Richards's saga, Garrett's barge also ran out of fuel one-third across, and his group, too, resorted to makeshift mast and sails. Their rations dwindled to a half tin of water and one teaspoonful of bully beef daily. When the wind died down, the men would jump into the water to push the barge forward. They endured an excruciating nine-day trip before they reached Sidi Barrani—a trip during which one soldier died from exhaustion and another committed suicide.[12]

The flight to avoid capture was not confined to large groups of men. Many others made the attempt, singly or in pairs; some met with success but most failed.

Major Sandover, the Australian who led his Eleventh Battalion so gallantly at Rethimnon, meant it when he told his commanding officer, Brigadier Campbell, that he would not surrender. He led a group of Australians from his unit across the mountains to a point east of Sfakia from whence he made his escape to North Africa.[13]

Private D. McQuarrie of the Eighteenth New Zealand Battalion had lain wounded in a hospital encampment in Suda. Cretan civilians kept him alive for two weeks by tending to his wounds and by feeding him and the other patients in the encampment. Deprivation and hardship followed soon after the Germans took over the area. McQuarrie was transferred to a hospital in Khaniá where he personally witnessed the wounded die from hunger and lack of care. He decided to escape on June 18. Trekking south to the village of Meskla, high in the White Mountains, he stayed with a Cretan family for two weeks; he ate well and his wounds had an opportunity to heal.

However, the Germans were closing in and threatening death to any Cretan who offered shelter or assistance to a British soldier. Fearing for the safety of his hosts, McQuarrie left for the surrounding hills. There he met another New Zealander, Private B. Carter, who had escaped from the prison camp at Galatas on July 1.

The two wandered about the mountains for a week and then headed north, back to Suda. They were joined by two Australians and finally reached the coast, where they found an abandoned dinghy. On July 16 they began their long trip across the waters to North Africa.

As soon as they set sail, they realized why the dinghy had been abandoned. They used their socks and shirts to plug the many holes, and each man took a turn sitting on a larger hole in the stern while the rest bailed water. Locomotion was provided by a makeshift setup of lashed oars for a mast and tied blankets for a sail. Luckily for them, a strong gale prevailed throughout the trip, blowing them the 400 miles to Sidi Barrani within four days. When the British soldiers at Sidi Barrani waded out to help them, the dinghy fell apart. It was a miracle, they thought, that this delapidated craft had remained seaworthy long enough to complete such a tempestuous sea voyage.[14]

Lieutenant R. Sinclair of the Twenty-second New Zealand Battalion and Lieutenant Roy Farran of the Third Hussars Tank Regiment had fought hard in the eleven-day battle in Crete. Sinclair had been involved in combat around Hill 107 from the first day of the invasion, and Farran had led the unsuccessful New Zealand counterattack against Pirgos with his three light tanks on May 22. With his tank, Farran also led the counterattack to recapture Galatas. Now Sinclair and Farran were prisoners of the Germans.

Both men had been shipped from the prison compound in Prison Valley to Kokkinias Prison, on the mainland near Athens. It was from Kokkinias Prison that they made their escape. The Greek underground got them onto a thirty-foot caïque bound for Alexandria, together with ten other Greeks and three soldiers. As the caïque entered the straits between Kaso island and Crete, a heavy storm struck them with high winds and mountainous waves. Only the captain's skill kept the caïque from being swamped, but the effort soon exhausted their fuel. The same dilemma that confronted Richards's and Garrett's groups now presented itself to Sinclair, Farran, and the rest. Makeshift sails were used to catch what little wind prevailed. Rations diminished daily. By the ninth day, the men lay in utter exhaustion—thirsty, hungry, too weak even to speak. That night they were picked up by a passing British destroyer. Sinclair and Farran finally reached the safety of Alexandria.[15]

As the months passed, the Germans tightened the cordon and increased their search for these stragglers, whom they called "deserters." The Germans did not hesitate to shoot any civilian aiding an escapee, nor did they hesitate to burn whole villages in retribution. Yet despite these brutal measures, the Cretan population continued giving guidance and sustenance to the New Zealand, Australian, and British stragglers and escapees who roamed the hills and mountains of Crete.

Some 1,000 Commonwealth soldiers were eventually able to escape from the stricken island. Those soldiers who made no such effort or were unsuccessful remained as prisoners of war. These numbered approximately 11,835 men, many of whom were first confined in makeshift compounds at Aghia and Prison Valley and later transferred to the mainland. However, by the end of the year, there were still about 500 escapees at large and roaming the hills, having filtered into the safety of the mountains, seeking and receiving shelter from the Cretans.

During the four long, dreary years of the German occupation that followed, the people of Crete were to suffer heavily under the tyrannical rule of the Nazi oppressor. From the first day of the occupation, which began on June 1, 1941, the Cretan population faced a terrible trial of terror for their resistance. Countless thousands of Cretans were gathered for execution upon the slightest pretext. A constant sense of fear pervaded the island as squads of Germans marched from village to village collecting hostages at random. The more fortunate villagers were mustered into labor gangs; the less fortunate were sent to the execution wall. Over

2,000 Cretans were executed in the first month of the occupation. During the next four years, more than 25,000 islanders were marched before German execution squads. Considering the island's census of 400,000 residents, this was a decimating toll. It was also a hell of which the outside world knew nothing.

Men like Nicholas Manolakakis from Spilia village, who had seen his wife and son slain by the Germans on the first day of the invasion, waged a one-man campaign against the destroyers of his quiet family life. In the ten days that followed, he personally killed some forty German paratroopers. Now the SS were looking for him. They announced that if Manolakakis did not surrender himself immediately, they would execute at random ten hostages from his village for each day's delay. When Manolakakis heard of this proclamation, he left the safety of the White Mountains and, returning to his village, surrendered himself to the Germans. The SS had Manolakakis dig his own grave, and when he finished, they executed him. The same fate befell Kostas Manousos, the six-foot six-inch Cretan from Sfakia, who had seen his father slain on the first day of the attack. When he learned that a similar bounty had been placed upon his head, he made the same decision as Manolakakis. His surrender would prevent a wholesale slaughter of villagers from Platanias. His personal revenge accounted for forty-three Germans, and now he had to pay the price. He kissed his wife and son tenderly before making the long trek north to Platanias.

Not a single village, not a single home, not a single family remained unscarred by this wanton execution of relatives and friends. In time, the whole of Crete was draped in black, and a floodtide of mournful tears fell from the eyes of the bereaved.

High in the mountains of southern Crete, ranging from the White Mountains in the west to the Lasithi Mountains in the east, bands of men and women, old and young, roamed the slate-gray escarpments of those rugged heights fleeing the yoke of German oppression. They banded together into an army of patriots who fought a continuous battle against their enemy. In the four years of occupation that followed the invasion, these Cretans were the nucleus of the Cretan resistance movement against the German occupiers.

Crete was the last place in Europe to be freed from the German swastika. When the Germans finally departed on May 15, 1945—

one week *after* hostilities had ceased on the European continent—they left thousands of dead soldiers behind.

In London the population heard the final reports of the tragic events that turned an opportunity for victory in Crete into another defeat for British arms. Churchill announced to the House that the evacuation had been terminated and that the only cause for satisfaction was the heroic effort of the Royal Navy. He did not detail, however, the cost in personnel and in ships.

In the United States, a small article in the *New York Times* mentioned that Crete had finally succumbed to the German airborne onslaught. Little reference was made to the gallantry of the Commonwealth soldiers, to their plight in the withdrawal, or to the heroic exploits of the Cretans in fighting side by side with the New Zealanders and Australians. Certainly no reference was made to the Cretan hostages being executed daily for their resistance to the invader.

Across the Aegean Sea in Athens, the Greeks listened attentively to reports of the battle taking place. Some of their information came from American Embassy personnel, while most of it was heard over BBC news reports received on clandestine radios. By the end of May, the tone of the reports forecast defeat in Crete for the Allies. The Greeks believed the Germans had received a rude and costly shock.

In July 1941 General Kurt Student was summoned from Athens to appear before Hitler at the Fuehrer's new underground headquarters near Rastenberg, in the dark gloomy forest of East Prussia. It was from there at the Wolfsschanze—the Wolf's Lair—that Hitler now directed the campaign against Russia which had begun at 3:30 A.M. on June 22.

Student was instructed to bring several of his senior commanders with him so they might be decorated. Hitler greeted them warmly in the conference room of his headquarters. Following a simple ceremony in which he awarded the Knight's Cross to some of the paratroop officers, he congratulated them on their success.

"You have accomplished an essential task," Hitler informed them, "which could only have been undertaken by an airborne assault."[16]

Student was proud of his men; all those early hours of pending defeat were now forgotten. He did not wish to review the heavy losses incurred in the battle. The paratroop commander did not wish to be reminded that he no longer had a combatworthy parachute division. Given time, the division would be reinforced, reequipped, and revitalized. It would be given greater strength for greater military deeds in the days ahead. At Corinth and certainly in Crete, the parachutists had proven their mettle. If Keitel, Jodl, and Halder agreed with Hitler, then Student's paratroop corps would be given the support it so richly deserved. As coffee was being served, Hitler turned to Student, but his remarks were to shatter the paratroop commander's hopes.

"Of course, you know, Student, that we shall never order another airborne operation. Crete has proved," Hitler continued without a pause, "that the days of the parachute troops are over."[17]

Student was thunderstruck by the remark. "But why, mein Fuehrer?" he stammered in his typical, slow drawl.

Hitler ignored Student's obvious dismay, giving the reason for his decision: "The parachute force as a weapon is one that relies entirely on surprise. The element of surprise has exhausted itself."

Hitler rose and gave the general his hand in dismissal. "It is unfortunate, Student," Hitler concluded, "but Crete has become the graveyard of the German paratrooper."[18]

Lieutenant General Kurt Student, the first and last commander of the German Parachute Corps, was taken prisoner in 1945 by the Allied Forces. The man who had planned and commanded the Cretan invasion had been promoted to Oberstgeneral after Crete, and subsequently commanded various army groups on the eastern and western fronts during the rest of the war.

The high point of Student's military career was the airborne invasion of Crete, which resulted in a Pyrrhic victory for the Germans. Hitler never forgot the heavy toll of casualties—one in every four perished, totaling some 6,116, of which 1,990 were officially listed as killed.

After Crete, Student proposed a plan to launch an airborne invasion of Cyprus as a stepping-stone for an attack on the Suez Canal from the east. Hitler rejected the proposal, citing the heavy casualties in Crete.[19]

Student remained undaunted by this rejection and in April 1942 proposed an air invasion of Malta. The ultimate plan called for a combined air and seaborne assault, with a tentative date set for

June 10. This plan was favorably received by the German General Staff, and the program moved into full operation. Student was to command the combined German-Italian airborne forces that were to be used in the attack. He would command his original Fliegerkorps XI, which would be comprised of the reconstituted Seventh Air Division, the Italian Folgore Parachute Division, and a light air-landing support division, all to be ferried to Malta in 300 JU-52s and HE-111s, together with 155 Savoia-82s of the Italian Regia Aeronautica. In addition, ninety gliders were to be used as an advance attack force.

As June 10 approached, Hitler had misgivings that led to a delay. Student flew to Hitler's headquarters for a personal conference, hoping to obtain final approval for Operation Herkules, as it had been designated. Once again Hitler rejected the proposal. The reminder of the casualties suffered on Crete rose again like a nightmare. "The affair will go wrong," he declared to Student, and in a tone that meant that his decision was final, he added: "It would cost too many lives!" Crete had left a deep scar on Hitler.[20]

It must have been a bitter pill for Student to swallow when he personally witnessed the massive Allied airborne assault on Holland in September 1944. The very thought that the Allies had copied his creation and were using it against him must have made him envious on the one hand and angry at Hitler's shortsightedness on the other.

Student's anguish over the fate of his beloved paratroopers was deepened when in 1944 he lost his only son, also serving in the Luftwaffe. With the war's end came the end of Kurt Student's military career. A military tribunal cleared him of any complicity in war crimes, releasing him in 1948, whereupon he returned to his home to live out his days in postwar Germany. Student died in 1978 at the age of eighty-eight.

For the remainder of the war, the German parachute units fought with distinction *as infantry* on all the major fronts. And they were well respected by all Allied units that opposed them. The survivors of the battle of Crete were regarded as an elite group. They were given permission to wear a special patch bearing the word *Kreta* on their sleeve-cuffs.

General Freyberg returned to battle in North Africa, where he was wounded again during the British withdrawal to El Alamein.

His failure in Crete was to deprive him of any future independent command for the rest of the war. He subsequently served as a senior staff officer in North Africa and later in Italy.

Wherever he went, Freyberg's fame as Great Britain's most decorated soldier preceded his shadow by a mile. Yet the outcome on Crete seemed to bother him. Throughout the war he continued to give reasons—not always the same—why Crete should never have been defended.

Freyberg must have asked himself repeatedly why he had not ordered a counterattack on the night of the first day of the German invasion; or why he yielded to the wishes of his individual senior sector commanders instead of ordering them to attack; or why he had not armed the civilian population with the weapons stored in the warehouses in Khaniá. What a formidable civilian army they would have made!

After the war Freyberg continued to serve his sovereign. In 1946 King George appointed him to be governor-general of New Zealand. At the end of this tenure, he returned to England to become lieutenant governor of Windsor Castle and to serve in the House of Lords. His service to his country continued until his death in 1963.

The greatest tribute that could be given to the Australians and New Zealanders—both officers and enlisted men—who fought so bravely on Crete was accorded by the Cretan people. When asked what they thought of these men who came from so far away below the Southern Cross to defend their island, the Cretans smiled admiringly and replied: *"They were fighters!"*

The passage of time has obliterated many of the deep scars that war brings to the land, but the wounds of the heart endure. Those wounds forge the creation of monuments that decades later stand as an epitaph to the deeds of both invaders and defenders. Today the whole island of Crete remains a memorial to the battle that was fought there.

The English memorial to their fallen heroes is located not far from the Suda docks where they first set foot on Cretan soil. In a sprawling green meadow, the symmetrical lines of tombstones radiate from a central granite cross. The cool breezes wafting in from the water carry the fragrance of the flowers that surround the Suda Bay War Cemetery, the final resting place for Freyberg's men. Here lie the New Zealanders, the Australians, and the British of the Commonwealth. Perhaps most poignant of all is the inscription at the cemetery gate reminding the visitor that "As the sun sets low over Suda Bay, we shall remember them."

The German dead are buried at the new military cemetery—the Deutscher Soldatenfriedhof—which was opened in 1974 atop Hill 107, overlooking Maleme airfield. Beneath a 25-foot wooden cross are buried, under flat tombstones in tidy lanes amidst blossoming red flowers, those who came to Crete to stay.

The Cretans gathered their dead and buried them in the cemeteries of the villages in which they had lived.

Of all these grim reminders of battle, of all the monuments that have been erected as memorials to the dead, one, perhaps, stands out because of its simplicity.

On a high hill not far from Khaniá, there is a huge black wooden cross that marks the gravesite of a fallen soldier. No one knows whether that slain warrior was a Greek, a New Zealander, an Australian, or an Englishman, for time and the elements have expunged his name from the marker on the cross. His identity is known only to God. Daily several Cretan women dutifully ascend the hill and place a bouquet of flowers at the base of that cross, to honor the memory of this unknown soldier.

Somewhere in Hades, where the fallen of Greek mythology go when they depart this earth, Leonidas and his 300 Spartans—renowned heroes of the ancient battle of Thermopylae—must have been proud to accept into their ranks this gallant warrior who fought a modern Thermopylae in May 1941. Like Leonidas and his Spartans, he fought fiercely; and like them he died bravely for liberty.

# EPILOGUE

Fortune touched each person involved in this battle differently.

Kurt Student's immediate superior, General Alexander Löhr, was not so fortunate as Student. The commanding general of the German Fourth Air Fleet, whose air force command was involved in the Balkan operations against Yugoslavia, Greece, and Crete, was held for trial as a war criminal in Belgrade after the war. Accused of complicity in the opening-day bombardment of the Yugoslavian capital, in which 17,000 civilians were killed, he was executed on December 27, 1947.

Another officer who served in Crete and who met the same fate as Löhr was Colonel Bruno Brauer, commanding officer of the First Parachute Regiment, which landed in Iráklion on May 20. After the battle Brauer remained as commander of the occupation force, with headquarters at Khaniá. He bore the onus of responsibility for the brutal mass executions undertaken by the SS against the Cretan civilians during the four-year occupation. Tried in Athens as a war criminal, he was executed on the anniversary of the invasion of Crete—May 20, 1947. Buried in Kokkinias Prison cemetery near Athens until 1974, his remains were reinterred in a grave at the new German military cemetery at Maleme in Crete.

General Wolfram von Richthofen, who commanded the aircraft that rained continuous death upon Crete, survived the war only to die of natural causes in an Allied prisoner-of-war camp.

Major General Eugen Meindl, commanding officer of the assault regiment, who had been severely wounded in Crete, recovered in Germany and returned to command a battle group on the western front during the Allied invasion of Normandy in June 1944.

Another officer in the assault regiment who survived wounds

received on Crete was Major Walter Koch. It was Koch who commanded the glider companies that landed on Hill 107 on May 20. After Crete, Koch rose to command the elite Fifth Parachute Regiment serving in North Africa, which was built around the surviving officers and NCOs of General Meindl's assault regiment. Koch was killed in an automobile accident in Germany in October 1943.

Most of the German officers who survived the battle in Crete achieved advancement in rank. Colonel Richard Heidrich, who commanded the Third Parachute Regiment in Prison Valley, rose to become a general in command of the reconstituted Seventh Airborne Division. In a major reorganization of the airborne units, the veteran Seventh Airborne was renamed the First Airborne Division and, with Heidrich commanding, fought the Allies brilliantly and stubbornly at the epic Battle of Cassino in Italy.

Commanding his old regiment was one of Heidrich's former battalion commanders, Colonel Ludwig Heilmann. Heilmann's former Third Parachute Battalion had been wiped out on the first day of battle in Crete.

Another of Heidrich's battalion commanders in Crete was Baron von der Heydte. A captain in Crete, Friedrich August Freiherr von der Heydte rose to a colonelcy and served on the eastern and western fronts. He commanded a special task force in the Battle of the Ardennes in 1944, and he was captured by American troops. After the war, he returned to Würzburg where he taught international law.

Colonel Bernhard Ramcke, the aggressive parachute officer who succeeded the wounded General Eugen Meindl in field command of the paratroopers in the Maleme area, led a brigade in the battle at El Alamein. As a major general he commanded the newly formed crack Second Parachute Division and moved into Brittany in June 1944. His defense of the encircled city of Brest held many American divisions at bay during that long siege, until he was forced to surrender in mid-September.

Captain Walter Gericke, who commanded the Fourth Assault Battalion in the Maleme area, subsequently rose in rank and saw combat service in North Africa, Sicily, and Italy. After the war Gericke became commanding general of the first West German airborne division in 1962.

Many of the soldiers of lower ranks also survived the war. Werner Schiller recovered from the wound he received in Crete and returned to combat duty in North Africa and later in Italy and France. He survived the war to become an engineer.

Corporal Hans Kreindler was released from captivity when the Germans took Galatas. Returned to combat duty, he fought in North Africa and Italy and was wounded at Cassino. He survived the war and emigrated to South America and thence to the United States.

Perhaps the greatest disappointment among the paratroopers who fought in Crete was Max Schmeling, the former world heavyweight boxing champion. He saw little or no action in Crete because of a stomach disorder. Nevertheless he became a central figure of Joseph Goebbels's propaganda machine, depicted in photographs and posters as a hero-Fallschirmjäger. Veterans of the Cretan campaign scoffed at this image. Schmeling survived the war and became a businessman in West Germany.

In Crete the officers and men of the Australian, New Zealand, and British units wrote the finest pages in their war history. However, in some cases the battle records men established on Crete tended to affect their destiny for the remainder of the war, and for some senior commanders, Crete had a telling effect on the rest of their military careers.

General Edward Puttick, who headed the New Zealand division in Crete, found that his actions there left a shadow on his ability as a leader in battle. He continued to command the division for a brief period after Crete, but when the division was transferred to Italy, Brigadier Howard Kippenberger took over.

Brigadier James Hargest of the Fifth New Zealand Brigade, the farmer-turned-politician-turned-soldier, could not overcome the lethargy he had shown during the first night of the invasion, when he allowed Hill 107 to be abandoned. Even his fine leadership during the withdrawal to Sfakia did little to erase his earlier conduct.

Colonel Howard Kippenberger, the feisty commander of the Tenth New Zealand Brigade in Prison Valley and at Galatas, proved that he had a penchant for fighting the enemy. In North Africa, Kippenberger was given command of a brigade, and in Italy he rose to command the New Zealand division. Wounded at Cassino, he survived the war with the rank of major general and was later knighted for his exemplary service.

The man who succeeded Kippenberger as commander of the

Twentieth New Zealanders—Major John Burrows—eventually commanded a brigade. Major Sandover, the Australian from the Eleventh Australian Battalion who escaped from Crete, also rose to command a brigade by the end of the war. However, his immediate superior, Brigadier Ian Campbell, remained to surrender at Rethimnon and had to spend the next four years in a German prison camp. Lieutenant Thomas, who led a platoon from the Twenty-third New Zealand Battalion at Galatas, was captured by the Germans as he lay wounded. Like Lieutenants Sinclair and Farran, he was transferred to the Greek mainland and later escaped to North Africa.

Another officer who rejoined his regiment and saw additional service in the campaigns in Europe was Captain Michael Forrester, whose exploits on Crete became legendary.

Some officers who escaped from Crete met sad ends on other battlefields. Colonel John Allen of the Twenty-first New Zealand Battalion fought and died in North Africa. Lieutenant Colonel John Gray, who aged perceptibly during the hot battle at Galatas, was also killed in action in Europe. Many others also escaped from Crete only to die in other theaters of war.

Of the Greek soldiers who fought with the New Zealanders and Australians at Galatas, Alikianou, Rethimnon, and Iráklion, most remained to become prisoners of the Germans. Very few Greeks were evacuated from Crete with the British forces, for no provision had been made. Some did escape to join the Cretans in the mountains and to fight in the resistance.

Captain Emorfopoulos—Captain E—survived the wounds he received defending Cemetery Hill before Galatas. For the rest of the war, he was a German prisoner. His adjutant, Lieutenant Aristides Kritakis, was also captured and spent four years in a prison camp in Germany. After the war he returned to Greece and resumed his profession as a correspondent.

The civilians in the story fared better.

Major John Drakopoulos, the "maintenance engineer" in the Grande Bretagne Hotel whose covert activities discovered the German intent for Crete, continued his work for the British until 1943. When the Gestapo uncovered his status as a double agent, he was forced to flee. He returned to Athens after the war where he lived until he died in 1977.

It is worth mentioning that the British had been aware of the pending operation against Crete from another source. An apparatus known as Ultra had enabled them to intercept and decode German messages originating in the highest German command echelons. As early as April 28, Churchill had informed General Wavell that an airborne invasion of Crete was to be anticipated. Nevertheless, General Wavell's replies to the prime minister indicated that he did not believe these reports. He felt strongly, as did the Imperial General Staff, that the impending attack on Crete was a ruse, and that the major assault would be directed elsewhere. By the time Wavell accepted the fact that the Germans did intend to invade Crete, it was too late to take stronger measures to defend the island.

The man who hired Drakopoulos as the maintenance engineer for the Grande Bretagne, George Canellos, survived the war and became director of the hotel.

As an afterthought, SS Colonel Heinz Gellermann, the Gestapo officer who interviewed Drakopoulos and approved his employment in German headquarters, remained in Athens until 1943. He was later transferred to the Russian front, and there is no evidence that he survived the war.

Athanasios Tziotis, the teenager who carried messages to the British secret wireless transmitter at 5 Canaris Street, also survived the war. In later years he married a coworker at the Grande Bretagne.

Most of the Cretans who fought the Germans and survived took to the mountains during the occupation. From there they continued the fight as members of the resistance. George Psychoundakis and Manoli Paterakis were no exception.

Psychoundakis, the lithe, olive-eyed shepherd from the village of Asi Gonia, became a runner for the British secret agents who were sent into Crete to work with the Cretan resistance. Paterakis became a legend. After fighting the Germans during the invasion, he continued the fight as a guerrilla during the occupation. He was awarded the Military Medal of the British Empire, and the walls of his home are adorned with letters of commendation from such famous people as Field Marshal Sir Harold Alexander, among others.

The West German National Federation of War Memorial Associations—Volksbund Deutsche Kriegsgräberfürsorge—purchased the ground of Kavsakia Hill at Maleme, better known as Hill 107, and in 1974 opened a military cemetery there. They reburied the 4,465 paratroopers who were killed during the Battle of Crete and those who died during the occupation. As caretakers for this new cemetery the Germans chose Manoli Paterakis and George Psychoundakis!

When Psychoundakis left his home village of Asi Gonia in 1941 to fight the Germans, he swore that he was "going to bury a German officer." He never had the opportunity to fulfill that vow during the battle or later during the occupation. But by an ironic quirk of fate and time, Psychoundakis was the caretaker when the Germans transferred the remains of General Bruno Brauer from the Kokkinias Prison cemetery in Athens, where he had been buried after his execution in 1947, to the military cemetery at Maleme. It was Psychoundakis who actually reinterred Brauer's remains into the new gravesite. After thirty-three years, George Psychoundakis had finally fulfilled his vow—he had buried a German officer.

# NOTES

## CHAPTER 1 NO, IT IS WAR!

1. Archer, *The Balkan Journal*, 117–120.
2. Liddell Hart, ed. *History of Second World War*, Vol. 1, 272.
3. *Ibid.*, 272.
4. *Ibid.*, 263.
5. Wason, *Miracle in Hellas*, 13.
6. *Ibid.*, 14.
7. Papagos, *The Battle of Greece*, 275.
8. Liddell Hart, ed., 1:264.
9. Stewart, *The Struggle for Crete*, 31.
10. Papagos, 414.
11. Trevor-Roper, *Hitler's War Directives 1939–1945*, 90.
12. Smith, *The Great Island: A Study of Crete*, 1-89.

## CHAPTER 2 WAR COMES TO THE LAND OF MINOS

1. Thomas, *Nazi Victory, Crete 1941*, 53.
2. *Ibid.*, 54.
3. Ritchie, *East of Malta, West of Suez: The Official Admiralty Account of the Mediterranean Fleet 1939–1943*, 101.
4. *Ibid.*, 102.
5. Liddell Hart, ed., 3:1327.
6. Lenton, *Navies of Second World War: British Cruisers*, 72, 73.

## CHAPTER 3 MERCURY IS BORN

1. Farrar-Hockley, *Student*, 88.
2. Manvell, *Goering*, 127.
3. Townsend, *Duel of Eagles*, 173, 238.
4. Frischauer, *Rise and Fall of Hermann Goering*, 187.
5. *Ibid.*, 188.
6. Whiting, *Hunters From the Sky*, 48.

7. Frischauer, 189. Frischauer is quoting the diary of General Karl Bodenschatz, Goering's military aide.
8. Clark, *The Fall of Crete*, 48.
9. Frischauer, 190. Quoting Bodenschatz.
10. Bekker, *The Luftwaffe War Diaries*, 261.
11. Halder, *Kriegstagebuch,* entry April 24, 1941.
12. Frischauer, 191.
13. Manvell, 66.
14. Windrow, *Luftwaffe Airborne and Field Units*, 28.
15. Farrar-Hockley, 6–80.
16. *Ibid.*, 81.
17. Student, *Crete*, 55.
18. *Ibid.*, 55.
19. Bekker, 261.
20. *Ibid.*, 261.
21. Student, 55.
22. Clark, 51.
23. Student, 55.
24. *Ibid.*, 60.
25. *Ibid.*, 60.
26. Clark, 51.
27. Farrar-Hockley, 81.
28. Frischauer, 195.
29. *Ibid.*, 195.
30. Trevor-Roper, 117.

**CHAPTER 4**　DETERMINE THE NEXT GERMAN OBJECTIVE

1. Churchill, *The Second World War*, Vol. 3, 246.
2. *Ibid.*, 244.
3. *Ibid.*, 246.
4. *Ibid.*, 247.
5. *Ibid.*, 246.
6. *Ibid.*, 251.
7. *Ibid.*, 261.
8. *Ibid.*, 272.
9. Cameron, *The Valorous Island: Malta*, 23.
10 *Ibid.*, 31.
11. Whiting, *The War in the Shadows*, 40.
12. *Ibid.*, 40.

**CHAPTER 5**　ANY DAY AFTER THE SEVENTEENTH

1. Waller, *With the 1st Armored Brigade In Greece*, 19.
2. Canellos, George. Interview with author. Athens, July 10, 1976.
3. Whiting, *The War in the Shadows*, 28.
4. Drakopoulos, John. Interview with author. Athens, July 14, 1976.

5. Tziotis, Athanasios. Interview with author. Athens, July 8, 1976.
6. Thompson, *Assignment: Churchill*, 218.
7. Churchill, 3:280.

**CHAPTER 6** SCORCHER ON COLORADO

1. Churchill, 3:227
2. Winterbotham, *The Ultra Secret*, 104.
3. Churchill, 3:271.
4. *Ibid.*, 272.
5. Churchill, 2:548.
6. Churchill, 3:273.
7. Clark, 30.
8. *Ibid.*, 31.
9. *Ibid.*, 31.
10. *Ibid.*, 31.
11. *Ibid.*, 32.
12. *Ibid*, 33.
13. Churchill, 3:274.
14. *Ibid.*, 273.
15. *Ibid.*, 273.
16. Stewart, 73.
17. Churchill, 3:277.
18. *Ibid.*, 281.
19. *Ibid.*, 280.
20. Clark, 33.

**CHAPTER 7** JUST A CIRCLE ON THE MAP

1. Lazerakis, Peter. Interview with author. Khania, June 30, 1977.
2. Stewart, 93.
3. Manolikakis, *The Golgotha of Crete*, 55.
4. Davin, *Crete*, 469.
5. Manolikakis, 57.
6. Stewart, 93.
7. *Ibid.*, 121.
8. Clark, 84.
9. Gyparis, *Heroes and Heroism in the Battle of Crete*, 99.
10. Kippenberger, *Infantry Brigadier*, 50.
11. Kritakis, Aristides. Interview with author. July 10, 1978.
12. Kazantsakis, Vasili. Interview with author. July 16, 1978.

**CHAPTER 8** THE HUNTERS FROM THE SKY

1. Clark, 57.
2. Kurowski, *Der Kampf Um Kreta*, 18.
3. *Ibid.*, 20.

4. Windrow, 3.
5. *Ibid.*, 4.
6. Liddell Hart, ed., 2:504.
7. Farrar-Hockley, 47.
8. *Ibid.*, 52.
9. Kurowski, 19.
10. Bekker, 123.
11. U.S. Department of the Army. *Airborn Operations—A German Appraisal*, MS P-051, 88, 89.
12. Bekker, 120.
13. *Ibid.*, 264.
14. *Ibid.*, 264.
15. Von der Heydte, *Daedalus Returned*, 40.
16. *Ibid.*, 43.

## CHAPTER 9  IT IS ONLY A RUMOR

1. Manolikakis, 12.
2. Rose, Thomas. Interview with author. London, August 12, 1974.
3. Michas, George. Interview with author. Khania, July 13, 1977.
4. Pavlides, Hector. Interview with author. Athens, July 20, 1976.
5. Gyparis, 110.
6. Pavlides, Hector. Interview. Athens, July 20, 1976.
7. Churchill, 3:272.
8. Kritakis, Aristides. Interview. Athens, July 10, 1978.
9. Kreindler, Hans. Interview with author. Vienna, August 20, 1974.
10. Schoerner, Karl. All information on Schoerner was furnished by Kreindler. Vienna, August 20, 1974.
11. Clark, 44.
12. Ryder, John. Interview with author. London, August 13, 1974.
13. Stewart, 130.
14. *Ibid.*, 131.
15. Ryder. Interview. London, August 13, 1974.
16. Stewart, 132.
17. Farrar-Hockley, 91.

## CHAPTER 10  MERCURY IS AIRBORNE

1. Von der Heydte, 14.
2. Thomas, *Nazi Victory*, 143.
3. *Ibid.*, 143.
4. Bekker, 263.
5. U.S. Department of the Army. Ms. B-639, 184.
6. Kreindler. Interview. Vienna, August 20, 1974.
7. Clark, 59.
8. Von der Heydte, 14.

9. Hausser, Franz. Interview. Vienna, August 21, 1974.
10. Bekker, 271.

## CHAPTER 11 THEY ARE COMING!

1. Stephanides, *Climax in Crete*, 95.
2. Kritakis. Interview. Athens, July 15, 1978.
3. Stewart, 148.
4. Stephanides, 144.
5. *Ibid.*, 149.
6. Clark, 61.

## CHAPTER 12 IT WAS LIKE A TERRIBLE DREAM

1. Kurowski, 32.
2. Bekker, 267.
3. Clark, 64.
4. *Ibid.*, 63.
5. *Ibid.*, 64.
6. Schiller, Werner. Interview with author. Zurich, August 22, 1974.
7. Davin, 130.
8. *Ibid.*, 129.
9. Clark, 65.
10. Striker, Ray. Interview with author. London, August 13, 1974.
11. Clark, 65.
12. Bekker, 270.

## CHAPTER 13 IT WAS MAGNIFICENT, BUT IT IS NOT WAR

1. Stewart, 182.
2. Clark, 66.
3. Stewart, 182.
4. Kurowski, 24.
5. Bekker, 271.
6. Von der Heydte, 59.
7. *Ibid.*, 62.
8. Kreindler. Interview. Vienna, August 20, 1974.
9. Von der Heydte, 69.
10. Clark, 62.
11. Bekker, 273.
12. Clark, 85.
13. *Ibid.*, 84.
14. Vlahakis, Mixali. Interview with author. Khania, July 19, 1978.
15. Manolikakis, 39.
16. *Ibid.*, 42.
17. Bedding report quoted in Clark, 86.

**CHAPTER 14**   THAT THE GERMAN SHALL NOT PASS!

1. Kippenberger, 52.
2. *Ibid.*, 53.
3. *Ibid.*, 52.
4. Davin, 147.
5. Schiller, Werner. Interview. Zurich, August 22, 1974.
6. Clark, 69.
7. Davin, 148.
8. Stewart, 157.
9. Davin, 142.
10. Kreindler. Interview. Vienna, August 20; 1974.
11. Clark, 71.
12. Davin, 143.
13. Gyparis, 99.
14. Stewart, 185, 186.
15. Manolikakis, 39.
16. Wie Wir Kampfen, *Parachute Engineers in the Battle of Crete*, 13.

**CHAPTER 15**   WITH AXES, WITH SHOVELS, AND WITH THEIR
                 BARE HANDS

1. Manolakakis, Manolis. Interview of brother with author. Khania, July 10, 1978.
2. Paterakis, Manolis. Interview with author. Khania, July 11, 1978.
3. Manolikakis, 54.
4. Davin, 468.
5. Bekker, 271.
6. Georgalakis, Maria. Interview with author. Athens, July 5, 1978.
7. Kreindler. Interview. Vienna, August 20, 1974.
8. Paterakis. Interview. Platania, July 12, 1978.
9. Schiller. Interview. Zurich, August 22, 1974. Schiller again met Paterakis in 1975 while visiting the German cemetery at Maleme. He recognized Paterakis as the Cretan who had stopped to stare at him in this episode. Paterakis denies seeing Schiller, but he claims that he paused to urinate. He adds that had he seen Schiller hiding in the bamboo glade, he would have shot him.

**CHAPTER 16**   HENCE, THEY HAVE TO PRESERVE MY HEAD

1. Stewart, 166.
2. *Idid.*, 171.
3. Henderson. J. *22nd Battalion, Official History of New Zealand in World War II*, 21.
4. Stewart, 167.
5. Bekker, 270.
6. Clark, 68.

7. Ross, *23rd Battalion, Official History of New Zealand in World War II*, 67.
8. Manolikakis, 54.
9. Bekker, 272.
10. Fredericks, Franz. Interview with author. Fort Lee, N.J., June 6, 1979.
11. Bekker, 273.
12. Stewart, 193.
13. Bekker, 273.
14. Clark, 107.

**CHAPTER 17** BE BACK BY 4:30 P.M.

1. Bekker, 273.
2. Student, 92.
3. Clark, 83.
4. Gyparis, 100.
5. Clark, 91.
6. *Ibid*, 86.
7. *Ibid.*, 86
8. Stewart, 216.
9. *Ibid.*, 217.
10. *Ibid.*, 217.
11. Underhill, *The Royal Leicester Regiment*, 55.
12. *Ibid.*, 55.
13. Buckley, *Greece and Crete 1941*, 205.
14. Stewart, 206.
15. Feist, *Fallschirmjäger in Action*, 16.
16. Stewart, 209.

**CHAPTER 18** IF YOU MUST, THEN YOU MUST

1. Henderson, 52.
2. Clark, 69.
3. Henderson, 53.
4. Gyparis, 182.
5. Kritakis. Interview. Athens, July 15, 1978.
6. Clark, 75.
7. *Ibid.*, 76.
8. Kippenberger, 57.
9. Clark, 70.
10. *Ibid.*, 70.
11. Davin, 110.
12. *Ibid*, 110.
13. Clark, 71.
14. Von der Heydte, 87.
15. Churchill, 3:286.
16. Davin, 180.

17. Clark, 99.
18. *Ibid.*, 99.
19. *Ibid.*, 100.
20. Bekker, 275.
21. Clark, 100.
22. Stewart, 238.
23. *Ibid.*, 224.
24. Cody, *28th (Maori) Battalion: Official History of New Zealand in World War II*, 95.
25. Henderson, 54.
26. Davin, 118.
27. *Ibid.*, 118.

## CHAPTER 19 PRESS ON REGARDLESS

1. Stewart, 247.
2. Clark, 101.
3. *Ibid.*, 105.
4. Davin, 188.
5. *Ibid.*, 188.
6. *Ibid.*, 190.
7. Paterakis. Interview. Platania, July 11, 1978.
8. Clark, 104.
9. *Ibid.*, 104.
10. Meyer, *Battle for the Stronghold of Crete*, 90.
11. Psychoundakis, George. Interview. Tavronites, Crete. July 15, 1978.
12. Davin, 189.
13. Kurowski, 95.

## CHAPTER 20 IT HAS BEEN A GREAT RESPONSIBILITY

1. Stewart, 229.
2. *Ibid.*, 229.
3. Prüller, *Diary of a German Soldier*, 32.
4. Kurowski, 90.
5. *Ibid.*, 91.
6. Manolikakis, 71.
7. Kurowski, 91.
8. Kritakis. Interview. Athens, July 15, 1978.
9. Kritakis. Interview. Athens, July 15, 1978.
10. Kritakis. Interview. Athens, July 15, 1978.
11. Kritakis. Interview. Athens, July 15, 1978.
12. Kippenberger, 57.
13. Clark, 121.
14. Cody, 104.
15. *Ibid.*, 105.
16. Clark, 105.

17. Long, *Australia in the War 1939–1945*, Vol. 2, 235.
18. Clark, 120.
19. *Ibid.*, 119.

**CHAPTER 21**  THE WHOLE WORLD IS WATCHING YOUR
SPLENDID BATTLE

1. Davin, 215.
2. *Ibid.*, 215.
3. Farran, *Winged Dagger*, 95.
4. Davin, 216.
5. Paterakis. Interview. Khania, July 11, 1978.
6. Farran, 95.
7. Stewart, 297.
8. Farran, 97.
9. *Ibid.*, 97.
10. Clark, 126.
11. *Ibid.*, 126.
12. *Ibid.*, 127.
13. *Ibid.*, 127.
14. Ross, 72.
15. Davin, 216.
16. Clark, 129.
17. *Ibid.*, 127.
18. *Ibid.*, 127.
19. *Ibid.*, 129.
20. *Ibid.*, 128.
21. Cody, 105.
22. Dyer, *The Way of the Maori Soldier*, 73.
23. Pack, *The Battle for Crete*, 117.
24. Thomas, D., 168.
25. *Ibid.*, 169.
26. Stewart, 309.
27. Churchill, 3:293.
28. *Ibid.*, 293.

**CHAPTER 22**  MALTA WOULD CONTROL
THE MEDITERRANEAN

1. Davin, 238.
2. Clark, 130.
3. *Ibid.*, 130.
4. *Ibid.*, 131.
5. *Ibid.*, 131.
6. *Ibid.*, 131.
7. Wittmann, *Von Kreta, der Insel der Rätsel*, 6.
8. Clark, 137.

9. Stewart, 351.
10. Clark, 134.
11. *Ibid.*, 134.
12. Stewart, 353.
13. Meyer, K., 110.
14. Wittmann, 6.
15. Gericke, *Da Gibt Es Kein Zurück*, 85.
16. Dyer, 60.
17. Kippenberger, 61.
18. Long, 240.
19. *Ibid.*, 241.
20. Stewart, 316.
21. Filipakis, Tasso. Interview with author. Khania, July 17, 1978.
22. Long, 241.
23. Beroukakis, George. Interview with author. Khania, July 25, 1978.
24. Minarakis, Tasso. Interview with author. Khania, July 18, 1978.
25. Mourellos, *Battle of Crete*, Vol. 1, 412.
26. *Ibid.*, 412.
27. Paterakis. Interview. Khania, July 11, 1978.
28. Manolikakis, 54.
29. Thomas, D., 161.
30. Davin, 328.
31. Schmidt, *With Rommel in the Desert*, 76, 77.

**CHAPTER 23**  STAND FOR NEW ZEALAND

1. Clark, 130.
2. *Ibid.*, 131.
3. *Ibid.*, 138.
4. *Ibid.*, 139.
5. Kippenberger, 63.
6. Von der Heydte, 120.
7. *Ibid.*, 120.
8. Kritakis. Interview. Athens, July 15, 1978.
9. Davin, 235.
10. Kritakis. Interview. Athens, July 15, 1978.
11. Davin, 235.
12. Clark, 141.
13. Stephanides, 100.
14. Von der Heydte, 123.
15. Kritakis. Interview. Athens, July 15, 1978.
16. Kippenberger, 59. Also reported by Clark, 132, 133 quoting A.Q. Pope of the 4th RTM Company; commented on by Kritakis in interview with author; commented on by Mrs. Eleni Beroukakis (nee Gregorakis).
17. Kippenberger, 63, 64.
18. Davin, 301.
19. *Ibid.*, 303.

20. *Ibid.*, 306.
21. Kritakis. Interview. Athens, July 15, 1978.
22. Kippenberger, 65.
23. *Ibid.*, 65.
24. *Ibid.*, 66.
25. *Ibid.*, 67.
26. *Ibid.*, 66.
27. Farran, 101.
28. Kippenberger, 67.
29. Clark, 147.
30. Thomas, W. B., *Dare To Be Free*, 24.
31. Stewart, 390.
32. Thomas, W. B., 26.
33. *Ibid.*, 28.


**CHAPTER 24**  WHY IS CRETE STILL RESISTING?


1. Clark, 152.
2. Kippenberger, 68.
3. *Ibid.*, 68.
4. *Ibid.*, 68.
5. *Ibid.*, 68.
6. *Ibid.*, 68.
7. Clark, 153.
8. Kippenberger, 69.
9. Clark, 153.
10. *Ibid.*, 153.
11. Davin, 294.
12. *Ibid.*, 325.
13. *Ibid.*, 325.
14. *Ibid.*, 326.
15. *Ibid.*, 326.
16. Kippenberger, 73.
17. Clark, 153.
18. *Ibid.*, 153.
19. Davin, 344.
20. *Ibid.*, 346.
21. Stewart, 411.
22. Davin, 348.
23. *Ibid.*, 349.
24. *Ibid.*, 361.
25. Clark, 154.
26. Davin, 378.
27. Stewart, 421.
28. Halder, entry dated May 27, 1941.
29. Manolikakis, 72.
30. Churchill, 3:295.
31. Stewart, 362.

32. *Ibid.*, 363.
33. Long, 265.
34. Manolikakis, 79.
35. Churchill, 3:295.
36. *Ibid.*, 295.
37. *Ibid.*, 295, 296.

**CHAPTER 25** 300 YEARS TO BUILD A NEW TRADITION

 1. Cunningham, *A Sailor's Odyssey*, 385.
 2. *Ibid.*, 385.
 3. *Ibid.*, 386.
 4. *Ibid.*, 387.
 5. Churchill, 3:299.
 6. Stephanides, 213.
 7. Kippenberger, 76.
 8. Stewart, 436.
 9. *Ibid.*, 159.
10. *Ibid.*, 453.
11. *Ibid.*, 453.
12. Davin, 399.
13. Stewart, 432.
14. *Ibid.*, 463.
15. Cunningham, 387.
16. *Ibid.*, 390.

**CHAPTER 26** CRETE HAS BECOME THE GRAVEYARD OF THE
GERMAN PARATROOPER

 1. Pack, 124.
 2. Davin, 446.
 3. *Ibid.*, 446.
 4. *Ibid.*, 447.
 5. Stewart, 467.
 6. Clark, 161.
 7. *Ibid.*, 162.
 8. Davin, 447.
 9. *Ibid.*, 447.
10. *Ibid.*, 447.
11. Clark, 178.
12. *Ibid.*, 178.
13. *Ibid.*, 166.
14. *Ibid.*, 169.
15. *Ibid.*, 181.
16. Farrar-Hockley, 101.
17. *Ibid.*, 101.
18. *Ibid.*, 101.
19. Stewart, 477.
20. *Ibid.*, 477.

# BIBLIOGRAPHY

Abshagen, K. H. *Canaris*. London: Hutchinson, 1956.

Addington, Larry H. *The Blitzkrieg Era and the German General Staff, 1865–1941*. New Brunswick, N.J.: Rutgers University Press, 1971.

Ansel, Walter. *Hitler and the Middle Sea*. Durham, North Carolina: Duke University Press, 1972.

Archer, Laird. *The Balkan Journal*. New York: W. W. Norton and Co., 1944.

Argyropoulos, Kaity. *From Peace to Chaos*. New York: Vantage Press, 1975.

Bailey. George. *Germans*. New York: Avon. 1972.

Bailey, Ronald. Ed. *World War II: Partisans and Guerrillas*. Alexandria, Virginia: Time-Life Books, 1978.

Baldwin, Hanson. *Battles Lost and Won: Crete—The Winged Invasion*. New York: Avon, 1968.

Barry, Gerald. *The Parachute Invasion*. London: Blackwoods, 1944.

Baumbach, Werner. *The Life and Death of the Luftwaffe*. New York: Ballantine Books, 1967.

Bekker, Cajus. *The Luftwaffe War Diaries*. New York: Doubleday & Co., 1969.

Bohmler, Rudolf. *Fallschirmjäger*. Munich: Verlag Hans-Henning Podzun, 1961.

Bragadin, Commander Antonio. *The Italian Navy in World War II*. Annapolis: U.S. Naval Institute, 1957.

Buckley, Christopher. *Greece and Crete 1941*. London: Her Majesty's Stationery Office, 1977.

Caidin, Martin. *ME 109*. New York: Ballantine Books, 1968.

Cameron, Ian. *The Valorous Island: Malta*. New York: Arbor House, 1963.

Carell, Paul. *Hitler Moves East 1941–1943*. London: G. Harrop & Co., 1964.

Cecil, Robert, et al. *Hitler's War Machine*. Secaucus, New Jersey: Chartwell Books, Inc., 1975.

Churchill, Winston S. *The Second World War, Vol. 2: Their Finest Hour.* Boston: Houghton Mifflin, 1950.

————. *The Second World War, Vol. 3: The Grand Alliance.* Boston: Houghton Mifflin, 1950.

Ciano, Count Galeazzo. *Ciano's Diary 1939–1943.* Garden City, New York: Doubleday & Co., Inc., 1946.

Clark, Alan. *The Fall of Crete.* London: Anthony Blond Ltd., 1962.

Cody, J. F. *28 (Maori) Battalion: Official History of New Zealand in the Second World War 1939–1945.* Wellington: Department of Internal Affairs, War History Branch, 1956.

Collier, Basil. *The Battle of Britain.* New York: Berkley Medallion Books, 1969.

Collier, Richard. *Duce!* New York: Popular Library, 1971.

Comeau, M. G. *Operation Mercury.* London: Kimber, 1961.

Congdon. Don, Ed. *Combat, World War II.* New York: Arbor House, 1963.

Cooper. Matthew. *Uniforms of the Luftwaffe 1939–1945.* London: Almark Publishing Co., Ltd., 1974.

Cunningham, Admiral of the Fleet Viscount of Hyndhope. *A Sailor's Odyssey.* New York: Dutton, 1951.

Davin, Daniel M. *Crete (Official History of New Zealand in the Second World War, 1939–1945).* Wellington, New Zealand: Department of Internal Affairs, War History Branch, 1953.

Davis, Brian L. *Luftwaffe Air Crews 1940.* New York: Arco Publishing Co., Inc., 1974.

————. *German Parachute Forces 1935–1945.* New York: Arco Publishing Co., Inc., 1974.

De Courcy, Captain J. *The History of the Welch Regiment 1919–1951.* Cardiff: the Western Mail, 1952.

Delarue, Jacque. *The Gestapo.* New York: William Morrow, 1964.

Dobiasch, Sepp. *Gebirgsjäger Auf Kreta.* Berlin: Stocker, 1942.

Dyer, Major H. G. *The Way of the Maori Soldier.* London: Stockwell, 1957.

Edwards, Roger. *German Airborne Troops 1936–1945.* New York: Doubleday and Co., Inc., 1974.

Farran, Roy. *Winged Dagger.* London: Collins, 1948.

Farrar-Hockley, Anthony. *Student.* New York: Ballantine Books, Inc., 1973.

Feist, Uwe, et al. *Fallschirmjäger in Action.* Michigan: Squadron/Signal Publications, Inc., 1973.

Fergusson, Bernard. *Wavel: Portrait of a Soldier.* London: Collins, 1961.

————. *The Black Watch and the King's Enemies.* London: Collins. 1950.

Fielding, Xan. *The Stronghold.* London: Secker and Warburg, 1963.

Fisher, Graham, and McNair-Wilson, Michael. *Black Shirt.* New York: Belmont Books, 1961.

Fitzgibbon, Constantine. *Secret Intelligence in the Twentieth Century.* New York: Stein and Day, 1977.

Frischauer, Willi. *The Rise and Fall of Herman Goering.* New York: Ballantine Books, 1951.

Galland, Adolf. *The First and The Last.* New York: Ballantine Books, 1973.

Galland, Ries and Ahnert. *The Luftwaffe at War.* Chicago: Henry Regnery Company, 1973.

Gardner, Hugh H. *The German Campaigns in the Balkans (Spring 1940).* Washington: Office of Chief of Military History, Department of the Army, 1954.

Gericke, Walter. *Da Gibt Es Kein Zurück.* Munster: Fallschirmjäger-Verlag, 1955.

German Air Force Handbook 1944. *Wie Wir Kampfen* (Parachute Engineers in Battle of Crete) Berlin: 1944.

*German Intelligence Digest, World War II.* Stamford, Connecticut: Blacksmith Corporation, 1943.

German Mountain Troops Corps H-Q., *Gebirgsjäger in Griechenland und auf Kreta.* Berlin: 1941.

Gibson, Major T. A. *Assault from the Sky, Crete 1941.* London: Journal of Royal United Services Institute, 1961.

Gill, Hermon. *Royal Australian Navy 1939–1942, Vol. 1.* Canberra: Australian War Memorial Press, 1957.

Gyparis, Paul. *Heroes and Heroism in the Battle of Crete.* (in Greek) Athens: 1954.

Halder, Col. Gen. Franz. *Halder: Kriegstagebuch.* Stuttgart: Kohlhammer, 1963.

Heckstall-Smith, Anthony and Vice-Admiral H. T. Baillie-Grohman. *Greek Tragedy, 1941.* New York: W. W. Norton and Co. Inc., 1961.

Heiden, Konrad. *Der Fuehrer.* Boston: Houghton Mifflin Co., 1944.

Henderson. J. *22 Battalion, Official History of New Zealand in the Second World War 1939–1945.* Wellington, New Zealand: War History Branch, Department of Internal Affairs, 1958.

Herzstein, Robert Edwin, Ed. *World War II: The Nazis.* Alexandria, Virginia: Time-Life Books. 1978.

Hetherington, John. *Airborn Invasion: The Story of the Battle of Crete.* New York: Duell, Sloan and Pierce, 1943.

Hibbert, Christopher. *Mussolini.* New York: Ballantine Books, 1972.

Howell, Wing Commander Edward. *Escape to Live.* London: Longmans, 1947.

Irving, David. *The Memoirs of Field Marshal Keitel, Chief of the German High Command, 1938–1945.* New York: Stein and Day, 1966.

———. *Hitler's War.* New York: Viking Press, 1977.

Ismay, General Lord. *The Memoirs of Lord Ismay.* London: Heinemann, 1960.

Keitel, Wilhelm. *Memoirs.* London: Kimber, 1965.

Kippenberger, Major General Sir Howard. *Infantry Brigadier.* London: Oxford University Press, 1949.

Koutsoulas, Dimitrios. *The Price of Freedom.* Syracuse, New York: Syracuse University, 1953.

Kurowski, Franz. *Der Kampf Um Kreta.* Herford und Bonn: Maximilian-Verlag, 1965.

Lavra, Stephen. *The Greek Miracle.* London: Hastings House, 1943.

Leach, Barry. *The German General Staff.* New York: Ballantine Books, 1973.

Lenton, H. T. *Navies of the Second World War: British Cruisers.* New York: Doubleday and Co., Inc., 1973.

Lewin, Ronald. *The Chief: Field Marshal Lord Wavell 1939–1947.* New York: Farrar, Straus and Giroux, 1980.

———. *Rommel as Military Commander.* New York: Ballantine Books, 1970.

———. *The War On Land: The British Army in World War II.* New York: William Morrow and Co., Inc, 1970.

Liddell Hart, B. H. *History of the Second World War.* New York: G. P. Putnam Sons, 1971.

———. Ed. *History of the Second World War, Vol. 1.* London: Marshall Cavendish Ltd., 1973.

———. Ed. *History of the Second World War, Vol. 2.* London: Marshall Cavendish Ltd., 1973.

Lochner, Louis, Ed. *The Goebbels Diaries.* New York: Doubleday and Co., Inc., 1948.

Long, Gavin. *Australia in the War 1939–1945, Vol. 2., Greece, Crete, and Syria.* Canberra: Australian War Memorial Press, 1953.

Macksey, Kenneth. *Panzer Division: The Mailed Fist.* New York: Ballantine Books, Inc., 1972.

———. *The Partisans of Europe in Second World War.* New York: Stein and Day, 1975.

Manolikakis, I. G. *The Golgotha of Crete.* (in Greek) Athens: Efstathiadis, 1951.

Manvell, Roger. *Goering.* New York: Ballantine Books, Inc., 1972.

Mathioulakis, C. Z. *Crete: Mythology and History.* Athens: Mathioulakis, 1974.

Mayer, S. L., Ed. *Signal: Years of Triumph 1940–1942.* Englewood Cliffs, New Jersey: Prentice-Hall, Inc., 1978.

Meyer, Kurt. *Battle for the Stronghold of Crete.* (War Correspondent with 100 Mountain Regiment) Berlin: 1941.

Mosley, Leonard. *The Reich Marshal: A Biography of Herman Goering.* New York: Dell, 1975.

Mourellos, J. D. *Battle of Crete.* Iraklion: Erotocritos, 1950 (in Greek).

Muller, Gunther. *Sprung Über Kreta.* Oldenberg: Stalling, 1944.

Neumann, Robert. *The Pictorial History of the Third Reich.* New York: Bantam Books, 1962.

Newton, Don, and Hampshire, Cecil. London: William Kimber and Co., Ltd., 1959.

Pack, S. W. C. *The Battle of Crete*. Annapolis: Naval Institute Press, 1973.

Papagos, General Alexander. *The Battle of Greece, 1940–1941*. New York: New World Publishers, 1946. (in Greek)

Payne, Donald. *Malta: Red Duster, White Ensign*. New York: Doubleday & Co., 1960.

Pia, Jack. *Nazi Regalia*. New York: Ballantine Books, Inc., 1971.

Playfair, Major General I. S. O. *The Mediterranean and Middle East: Vol. 2: The Germans Come to the Help of Their Ally (1941)*. London: Her Majesty's Stationery Office, 1956.

Poolman, Kenneth. *The Kelly*. London: William Kimber and Co., Ltd., 1954.

Price, Alfred. *Luftwaffe: Birth, Life and Death of an Air Force*. New York: Ballantine Books, 1969.

Pruller, Wilhelm. *Diary of a German Soldier*. New York: Coward-McCann, Inc., 1963.

Psychoundakis, George. *The Cretan Runner*. London: John Murray, 1955.

Ringel, Gen. Julius. *Hurra Die Gams*. Berlin: Leopold Stocker Verlag, 1965.

Ritchie, L. A. *East of Malta, West of Suez: The Official Admiralty Account of the Mediterranean Fleet 1939–1943*. Boston: Little Brown, 1944.

Rokakis, Manousos. *The Story of Crete, 1941–1945*. Khania, Crete, 1953.

Ross, Angus. *23 Battalion, Official History of New Zealand in Second World War 1939–1945*. New Zealand: War History Branch, 1959.

Rothberg, Abraham. *Eyewitness History of World War II*. New York: Bantam Books, Inc., 1962.

Rudel, Hans Ulrich. *Stuka Pilot*. New York: Ballantine Books, 1973.

Russell, Francis, Ed. *World War II: The Secret War*. Alexandria, Virginia: Time-Life Books, 1978.

Schmidt, H. W. *With Rommel in the Desert*. New York: Ballantine Books, 1967.

Sheffield, Major O. F. *The York und Lancaster Regiment 1919–1953*. Aldershot: Gale and Polden, Ltd., 1956.

Shirer, William L. *The Rise and Fall of the Third Reich*. New York: Simon and Schuster, 1960.

———. *Berlin Diary*. New York: Popular Library, 1941.

Singleton-Gates, Peter. *General Lord Freyberg, V. C.* London: Joseph, 1963.

Smith, Michael Llewellyn. *The Great Island: A Study of Crete*. London: Longman, Green and Co., Ltd., 1965.

Speer, Albert. *Inside the Third Reich*. New York: Avon Books, 1971.

Stephanids, Theodore. *Climax in Crete*. London: Faber and Faber, Ltd., 1946.

Stevenson, William. *A Man Called Intrepid*. New York: Harcourt, Brace, Jovanovich, 1976.

Stewart, I. McD. G. *The Struggle for Crete: 20 May–1 June, 1941.* London: Oxford University Press, 1966.

Student, General Kurt. *Crete (Kommando).* South Africa: Ministry of Defence, 1952.

Sulzberger, C. L., Ed. *The American Heritage Picture History of World War II, Vol. 1.* New York: Simon and Schuster, Inc., 1966.

Thomas, David A. *Crete 1941: The Battle at Sea.* London: New English Library, 1976.

———. *Nazi Victory: Crete 1941.* New York: Stein and Day, 1972.

Thomas, W. B. *Dare to Be Free.* London: Wingate, 1957.

Thompson, Walter H. *Assignment: Churchill.* New York: Farrar, Straus and Young, 1955.

Toland, John. *Adolf Hitler.* New York: Doubleday and Co., Inc., 1976.

Townsend, Peter. *Duel of Eagles.* New York: Simon and Schuster, 1971.

Trevor-Roper, H. R., Ed. *Blitzkrieg to Defeat: Hitler's War Directives, 1939–1945.* New York: Holt, Rinehart and Winston, 1965.

Underhill, Brigadier E. W. *The Royal Leicestershire Regiment 17th Foot: A History of the Years 1928–1956.* South Wigston, Leics., Regimental Printing Office, 1958.

U. S. Department of the Army. Office of the Chief of Military History. *The German Campaigns in the Balkans-Spring 1941.* Washington: 1953. Ms 20–260.

U. S. Department of the Army. Office of the Chief of Military History. *General Hans-Joachim Rath, 1st Stuka Wing (February–May 1941).* Washington: 1953. Ms No. D-064.

U. S. Department of the Army. Office of the Chief of Military History. *Airborne Operations—A German Appraisal.* Washington: 1952. Ms No. P-051.

U. S. Department of the Army. Office of the Chief of Military History. Major General Rudiger Von Heyking, *Commitment of Parachute Troops by the Second Air Transport Wing (Special Purpose): Crete, 21 May 1941.* Washington: 1953. Ms No. B-639.

U. S. Department of the Army. Office of the Chief of Military History. *Warlimont, General of Artillery: Answers to Questions Concerning Greece, Crete, and Russia.* Washington: 1953. Ms No. B-250.

Von der Heydte, Baron F. *Daedalus Returned, Crete 1941.* London: Hutchinson and Co., 1958.

Von Mellenthin, Major General F. W. *Panzer Battles: The Balkan Campaign.* New York: Ballantine Books, Inc., 1973.

Von der Porten, Edward P. *The German Nazi in World War II.* New York: Apollo Edition, 1972.

Von Wittmann, A. *Von Kreta, Der Insel Der Rätsel.* Munich: Die Gebirgstruppe, 1954.

Waller, Lt Col. R. P. *With the 1st Armored Brigade in Greece.* London: Journal of Royal Artillery, 1945.

Warlimont, Gen. Walter. *Inside Hitler's Headquarters 1939–1945.* New York: Praeger, 1964.

Wason, Betty. *Miracle in Hellas.* New York: The Macmillan Company, 1943.

Waugh, Evelyn. *Officers and Gentlemen.* London: Chapman and Hall, 1955.

Weeks, John. *Assault from the Sky.* New York: G. P. Putnam's Sons, 1978.

Whipple, A. B. C., Ed. *World War II: The Mediterranean.* Alexandria, Virginia: Time-Life Books, 1978.

Whiting, Charles. *Canaris.* New York: Ballantine Books, 1973.

———. *The War in the Shadows.* New York: Ballantine Books, 1973.

———. *Hunters from the Sky.* New York: Ballantine Books, 1974.

White, Leigh. *The Long Balkan Night.* New York: Charles Scribner's Sons, 1944.

Wilmot, Chester. *The Struggle for Europe.* New York: Harper, 1953.

Windrow, Martin. *Luftwaffe Airborne and Field Units.* London: Osprey Publishing Ltd., 1972.

Winterbotham, F. W. *The Ultra Secret.* New York: Dell, 1976.

Winterstein, Ernst Martin, and Jacobs, Hans. *General Meindl und Seine Fallschirmjäger.* Munich: Gesammelt und Neidergeschrieben, 1949.

Woodhouse, C. M. *The Struggle for Greece: 1941–1949.* London: Hart-Davis, MacGibbon, 1976.

Wunderlich, Hans Georg. *The Secret of Crete.* New York: MacMillan Co., Inc., 1974.

Wykes, Alan. *SS Leibstandarte.* New York: Ballantine Books, 1974.

———. *Hitler.* New York: Ballantine Books, 1970.

Young, Brigadier Peter. *Atlas of the Second World War.* New York: Berkley Publishing Corp., 1977.

Zotos, Stephanos. *Greece: The Struggle for Freedom.* New York: Thomas Y. Crowell Co., 1967.

# INDEX